FOR HONOR WE STAND

Other Titles by H. Paul Honsinger

The Man of War Trilogy

To Honor You Call Us

For Honor We Stand

Brothers in Valor (forthcoming)

H. PAUL HONSINGER

FOR HONOR WE STAND

The Man of War Trilogy: Book 2

The characters and events portrayed in this book are fictitious. Any similarity to real persons, living or dead, is coincidental and not intended by the author.

Printed in the United States of America.

Cover design by: Gene Molica
Published by 47North, Seattle
www.apub.com

ISBN-13: 9781477849484
ISBN-10: 1477849483
Library of Congress Control Number: 2013944848

To my dear wife, Kathleen. You are my inspiration and joy, my companion and my friend, my safe harbor and my love. You bring light to every day, blessings to every hour, and happiness to every moment. If my creativity is a flame, you are the spark that set it alight. But for you, all would be darkness.

A NOTE FROM THE AUTHOR

For the benefit of lubbers, squeakers, and others unfamiliar with Union Space Navy terminology and slang, there is at the end of this volume a Glossary and Guide to Abbreviations, which defines many of the abbreviations, terms, and references used in these pages.

FOR HONOR WE STAND

CHAPTER 1

05:27Z Hours, 15 March 2315

Lieutenant Commander Max Robichaux, captain of the Union Space Navy destroyer USS *Cumberland*, was in trouble. Not the kind of trouble that could get his ass chewed out by Vice Admiral "Hit 'em Hard" Hornmeyer, whose ass chewings were a thing of legend. And not the kind of trouble that could get him hauled before a court martial and sentenced to life at hard labor at the deuterium separation plant on Europa, Jupiter's icy and desolate sixth moon. This was the kind of trouble that could get him killed. And not just him but also his shipmates. The lives of the 215 men and boys on board the *Cumberland* were in the twenty-eight-year-old skipper's hands, and if he couldn't pull a rabbit out of the hat sometime in the next thirty minutes, Max and his crew would all meet eternity together, in the cold, black battleground of space, a thousand light years from home.

The tactical overview display at Max's console in the *Cumberland*'s Combat Information Center (CIC) made the situation plain enough. It showed three ships, forming a long, narrow isosceles triangle, accelerating through the Mengis system, all three moving at about half the speed of light. At the apex of the triangle was Max's ship, the *Cumberland*, a *Khyber* class destroyer in the service of the Union Space Navy. *Cumberland* was fast, smart, stealthy, and—for her size—powerful. And she was running for her life.

The other two, slightly less than fifty thousand kilometers behind and about seven thousand away from each other, were "Hotels," standing for "H"—hostile warships. These Hotels were crewed by Krag, aliens descended from Earth rodents that an alien race had transplanted, along with other Earth plants and animals, to a distant world for purposes unknown, over eleven million years ago. The Krag had been waging a brutal war of extermination against mankind for more than thirty years—a war that, unknown to most of the public and even to most of the men in the Navy, the Krag hegemony was slowly but surely winning.

After the labels "H1" and "H2," each icon representing an enemy ship on the display bore the computer-generated label "KRAG CRSR CRUSTACEAN," designating the Hotels as enemy cruisers, which in general were much larger than destroyers like the *Cumberland* and *much* more heavily armed. Naval Intelligence had conferred upon this type of cruiser the only moderately ridiculous name *Crustacean* class. Big, powerful, and fresh from the Krag yards, they had the newest and most effective engines, deflectors, point defense systems, sensors, countermeasures, and weapons that the advanced Krag civilization could produce. The *Cumberland* would have been badly outmatched against just one such ship, but against two, the computer's tactical scenario evaluation algorithm (T-SEA, pronounced "tee-see") determined that "the correlation of forces very heavily favors H1 and H2."

No shit.

T-SEA rated the odds of survival as being stacked against the *Cumberland* to the tune of "approximately 7824.7 to 1."

At least we have a chance.

"Hotels are still on our six and closing the range," Lieutenant (JG) Bartoli announced from Tactical a little more than twenty minutes later, his Mobile, Alabama, drawl becoming more noticeable as the tension increased—"still" came out "stee-yul." "Now at thirty-four thousand kills. Closure rate is 773 kills per minute."

More important than what Bartoli said was what he did not say, what everyone in CIC knew: that the closure rate was a death sentence. Pounced upon and damaged by the cruisers when she jumped into the system, the *Cumberland* was no longer faster at sublight than the Krag vessels, which now had a slight speed advantage over the nominally faster destroyer. As a result, the two enemy ships would close until they reached a range of 27,253 kilometers (a nice, round number in the Krag measuring system) and each fired a salvo of six Foxhound missiles.

Although the *Cumberland*'s excellent point defense systems, plus some fancy maneuvering, might manage to destroy, deflect, decoy, intercept, or evade eight or nine Foxhounds at a time, *twelve* would be just too many. At least one would get through, detonate its 102.8-kiloton thermonuclear warhead, and the *Cumberland*, along with the 215 souls aboard her—the closest thing to a family that Max had in the universe—would silently and instantaneously die in a brilliant flash of fusing hydrogen, leaving behind not so much as a single particle of solid matter to mark that they had ever existed.

Max shook his head. *Not today. Today is not a good day to die.*

Unconsciously squaring his shoulders and jutting out his jaw, Max pulled his seat closer to his console and accessed the controls for the tactical display. He adjusted the scale to show everything within 1 AU, or about 150 million kilometers of the ship. Nothing.

Then 5 AU. Nothing. Then 10 AU. He smiled. Max punched up a voice channel and stabbed the comm button.

"Engineering. Brown here." Max always found the engineer's cultured English accent reassuring.

"Wernher! I know you said that the compression drive was out, but when you said 'out,' did you mean 'out' out or just 'not available for high c factors over long distances'?"

A chuckle came over the comm circuit, followed by an English accent that sounded as though it belonged on a foxhunt in Kent. "You want to know whether the compression drive is 'out out'? Notwithstanding the inartful phrasing, I do take your meaning, sir. You want to know whether there is *any* capability for superluminal propulsion at all, no matter how limited it may be. Pray tell, oh silver-tongued leader, what did you have in mind?"

"I'd like to get to that gas giant, Mengis VI." Max said. "It's only about seven AU away." Seven times the distance from the Earth to the Sun. Only about a billion kilometers. Just a biscuit toss. *Come on, Wernher.*

"Thinking about ducking into the upper layer of its atmosphere and hiding the ship in the electrical discharges from all those storms?"

"Exactly."

"But sir, the way that plays out tactically, that maneuver buys us only another... four hours or so. What does that get you?"

"Another four hours or so."

"Oh." Five seconds of silence. He was probably pulling up the tactical display on his console. "I see."

Yes, Wernher, it really is that bad. "Well?"

More silence. The engineer was thinking. "Sir, I don't need to tell you the compression drive was heavily damaged when we took that last hit to the aft section...."

Please, let there be a "but" coming.

"But I believe I could manage to provide very *low-order* superluminal propulsion for a *highly limited* period of time. I expect that by violating something like 150 Safety and Equipment Utilization Regulations, I could give you ten c for something like six minutes, which should get us where you want us to go."

"Outstanding." *Life. Four more hours of it anyway.* "I'll sign half a million SEUR waivers and have them plated in pure gold if you'll just get me to that planet. Oh, Wernher, since we're going to go on the compression drive already…"

"I'm afraid not, Captain. I could probably get you to the jump point, but we'd be all dressed up with no place to go. The main jump drive power junction is demolished, and there's no auxiliary or replacement unit on a ship this small. And before you ask, yes, my lads can build another from spares, but the unit is very intricate. It's a twenty-four hour job, if not a thirty-six."

"Understood. Then just get me to that gas giant. Do what you have to do, and let me know when you're ready."

"Aye, sir. Give me about five minutes."

"*I'd* give you all the time in the world, Wernher. The Krag, on the other hand, give you no more than five minutes and," he glanced at the tactical display, "forty-seven seconds. Your tea will have to wait."

"Understood. No matter, the scones are still cooling. Brown out."

Max called the engineer "Wernher," because his first and last name, Vaughn Brown, sounded to Max like *von Braun,* the surname of the famous German–American rocket engineer. Max, accordingly, called Brown by von Braun's given name, "Wernher," thinking the appellation both a joke and a compliment.

"Well, XO," said Max, turning to the man seated at his right, "what do we do when we get to the gas giant, other than join our chief engineer for some scones and Earl Grey with lemon?"

The man to Max's right, a die-hard coffee man born in Brazil on Earth, who had never tasted a scone, was Lieutenant Eduardo DeCosta, age twenty-three, the *Cumberland*'s new executive officer. DeCosta filled the berth of the late Texan, Robert Garcia, who had perished at the Battle of Pfelung a few weeks before. Until a week ago, DeCosta had been a hot-shot whiz kid in the Tactical section of the battleship *Hidalgo*. Now he was Max's XO.

Newly promoted, the young man was just discovering that the galaxy as viewed from the perspective of the tactical staff support room of an enormous battleship and the galaxy as viewed from the XO's station right in the middle of the action in the CIC of a destroyer were vastly different places.

As soon as he had discerned what the skipper's plan was, DeCosta pulled up a tactical plot and the main database entry for the destination planet on his console, and by the time Max asked the question, he was already working through the situation.

"Planet Mengis VI, number six in a twelve-planet system, 1.85 Jupiter masses, eight major moons—none inhabited, uncounted dozens of minor ones that are mostly captured asteroids, sketchy ring system, huge and very powerful magnetic field, hydrogen-helium composition with the standard trace elements and compounds for a gas giant, typical atmospheric dynamics with distinct cloud bands, extreme turbulence, violent electrical storms, multiple decks of ammonia and ammonia hydrosulfide clouds—it's pretty much a standard naval issue gas giant—Jupiter or Epsilon Eridani V on steroids."

"They don't vary much from system to system, do they?"

"No, sir."

"So, what does that give us to work with?"

"Well, sir, I suppose that, at least in the short term, we hide out in the cloud deck in an area of higher than average electrical activity to conceal our mass and EM signature, and engage our thermal stealth systems to keep from showing up as a hot spot against the cold of the planet's atmosphere. It's about 160 Kelvin in there, not as cold as the interstellar background, but still only twenty-five degrees or so warmer than liquid nitrogen. A bit on the nippy side."

"That's right. Now, think from the Krag perspective. When they pull into orbit at sublight about two hours after we get there, what'll they know? What'll they do?"

DeCosta considered for a few seconds. But only a few. "There's no way to avoid leaving an easy-to-follow trail through all those particles and fields, so they'll know approximately where we are. Not enough to target their weapons, but enough to know where they want to sit and wait us out.

"In their shoes, I would set up a standard high–low interdiction. They do it the same way we do: park one ship in low orbit right on top of their best guess as to our location, and park the other one in a higher orbit to cut off our escape if we try to slip out from underneath."

"Right. That's my read on it too. Once we've ducked under the clouds and out of sight, why don't we just crawl out from under the Krag and then run for it when we get far enough?"

"Won't work, Skipper. The main sublight drive's thermal signature suppression systems will keep the Krag from seeing the heat from the drive itself. That's great in space, but in a planetary atmosphere, running the drive will heat the surrounding atmospheric gases and leave a hot trail for the Krag to spot on infrared."

"What about creeping away on maneuvering thrusters?"

"Way too slow, sir. Down where we'll have to be, we'll be plowing through that thick atmosphere. We won't be able to get much speed going on those dinky little thrusters. We've only got four hours, and we won't get far enough. We'd gain about…twelve degrees in the intercept vector, which translates into seven additional seconds before they vaporize us. Maybe eight."

"And if we hide and do nothing more?"

"About two hours after we go on thermal stealth, our heat sink reaches capacity, and we have to do a thermal dump. Of course, if we dump, we give away our location. Even if we extend only the radiator fins shielded from their view by our ship, we'll create a hot spot in the planetary atmosphere that will stand out from orbit like a snowball in a coal bin. If we don't dump, then the heat sink fails, which will do the dump for us and damage half the systems in the ship as a bonus. In either event, they lock on their pulse cannons and blow us to hell."

Max nodded. The kid had it figured just the way he did. "And what if Wernher gives tea time a miss and effects repairs to give us back our speed advantage over the cruisers?"

"We still lose," DeCosta replied. "Even with our 23 percent acceleration advantage and our 7 percent top speed advantage over the *Crustaceans* restored, the interception geometry and the physics are totally against us. The high cruiser will be nearly out of the gravity well and at orbital velocity, so he's got a huge head start before the race even begins. If we try to run, he can cut us off and destroy us before we can develop enough speed to get away."

"What if we try to even the odds by taking on the low ship one-on-one once the two ships are settled in different orbits?"

"No go, Skipper. It's basic orbital mechanics. Because of the similarity in the kinetic energy values, it's a lot easier to transfer from high orbit to a low orbit in the same plane than to boost up to low orbit from the upper atmosphere, where we're going to be. The high cruiser can drop down into the lower orbit to help the low cruiser faster than we can climb up to fight him. They'll mop the deck with us."

"Okay, you've summarized the problem. We've got about four hours to solve it. Get with Kasparov and his people. Their sensors expertise makes them the closest thing to planetary scientists we've got. Make yourself an expert on Mengis VI and its environs. I need to know the lay of the land we're going to be fighting on. While you're doing that, I've got a bit of research of my own to do."

DeCosta got up from his station, walked over to the Sensors console, and began conversing with Lieutenant Kasparov animatedly. The two men talked in low voices, DeCosta sitting next to Kasparov in what was known as the "second-fiddle position" at the large and complex Sensors console.

The two pulled up screens in rapid succession and switched from one data channel to another, apparently plowing through a great deal of information and exchanging ideas. Kasparov was also talking a lot to his SSR, or "back room," to get information and advice from the specialists who gave him in-depth support and detailed monitoring of every sensor every minute of every day. Meanwhile, Max started pulling up data on the flight and control software parameters for the Talon antiship missile, the *Cumberland*'s primary weapon.

A few minutes later, Max's comm buzzed. "Skipper."

"Captain, this is Engineering." It was Brown. He sounded winded. "Compression drive is ready. Be aware that the compression drive control interface at the Maneuvering Station functions as OFF/ON only—there is currently no ability to regulate speed from CIC."

"Understood. We'll manage. Outstanding job, Wernher. Thanks. CIC out." He cut off the channel.

"XO, get us to Mengis VI."

"Aye, sir." DeCosta had started back to his station when Brown said the C-drive was working.

"Maneuvering, set course for Mengis VI, compression drive, prepare to engage at my command," DeCosta ordered. "Deflector control, forward deflectors to full, lateral and rear to cruise." Both men acknowledged the commands.

"Course computed," announced Maneuvering almost immediately. He had plotted the course five minutes ago and configured his console to update it continuously as the ship moved through space.

"Maneuvering, main sublight drive to standby. Maneuvering thrusters to standby."

"*Nulling main sublight* and bringing it to standby," said Maneuvering, tactfully supplying the XO's omission. In charge of Maneuvering was Chief Petty Officer First Class Claude LeBlanc, the deeply experienced Cajun in immediate command of the three spacers who actually had their hands on the controls directing the motion of the ship through space: one for yaw and roll, one for pitch and trim, and one to govern the propulsion systems. Those stations, and the men who manned them, were known respectively as Yaw, Pitch, and Drives. With a few muttered words to those three, he gave effect to the XO's commands.

On LeBlanc's console, the power indicator for the main sublight drive dropped to zero, and the drive's status light went from green for "engaged" to blue for "standby," followed immediately by the lights for the maneuvering thrusters. "Main sublight nulled and at standby. Maneuvering thrusters at standby. Attitude control by inertial systems only."

"Prepare to engage compression drive. C factor under control from Engineering."

"Aye, sir," LeBlanc acknowledged. "C factor controlled from Engineering. The status light on the drive just went from red to amber. Compression drive is ready for superluminal propulsion but is not nominal."

"Hotels One and Two approaching missile range. They just powered up their missile targeting scanners," announced Bartoli from Tactical, unable to keep the urgency from his voice. After a few seconds, "Missile targeting scanner beams from both ships are now traversing and phase scanning. Looking for a lock."

"Not today. Compression drive... engage," DeCosta ordered.

"Engaging," LeBlanc announced. He patted his Drives man twice sharply on the shoulder.

"Fleishman, go." Drives moved the control all the way forward. "Compression field forming. Instability in the compressed space forward... manually corrected from Engineering. Field going propulsive. Speed is zero point six. Zero point nine." Everyone gritted their teeth at the ear-piercing shriek of "Einstein's wail" as the ship breached Einstein's Wall by exceeding the speed of light.

"Ship is now superluminal. One point three. Two. Six. Nine. Field approaching equilibrium... Equilibrium achieved. Field is propulsive and stable at nine-point-eight-six c. ETA at Mengis VI is... five minutes and forty seconds from... MARK."

"Leaving Hotels One and Two behind. Range opening up rapidly. Twelve million kilometers. Eighteen million. Twenty-four million. No longer showing up on sensors."

"Never fear, Tactical, we'll see them again in about two hours," said Max.

"Thank you, sir, I was afraid I'd miss them," Bartoli said, his voice returned to normal.

"You know, sir," DeCosta said "when I got this assignment and read about the extra set of compression phase modulators on this class, I thought, 'So what? Big deal. Maybe it'll save a little time crossing from jump in to jump out, but it's not a significant combat capability.' But it's pretty obvious to me now that it *is* a big deal. The Krag don't have it and we do. When we scoot away at ten c, they can poke along at sublight and get left behind, or they can run at eighty or a hundred c inside a star system, which is like trying to drive a ground car at three hundred kph in a parking structure."

"It has been handy, no doubt," Max agreed. "It's always good to have a capability that your enemy lacks. Now, back to our problem. You're the one that Admiral Hornmeyer sold to me as the budding tactical genius. What can we do?"

"All I can think of is to find some way to even the odds. Find something that gives us a tactical advantage so we can take on one ship at a time on favorable terms."

"And how do we do that?"

"Nothing's coming to mind, sir."

"What did General Konovalov say right before the Battle of Belogorsk in the East–West War?"

"Other than, 'Oh, shit, I'm surrounded by half a million Chinese?'"

"Yes, other than that." Max smiled at the joke. As much for the benefit of the rest of the tactically inexperienced people in CIC as for DeCosta, Max continued.

"General '*Stolb,*' or 'the Pillar' Konovalov was surrounded by about *four hundred and eighty-five thousand* Chinese." He looked pointedly at DeCosta as he supplied the correct number. "But he and his scratch force of only a hundred and ten thousand men—and remember that they were mainly reservists, garrison forces, and rear echelon truck drivers, cooks, and file clerks—managed to hold off a numerically superior force comprised of crack troops, and did so without resupply for eleven days until the joint United States/British/German relief force arrived. Like Trafalgar, Midway, Jutland, Marathon, Sirius B, and a dozen other battles I could name, turning back that attack was the turning point of the war."

DeCosta nodded. "Didn't Konovalov say something like, 'Use terrain to even the odds'?"

"Very good. I'm told it sounds a lot catchier in Russian. Use the terrain. But we're in space, not along the Trans-Siberian Railway near the Chinese border, so what terrain do we have to use?"

"Well, sir, the planet is a Jovian-type gas giant. That means it's got a complex moon system, a ring system, all manner of crazy magnetic fields, electromagnetic effects, Trojan asteroids in its orbital path..."

"Is there any way to use any of that to gain a tactical advantage?"

"There will be lots of hiding places for something as small and stealthy as a *Khyber* class destroyer, and lots of moons and electromagnetic phenomena that could temporarily conceal maneuvers or weapons deployments to prevent enemy detection of what we're doing."

"Yes. There are..." An idea came to him. "Would it be too much to hope for that one of those moons happens to be volcanic?"

"Not too much at all, sir. One of the moons..." He glanced at his display and poked at a few buttons to pull up the data, "it's the third major moon, the eighth one out from the planet if you count the little ones too. That one is strongly volcanic. A lot like Io in the Sol system, spewing sulfur and other material out into space."

Max slapped his knee. "*That's* our terrain. Now, how do we use it?" He turned toward the Weapons station, enthusiasm beginning to show.

"Mr. Levy, I seem to recall a report in the last few days saying that the *Crustacean* class cruisers have a new countermeasures capability. They blast some sort of signal at our Talon missiles, and they veer off into useless trajectories. Well, about 60 percent do, anyway. Have I got that right?"

Ensign Menachem Levy had just joined the ship a week ago. He was only nineteen years old, greener than a seasick tree frog, and was pretty weak on CIC procedures, but Max would have bet he could assemble a Talon missile from spares without checking the database for instructions. The young man knew the answer off the top of his head.

"Yes, sir, that's right, but we've already developed and installed a software patch that's supposed to cut that to less than 10 percent. And if you ask me sir, I think that estimate is very conservative. Now that we've installed the patch, I don't think that the new Krag countermeasures would have any effect at all."

"Thank you, Ensign. Now, I need another opinion. Do the Krag know we've implemented a counter-countermeasure?"

"I don't know, sir." Apologetically, he added, "I don't get those reports."

"Fair enough." *The boy can't know everything, after all.* Max turned in another direction.

"Intel. Mr. Bhattacharyya." Another young officer who didn't need to be told much. "Mr. Levy doesn't get those reports. You do. Start feeding him the ones relating to weapons and countermeasures, and put together a package of the older ones you think he might find useful. Get it to him by 06:00 tomorrow."

In response to a questioning look, "And yes, Mr. Bhattacharyya, at 06:00 tomorrow you will still be alive to send him the package; he will still be alive to read it; and I will still be alive to be very unhappy if you don't send it to him. Take that to the bank. Now, Ensign, do the Krag know about the software patch?"

Ensign Bhattacharyya considered for a moment. "I don't see how they could, sir, except by means of some kind of mole or signal intercept. The patch was implemented just over forty-eight hours ago, and I have no report of anyone having fired a Talon at a *Crustacean* in that time. That makes sense, sir. Because they're such big ships, people generally attack them with Ravens. There's not much of anything that can stand up to a one-point-five megaton warhead."

"Right. Maximum yield on a Talon is a hundred and fifty kilotons. That won't kill one of those big bastards." Max paused, his lips curling into what some CIC personnel were starting to call his "crafty grin." "Unless you can get in a sucker punch. All right. I've got the terrain. I've got the weapon. I've got the tactics. Mr. Levy, you and I have some missile software to rewrite."

"Sir, we're starting to get the data stream from our stealthed sensor probe in orbit," Bartoli reported from Tactical. "There's lots of interference and the signal breaks up from time to time, but what we're getting is good enough for us to monitor what the enemy ships are doing. Hotel One and Hotel Two are settling in right where you expected, Skipper. Hotel Two is in a low forced orbit, staying right over our heads, 277 kills above the cloud tops, and Hotel One is in the high position at just over 32,000. Both are using active sensors, but not in any way that would detect us in these conditions. It looks more as though they're just making sure we know they're here so we'll stay under the clouds until we're truly desperate. Looks like they're making themselves comfortable."

"We need to be comfortable ourselves," Max said. "If we make our move too soon, they might not take the bait."

At that moment, the security door to CIC cycled to admit Dr. Ibrahim Sahin, the ship's chief medical officer and, at least for another few days, the Acting Union Ambassador and Minister Plenipotentiary to the Pfelung. The species of large, highly artistic, and insightfully intelligent lungfish-like aliens had recently made common cause with the Union against the Krag.

Max had taken the unusual step of giving the doctor unrestricted CIC access after his insights into Pfelung psychology saved the ship from being blown to flaming atoms at the Battle of Pfelung. Sauntering into the compartment right behind him came Clouseau, a large (some might even say somewhat fat) black cat that had joined the ship a few weeks before by darting through a docking tube from a freighter carrying Krag contraband.

As on sailing ships of old, spacers considered ship's cats lucky, black ship's cats luckier, and black ship's cats that joined the ship of their own accord luckier still. Clouseau, as a result, was much prized by the men and boys alike. He lacked for no conceivable feline necessity, comfort, or (truth be told) even luxury. The feline acted as though he owned the ship, which, from his peculiar cat perspective, he did.

The doctor sat at the Commodore's Station, a console on the command island to the CO's left. On most ships, the commodore's station was used very rarely, a place for the occasional visiting senior officer or dignitary to sit in CIC out of everyone's way and, more or less incidentally, to have a general-purpose console for viewing tactical and status displays, reading and sending messages, and performing other basic functions that let him stay informed and keep busy without getting into any trouble.

On the *Cumberland*, this spot had become Dr. Sahin's unofficial action station whenever something interesting was happening and he didn't have patients to attend to. Clouseau, as had become his habit, sat beside the doctor, whose spare frame left plenty of room in the seat for even a large cat. The doctor pretended not to notice the cat, while the cat pretended not to care. Clearly, their mutual affection ran deep.

"I'm sure you have a plan," Sahin said to Max, in a confidential tone.

"No, Doctor, I just make this stuff up as I go," Max replied in the same fashion. "Of course, I have a plan."

Sahin sniffed. "And no doubt, this plan of yours is extremely convoluted, highly dangerous, requires split-second execution, and involves a large measure of deception, misdirection, trickery, sneakiness, and unabashed underhandedness."

"No doubt."

"And you wouldn't dream of explaining it to me in advance."

"Certainly not, that would spoil the suspense."

"Did it ever occur to you that I don't like suspense?"

"Did it ever occur to you that I do? And I *am* the captain. Besides, the ride will be more entertaining if you don't know what's around the next bend."

"A splendid philosophy, indeed...for an amusement park attraction." Sahin, who had become fairly proficient at inducing the console in front of him to display the information he wanted, quickly surveyed the tactical situation. "The enemy ships, why are they not firing on us?" he asked Max.

"Because we're not showing up on their sensors."

"How can that be? We are only a few hundred kilometers away from the nearest one. They could practically spot us with the *model one eyeball*." He placed a not so subtle emphasis on what he thought to be a bit of deftly deployed naval slang.

"That's *Mark* One Eyeball. They can't spot us because we're sitting in the best place in this whole system to hide a warship. First, there's the electrical discharges in the planet's atmosphere, lightning storms like all of the thunderstorms on a terrestrial planet times a hundred thousand.

"Second, all the volcanic ejecta that one of the planet's moons is spewing into space interacts with the planet's magnetic field to create Alfvén waves. They ionize all that volcanic stuff, and it flows down the magnetic lines of force to the planet. On the way, the stream of those particles zipping through the planet's magnetic field sets up powerful synchrotron maser radiation—high-intensity radio waves that have a wonderful sensor-scrambling effect. Combine that with the gravitation, atmosphere, clouds, and magnetic field of the planet itself, and we're almost impossible to spot unless you come on down into the atmosphere with us and hit us with an active sensor scan at close range, or our thermal stealth gives out and we make a hot spot in the atmosphere."

"I had no idea that you were such a physics maven," the doctor said.

"I'm not. One of my worst subjects, right up there with English Literature 1600 through 1900. *Paradise Lost.* The Brontë Sisters." He shuddered. "I'm just an expert in the physics that gives me ways to hide from, confuse, evade, bamboozle, or misdirect an enemy. At that kind of physics, I could teach graduate-level seminars."

"A fine area in which to be expert in your line of work, although I rather like *The Tenant of Wildfell Hall.* In any event, since we are so well hidden, can we not stay here indefinitely? Perhaps the Krag will grow tired of waiting for us and scurry along on their Krag way to do their other Kragish business."

"No chance. First, they don't do that. Krag are the most relentless creatures in the galaxy," Max said with perhaps a little too much vehemence. He continued more calmly. "They'll stay here until they die of old age. Then, with the feeble gasp of their last, dying rat breath they'll command their ship's computers to destroy us if we ever come out of the clouds even if it's a hundred years later and the ship is crewed by our great grandchildren. But they won't have to wait that long. In just about two hours our heat sink will reach capacity. You know what that means."

"I do. You have explained it to me at tedious and redundant length. What perplexes me, though, is how we are remaining at this altitude and in this position without making ourselves known? If I am not mistaken, being in the atmosphere, we cannot be coasting around the planet in orbit. Therefore, we would have to use our drives, expelling hot gases that heat the atmosphere around us, thereby making the ship liable to be detected."

"You're right. We're not in orbit. And if we were in most any other ship, we'd be dead. Most warships have two maneuvering thruster systems: a main that runs off of plasma from the fusion reactor, and an auxiliary that uses liquid hypergolic bipropellant held in pressurized storage tanks. Because of the extraordinary emphasis on stealth in our design, we have a third—known by a clever acronym that I won't bother you with, as you'd forget it instantly—that operates off of cold gas.

"We take gas—either in the form of our own supplies or drawn in from any atmosphere that we might happen to be in—compress it to the liquid state, and then vent it without combustion through the thruster nozzles, with the rapid expansion of the gas providing thrust. We vary the expansion and compression ratios to manage the temperature of the exhaust to match ambient, so we don't create a hot spot. So long as the fusion reactor keeps pumping out power to operate the system, we could hover here almost indefinitely."

"An ingenious system, no doubt," the doctor said, thoroughly unimpressed. Even the most brilliant feats of aerospace engineering made little impression on him. "It would be even more ingenious if the designers had included a heat exchanger system to allow the cold gas to carry away the thermal energy from the heat sink, allowing you to do an almost continuous 'thermal dump' without creating a thermal signature. But then, I am just the Sawbones around here."

Max was briefly dumbfounded. Why didn't anyone think of that before? He'd have to talk to Wernher about that one. There might be a way to build that modification into the *Cumberland* with spares already on board or parts they could fabricate.

Not recognizing that he had just made a suggestion that might significantly affect the design of stealth vessels for decades to come, the doctor plowed on. "But how did we get in this precarious predicament? I had no idea anything was amiss until we were hit by enemy fire and my patient rolled off the examining table. He was heavily sedated at the time and made a most unsettling thud."

"That's why your treatment beds all have restraint loops," Max said. "Or didn't you know that?"

"I do now, and I plan to make scrupulous use of them hereafter. I hasten to add, however, that they wouldn't be necessary if we were not hit unexpectedly by enemy weapons fire, an event for which you have yet to provide a satisfactory explanation."

"Simple ambush. There's a convoy due through here in about sixteen hours. The admiral sent us here to sanitize the system and make sure it was clear for the convoy. When we jumped into the system, these two cruisers were already here, probably tasked to lie in wait for the same convoy."

"How did we escape? I seem to recall your having told me on more than one occasion that cruisers are much mightier ships than destroyers."

Max restrained himself from rolling his eyes at the doctor's apparent inability to assimilate even the most rudimentary naval knowledge, notwithstanding that he was the most conspicuously brilliant man Max had ever known.

"Much more powerful than we are, Doctor. *Each* of those ships packs about eight times our firepower. How did we get away? First, they weren't expecting us. Usually, the picket or scout destroyer jumps in six or seven hours before the convoy comes through. But Admiral Hornmeyer sent us in early because, well, that's just the sort of thing that he does. That crafty old bastard's got unpredictability down to a science. If a task force has a habit of dividing itself into two groups to attack, when *he* attacks it will be with three groups this time, with five the next, with four the next, and then he'll throw everything he's got at the enemy in one huge formation. Krag prisoners tell us that they've got a whole department, staffed by hundreds of officers, with no function other than to try to predict what Hornmeyer is going to do next, and three times out of four they get it wrong." He chuckled in admiration.

"Anyway, when we jumped in and surprised them, neither of us was ready for a fight, but they were closer to being ready than we were. All our critical systems were safed for the jump, whereas all the Krag had to do was to arm their weapons and start shooting. We were a little bit better off than if they had been expecting us at that moment, but not enough for us to be able to get away unscathed." He shook his head, remembering the shock of being hit by enemy weapons fire less than a minute after coming out of jump, before he was even aware the enemy ships were present.

"You said 'first.' Is there a 'second'?"

"Oh, yes. Remember Midshipman Goldman? The lieutenant I demoted temporarily for verbally abusing an enlisted man?"

"I remember him well." He dropped his voice to just above a whisper. "You may recall that I treated him for a stims addiction."

"Right. Well, it turns out he knows the ins and outs of Krag sensors better than anyone imagined. Apparently, when he was serving on the *Themistocles*, he made the mistake of smarting off to Captain Tobias. You know, 'Temper Tantrum' Tobias? Well, Captain Tobias decided to teach Goldman a lesson and assigned him to spend five months doing nothing but disassembling, reassembling, and testing to destruction hundreds of Krag sensor multiplex relay assemblies he had just taken off a captured Krag tender.

"After that experience, Goldman knew just how to configure our active sensors to emit a pulse precisely tailored to fry the multiplexers. The trick is no good as a standard battle tactic because the emitter isn't built to transmit a tight coherent beam, so unless you're within ten thousand meters or so, the beam spreads out too much and you aren't hitting the multiplexer with enough power to do the job. But since all our weapons were offline, the rat-faced bastards had closed to about eighty-five hundred meters to finish us off.

"We hit both ships with it, effectively blinding them, and ran like scalded dogs. We're not in their sights any more, but in a few hours they'll catch up with us again and have significant advantages in numbers, firepower, and tactical position."

"So what do we do?"

"Have you ever read Sun Tzu?"

"Sun Tzu?" He shook his head. "I thought that was a particularly ridiculous breed of dog. The ones that look like tiny, animated dust mops."

"No, that's *Shih* Tzu. Very lovable pets, I hear. *Sun* Tzu was a Chinese general and philosopher of war. Sixth century BCE. Brilliant. Commodore Middleton made me practically memorize his book, *The Art of War.* Old Sun Tzu is the one who said, 'All warfare is based on deception.'"

"A principle by which you live scrupulously."

"Of course. My most cherished military maxim. But he said something else that is particularly relevant here—this is a paraphrase, of course—but he said basically that when you engage your enemy, it should appear to him that you are doing exactly what he expects you to do."

"What conceivable good does that do?"

"A great deal, actually. Knowing what he expects, you *appear* to do exactly that. Give him one or two clues that point to what he has been thinking you're going to do and that's what he's going to see, even if the clues could point to a hundred other things as well. After all, we all love being right, don't we? The rub is that you are *not* doing what he expects, but rather something completely different.

"You do something that *looks* like you are doing A. He jumps to the conclusion that you *are* doing A and launches his planned response for A, but you are doing *B*. And not only are you doing B—which he didn't expect—but when you made your plans for B, you took into account your exact knowledge of what he would do when he thinks you are doing A. So, he is not ready for you, but *you* are ready for *him*."

"Very clever, indeed. Use his preconceptions against him. That goes along with modern cognitive theory that says people tend to perceive reality in light of preexisting expectations and will ignore large amounts of contrary data before finally changing their minds."

"Right. That's just what I'm counting on."

"So what are you going to do?"

"Exactly what the Krag expect. And no, I won't tell you what that is. You'll just have to be surprised." His face took on a predatory look as he tapped his finger on the icon for one of the Krag cruisers. "Just like our friends with the tails."

Two hours and eleven minutes passed. During that time, Max had ordered the entire crew by turns to go to the mess or the wardroom, as appropriate, for a hot breakfast. Just as her captain would not send the *Cumberland* into battle unfueled, so he saw that the men who served her went into battle with a hot meal in their bellies.

"Coming into position," announced Bartoli. The *Cumberland* had not been maintaining a constant position in the atmosphere; rather, as the moon that was the source of the particle stream had moved in its orbit, causing the stream to shift along with it, the ship had followed the erratic movement of the stream's terminus in the atmosphere. The doctor could sense the tension in CIC gradually increasing as the time to implement the skipper's plan approached. He noticed several of the watch standers covertly wiping sweaty palms on their pants or shifting nervously in their seats. There also seemed to be unusually heavy traffic in and out of the CIC's "head," or lavatory. Obviously, whatever Captain Robichaux had in mind, the crew perceived it to be difficult, risky, or both.

When the ship was in the correct position, and at about the time when the Krag would be surmising that the *Cumberland*'s heat sink was reaching capacity, Bartoli called out, "Now, Skipper."

Max's adrenalin got the better of him. He came to his feet. "EXECUTE," he said, a little too loudly. He did his best not to cringe at how his powerful voice boomed in the CIC's confined space.

LeBlanc gave two sharp pats to the shoulder of Able Spacer First Class Fleishman, the man on Drives, who pushed his control all the way to the stop. "Main sublight ahead at Emergency," said LeBlanc.

Like a rabbit darting out from under a bush, the *Cumberland* shot out from the clouds, her acceleration just over 95 percent of nominal, thanks to hasty repairs by Lieutenant Brown and his band of improvisational engineers. In a few seconds, the destroyer cleared the atmosphere of Mengis VI, accelerating away from the planet and making straight for its closest moon, known prosaically as Mengis VI A, an unremarkable rock just over 3000 kilometers in diameter, orbiting the planet at an altitude of 56,423 kilometers.

"Mr. Nelson," Max said to the man at the Stealth console. "Now that we're out of the atmosphere, let's dump some heat, shall we?"

"Aye, sir. Extending radiator fins seventeen through twenty-three." On the sides of the ship blocked from the enemy vessels' view, radiator fins extended themselves and turned cherry red, radiating into space the heat that *Cumberland* had stored in her heat sink. With no atmosphere around the hull to be heated, the ship could shed its thermal energy without giving away its position, so long as the fins were not in a direct line of sight with either enemy ship.

"Would you please tell me at least the first part of what we are doing, Captain?" asked Sahin in a tone bordering on whining, his almost pathological curiosity getting the better of him.

"Actually, I think I'll yield that honor to Lieutenant DeCosta. XO?"

The executive officer smiled self-deprecatingly and waved the doctor over to his own console, which had more and larger displays tied into more data channels than the doctor's.

"Here we are, Doctor." He pointed to the icon representing the *Cumberland.* "The enemy expected us to keep station in the planet's upper atmosphere until our heat sink reached its capacity, and then, having no other options, make a run for it. Even with stealth systems engaged, at this range and accelerating this hard, we can't completely mask our drive signature, so they can detect us well enough to follow. Now, we are doing exactly what they thought we would do, running right when they expected us to run, falling right into the trap they have prepared for us." The doctor grimaced. This wasn't comforting at all.

DeCosta continued. "Here is the cruiser that was in low orbit," he pointed to an icon moving away from the planet to fall in behind the destroyer. "This one is the 'chase man.' He has gone to flank speed and is doing his best to follow us. He's falling behind right now, but he can already tell from our acceleration curve that, even with our repairs, he has a higher top speed and will eventually overtake us. Right now, we're ducking into the stream of ionized matter from the volcanic moon. Here is the path of the stream," his finger traced a long curve from the moon to the planet.

"Notice that the planet's inner moon is just about to enter it. He thinks we're using the stream to help us lose him or prevent him from getting a missile lock, so he isn't concerned. We're doing just what he expects fleeing prey to do. Run and hide.

"Here is the cruiser that was in high orbit." The XO pointed to another icon on the display. "If the low cruiser is the 'chase man,' then the high cruiser is the 'cutoff man.' The cutoff man's job is to station himself athwart our line of escape, forcing us, he thinks, to do one of three things: One, attack him head on, in which case we will be destroyed by his superior firepower. Two, try to go around him, in which case we are cut off using his superior speed and advantageous starting position and then destroyed by his superior firepower. Three, try to hide in the space between the chase and the cutoff man, the high cruiser serving as the anvil to the low cruiser's hammer. In that case, they use their excellent active sensor capability to locate us and their superior speed to hem us in between them, at which point we are then…"

"Destroyed by their superior firepower," the doctor completed. "It looks gloomy, but you do not seem in the least weighed down by it."

"Here's where reality first starts to diverge from their expectations. See the computer's projection of the cutoff man's most likely intercept course right here?"

"I do, but it is blinking red and seems to go right through this moon."

"Right. That's because we timed our escape maneuver and aimed the direction of our exit so that this moon, Mengis VI A, blocks the cutoff man's direct intercept vector. Unless he wants his current speed to carry him thousands of kills out of his way, he needs to drop a lot of velocity and go around it, following the limb of this moon like this." The XO's finger traced along the curvature of the moon on the side facing away from the planet.

"How do you know he's going on that side rather than on the one nearer the planet?"

"Good question. Because, when the Krag go around a moon or planet, they do it posigrade, that is, along with the direction of the body's rotation, if they can possibly manage it. That's so if they need to make an emergency landing, they have to dump a lot less velocity in order to set down safely. Now, here's his play. He's only going to follow the curvature of Mengis VI A until the shortest distance between him and his estimate of our course projection doesn't go through that moon. At that point, he pulls out of his curve and heads straight toward the line of our course. As soon as he clears the limb of the moon, he turns on his active sensors and starts sweeping the area where he calculates we will be.

"The tail man will do the same thing, sweeping the area ahead of him, with the idea that if we're being painted by the full sensor output from two cruisers roughly ninety degrees apart, we'll show up despite the ionized particles and the maser radiation."

"Won't we show up?" asked the doctor.

"We probably would. But it'll never get that far."

"Weapons," Max interrupted. "Are we clear on the firing procedure and timing for those missiles?"

"Affirmative, Skipper. Talons loaded in all three tubes. Missiles are armed, drives enabled, safeties disengaged, targeting data entered—they're ready for firing in all respects, excepting only that the missile doors are closed. The missiles will be fired by computer when the programmed launch criteria are met, with Chief Wendt in the Weapons back room on the manual firing controller just in case."

"Very well."

"Why Wendt?" DeCosta asked the skipper. "He's got to be in his fifties."

"He may be one of the oldest men on the ship, but he still tests out as having the fastest trigger pull. He beats the young guys every time. Plus, every man on board trusts his judgment—he *is* the Chief of the Boat. No one's going to be distracted worrying about whether he'll make the fire/no fire call correctly."

Sahin could see on the XO's tactical overview display that the icons for the enemy high cruiser and the *Cumberland* were now coming very near to the circle that designated Mengis VI's inner moon, the *Cumberland* inside the particle stream on a course that would take it past the moon on the right-hand side as viewed on the display, and the Krag cruiser on a course straight at the moon from the left, each screened from the other by the moon. Even on the scale shown by the console display, the icons representing the ships seemed to be moving very, very fast.

Max sat down again, the better to see the displays at his console. "Weapons, open missile doors on tubes one, two, and three. Stealth, engage all stealth systems."

"Opening doors." Short pause. Three lights on the Weapons Console changed from blue to green, and Weapons checked three optical feeds. "Visual verification: tubes one, two, and three are open and are clear of obstructions."

"Stealth systems engaged," said Nelson.

"Very well. Prepare to execute first maneuver on my mark." Max stood watching the tactical plot for nearly half a minute, the icons on the screen moving in a slow motion ballet along geometrically perfect arcs. Several of the men in CIC were shifting or fidgeting nervously at their stations. Max noticed.

"Steady, boys, steady," he said evenly, the words from the Union Space Navy's official song. He felt the men take a collective breath, steady themselves, and steel their nerves for what they were about to do, and go through, together.

"First maneuver. Ready... ready... *execute.*" Maneuvering pulled a hard turn, demonstrating the nimbleness for which this class of ship had already become legendary. Within only a few seconds, the destroyer turned through a 94-degree course change, pointing the ship straight at Mengis VI A. As soon as the turn was executed, LeBlanc had his Drives man engage the braking drive at maximum. This maneuver went unobserved by the high cruiser because its line of sight was blocked by the bulk of the nearby moon. The low cruiser likewise did not detect the maneuver because of the *Cumberland*'s highly effective stealth systems, interference from the charged particle stream, and because by doing something unexpected, the ship had in only 1.84 seconds traveled laterally out of the zone covered by the cruiser's most sensitive passive sensors, which had an accumulate and refresh cycle of just over two seconds.

When the destroyer dropped off their sensors, it never occurred to the Krag in the low cruiser that the monkey-blasphemer humans were doing anything but continuing on the same course to fly from their better-armed attackers.

"Are we committing suicide? I see that we are headed directly for the surface of that moon." There was discernable alarm in the doctor's voice.

"No, Doctor, we are not going to hit the surface. We are just going to get very, very close to it."

"How close?"

"The highest surface feature on that moon is right at seven thousand meters, so we will be at seven thousand two hundred."

"Isn't that, according to the old American idiom, 'cutting it a little close'?"

"Yes. It is."

"As long as you are aware of it." It took a very acute ear to detect the sarcasm in the statement. Max had a very acute ear. "In addition to cutting it a little close, aren't we going a little fast for a ship that is going to be that close to the surface?"

"Not really. We'll not be going much more than one thousand kilometers per second."

"Oh, a snail's pace. You *so* ease my mind." This time the sarcasm was not so subtle.

Max kept a close eye on a display on his console, which he had configured to show distance to the surface of the moon. Chief LeBlanc had a similar display. Both men watched the numbers as they fell rapidly. Watched them *very* closely. By Max's orders, this next maneuver would be executed at the chief's command, as he had the better "feel for the ship." Nevertheless, more for his own reassurance than to communicate anything new, Max said to LeBlanc, "Second maneuver at your discretion, Chief."

"Second maneuver at my discretion," the older Cajun acknowledged. On various displays around CIC tied into the forward video feed, Mengis VI's moon approached at terrifying speed. It seemed impossible to avoid a collision, inscribing a new canyon that some wit would probably name the *Cumberland* Valley. People had to remind themselves to ungrit their teeth, to unclench their hands, to breathe.

"All right, men," LeBlanc told the three men at their stations in front of him, "just like we talked about. In five seconds. Four. Three. Two. One. Now!"

At Chief LeBlanc's signal, the man controlling pitch and roll pitched the bow of the ship up so that it was precisely following the contour of the moon's surface and rolled the ship so that its missile tubes, one of which was mounted in the bow exactly between the one and the two o'clock positions, and the other between the seven and the eight, were level with one another. The braking drive disengaged and the main sublight drive went to Flank to push the ship through this maneuver, then to one-tenth power to hold the ship to the trajectory Max had ordered for it, which was anything but an orthodox Keplerian orbit.

The craters and mountains of the desolate world below them whizzed past so rapidly that they could hardly be discerned on the optical feeds. The smallest errant twitch on the pitch controller could slam the *Cumberland* into the surface so hard that the only evidence she had ever existed would be the kilometer-wide crater, the rapidly expanding ball of incandescent gas, and the "we regret to inform you" commgrams to the parents, orphans, and widows.

Dr. Sahin looked at his tactical display. The icon for the *Cumberland* and the icon for the Krag cruiser were approaching one another so fast that they would meet in only a few seconds. He noted from the "data source slot" at the top of the display that the information on the positions of the two ships was being received from the *Cumberland*'s sensor probe launched hours earlier. To all appearances, nothing would stop the two ships from colliding head-on at catastrophic velocities.

"This appears to be an extremely hazardous maneuver," Sahin said. The pitch of his voice was at least a major third above normal. Maybe even a perfect fourth.

"Yes. It is," Max admitted. "But it's a lot less hazardous than fighting it out on even terms with those cruisers."

Just when Sahin was going to ask how much less hazardous it was, the two ships came into sight of one another. Apparently by prior arrangement, this fact required no announcement from the Sensors or Tactical officers. Max simply said, "Now."

Two sharp pats on the shoulder from Chief LeBlanc to the man at Pitch, and the *Cumberland* dove sharply toward the surface of the airless moon and then almost immediately leveled out, barely fifty meters above the crater-scarred terrain. At the same moment, the ship's computer, following the instructions given to it a few hours before, fired two Talon missiles, one from each of the forward missile tubes. In order to give the seeker systems time to lock on, given the close range and high closing velocities of the two vessels, the acceleration coils were set to give the weapons just enough velocity to clear the launch tubes and the bow of the ship, instead of the .61 c that was nominal for the system. At their highly reduced speed, the time from launch to impact was just under a second.

The Krag had no time to react. They were not expecting the humans. Not there. Not then. The blaspheming monkeys were supposed to be in the midst of the particle stream, frantically running for their lives, where they would be located by sensors and attacked minutes from now, not popping up over the limb of this moon and attacking head on.

Accordingly, the Krag didn't have their missile launch systems energized, the missile drives enabled, or the warhead safeties disengaged. Neither had they prepared the ship to receive enemy fire. In fact, the only element of the Krag cruiser's defenses that was in place was its electronic warfare and countermeasures suite, which Union Naval Intelligence had correctly advised was always active.

The ever-alert Krag computer sensed the incoming missile and reacted appropriately, transmitting a highly focused, randomly modulated EM pulse designed to disrupt the Talons' guidance software. One missile behaved as the Krag expected, veering wildly off into deep space, zooming out of sight and off the Krag sensor scans. But the other flew true, straight at the Krag warship, past the powerful Krag deflectors, at the moment configured to repel space debris but not weapons fire, through the multiple point defense zones protected by interlocking layers of four distinct kinds of antimissile weapons, all safed and deactivated, and to within just over a meter of the cruiser's hull, equipped with structural integrity fields and blast suppression emitters that would allow it to withstand the detonation of a nuclear warhead the size of that carried by the Union's Talon missile—all switched to standby.

The 150-kiloton fusion warhead blew just as the *Cumberland* streaked between the cruiser and the surface of the moon below. The resulting globe of white-hot plasma hungrily ingested the forward two thirds of the cruiser, fracturing its very atoms into free nuclei and electrons, while melting or shattering the rear third into a spray of pea-sized droplets of molten metal and plastic, interspersed with tens of thousands of solid chunks of the harder parts of the hull and the more heat-resistant engine parts, none larger than a man's head.

Some of these solid pieces arced off into space to join the other debris, moonlets, and other bodies that swarmed around the enormous gas giant, whereas others slammed into the surface of Mengis VI A, an artificial storm of meteoroids littering the tiny world like deadly metallic hail. The fireball blossomed behind the destroyer as, apparently due to accident triggered by the proximity of the nuclear explosion, the *Cumberland*'s rear tube fired another missile that also zoomed away from the moon in a peculiar-looking trajectory. If the Krag happened to have any sensor drones in the neighborhood, they would see an accidental firing and a wasted missile.

In fistfighting, it's called a "sucker punch." In warfare, it's called "tactical surprise." To the crew of the *Cumberland*, it was a definite kill.

The fireball now astern, Max called out, "Weapons, reload all tubes with Talons. Maneuvering, fourth maneuver . . . *execute*."

As Weapons acknowledged the order, a few quick pats on the shoulder from Chief LeBlanc prompted the Yaw and Pitch men to steer the agile warship through another violent maneuver, bending the *Cumberland*'s course under full acceleration in a sharp hairpin turn back toward the middle of the particle stream and then turning her again, this time gradually, until after a few moments the *Cumberland* settled into its former path, with the enemy ship that had been the low cruiser about twelve thousand kilometers behind and slowly gaining. As soon as the ship was reestablished along its former course, Max turned to Nelson at Stealth.

"Mr. Nelson, I think it's time for that malfunction we discussed."

"Aye, sir." Nelson touched a key on his console. A few seconds later, he announced. "Apparent malfunction in Stealth systems caused us to leak EM aft for five point three seconds, after which the malfunction was 'repaired' and the leakage stopped."

"Well done, Mr. Nelson."

"Malfunction?" The doctor sounded concerned.

"Not a real one," Max mollified him. "I wanted to be sure the cruiser knew we were here, so we shut down a few of the electromagnetic suppression systems for a few seconds so that some of the electromagnetic radiation the ship generates in normal operation leaked in the Krag's direction.

"We gave him a contact for just over five seconds, which is long enough for him to get a definite detection as well as a rough bearing, but not enough time to give his computer sufficient data points over time to do target motion analysis and spit out a firing solution. With all the sensor interference in this particle stream, he's going to have to close within about fifteen hundred kills to get a strong enough detection to be able to fire his weapons accurately."

"Why, look at that. We're doing as we were doing before! Running away from the enemy cruiser inside this river of ionized material." The doctor looked perplexed. "I'm certainly pleased that we dispatched that other ship so deftly, but are we still not in an impossible tactical situation with regard to this other vessel? Is she not speedier and more powerful than we, such that she will eventually catch up with us and defeat us in combat?"

"It certainly looks that way, doesn't it," answered Max. "As far as Mr. Krag is concerned, we never left the stream, and we've been running for our lives the whole time. All he's seen of us tells him that we're panicked prey, so that's all he's going to expect."

Max looked at a chrono display that, for reasons unknown to the doctor, had been counting down and was now at just under one minute. He then glanced at the tactical overview display, which was now set on a large scale, with the *Cumberland* at the bottom of the screen, the cruiser at the top, and a small green "x," which was apparently a stationary point in space, creeping just to the left of the destroyer. Now it seemed to be moving toward the cruiser as the ships moved through space and the display adjusted, keeping them in the same relative positions so that they did not run off the edge of the screen. "Speaking of which..." Max hit the comm button.

"Engineering. Brown here. I surmise that this is my cue."

"Spot on, my good chap. You've got thirty seconds. I'll give you a countdown from five."

"Understood."

A tense twenty-five seconds went by, Sahin wishing he had time to ask a quick question so he could understand what was happening, but knowing that he did not.

"Five. Four. Three. Two. One. NOW!"

"Executing," said the engineer over the comm. Everyone in CIC, and presumably throughout the ship, felt a lurch as the main sublight drive abruptly stopped providing acceleration. "Main sublight on standby," Brown informed Max. "As far as the Krag are concerned, they saw a plasma dump followed by a drive shut-down. They're going to conclude that the damage they did to us earlier caused a catastrophic drive failure and that we are now without propulsion."

"Outstanding," said Max gleefully.

"*Outstanding*?" Sahin was aghast. "Now that we are no longer accelerating, that huge ship full of voracious man-sized rats is going to catch up with us and send us all to Jannah. I had hoped to go there, but it was my cherished desire to delay the arrival for at least a few more years."

"It's not what it looks like, Doctor. If you go to paradise anytime soon, it won't be because of anything I did today." Max spoke slowly and calmly. "I just need to get the Krag ship, for targeting purposes, to stop accelerating. Talon missiles aren't very good at side shots on rapidly accelerating targets."

"Side shots? I don't understand."

"You will."

"And we can fire only two missiles at a time," the doctor continued. "My understanding is that, if a ship of that kind is prepared for our attack, with his deflectors . . . what is the term . . . *deflecting*, it is unlikely that only two missiles will take him out of action. Is my understanding in error? You know how often I am wrong about such matters."

"No, you've got it right this time."

"I don't understand."

"You will."

"You are becoming repetitious."

"I know."

"The Krag cruiser has engaged its braking thrusters and is slowing rapidly," Mr. Bartoli sang out from Tactical. "He's right in the groove, sir, and he's matching our velocity."

"Excellent, Mr. Bartoli."

The doctor could see from the tactical display that the icon for the Krag ship was now almost on top of the little green x.

"Maneuvering," Max said in a quiet voice, obviously reining in his excitement. "Are you ready?"

"Yes, *sir.*" LeBlanc sounded eager.

"Then... fifth maneuver... *execute.*"

Pitch and Yaw steered the ship through a "flapjack," the maneuver that rapidly flipped the ship bow for stern, after which Drives decisively shoved his main sublight controller all the way forward. In just under five seconds the destroyer had gone from coasting with her bow pointed in the direction of travel to thrusting at emergency power against its forward velocity with her bow pointed at the enemy cruiser. While the sublight drive would not stop the ship any time soon, thrusting against the direction of travel would increase greatly, and unexpectedly from the Krag point of view, the closure rate between the two ships.

The doctor could see that the Krag ship was now almost right on top of the little green "x" on the tactical display. "Weapons," Max called out, "abbreviated firing procedure. Make weapons in tubes one and two ready for firing in all respects, and open missile doors. Set both warheads for maximum yield, and program terminal guidance for custom attack pattern zero one. Set launch tubes for minimum speed."

With the efficiency that Max had already come to expect from him, Levy at Weapons had anticipated this order and had his hands resting near the appropriate controls. Acknowledging the order, his fingers flew into action. It took only a few seconds for the appropriate lights to change from blue to green and for Levy to check the two relevant optical feeds.

"Missiles in tubes one and two ready for firing in all respects. Doors for tubes one and two are open and visually verified to be free of obstructions. Warheads set for yield of one-five-zero kilo tango. Custom attack pattern zero one loaded and selected. Launch tube acceleration at lowest setting."

"Very well."

"Lowest setting? I thought that missiles needed to travel as fast as possible to get through the enemy point defense systems." The doctor sounded genuinely concerned. "That was the point of bolting the missiles onto the cutter when we destroyed the Krag battlecruiser a few weeks ago."

"Relax, Doctor. Today, we're firing Talons. The missiles we fired at the battlecruiser were Ravens. Ravens have a much bigger warhead but are a lot less nimble and with a less effective countermeasures suite. The Talons are sly and fast. They'll get through."

"But why not use the high speed, anyway? I remember more than one occasion on which you told me that faster is better in these cases."

"It usually is, but at this range, faster is *not* better. As close as the Krag ship is to us, if we launched at 61 percent of the speed of light, the missiles would be past the Krag ship before their targeting systems could lock on." During this discussion, Max's eyes had never left the tactical display. "And now, Doctor, speaking of firing..." He watched the display carefully. Just as the cruiser touched the green "x," he gave the order: "Tubes one and two...*fire.*"

The ship shuddered as it spat the two missiles out of the launch tubes, applying just enough acceleration to eject the weapons. Their drive systems kicked in immediately and steered them on oblique trajectories away from the straight line between the two ships, so they could strike the cruiser from its belly and its flanks, where it was more vulnerable. As soon as the missiles cleared the tubes, Max spoke, "Maneuvering, sixth maneuver, *execute.*"

Under Chief LeBlanc's direction, the ship veered violently once more, this time heading straight for the nearest edge of the ionized particle stream and accelerating as hard as could be managed by her damaged propulsion systems. "Captain," announced Kasparov from Sensors a few seconds later, "we have cleared the particle stream."

"Very well. Sometimes the darn things act like a pipeline for the warheads' EMP. Don't want to be in there when they go off if we can help it," said Max. As soon as the destroyer cleared the particle stream, the doctor saw two ^ symbols appear on his tactical overview display, moving rapidly and converging on the Krag cruiser from slightly different vectors. The symbols seemed identical to those representing the two missiles fired by the *Cumberland* just a moment before. "Sir, may I ask, what exactly are these?"

Max glanced down at the display as a grin spread across his face. "Those are our other missiles."

"Other missiles?"

The doctor had barely articulated his question when Levy at Weapons interrupted. "Receiving telemetry from all four missiles. All show successful target acquisition. Handshaking protocol completed. They have switched from Independent Attack to Cooperative Interactive Logic Mode. Maneuvering for simultaneous circumferential detonation. The CILM upgrade in the new Talons is functioning nominally."

The doctor could see the ^ symbols moving quickly to encircle the enemy vessel and approach it from four different directions, preventing the cruiser from being able to concentrate its defenses against a single attack vector. "Missile impact in three, two, one, *now*."

Somewhere between Mr. Levy's "n" and his "w," each of the thirteen or so displays in CIC tied into the optical feeds that were following the Krag Cruiser burst into unwatchable brilliance, their protective circuitry kicking in to limit the brightness to levels that would not damage human retinas or overdrive the video outputs on the panels.

Slowly the flat white of the screens dimmed to show a four-lobed fireball in the shape of a grotesquely obese "x," marking the spot where the Krag cruiser died, expanding and fading, rapidly becoming dimmer and more diffuse as it merged with and disappeared into the cold, tenuous gases of space.

The iron band that had been compressing the chest of every man in CIC vanished. As one, they drew in the *Cumberland*'s processed, recycled, conditioned, bottled, artificial, metal- and lubricant- and ripe-man-tasting air. This stale mélange was, to them, sweeter than the purest breeze from a virgin beach and more bracing than the cleanest, icy blast from a wind-swept glacier. It was the taste of life. These men knew they would not die.

Not today.

Having shared in the collective breath of thanksgiving, Max turned to Chief LeBlanc. "Maneuvering, reduce speed to zero-point-one c, standard deceleration. Make your course for Jump Point Charlie. Good job, everyone. This one will make a good story to tell your kids."

A few of the more exuberant enlisted men slapped each other on the back. The chief had hardly finished acknowledging the order before the doctor, who had been almost beside himself with frustration stemming from unsatisfied curiosity, interjected.

"But Captain, who fired those other two missiles?" the doctor asked, his face a veritable study in confusion. He stood, too frustrated to remain sitting.

Max shrugged. "We did. Who else was there?"

"But I saw us fire only two. I remember. I was sitting right here." He pointed to his seat in indignation, as though its mere presence helped prove the truth of what he was saying.

"And you were sitting right there when we fired the other two," Max said placidly.

"Certainly not. I can state most emphatically that I recall no such missiles being fired. In fact, the only other missiles were the one that hit the first cruiser. Except for those other two that went..." He trailed off and started to nod appreciatively. "Ohhh...I think I begin to see. 'All warfare is based on deception.' You are a sly fox. I think old Sun Tzu would be proud. What did you do, then?"

"All along, my problem was how to take out these cruisers when we really didn't have enough firepower to do it. We can fire only two missiles at a forward target at a time. But it takes four missiles to throw enough counter-countermeasures at them and to make their systems divide their attention enough so the missiles can get through. I had to get one of those cruisers with a sucker punch—you saw how we did that by appearing right in front of the first one where he least expected us.

"With the second ship, the trick was how to launch four missiles without him knowing in enough time to evade them. So I fired two when the second cruiser's view of us was blocked by that moon and made it look like a miss and a misfire in case he had any sensor drones in the system. Levy and I programmed those two missiles to drop down to their slowest speed, take fuel-efficient trajectories around that moon, and then attack from the flank. That's what that business about the supposed engine failure was about.

"We just had to be very careful about the timing and the velocities to put the enemy cruiser in just the right spot at just the right time so that the missiles could find it. The faked malfunction also made sure that he arrived expecting wounded and panicked prey, not a circumferential missile attack. We had very little margin for error. So, we followed Sun Tzu's advice by appearing to do exactly what the Krag expected. They responded just like Sun Tzu said they would. They were predictable."

"You say 'predictable' as though it left a bad taste in your mouth."

"It does. In this business, predictability is a cardinal sin. When you become predictable in combat, there is only one outcome—you die."

CHAPTER 2

18:02Z Hours, 15 March 2315

"Church, I'll be right behind you. I merely want to make certain that this equipment is properly stowed." Dr. Sahin watched as Nurse Church and Corpsman Worth trundled midshipman Gilbertson away to the Casualty Station. His injury, a supracondylar fracture of the humerus, was painful but presented no special problems in treatment. The boy had been hurrying while carrying some part or other and hadn't looked where he was going, tripped over a properly marked step in the floor, tried to stop his fall by putting out one of his arms, and had broken the upper arm bone. The supracondylar fracture was one of the most common in children and was endemic among midshipman. Among naval doctors, it was, in fact, known as the "midshipman's break."

Once he restored the first aid kit to its proper location and noted what supplies in it would require replacement, Sahin looked around. As was true of every other compartment on board, this one wore its name prominently stenciled on the wall: Jump Drive Power Junction Compartment. One wall of the compartment was the outer hull of the ship. Dr. Sahin could see a sturdily but roughly patched three-meter section of hull that had been blasted out of existence by a Krag plasma cannon, near which there were six locations where work was being performed. It appeared that the men were constructing a complex piece of equipment from parts being brought in from another compartment.

In response to his question, one man informed him that they were "rebuilding the whole bleeding Jump Drive Power Junction from spares, and not taking their time about it, neither." Bram could see that; at each of the six places where work was going on, there were two men installing parts and one man with a padcomp providing instructions and relaying requests for additional parts through midshipmen who retrieved the parts from stores. Other midshipmen grabbed tools for the workers as needed, with a few burly spacers and a man with a small hoist available to do heavy lifting as needed. The chief engineer stood by, ready to answer questions and solve problems.

Every man had a job. Every man was busy. No one was standing around waiting for a part, for instructions, or for someone else to get out of the way so he could do something. It wasn't chaos—it was a symphony. Outside of an operating theater, the doctor could not remember ever seeing any operation being carried out on board ship with as much precision and coordination as this one. He had heard that Lieutenant Brown was remarkably efficient and often managed to complete repairs in record time. In light of what he saw, it was not hard to understand why. With a nod to the engineer, he returned to the Casualty Station.

Chief Engineer Brown had not been entirely truthful. He had estimated that the construction of the new jump drive power junction would take at least twenty-four hours and, according to the book, as many as thirty-eight. The job actually took eighteen and a half. The jump drive repaired, Brown could turn his attention to completing repairs to the fusion reactor cooling systems so that the *Cumberland* could recover all of her remarkable speed—speed that the tiny ship needed desperately to complete the kinds of missions for which she was built.

Meanwhile, Max was writing the Contact and After Action Report, relating the engagement in the Mengis system, to be sent to his immediate commander, Admiral Hornmeyer at Task Force Tango Delta, with a copy to the Office of the Chief of Naval Operations at Norfolk on Earth. As usual, he was struggling with where to strike the balance between the two competing goals of any after-action report: on the one hand, communicating to one's superiors the commander's aggressiveness, courage, dash, and daring while, on the other, reassuring those same superiors of this same commander's prudence, reasonableness, caution, and circumspection. Maybe it would be easier to write if he had multiple personality disorder.

Max was particularly keen on getting this report right. The last time he had met with the admiral, old Hit 'em Hard had hinted that he had some sort of interesting assignment in mind for the *Cumberland*, and Max didn't want to say anything in the report that might change the admiral's mind.

In any event, it would be several days before the *Cumberland* was going to be doing much of anything, interesting or otherwise. With her compression drive out of commission until she could rendezvous with a repair tender, the *Cumberland* could travel through space in only two ways: propelled by her main sublight drive through normal, Einsteinian space, and hurled by her jump drive from one presurveyed jump point to another, similar point in a nearby solar system, skipping over the intervening light years in an instant. With these limitations, it took the *Cumberland* something like sixteen hours to travel at roughly half the speed of light the average 60 AU distance within a star system from the jump point by which it arrived to the jump point by which it left. And the task force was four systems away.

Given the present performance level of this crew, though, there was always plenty to keep the men busy while the ship crossed one star system after another, mainly training, training, and more training. There were GQ drills, combat drills, firefighting drills, damage control drills, and boarder repulsion drills. There was rifle practice, shotgun practice, sidearm practice, grenade practice, and practice with the various edged weapons issued to or allowed to be used by the officers and men, including the boarding cutlass, the dirk, and the battle-ax.

Maybe, if they work very, very hard, the crew's proficiency level will rise to the task force average. Average would represent a substantial improvement because, when Max took command, the crew's performance rating was the worst in the task force. Max was about to summon his XO to come see him about trying to squeeze more training into the schedule, when his comm buzzed.

"Captain, here."

"Skipper, this is Chin. I've just decrypted a signal that I think you need to see. And sir, this is going to sound a bit odd, but I think you're going to want to have Dr. Sahin there with you when you see it."

Unlike some officers, Max believed that the obligations of command ran in both directions. Obviously, subordinates owed their superiors obedience and respect. Perhaps not so obviously, but of equal importance, superiors owed their subordinates duties as well: loyalty, compassion, respect for their dignity, recognition of their value as individuals, teaching and guidance, correction and discipline, praise and reward for excellence and outstanding effort, and—maybe above all—trust. For Max, when a subordinate made a recommendation of that kind, particularly when all that was at stake was a little time and inconvenience, you didn't cross-examine the man about his reasons. Instead, you took his advice, proving by your actions that he has your trust. It nearly always paid off.

"Come to my day cabin in half an hour. I'll have the doctor here by then."

Chin got there first, with the doctor arriving a few moments later. The captain's steward served all three men some of the excellent and ruinously expensive coffee given to Dr. Sahin by Ellington Wortham-Biggs, an art dealer on Rashid IV. As always, the taste was sublime. When Chin took a sip of the coffee and recognized the flavor, an ironic smile slowly wrote itself on his lips.

"Okay, Chin, what have you got?"

The communications officer, only a twenty-year-old ensign who had never before sat drinking coffee in the captain's day cabin, took a second or two to compose himself before beginning.

"Sir, the *Cumberland* has assigned to it metaspacial data channel 77580, and we monitor it constantly. We get ten or twelve transmissions on it per watch, in addition to the signals we get on the ALL FLEET channel, the Task Force Tango Delta channel, *et cetera*.

"Well, about an hour ago we received a signal on channel 77580—only it didn't start off with an authentication code prefix." To the obviously confused doctor: "That's a twenty-seven-character identifier, changed daily, assigned to each authorized naval sender, which is how we know a signal is from Norfolk or Admiral Hornmeyer instead of from the Krag or a bunch of schoolkids in North Tonawanda, New York. Ordinarily, we would have discarded it, since civilians send signals on the wrong channel all the time. They get the digits transposed, punch in the wrong number, have a glitch in their equipment, bump the channel selector in the middle of sending, *et cetera*. Most of those signals are in clear. No code. No encryption. But this signal was encrypted. Not only that, it's a Union Space Navy encrypt. *Permafrost*."

Max suddenly sat bolt upright. "*Permafrost*? You're sure they used that one?"

"No doubt, sir. We get a perfectly comprehensible, if a bit cryptic, message if we use *Permafrost*. Otherwise, we just get a lot of gibberish."

"Pardon me," the doctor verbally threw an elbow to get into the conversation. "But not everyone present is versed on the latest developments in military and naval cryptography. What is so special about *Permafrost*?"

The entire ship's company had tacitly agreed that it was the captain's job to answer this kind of question for the doctor. Max tried to keep his voice from sounding too pedantic. "It's the code name of a high-level naval encrypt. In fact, it's Indigo level, which is the second highest. We replaced it with *Icicle*—what? About four months ago?" Chin nodded a confirmation.

"Even if we have no indication of it having been broken, we never use any encryption for more than a year. That way, even if someone does break it, the damage is limited, and the enemy has to start off breaking a new one.

"*Permafrost* was the main high-level encrypt we used for sending intelligence reports, operational orders, tactical and strategic communications—basically the kind of information that would do the most damage if it fell into the hands of the enemy. There's only one higher level, Violet, that we use for our deepest, darkest secrets. I've never received anything encrypted at that level—I'm not important enough, you see—so I really don't know what is more important than the Indigo material. Who other than the Navy would have the ability to send a message in *Permafrost*, and why would they do it?"

"I have an idea, sir," said Chin, somewhat tentatively.

"Let's have it."

"Another government with a strong defense and intelligence establishment could pull it off: Romanova, Rashid, Ghifta, Pfelung. Now, suppose a private party wanted to hint that he had high-level connections with one of those governments but did not want to come right out and say so. Or if a government wanted to communicate something to us unofficially through a private party, but in a way that said the communication had official sanction. This would be a good way to do it. The sender would be providing us with his bona fides right there, in the structure of the message. Of course, I've seen the message, and that theory fits with what it says."

"Let's see the message then."

Chin reached into a pocket of his uniform and pulled out two slips of paper. Actual paper. Very few things on a warship were printed on paper. With each man having two or three padcomps and computer workstations and consoles with computer access all over the ship, there was little need to print anything. Perhaps more than anything else, committing the message to hard copy showed how much importance Chin attached to the communication.

He slid the printouts across the small table to the captain and the doctor. They read: "TO THE DISCIPLE OF APOLLO STOP THE MAN WITH WHOM YOU LAST TOUCHED SWORDS URGENTLY DESIRES TO MEET WITH YOU AND YOUR PRINCIPAL IN CONFIDENCE ON A MATTER OF THE HIGHEST POSSIBLE IMPORTANCE TO THOSE WHO SHARE YOUR QUESTIONABLE TASTE IN ATTIRE STOP COME TO THE PLACE WHERE THE MASTIFF SLEEPS AS SOON AS YOU ARE ABLE STOP WEAR SOMETHING TURQUOISE AND ARRIVE RIDING THE SAME HORSE AS PREVIOUSLY STOP MESSAGE ENDS."

"Now I don't understand all of this," Chin said, "but based on the reference to Apollo, I thought it was probably addressed to you, Doctor, and that he wants to meet with the both of you. I don't know the rest, but it looked extremely important to me, so I brought it to your attention right away."

"Outstanding work, Chin," Max said. "Your instincts were perfectly correct. Thank you. The doctor and I will take this from here. You're dismissed." Chin drained his coffee cup, set it down, and left.

"Well, Bram, I hope you can make more sense of this than I can, because other than knowing who Apollo is, the rest of it is Greek to me."

"Apollo. Greek. Your wit never ceases to amaze. But as a matter of fact, Max, I believe I understand every word of it perfectly. This is only fitting. The message is, after all, addressed to me. One might expect, therefore, that the writer would adapt the message to my particular understanding."

"All right, then, translate it for me."

"Very well. As Ensign Chin correctly surmised, I am the disciple of Apollo. The physician's Hippocratic Oath begins with the invocation of several ancient deities, the first of whom is Apollo. The man with whom I recently touched swords is the merchant Ellington Wortham-Biggs. As part of our recent dealings we swore a Rashidian 'sword oath' that involved drawing our swords and touching them flat to flat, near the tips. You, my friend, are my principal. Those who share my questionable taste in attire are, I believe, the Navy, as we all wear the same uniform, which, I believe, the perfectly turned out Mr. Wortham-Biggs would regard as most unbefitting a gentleman. The directive to wear something turquoise is most likely a reference to the turquoise sash that goes on my uniform when I am acting as an ambassador. He wishes that I be empowered to act in that capacity when

I meet with him, just as I was with the Pfelung. 'The place where the mastiff sleeps' is his private office. There was a most enormous, somnolent, loudly snoring mastiff there when we met."

"And 'the same horse' means that we are to arrive in the microfreighter rather than bringing the *Cumberland*, a rated warship of a foreign power, to the capital world of the kingdom," Max finished.

"A reasonable interpretation."

"But what would be the 'matter of highest possible importance'?'"

"I have no idea, but as you could tell from my report regarding my negotiations with him, this gentleman is wealthy, exceptionally well-connected, and possesses impressive intellectual gifts. If he wants to meet with me in an ambassadorial capacity and says that the subject matter of that meeting is something of the highest possible importance to the Navy, I am inclined to believe him."

"So am I."

CHAPTER 3

06:42Z Hours, 19 March 2315

The doctor wasn't the only person who seemed to believe the veracity of the coded message. The admiral also seemed to be convinced it was legitimate. Max pulled up his most recently issued orders:

09:55Z 17 March 2315
TOP SECRET
URGENT: FOR IMMEDIATE IMPLEMENTATION
FROM: HORNMEYER, L.G., VADM USN CDR TF TD
TO: ROBICHAUX, MAXIME T., LCDR USN

1. USS CUMBERLAND, DPA 0004, IS ORDERED TO RAIPUR II AT BEST PRUDENT SPEED TO RENDEZVOUS WITH ROTTERDAM CLASS TENDER, USS NEWPORT NEWS, TMA 1968, TO UNDERGO REPAIRS AND REFIT CONSISTENT WITH SEPARATE ORDERS ISSUED THIS DATE.

2. YOU AND DOCTOR SAHIN ARE TEMPORARILY DETACHED FROM VESSEL AND DIRECTED TO

PROCEED TO RASHID IV, TRANSPORT VIA SHETLAND MICROFREIGHTER PREVIOUSLY ISSUED. WHEN IN RASHID SYSTEM, AS WELL AS EN ROUTE TO AND FROM, YOU AND DOCTOR SAHIN ARE AUTHORIZED TO WITHHOLD DISCLOSURE OF NAVAL AFFILIATION AS YOU DEEM APPROPRIATE TO COMPLETION OF MISSION. UNIFORM REGULATIONS ARE WAIVED FOR THESE PERSONNEL FOR DURATION OF THIS MISSION.

3. DOCTOR SAHIN IS HEREBY APPOINTED ACTING UNION AMBASSADOR AND MINISTER PLENIPOTENTIARY TO THE UNIFIED KINGDOM OF RASHID, ALLIED EMIRATES, AND PROTECTED ISLAMIC WORLDS FOR THE PURPOSE OF CONDUCTING ANY NEGOTIATIONS AND CONCLUDING ANY AGREEMENTS WITHIN THE SCOPE OF THE INSTRUCTIONS ISSUED TO HIM UNDER SEPARATE COVER. IN THIS REGARD, HIS AUTHORITY SHALL BE DEEMED TO SUPERCEDE THAT OF THE REGULARLY APPOINTED UNION RESIDENT MINISTER NOW IN PLACE. SIGNED AND SEALED COMMISSION TO THAT EFFECT ALREADY IN POSSESSION OF LCDR ROBICHAUX.

4. DURATION OF DIPLOMATIC MISSION TO BE AT DISCRETION OF DOCTOR SAHIN BUT SHALL NOT EXCEED FIFTEEN DAYS ABSENT EXPLICIT ORDERS FROM THIS COMMAND.

5. LCDR ROBICHAUX IS REMINDED THAT WARSHIP HULL MATERIAL, NOT TO MENTION JUMP DRIVE COMPONENTS AND COMPRESSION DRIVE PRIMARY PHASE REGULATORS, DO NOT CONDENSE FROM NEBULAE, NOR ARE THEY EASY TO REQUISITION WHEN THE FLEET IS 1000 LIGHT YEARS AWAY

FROM THE CORE SYSTEMS. EXERCISE GREATER CARE IN THE FUTURE.

6. GIVEN THAT CUMBERLAND IS IN FOR REPAIRS, I MIGHT AS WELL AUTHORIZE THE REPAIR CREW TO ATTACH A SECOND BRONZE BATTLE STAR TO THE VESSEL IN RECOGNITION OF RECENT COMBAT VICTORY OVER TWO CRUISER ENEMY FORCE AT MENGIS VI. THIS CREW HAS COME A LONG WAY.

7. I HAVE REVIEWED REPORT RE ENGAGEMENT AT MENGIS VI. WHILE I HESITATE TO ENDORSE SUCH AN IMPROBABLE SEQUENCE OF HARE-BRAINED STUNTS AS ACCEPTABLE NAVAL COMBAT MANEUVERS, MAGNITUDE OF LOSSES INFLICTED UPON THE ENEMY COMPELS ME AGAINST MY BETTER JUDGMENT TO RECOMMEND YOU FOR THE ORDER OF TACTICAL MERIT. IF THE COMMENDATIONS BOARD HAS ANY SENSE, THEY WILL DENY MY REQUEST.

8. STAY OUT OF TROUBLE, ROBICHAUX. IF YOU DO ANYTHING STUPID, I WILL KICK YOUR ASS

At least, Max thought, there is no doubt that the admiral wrote these orders himself. He loved the warm, secure feeling he got from knowing that he was on Admiral Hornmeyer's good side.

Given the microfreighter's speed limitations, it was a two-day trip from Raipur II to Rashid IV, a journey that the two men spent mostly catching up on things. Max worked on what was still referred to as "paperwork," notwithstanding the almost complete absence of paper employed in its completion. Running a warship, even a warship as small as the *Cumberland*, required that her commander generate, read, review, comment upon, complete, fill out, check off, authenticate, sign, verify, forward, and reply to a staggering volume of documents and communications, a process that consumed several hours a day.

The doctor was reading various medical journals, treatment bulletins, and other newly available information on advances in medical science. This process as well was quite time-consuming, particularly given the number of fields in which the doctor was interested and tried to keep up his expertise.

They also caught up on sleep. Neither man had gotten much rest since the two had reported aboard the *Cumberland* on 21 January 2315. The microfreighter's automated cabin monitoring system recorded many, many hours of deep, vigorous, bulkhead-rattling, manly snoring during the journey.

Both men were well rested and relaxed when they jumped into the Rashid system on 19 March and made contact with Rashidian System Traffic Control. Having completed the standard electronic identification, interrogation, and response process, the microfreighter, known only by the prosaic registry number GPGC 72114, had been waiting about five minutes to receive instructions from the traffic controllers. The doctor was getting impatient.

"Do you think that something is amiss? I cannot imagine why anything would take this long."

"Relax, Bram. Traffic controllers are just another species of government bureaucrat." He smiled and turned toward his friend. "You are familiar with the three imperatives of bureaucratic behavior, right?"

The doctor shook his head. "Other than 'cause as much frustration as possible to Ibrahim Sahin,' I'm sure I have no idea."

"Well, then, it's a good thing you have me in your life to impart these nuggets of pure, triple-distilled wisdom to you. I am tasked with the completion of your already considerable education. Attend closely, my friend. Here are the Three Rules of

Bureaucratic Behavior that Commodore Middleton taught to me years ago.

"One: Never, ever hurry. If you do something fast once, people will expect you to do it that fast every other time. Two: Never be the first person to do anything. To err is human, but to err in a way no one has erred before makes people question your judgment. Three: There is no mistake that cannot be papered over by enough of the right kind of documentation. Once the dust settles, it's not what you do, but what you say about what you did, that matters."

The doctor chuckled. "There is more truth to those statements than I really care to admit. There is a surprising amount of bureaucracy in a military hospital, you know. I was truly surprised because I thought that the objective external constraints of the life and death of patients would limit the development of bureaucratic tendencies. Unfortunately, however..."

The doctor's exposition on the subject of medical bureaucracy was interrupted by the three quick beeps of an attention signal from the comm panel indicating that traffic control was about to issue instructions. Twenty seconds later, the speaker came to life.

"Union Microfreighter Galaxy Papa Galaxy Charlie seven-two-one-one-four, this is Rashidian jump point traffic control. We are prepared to transmit navigational instructions. Are you ready to copy? Over."

Max hit the transmit key. "This is one-one-four, acknowledging. Ready to copy instructions. Over."

"One-one-four, you are cleared to enter system immediately. Safety, cargo inspection, and customs clearance have been waived. Entry visas are conferred upon both vessel occupants without personal interview. Standard traffic pattern approach requirement is waived. You are being given a direct approach to

Rashid IV and direct clearance to land on Victor India Papa Pad zero-zero-two at Amman Spaceport. Set your transponder to squawk Kilo Papa Lima Charlie, and that will get you all the way to the surface. Trajectory being downloaded to your navcomp right now. Please acknowledge receipt. Over."

Max keyed the navcomp and saw that a nearly straight line trajectory from the ship's current position to the surface of Rashid IV had been plotted without any of the usual weaving about to avoid other traffic, curving to avoid communications beam corridors, or oblique angles designed to bring the ship through traffic control points. Usually, the only time a ship got to follow so straight a path was when it was a warship going into combat and was more interested in nuking the traffic control center than in following any instructions it might happen to issue.

"This is one-one-four. Thank you, control. Trajectory received, instructions acknowledged. Initiating approach. One-one-four out." He killed the pickup, set the course, and engaged the drive. Then he turned to his companion. "Son. Of. A. Bitch."

"Clearly, you are astonished."

"Astonished? I'm flabbergasted. In the twenty years since I went to space, I've never heard of a dinky little banged-up foreign-flag microfreighter jumping into one of these independent systems and being given priority clearance all the way from the jump point to the ground, on a VIP landing pad, and on a nearly perfect direct trajectory at that. Normally, jump point control would have handed us off to system control, who would have handed us off to Rashid IV planetary zone control, then a hand-off to low orbit and proximity control, hand-off to approach control, hand-off to descent control, hand-off to spaceport and landing control.

"Plus, in a trading center like Rashid, we would normally have to follow an approach pattern in line behind a dozen or two other ships, go through four or five traffic control points, at any one of which we could be held for hours awaiting other traffic and clearances. It would all take at least twenty hours and probably closer to thirty-six. As it stands, we'll be on the ground in about eight hours or so, almost all of which is just the time it takes at our cruising speed to go from point A to point B. Didn't you have to go through all of those stages when you came here in the micro-freighter back in January?"

Sahin's eyes took on a faraway expression. "I suppose that we did, but Spacer Fahad was piloting the ship, and I wasn't paying very close attention. As I recall, I was reading an amazing journal article on Krag molecular biology and the relationship between the genetic sequences that they evolved for the creation of large, powerful brains to those evolved by humans. What made the article so intriguing is that, although we share many DNA sequences with the Krag, when you consider that we have forty-six chromosomes and they have forty-two, the allocation of particular base sequences to certain chromosomes doesn't correspond with the similar allocation in humans. The instances of correspondence versus the instances of difference...

"I see your eyes glazing over, my friend. I am certain that I am boring you. In any event, you may take my word that the article was fascinating in the extreme and was more than sufficient cause for my lack of attention to the mundane details of how Spacer Fahad and I were routed from the jump point to the surface."

"Perfectly understandable," Max said, hoping that the semblance of sincerity with which he invested the statement was convincing. "Anyway, clearly we're being given the VIP treatment. Your friend Mr. Wortham-Biggs must be expecting us and apparently has the clout to see that we hit on the ground as fast as that can be made to happen. He must have something very important in mind."

"I think that we were able to surmise that already from the contents of his message. Incidentally, why do all of the Rashidians calling this ship call it by a series of letters and numbers instead of its name? It would seem much more efficient to call us the *Bosporus* or the *Lemur* or whatever our name is instead of GCPP and a bunch of numbers."

"That's GPGC."

"Whatever. Who can remember something like 'GPGC,' anyway? So, why not use our name?"

"We don't have one."

"Don't have one? I thought there was some sort of interstellar navigational treaty or other that requires all ships to have names."

"There is. But only ships displacing more than ten thousand metric tons get names. Anything smaller just gets a registry number."

"Can't we give it an informal name then, just between us? It would be so much more convenient than always having to say 'the microfreighter is going here' or 'the microfreighter just came from there,' or 'let's hop in the microfreighter and go to Asimov III B ii 4 g—I hear the Hariseldonfish are running this time of year.'"

Max found himself grinning at the doctor's fictitious world with its fictitious fish. "What kind of name, then?"

"Something easy and logically related to 'Cumberland.' I am not from Earth and my forbears are not from North America, so North American Earth geography is not a strength for me, so I ask this to you. Isn't 'Cumberland' the name of both a mountain pass and a river as well?"

"Sure. The river was named first, and then several features in the area were given the same name—the Cumberland Gap, the Cumberland Valley, and so on. A creek that flows into the Cumberland River is what created the Gap."

"In addition to this creek, does the Cumberland have other tributaries?"

"I believe it does. Why?"

"What are the names of the tributaries of the Cumberland River? One of those might do."

"Let's look." Max pulled up the proper database. "Two main tributaries. They are called 'forks' of the river; that's just how people named things in those days, but they do have specific names: the Poor and the Clover. There we go, then. Between us, we'll call her the *Clover*, because she serves, or is *tributary* to the *Cumberland*. It's something of a pun, you see, on both meanings of 'tributary.'"

"I get it. Surprisingly, though, I actually like it."

"*Clover* it is," said Max. "I'll cut the order when we get back to the *Cumberland*. Among our crew, she will be known as the *Clover*."

A noise from the pilot's console demanded Max's attention. He turned from his friend to the main console, which had automatically pulled up the Vessel Intercepts and Collisions display.

"Looks like we're about to get some company," he said. "Two incoming vessels, small and fast. They're scanning us with powerful and reasonably sophisticated, but not state-of-the art, sensors. Constant bearing, decreasing range. Look like fighters. The last intelligence report I read said that the Rashidians weren't maintaining fighter patrols near either of the inhabited worlds in this system. I wonder what's up."

"Do you suppose that they are sent to destroy us?"

"Not likely, Bram. After all, they have a major battle station covering the jump point. That monster could have easily blown us to flaming atoms two seconds after we jumped in. Besides, I don't think it likely that they would roll out the red carpet with one hand and stab us in the back with the other. That doesn't sound like the Rashidians who, after all, are renowned throughout Known Space for their honor and hospitality. You've been there. You know them better than I do. Does that sound like them?"

"No. You are correct. What do you think the fighters are doing?"

"Escort. They're here to make sure we get on the ground safely, which worries me.... It worries me a lot."

He advanced his pilot's seat all the way up to the console and began flipping switches, pulling up displays, and configuring soft key panels. From his own somewhat limited expertise as a pilot, Dr. Sahin could see that Max was enabling the targeting scanners for the ship's weapons systems, bringing the auxiliary fusion reactor and its cooling system on line to provide the *Clover* with speed and maneuverability that no opponent would suspect she had, and powering up its full array of active sensor equipment.

The doctor's face showed his confusion. He started to open his mouth, but Max, still working his console very quickly but without any trace of haste, articulated his question for him and offered an answer.

"Why am I worried because the Rashidians are sending an escort to make sure we get to the surface safely? Because, my friend, the Rashidians would not be providing an escort to make sure we get on the ground safely unless they believe there might be someone else out there somewhere trying to make sure that we don't."

An ominous silence followed, broken only by the sound of Max pulling up several different screens on the main comm console and then typing furiously. He had also suddenly decided to get some message traffic out. Just as he sent the last message, the comm panel gave two quick beeps indicating that the *Clover* was being hailed by another ship. Twenty seconds passed. "Union microfreighter Galaxy Papa Galaxy Charlie seven-two-one-one-four, this is a Royal Rashidian Naval Fighter; my call sign for this mission is Escort One. My counterpart is Escort Two. Please acknowledge. Over."

"Escort One, this is one-one-four, reading you five by five. Do you have any special instructions for me? Over."

"Negative one-one-four. Maintain course and speed as previously instructed by jump point control, without reference to our maneuvers. *We* will maintain formation with *you*. If any unauthorized ship approaches, simply maintain your course and speed, do not attempt any evasive maneuvers, and we will take care of the situation. Over."

"Affirmative, Escort One. We will steer a lubber line and leave any Richthofens to you. By the way, are you expecting any 'unauthorized ships' in particular? Over."

A few seconds passed. Max knew why: the pilot was not authorized to tell Max what he knew but had probably been told who he was escorting and therefore knew that even though Max did not fly a fighter, he was a pilot, and a bona fide military pilot with extensive combat experience at that. And all space pilots obeyed one rule, a rule that went double for combat fliers: No pilot ever lies to another pilot about the condition of his craft or what he will meet in space. Ever. Even if they are from different planets. Even if they fly different flags. Even if they are of different species. They are all Brothers of the Black Sky, facing alike the eternal, deadly perils of the endless void. Max knew that Escort One would find a way to let him know what he would meet.

A minute passed with nothing but digitally scrubbed silence over the comm. Then, the slight hum of a carrier signal. "One-one-four, this is Escort One. You sound as though you might be a scholar of military history. Is that true? Over."

"My favorite subject, Escort One. Over."

"Excellent. Well, then, you have come to the right world because Rashid IV *and its environs* are home to a great many antique rifle collectors. Over."

"Is that so? What kind of rifle collectors? Over."

"All kinds. Most of them are friendly enough. The ones you want to avoid, though, are the ones who have great affection for the United States Army rifle that preceded the Model 1903 Springfield. I forget the *name* but I'm sure you'll remember it specifically. Not that these people actually make the rifle, mind you. But they are extremely fond of it and are happy to *work with it*. Over."

Max snorted, then keyed to transmit. "Message understood. And thank you. You can ride my wing any day of the week. Glad to have the company, Escort One. One-one-four out."

"I'm glad *you* understand, because I am utterly clueless," said Dr. Sahin.

"Well, Bram, it's like that message from Wortham-Biggs. It was written for you, so you got it and I didn't. Well, this message was meant for me, so I got it and you didn't."

"Are you going to translate for me, or do I have to access the ship's database and start reading about antique military rifles?"

"Not that some time in the database wouldn't do you some good, but I would rather have you reading about naval customs, military procedures, and filling in the gaps in your knowledge of warships than looking up material about old rifles.

"Before the Model 1903 Springfield, a bolt-action rifle firing the thirty-aught-six cartridge, the standard issue rifle in the United States Army was the Model 1896, a bolt-action rifle chambered for the '.30-caliber army' cartridge, also known as the thirty-forty.... It was better known by the names of the men who designed it: the *Krag*-Jorgensen."

"Aahh. So, whoever would want to stop us from landing would be someone who is friendly with the Krag. Interesting. That gives me a very good idea of what we are doing here."

Just as Max was about to ask precisely what that idea was, he noticed that the proximity display showed Escort Two pulling rapidly out of formation and accelerating more or less at right angles to the course of the other two ships. Two beeps. Escort One was about to talk to them. In the intervening twenty seconds, Max started to configure the active sensors to do a focused scan in the direction the fighter was going.

"One-one-four, this is Escort One." The pilot's voice had the tone that everyone who has ever served in the military associates with an officer giving orders, "Maintain your current status. Do *not* change course or speed unless directed by us. Do *not* alter the directionality of your active sensor scans. Please acknowledge this message and your intention to comply with these instructions. Over."

"Escort One, this is one-one-four. Message received. No yoke and throttle action. No waving the flashlight. Will comply. Any word on what's going on? Over."

"Only that we have some visitors. Nothing that Escort Two can't handle. Escort One out."

"Well, that was not particularly informative. What are you doing, Max? He said not to do anything with our sensors."

"Actually, he said 'do not alter the directionality of your active sensor scans,'" corrected Max as he continued entering commands on the *Clover*'s small but capable sensor console. "He didn't say a word about passive sensors. Let's see how much I remember from my years in Sensors. I'm just altering the gain on this sensor"—he pulled up a screen and entered some commands—"tweaking the resolution on that one"—more commands—"changing the bandwidth and the sampling frequency here"—about twenty seconds of configuration changes—"integrating the feeds through a tactical interpretive algorithm, and then telling the algorithm that it is looking at interception of an unknown number of vessels of unknown type by one small Rashidian fighter"—that took almost a minute—"and... *comme ça*."

The display in front of him, which had been showing various graphs and waveforms that meant nothing to the doctor, went blank for an instant, after which three icons appeared on it. One was labeled "RASHID FGTR" and the others had labels that said "UNID FGTR 1" and UNID FGTR 2."

"See here, Doctor, this is what's going on. Here are two fighters. Let's call them Uniform one and two. With the limited sensors on this ship, I can't give you an ID. I can give you their bearing, range, course, speed, and their mass, but that's all. Uniform One and Two are on an intercept course with us. If nothing changes, they will be within missile range in about six and a half minutes.

"And here's our friend, Escort Two, accelerating to intercept the fighters." He grunted appreciatively. "*Nice* acceleration profile. I didn't know the Rashidian fighters could crack on like that. That's some useful intel. He'll be in missile range of the fighters in about forty-five seconds, but if he's smart, he won't shoot just then. Uniform one and two would see the firing and be able to track the missiles' seeker heads, maybe giving them a chance to evade. So, he will probably take a bit longer to get into the optimal firing position. The other fighters probably don't see him, so it'll be a rude surprise."

"Why is it that we can detect him and that the fighters likely cannot?"

"Simple geometry. Escort Two's engines are pointing in our direction, so they show up like a spotlight on practically every sensor I've got. Hell, if you went in that little passenger compartment back there and looked out a porthole, you could probably see the damn thing with the Mark One Eyeball. A fighter is a whole lot harder to spot from nose on."

"But the attacking fighters have their fronts to us, do they not? Why can we detect them?"

"Because I'm not detecting the fighters exactly. I'm detecting their missiles. They have activated the missiles' seeker heads, so they can acquire the target the moment they're in range, fire quickly, and get away. The seeker heads are broadcasting conventional RF and tachyo-graviton radar, which our sensors are picking up. Remember, they think they're hunting a standard microfreighter with only rudimentary sensors. So, the seeker head detection gives me a bearing to focus our mass detector on, and based on their mass I can verify that they are fighters and not just slow missiles."

"What happens now?"

"Very shortly, there will be an engagement. Since this is a fighter engagement in space fought with nuclear weapons, I can guarantee that someone will die, and based on the tactical situation, I can almost guarantee you, it'll be Uniform One and Uniform Two. The only question is how."

"How can you be so certain? The Uniforms do, after all, have a numerical advantage."

"In this case, that won't matter. The greatest tactical advantage known to man is for you to be aware of your enemy while he is not aware of you. That means, if you have the firepower, you can kill him before he even knows you're there, and that is what Escort Two is going to do."

"How will he do that?"

"I don't know how he *will* do it, but I know how I *would*."

"How then?"

"The sneaky way, of course."

"Of course. And that is?"

"Let's watch and see if he does it." A few moments of silence ensued while both men watched the tactical display.

"Yep. There he goes. Just what I would do. He's going ventral—that's under their bellies. Inexperienced pilots tend to rely on their eyes too much and go by what they can see out the canopy, which is generally ahead of them and above. Even when they do use their sensors, fighter sensors are very good at looking straight ahead, and pretty poor in every other direction. Fighter pilots tend to ignore what's under their bellies so naturally that's where I like to go.

"You put yourself three or four thousand kills ventrally to his course, cut your drive, and let the targets zip by right over your head. Look, you can see him going ventral right now. The two attackers aren't even twitching either. They have no idea he's there. Now he cuts his drive and lets them pass. And there they go. He lets them get far enough past that he won't pick up too much of their drive trails. About now. Now, watch as he turns around—there he goes—and slips himself in right behind them. Like that. Then he sets his missiles for passive thermal-seeking mode so that there isn't even a missile seeker radar for the target to pick up as warning—we aren't going to be able to detect that—and closes the range a little...to right...about...*there*, and then he stops closing. We can't see it, but I bet he just fired his missiles. They lock in on the heat of the bad guys' drives and fly right up their tailpipes."

The icons representing the unidentified fighters disappeared from the display. "Score two kills. It's one of my favorite tactics. The enemy doesn't know I'm there until after he's dead."

After the requisite attention signal, Escort One was back on the comm. "One-one-four, this is Escort One. Please respond. Over."

"One-one-four here. Over." Max responded.

"One-one-four, please be advised that Escort Two has just extended to our visitors the *warm* hospitality for which Rashid is justifiably famous. Over."

"I'm sure you baked them a Teller-Ulam soufflé. You know, the one with the recipe that starts off with 'preheat oven to ten million degrees Kelvin.' Over."

"Indeed. That is the very dish. We have had a few opportunities to serve it in the last hour or so. Now, one-one-four, I have new instructions for you. Am I correct in surmising that your vessel is a horse disguised as a camel? Over."

The pilot probably spotted the subtle modifications to the engine nozzles, the well-disguised but larger than normal bulge in the hull to accommodate the enlarged fusion reactor, and the military-grade sensor emitters, all of which—to a well-trained eye—said that the *Clover*'s performance would be decidedly more sprightly than that of a stock Piper-Grumman *Shetland* class microfreighter.

"You have keen eyes. Over."

"How many Gs can you sustain safely? Over."

"Fifteen. Over." That was the rating anyway. Max and Brown had gone over the design and the naval upgrades and jointly decided the real number was closer to eighteen or twenty, but Escort One didn't need to know that. Before the Navy modified it, the little vessel could pull no more than 3.3 Gs.

"Very good. That will blow some sand in our adversaries' faces. I have new instructions for you. It's too dangerous for you to proceed to your landing as planned. Rather, you will rendezvous with some of our forces in space, and they will see you safely to the surface. I am transmitting a set of coordinates. Pull your best acceleration all the way to that point. No terminal deceleration—the vessel with which you are rendezvousing will match velocities with you. Escort Two will clear your twelve and I will cover your six. From their present trajectories, none of our visitors can pull enough delta V to catch you at fifteen Gs. There are several that were stealthed in orbit here, and they are accelerating hard now, thinking that they can catch the camel. They will be very disappointed to see that you are a horse, especially now that by redlining their drives they have given away their positions. They will not live very long to regret the miscalculation. Over."

"I wonder who actually sent those fighters," said Max. "Escort One hinted that it was someone who was working with the Krag, but I have no idea who that might be."

"I have a reasonably probable hypothesis," said Dr. Sahin.

"And?"

"It's one of the emirs. In the Union, most people think of the 'Unified Kingdom of Rashid' as a truly unified kingdom when, in reality, it is anything but. It is a singularly complex polity. Roughly half of its worlds are ruled directly by the crown, as in any other hereditary monarchy. Another 40 percent or so are emirates, small groups of two to seven worlds ruled by one of the six emirs—the heads of the ruling families. The remaining 10 percent are the Protected Islamic Worlds, mostly low population planets consisting mainly of universities, seminaries, Islamic scholars, and independent scientific research institutes. The emirs, of course, owe allegiance to the king but can, from time to time, be somewhat wayward. This 'waywardness' can become somewhat awkward, as each of them commands a small but capable set of defense forces loyal only to him."

"So, you think that one of the emirs might want to stop us from meeting with your friend?"

"That would be a distinct possibility, Max. The hypothesis certainly fits the data quite closely."

"It does. It's not very comforting, though. Not very comforting at all."

At the specified coordinates, the *Clover* encountered the immense Rashidian carrier, the RRS *Riyadh*, which had been conducting operations just outside the orbit of Rashid VI only 2 AU from the *Clover*'s initial position. About forty-five minutes after the new instructions from Escort One, twelve Rashidian SF-89 Qibli ("Scirocco") fighters appeared to escort the micro-freighter the rest of the way to the carrier. Max had hardly set the landing skids on the carrier's deck before it the giant ship pulled a high G, two-axis course change that must have raised her chief engineer's blood pressure thirty or forty points. When the carrier straightened out on her new heading, Max could feel dissonant vibrations transmitted through the deck to the soles of his feet as he and Dr. Sahin walked through the ship; they told Max's exquisitely sensitive sense of warship machinery that all three mains and both auxiliary coolant circulating pumps for the carrier's four massive fusion reactors were being redlined.

The Rashidians assigned an earnest but selectively communicative lieutenant commander to escort (and keep an eye on) Max and the doctor. The young man, about Max's age, explained their course, rate of acceleration, and how the *Clover* would be ejected upon arrival at Rashid IV at a suitable distance. He went on to detail how, by redlining its drive, there would be just enough time and space for the *Clover* to decelerate from the carrier's velocity to entry interface, how Rashidian flight controllers would clear a path for it from entry to the landing pad, and how fighter/interceptor aircraft would escort it to a safe landing. The only thing he did not explain was why the entire Unified Rashidian Kingdom was putting forth such a profligate expenditure of men and resources dedicated to seeing that one lieutenant commander and one doctor/acting ambassador were deposited safely on the surface of Rashid IV at the earliest possible moment. What could be so urgent?

At least, now that they were on a gigantic carrier surrounded by the aggressively defensive swarm of its Combat Area Patrol fighters, there was no chance of any further attempted ambush. Which, of course, was the point.

The ejection maneuver took place exactly as planned. The *Clover* simply lifted off the hangar deck and nudged itself out the port side of the carrier on maneuvering thrusters. Even though the microfreighter had the same forward velocity as the carrier, the larger ship was under full acceleration, while the *Clover* was not. As a result, the two vessels rapidly separated. The carrier's enormous, blunt shape dwindled in only a few moments to nothing more than the brilliant pinprick of light created by its huge fusion drive, seeming to move ever so slowly against the background of fixed stars, the vastness of space reducing the carrier's great speed and enormous bulk, as it reduces all the puny handiwork of man, to insignificance.

After separating from the carrier, Max programmed the *Clover*'s ID transponder, in accordance with Escort One's instructions, to broadcast Kilo Papa Lima Charlie. Within a minute of leaving the carrier, the microfreighter was surrounded by a veritable cloud of thirty-six Qibli fighters arrayed in a flying wedge, defying any foe to challenge them. Max never knew whether these fighters were launched from the carrier, in which case they would have a long flight back home, or whether they were based on or near Rashid IV.

After several minutes of hard deceleration, the *Clover* encountered the tenuous outer fringes of Rashid IV's atmosphere. The leading surfaces of the vessel began to heat as the ship entered the transitional regime in which space gives way to atmosphere, and where fusion and rocket engines propelling ships in silent obedience to the tidy maxims of Kepler and Newton give way to air-breathing jets pushing aircraft, with a deafening roar, through buffeting gases subject to the laws of Bernoulli, Navier, and Stokes.

When the formation had descended to about a hundred kilometers, the space fighters peeled away, a single two-ship element at a time in quick succession, their brightly blue-white drives tracing graceful curves against the deep blue-black sky as they soared back to the infinite dark that was their natural abode.

Each element was instantly replaced by a pair of sleek AF-97 "Haboobs" ("Sandstorm") atmosphere fighters built jointly by the Rashidian Kingdom and the Romanovan Imperium (the Romanovans called it the "Gladius"). The hand-off took place in a series of maneuvers so beautifully choreographed and so quickly and precisely executed that Max knew he had just seen a crack atmosphere fighter squadron take the place of a crack space fighter squadron. This was yet another sign of how important his and the doctor's safety were to the Rashidians. As an old saying of obscure origin goes, "They cared enough to send the very best."

As Max explained to the doctor what was going on and why he was so impressed, the comm panel called for attention with two beeps. Twenty seconds later, the business-like, yet studiously relaxed, voice of a Rashidian pilot came into the cabin.

"Union Microfreighter Galaxy Papa Galaxy Charlie seven-two-one-one-four, this is the Tabi'a Commander, my call sign is Yarmouk Three, please acknowledge. Over."

"Yarmouk three, this is one-one-four. We read you. Over."

"One-one-four, does your database include the communication protocols from the *Equilateral* exercises held last year? Over."

Dr. Sahin watched while Max checked. All the materials from the joint Union/Rashid/Romanova exercises held ten months previously were in the database—an entire database full of comm protocols, transponder codes, command and control rules, and the other minutiae that allow elements of different armed forces to work together as a unit.

"Yarmouk Three, this is one-one-four. Affirmative. We have a complete set of documentation for the ex, including the Oscar Hotel and the Romeo Oscar Echo. Over." Meaning, the Operational Handbook and the Rules of Engagement.

"Excellent, one-one-four. Then please implement Formation Comm Protocol Bravo with you as the pigeon. You are assigned new call sign 'Sadeek One.'" Max saw the doctor smile broadly at that. He made a mental note to ask what 'Sadeek' meant. "If we are not successful in establishing communications in two minutes, return to this frequency and the current encryption. Over."

"Roger that. Formation Comm Protocol Bravo, I'm the pigeon, new call sign Sadeek One, and if we are not talking in two minutes, come back here using the same encrypt. Changing frequencies now. Over and out."

Max called up the protocol and started punching in the frequencies. He also loaded the applicable encryption scheme, known as *Casablanca*, into the *Clover*'s ENDEC, or ENcrypter/DECrypter, better known as the "Blue Box," even though as long as anyone could remember, they were all painted reddish-orange.

While he was doing this, Max asked, "What does 'sadeek' mean?"

"It is a felicitous choice of appellations. It means 'friend.'"

"Sounds good to me." Pause. "Or maybe not. 'Speak, friend, and enter.'" He gave a brief, apprehensive, chuckle.

"What is 'speak, friend, and enter'?"

"An inscription over a doorway in one of my favorite books when I was younger."

"What was on the other side of the door?"

Max thought for a moment, wondering how to summarize something like twenty pages of a complex and classic work of

English literature. He did his best. "A long, dark journey, full of wonder and deadly peril. But a journey that had to be made."

"Let that not be an omen."

"Amen. That author wrote about omens a lot. But now that I think of it, I don't think he believed in them. All right. I've got everything set up." He keyed for transmission. "Yarmouk Four this is Sadeek One. Do you read? Over."

The response was immediate. "This is Yarmouk Four reading you five by five, Sadeek One. I have new instructions for you." The other pilot described a series of maneuvers, altitude changes, and a new landing point in such densely woven aerospace jargon that, excluding articles, adjectives, and the occasional adverb, the doctor was certain he understood only one word in twenty. When Max had repeated the instructions back to Yarmouk Four in equally impenetrable language and followed the fighter squadron through a change in course and altitude, he turned to his companion. "Let me guess. You didn't get any of that."

"Scarcely a word. You might as well have been speaking Pfelungian. I can't imagine why you would have to guess. You conducted a conversation, for minutes on end, consisting of nothing but incomprehensible pilot argot, which I have long suspected pilots specifically evolved as a coded language so that members of your elite club of drive-and-rudder men can speak without being understood by the uninitiated and, further, as a kind of secret handshake so that you can recognize one another. It should entail no guesswork at all to conclude that I, an ignorant cretin who merely speaks a dozen and a half languages or so and who possesses a veritable plethora of university degrees in six different fields, would be unable to comprehend a word of the proceedings."

"That's 'drive-and-*thruster* man.' Thruster."

"See what I mean? You people have your own language, constructed with incomprehensibility and exclusion as an objective, and you have the undisguised temerity to wonder that you are not understood. You might as well build a fire and marvel that it generates heat, light, and smoke."

Max knew better than to offer the rejoinder that medicine was just as bad or even worse. Although aerospace jargon had its basis in Standard, most medical terms are derived from Latin, the language of a long-dead civilization that was currently spoken only by the Romanovans, and Greek, a beautiful but now obscure language spoken by only a few million of humanity's hundreds of billions. He knew from experience that Sahin would never admit the comparability of the two cases. He decided just to go ahead and explain what was going on.

"In the plainest possible terms, here is what is happening. It is believed that our original flight plan has become known to people who want to kill us. Accordingly, our descent and flight path have been changed. As much as possible it now takes place over the sea. We will travel with this escort until the last two and a half minutes or so, or just before we cross the coast. Then, the escort will peel off so that no one will see a microfreighter with a fighter escort, which would attract attention and, apparently, cue the people on the ground that something unusual is happening. We will land at a different field from the one originally planned. This one is technically not a spaceport, but the Rashidian authorities are waiving that requirement and will let us set down there. It's a military airfield, well garrisoned. Someone will meet us there and take us where we need to go."

"Why approach from the sea?"

"It's hard to hide a portable surface-to-air missile launcher or pulse cannon on the surface of the ocean. You have to put it on a ship or a boat, and those have been cleared from our flight path."

As the two men spoke, Max steered the ship through a series of turns and descents. Just before they crossed the coast, the fighter escort peeled off, the leader wagging his wings as they departed, a fact reflected by a similar motion of the icon representing the fighter on Max's proximity display. Before Sahin knew it, with a gentle bump the *Clover* was on the ground.

After a few moments to equalize pressure, the hatch cycled and opened outward with a clunk and a hiss. The doctor was standing at the hatch when the first glimpse of the outside became visible. "But... it is dark," he blurted indignantly.

"I noticed. The phenomenon is technically known to planetary scientists as 'night.' I hear that it happens on a regular basis around here."

"Do not be obtuse." He practically stomped his foot with uncharacteristic petulance. "I mean that it is dark when it should be light. I programmed my wrist chrono for the rotational period of Rashid IV and set it for the local time at Amman where we were to meet Mr. Wortham-Biggs. I was expecting it to be 13:42 standard time, which is the middle of the afternoon in Amman's time zone. But it is fully dark."

They stood in the hatch. which was about three meters off the ground, and waited for the *Clover* to extend its embarkation ramp, a process that took a little more than two minutes.

"That is because we did not land at Amman, but at Harun, the planet's capital city, to confuse anyone who might be planning to do us harm in Amman. Local time here is seven hours later than at Amman. Mr. Wortham-Biggs took a suborbital shuttle and is already at the meeting site. We're going to be taken by ground car, just like ordinary off-world trade delegates, to the Ministry of Trade building, where we will have our meeting."

"When did you obtain that valuable intelligence, and why did you not inform me? It is not as though I am along solely as a passenger, you know."

"Yarmouk Four and I talked about it on an open comm with you sitting right beside me."

The doctor harrumphed. "It has already been established that I did not comprehend any of your pilot treehouse-gang code conversation. Must you belabor the point? You know, I am rather put out by all of this. I should have liked to have received this disappointing news in a less abrupt fashion."

"Disappointing news? What's so disappointing about having the meeting here rather than in Amman?"

"Because if we are meeting Mr. Wortham-Biggs at a government office rather than in his private study, the coffee will not be nearly as good."

Max chuckled inwardly. *Coffee my ass.* Ibrahim Sahin was clearly hoping to spend a few moments with Wortham-Biggs's perfectly lovely daughter. According to Spacer Fahad, who had attended the first meeting between the doctor and Wortham-Biggs, a blind man could have seen the sparks flying between the young lady and Bram for the few moments they had been together.

By this time the ramp had extended. and a small party had gathered at its foot. Max and the doctor, each carrying a small, plain-looking duffle, descended to meet them. Two of the men were in Rashidian Air Force uniforms, which looked vaguely like twenty-first-century British Air Force uniforms. Ten more were dressed like Max and Sahin, in the medium brown and tan, flowing robe of the kind worn by virtually everyone on Rashid IV who did not have a specific reason to wear something else.

The man with the more elaborate uniform and, apparently, the higher rank of the two, approached Max when he reached the bottom of the ramp. He was a handsome man, a bit taller and broader than Max, wearing a thin, closely trimmed beard that seemed to be the style on this world, and he looked to be just on the near side of sixty. He had a bearing that Max was accustomed to seeing in highly effective senior officers. Max would have bet he was the base commander.

"Good evening, gentlemen," he said. "I am Colonel Mubarek and this is my executive officer, Major Hassam. You are Captain Robichaux?"

"That's correct, Colonel. I'm Max Robichaux. This is my chief medical officer, Lieutenant Ibrahim Sahin. He is also acting Union ambassador to the Kingdom." The colonel shook hands with both of them in the manner common in the Union, although hand shaking was not the custom on Rashid IV.

"Very pleased to meet the both of you," said the colonel. "Please forgive me for not introducing these other gentlemen, but they are in a profession in which their names are not the subject of casual discussion. Please also forgive us for the disruption of your visit by certain lawless elements. We will do everything possible to prevent further incidents of the kind. Now, let us attend to your transportation to the Ministry of Trade."

While an Air Force crew secured the *Clover* and hustled it into a nearby hangar, Colonel Mubarek led the group into the hangar closest to the landing pad where the microfreighter had set down. In it were three identical, large, luxury-type ground cars. The colonel explained that all three cars would head to the ministry, with two as decoys. Each car would carry four men, with two cars carrying four of what Max mentally labeled the "special ops men"—they were obviously highly trained special forces troops: lean, hard, and deadly. The other would carry Max, the doctor, and two of the special ops men. The three cars would travel in line-ahead formation, swapping positions from time to time.

The three vehicles took off into the night at what seemed, to Max and the doctor at least, to be an imprudently high speed.

There were several checkpoints inside the air base at which the motorcade did not even slow down. Within moments, they had crossed the base perimeter and reached a highway that led the short distance from the base to Harun, the capital of the planet and the entire Unified Kingdom of Rashid, Allied Emirates, and Protected Islamic Worlds. Just as the vehicles left the base, Max noticed an aircraft that seemed to be flying in formation with the motorcade.

Max gestured at the vehicle and turned to one of the special ops men. "Is that rotorcraft providing cover for us?"

"That is correct," he answered. "Only, we use the older term 'helicopter.' It's there to help protect from attack by air and to act as a gunship to strike at any ground targets that should constitute a threat. There are also two atmosphere fighters at higher altitude to provide additional air cover, although they would not be much help with anything on the ground."

Max nodded, sat back, and relaxed a bit for the first time since the initial Rashidian space fighter escort had first shown up on the *Clover*'s sensors. He noticed that, as he leaned back in the seat and rested his elbow on the armrest, a console deployed from the space between the seats. The console's display showed a menu, containing several entertainment and music programs, local broadcast channels, and a navigation display. Max called up the display and examined the layout of the city, paying particular attention to the projected route of the motorcade, the location of the Ministry of Trade, and other landmarks and facilities. Like most naval officers in combat assignments, Max had a good head for maps and spatial relationships, so much so that he was able to get his bearings quickly and before long knew where they were in the city.

Several times so far, the cars had swapped positions. After the last swap, the car carrying the Union men was in the rear. The number two car was about 150 meters ahead, and the number one the same distance ahead of the number two.

The motorcade passed an impressively large Muslim seminary and a large regional retail facility. which the navigational display identified by the peculiar title of "shopping mall," and Max noted that the ministry was now only five kills away. Maybe, Max thought, whoever had been behind the attempted fighter attack in space didn't have any assets on the ground in Harun.

Or maybe, they did.

A tiny point of brilliant orange light climbed into the sky from behind a nearby building. It accelerated rapidly, trailing smoke and glowing gas as it swerved erratically through the air before locking in onto its target and making a beeline for the rotorcraft flying about four hundred meters directly over the lead vehicle. Before Max could give voice to the words that came immediately to mind, which were, "Oh, shit, that's a portable surface-to-air missile; we're really screwed," the object had struck the rotorcraft, leaving it a roiling thundercloud of flaming smoke, a hailstorm of metal and plastic shards, and a rain of still-burning fuel that showered the first vehicle as well as half of a city block, setting fire to every combustible object it touched.

Max knew exactly what that meant and what had to be done. "Driver, change course! Turn around and go down a side street—anything but continuing on our planned route." Either at Max's prompting or having come to the same conclusion independently, the driver expertly spun the vehicle 180 degrees, as though it were a stunt car, and in a screech of tortured tires, had it moving in the opposite direction in less than two seconds, trailing a blue cloud of burned Plasti-tyre.

Just as the car began to accelerate, the first vehicle exploded, probably ignited by the burning aircraft fuel in which it was now coated. The ground car's hydrogen fuel made for a remarkably transparent fireball, a chaotic vortex of blue flame threaded with strands of black smoke and swirls of yellow-orange fire produced by combustion of the plastic, electronics, and human flesh.

The gut-rattling *CROOOMP!* of the shock wave from that explosion struck Max and Bram's car, at the same moment another light caught their attention. A yellow-white streak lanced out from the window of a building near the street, striking the second car and obliterating it just as thoroughly as the first. In contrast to the first car's explosion, this one's consisted of a sharp *BLAM!* from the warhead of the weapon, followed nearly two-thirds of a second later by a *CROOOMP!*, marking the secondary explosion caused by the detonation of the vehicle's cryogenic hydrogen.

The shock wave struck the side of the still-accelerating car carrying Max and Bram as it turned sharply, fleeing down a side street to escape the shooting gallery, rocking it hard to port. but not slowing its rapid acceleration. One six-second reload later, another yellow-white streak reached out from the same building, but the longer range, poor shooting angle, and the shooter's haste to fire his weapon before his shot was blocked by the building on the corner, caused the shoulder-launched antitank weapon to miss the car by a good fifteen meters, instead slamming into the side of a building across the street from the firing site.

The ground car carrying Max and the doctor rocketed down the side street, then took a squealing right down what Max recognized as one of the city's main boulevards. The second special ops man was talking busily on the vehicle's Rashidian version of a secure comm unit, informing someone, somewhere, of what was going on—whatever the hell that was.

At that point, as the buildings and parked ground cars flew past his window at about 180 kph, Max decided that it was time he found out what was happening.

"Hey, Driver, do mind telling us what in the fucking hell is happening here?"

Much to Max's surprise, the driver felt a straightforward question deserved a straightforward answer. "It's the emir. The emir of the House of Habib. The bastard son of an infidel whore opposes any agreements with the Union. He rules two worlds in the New Damascus system, commands a small system defense force, and has managed to slip a few hundred of his best troops into the city under the ruse that they were soldiers on leave, coming to the capital as tourists. There were caches of hidden weapons waiting for them. He also has supporters in the royal palace, the Ministry of Defense, and several other government departments, who have been providing him with information. Just a few moments ago his men seemingly came out of nowhere, converged on the Ministry of Trade, and ringed it with hastily constructed barriers and field fortifications."

"What about the Second Motorized Infantry Brigade? I thought they were stationed just outside the city."

"You are very well informed, Captain. Yes, the Second is stationed nearby precisely for the purpose of protecting the capital against this sort of attack. Unfortunately, our commanders were taken in by a diversion that drew them to another city, Aswan, about two hundred kilometers away. The emir staged a 'revolt,' which, when the troops arrived, turned out to be only a dozen or so of the emir's men and several hundred paid recruits from anti-Royalist student organizations at the university. The students knew nothing of the purpose for which they were hired to throw rocks and light trash fires, but were cleverly coached in how to lure the troops into dispersing and pursuing them on many wild goose chases all over the city. It will be hours before the brigade is reassembled, can remount their vehicles, and return to the capital."

The driver turned down a different street at the same breakneck speed. There was no traffic. Apparently, the word had gone out that there was some sort of unrest and that people were to stay off the streets. The man who had been talking on the comm spoke quickly to the driver in what sounded like Arabic. The driver nodded quickly and made another turn.

"We are instructed to return you to the air base, where you will be protected by the base garrison until the emir's troops are captured or killed, at which point 'Mr. Wortham-Biggs,'" Max and the doctor could almost hear the amused quotation marks around the name, "will be transported to the base where he can meet with you under secure conditions. Is that acceptable?"

"Of cour—" Max started to say.

"No. It is not," the doctor interrupted, in a peremptory tone that Max had never heard Sahin use outside of the Casualty Station. "I'm sorry, Captain, but this information changes things. The written instructions given to me by Admiral Hornmeyer contain information that puts what the emir is doing in a different light. The emir's action means that it is urgent the meeting take place immediately. Within the hour is preferable. Two or three hours from now may be too late, with consequences that make words like 'disaster' and 'catastrophe' seem like bland understatements. I believe that the emir may be the least of our problems."

The driver shook his head. "I don't see how that would be possible. We're now several minutes away from the ministry. Even if we turned around and went back in that direction, the emir's troops—who are quite proficient—have the building surrounded and the streets blocked. Yes, there are troops at the base that could be used to break the cordon, but it could not be done in the time frame you describe.

"By design, there are no armored or artillery units, or armored fighting vehicles, in or near the capital. We couldn't mount any kind of air strike against such small targets in a crowded city without causing unacceptable civilian casualties. That leaves cracking the perimeter by conventional infantry assault without prior bombardment."

He shook his head at the prospect, obviously an experienced combat soldier evaluating how the engagement would proceed. "We would have a numerical advantage, but the airbase troops are mere garrison soldiers. Their boots are very shiny and their bayonets exceptionally bright, but I doubt any of them have ever made a ground attack without air or artillery support against a prepared defensive position. The emir's troops, on the other hand, are an elite, space mobile, special operations unit, veterans of many battles. I'm afraid we cannot get the ambassador through the emir's lines in time."

The doctor looked at his feet dejectedly. Max, however, smiled broadly and slapped the driver on the back. "Just get us to the airbase, my man, and I will deliver the ambassador to the meeting."

The doctor looked at him sourly. "And just how do you expect to do that? Didn't you hear this gentleman, who apparently possesses considerable expertise in this area, state that getting me through the lines is impossible?"

"Of course I heard him. Not only that, I believe him and agree with him 100 percent. We can't get you *through* the lines in time."

"Max," Sahin said with exasperation, "you're not making any sense. How can you say you're going to get me to the meeting but that you know you can't get through the lines?"

"Easy. We're not going through. We're going *over*."

CHAPTER 4

18:23Z Hours, 19 March 2315

"I thought your convoluted and exceptionally hazardous plan back at Mengis VI was the epitome of foolhardiness," said Sahin, his voice inching across the boundary that separated the merely high-pitched and tense from the truly shrill and panicked. "Little did I know that you had *vast*—truly, truly vast—untapped resources of foolhardiness, the magnitude of which could scarcely be imagined, much less articulated."

"What we're doing isn't as dangerous as what we both think is going to happen if I don't get you to that meeting."

"What do *you* think is going to happen?"

"Let's say that, although I never saw your written instructions from the admiral, I spent enough time in the Intel back room of enough warships to have a good idea what's going on with the emir and—"

"MAX!" the doctor interrupted, this time his voice definitely reaching the level that can only be described as a terrified scream. "You almost hit that building!"

"No, I didn't. I must have cleared it by seventy-five centimeters—maybe even a whole meter. Relax. I know what I'm doing."

What Max was doing was flying a single-engine, pusher propeller–driven, high-wing monoplane trainer aircraft he had "borrowed" from the airbase. It was a Beechcraft T-96 Skylark, an 85-year-old trainer design manufactured by license on Rashid V A. The Skylark was not particularly fast, but it was stable, highly maneuverable, known to be extremely forgiving, and possessed enormous flaps, enabling it to make very short takeoffs and landings. Max had done his first atmosphere pilot training in an almost identical plane and always loved flying it.

Dr. Sahin was able to talk the reluctant base commander into allowing Max to use the plane, based on the doctor's representations of the diplomatic urgency of the situation. The doctor had no problem with riding in a small aircraft, but he did have a problem riding in a small aircraft flying barely fifteen meters off the ground, dodging utility poles and trees, missing obstacles by millimeters, all the while keeping lower than the tops of the surrounding buildings so that the plane could not be picked off in the same manner as the ill-fated helicopter, unless it happened to fly right over the missile launcher. At one point the left wheel of the fixed tricycle landing gear had actually struck the top of a palm tree, causing one of the fronds to tear off and become entangled in the gear strut. It was now flapping madly in the 110 kph slip stream, making a sound somewhere between tearing cloth and machine gun fire, and looking absurdly like some sort of poorly applied vegetative camouflage.

"Okay, Bram, we're about a kill away from the ministry. The troops on the ground are likely to take some shots, so be sure to sit on the spare vest those fly boys gave us and keep your head down." The Air Force base commander had provided them both with body armor vests, two apiece, one to wear, and one to sit on to stop rounds fired from below, as the trainer was unarmored.

Rather than putting his head down, Sahin sat absurdly and improvidently upright, craning his neck for a look at the ministry compound as bullets started to fly past the small plane, some of them making distinctly audible whirring and buzzing sounds. "I don't see the landing strip," he said.

"There isn't one," Max said blandly.

"No landing strip! Did you notice before getting into this machine that it is an airplane and not a rotorcraft? I distinctly remember observing that the noisy spinning thing is on the rear pushing us rather than on the top holding us up. I am a keen observer and rarely miss such things. Where, pray tell, do you intend to land if there is no landing strip?"

"The courtyard."

"But that's only—"

"I know its dimensions. Now, be quiet and get down before I knock you upside the head and shove you down myself."

The doctor complied just as a burst of three assault rifle rounds stitched their way through the door of the aircraft and exited through the roof of the plane, transecting the intervening airspace occupied less than a second before by the doctor's head. Another rifle round shattered Max's window, showering the left side of his face with shards of Visi-Plex and slicing open his cheek, which immediately began to bleed profusely. He didn't even notice the blood until a bit got in his eye. He wiped it away absently and kept flying.

About two hundred meters before reaching the hasty fortifications erected by the emir's men, Max pulled up hard on the yoke and advanced the throttle, pushing the small plane into a steep climb that reached its apex right over the emir's lines. At that point, Max chopped the throttle, extended the tiny plane's huge flaps and held it just on the far side of a stall. With the wing tilted to so high an angle, the formerly smooth laminar flow of air over its surface broke down into a chaotic collection of vortices causing it to lose lift. The plane fell from the air, still carried forward slowly by inertia and with its descent slowed by the aerodynamic drag of its broad wings, which, divested of their former role as airfoils generating lift, were now charged with a function not unlike that of a parachute. Max skillfully managed the throttle, the flaps, and the yoke to steer the plane in a wobbling, sliding path, sometimes almost balancing atop the thrust generated by its propeller, directly toward what looked like a forty meter–by–forty meter decorative garden surrounded by the two-story ministry building: the ministry's courtyard, enclosed from all sides and shielded by the building from gunfire.

Like a perfectly tossed horseshoe dropping directly onto the spike, the airplane, maintained by Max in a precisely controlled and deftly steered stall, dropped in a nearly vertical descent right into the center of the courtyard. It came to earth, noisily smashing through the lovely and delicate white trellis donated by the Benevolent Order of Rashidian Diamond and Precious Gemstone Traders, knocking over and irreparably shattering two fountains personally selected for the courtyard by the king's much-revered and exceptionally pious late grandmother; snapping off two of the plane's three landing gear struts; and turning its propeller into something that looked like it belonged in a Salvador Dali painting.

Just as the plane's engine sputtered to a stop from a snapped fuel line, a second-floor awning loosened by a wingtip tore loose from its supports and tumbled into the ministry rose garden, crushing the roses that had been selected and meticulously tended by the minister himself, ruining them utterly. The plane's left wing, severely jarred by the impact with the ground, chose that moment to break in half, the outboard section falling with a metallic clatter, smashing a third fountain, which until that moment had been undamaged.

Amid this chaos, Max managed to shoulder his door open and climb out of the aircraft, said door falling off its hinges and crushing a small cluster of ornamental ferns—a gift from the Prime Minister of New Formosa, lovingly transplanted from his personal garden 973.8 light years away. Just as Max got his feet planted on terra firma, a dozen of the king's troops, led by a full major general, his sword drawn and blood in his eyes, burst into the courtyard and leveled their assault rifles at the unexpected arrivals.

"Surrender immediately or you will be shot!" the general shouted.

The absurdity of his situation not lost on him at all, and knowing no quick and accurate way to explain the situation to the general, Max fell back on the most basic military definition of the situation: he was a lieutenant commander newly arrived in the presence of a general officer. There was only one thing to do.

Max pulled himself to attention, gave the general his best salute, and announced in a booming parade-ground voice "Sir. Lieutenant Commander Maxime Robichaux, Union Space Navy, along with the Acting Union Ambassador, Dr. Ibrahim Sahin, here for our appointment with Mr. Wortham-Biggs. I believe we're expected."

"I must say, Captain Robichaux, that you *do* have a flair for the dramatic," Ellington Wortham-Biggs observed. "You should remember, however, that such predilections are not always appropriate. You could very easily have gotten yourself and the doctor killed, not to mention severely damaging the ministry building, if not burning it to the ground. I am officially required to convey the extreme displeasure of my government with the means by which you chose to arrive at this meeting. My government reserves the right to seek reparations from yours for the rather expensive damage caused by this little adventure."

Wortham-Biggs stirred his coffee with deliberate precision, his accent more perfectly British than that of any true Englishman. He took a sip, poorly concealing his disapproval of the taste. "As I said, the disapproval is *official.* Given your rather inventive solutions to prior problems, on the other hand, I was actually expecting something... what is the expression? Oh, yes, 'out of the box.'"

He treated the idiom the way a fussy butler would handle a soiled diaper. "I do regret extremely, however, the incidents that forced you to engage in this adventurous behavior. You may be assured that the individuals responsible, including the emir, will pay a heavy penalty."

Profoundly unconcerned with the emir's fate, Max and Sahin sipped their subpar coffee. The three men were in one of the ministry's many conference rooms, originally designed for trade negotiations. They were seated around a table for eight, roughly five times as long as it was wide, with places for three on each of the long sides and one more at each of the ends. Max and the doctor sat together on one side of the table, and Wortham-Biggs sat at the near end rather than opposite them as they'd expected.

Sahin had tended Max's injury quickly, using the medical kit he had brought with him in his duffel. His ministrations had left Max's face spotted in several locations with liquid wound dressing and bearing a 75-millimeter bandage on his cheek. For some reason, the injury seemed to have deadened Max's sense of taste, or maybe the topical anesthetic in the wound dressing was seeping into his system and deadening his taste buds. In either event, the coffee seemed flavorless to Max.

Between the injury and the ebbing of the adrenalin from his borderline-insane piloting stunt, he was finding it hard to pay attention. He found himself wanting a donut. Or maybe a candy bar. Something full of sugar and utterly devoid of any known nutritional value. Max looked at his colleague, as if to give him a signal to get down to business. The clock was ticking. The doctor got the hint.

"Mr. Wortham-Biggs, as you can surmise, we received your ingeniously conceived message and have come, as quickly as we were able, in answer to it. When we last met, you did me the very great favor of speaking in a manner marked by directness and honesty. It was my pleasure to reciprocate in that regard. Given what my friend and I have just been through, and in light of the exigency of events, might I suggest that we consider our previous meeting a precedent and that we conduct our discussions here today in a similar manner?"

"My thoughts precisely," Wortham-Biggs said. "Perhaps the most efficient use of our time would be for me to provide you with a brief summary of the relevant aspects of the political and dynastic situation in the Kingdom, and then present to you the precise proposal that we believe needs to be communicated by the most expeditious means to your government." He inclined his head in inquiry. The doctor nodded his approval.

Wortham-Biggs smiled in gratitude. As though collecting his thoughts, he removed his gold pocket watch from his vest and unhooked the chain. Max could see that it was not, as he had expected, a "fancy" dress pocket watch of the kind carried by many gentlemen of the day. Such watches were like the pocket watches of old in appearance only: an antique-style gold case fitted with a laser-regulated, wireless network synchronized quantum chronometer that was never more than a few thousandths of a second fast or slow, moving old-fashioned watch hands in digitally calculated nudges around a "retro design" analog face.

This watch was not antique *style* but *antique*. It was an open-faced model, with each hour marked by an Arabic numeral, clear minute marks around the circumference of the dial, and a second hand that swept a small circle near the bottom of the face rather than the entire watch. The maker's name, "Hamilton," was printed clearly on the dial. The words "railroad watch" came to Max's mind, for this was an Earth artifact made sometime in the last few decades of the nineteenth century or the first few of the twentieth. Max could not begin to imagine how much it would cost to purchase a four-hundred-year-old mechanical timepiece in working order and in such beautiful condition.

The man quietly wound the watch by turning a knob on the stem between his thumb and his forefinger, storing mechanical energy in a coiled metal mainspring inside the mechanism, to be released in tiny increments by the interaction of the escapement and balance wheel, precisely repeating the steps of their exquisite mechanical duet exactly five times a second.

Because Commodore Middleton had collected antique timepieces and talked about them endlessly, Max knew that railroad watches were meticulously tested and certified to be accurate to within thirty seconds a week, meaning that they measured the passage of time to an accuracy of one part in 20,133, without electronics or external regulation of any kind, and with no source of power other than a human thumb and forefinger supplying torsion to a delicate spiral of metal. It was the equivalent of measuring something a meter long to an accuracy of a twentieth of a millimeter, a few times the width of a human hair. As though recognizing the level of engineering achievement such a device represented when it was made, Wortham-Biggs placed it gently, almost reverently, on the table, face up.

"To summarize then. At the risk of sounding like a guidebook, I remind you that the Kingdom was settled by the Pan Arab Alliance shortly after the construction of Earth's first jump drive ships, even before the Earth was fully unified. Our fifteen star systems with their twenty-five inhabited planets and moons, all packed into an irregular egg-shaped area less than ten light years across, formed a natural political and economic unit from the very beginning. We have always had a cultural and economic identity distinct from the rest of Human Space and, but for a few decades as members of the Confederation, have not been part of the great political systems that have ruled most of humanity over the centuries. Our current relations with the Union are friendly, but we are not allies with you in your war against the Krag or otherwise.

"Our government is a monarchy. We have a Parliament, but as we are engaging in frank speech among gentlemen, I will not pretend that it plays a meaningful part in the governance of the Kingdom. True power rests in the hands of the king, and to a significantly lesser extent, the six emirs. Unlike most monarchies, we have six royal families, not one, each of which is descended from one of the six dynasties that ruled one of the leading Arab states at the time of our founding. The throne rotates from dynasty to dynasty in a prescribed order, such that when one king dies, whether after a day or a century, the next family places its chosen member, usually its emir, on the throne—except of course that no one may take office through assassination.

"In 2280, King Majali of the House of Qudah died at the ripe old age of 108, and the kingship fell next on the House of Jaafar. As this part of the galaxy was then stable and at peace, Jaafar sought to conciliate the other families and build harmony among the ruling houses by naming Rafi to hold the throne. Rafi's deserved reputation is that of an amiable man loved by all and, foremost, with an astonishing ability to inspire loyalty and good feeling, build bridges and alliances, and unify people of differing backgrounds and interests.

The Kingdom genuinely rejoiced at his coronation because everyone knew he was a genius at bringing people together, even though he did not have much of a reputation for strength of will or discerning intellect. This choice proved, however, to be a less than perfect one, as the Krag attacked the Union the following year.

Within minutes of the attack and before we learned of it, the Krag approached Rafi through a so-called neutral envoy belonging to a still unidentified species. He conveyed the Krag message that their putative war objective of the extinction of mankind was merely bellicose language for the internal consumption of a fairly small but highly vocal and influential religious minority. He assured Rafi that their true war aim was merely to break the Union's military and humble its leadership, at which point they would extract some sort of territorial concessions and other pro-forma tribute, and then return to their space, leaving Rashid and the other independent human powers alone. Rafi believed them, and we have remained neutral.

"Two things have happened to change that, the first of which you are aware of. The Krag dishonored our people by tricking us into a series of 'straw man' sales, in which we sold them war matériel through intermediaries—war matériel that the Krag then used to kill other Muslims, not to mention other Peoples of the Book, and many others who are our brothers and sisters on no basis other than that our ancestors and their ancestors lived together on Earth, breathed the same air, were watered by the same rains, and lived under the same skies.

As this fact has gradually become known, many of those with influence in the Kingdom have come to believe that the Krag cannot be trusted and that, once they defeat the Union's Navy, they will turn their attention to the other 'infesting vermin' as they call us, destroy the forces of all the independent powers, and then erase the human race from the galaxy."

"And the second thing that has changed your situation?" The doctor asked the question before Max could open his mouth to say the same thing.

"Rafi is dead. We have been withholding the announcement for the past several days so that we could conclude this meeting first, but it will become generally known tomorrow. Rule of the Kingdom next falls to the House of Saud. In light of the perilous state of affairs in the galaxy, the Elders of the House have decided not to place our elderly and ailing emir on the throne. The next King will be Admiral Khalil."

Max nodded in recognition. "You've heard of him?" asked the doctor.

"Yes. Used to be a battleship captain. A good one. He commanded the *Abha* at the Battle of Napoli Prime in that scratch Union/Rashid/Romanova task force that got put together when the Najin invaded from the Perseus arm two years ago—the only battle in which Rashidian and Union forces ever fought side by side. That was the impetus for the *Equilateral* exercises a while later. Khalil commanded the *Abha* and the five Rashidian ships in that engagement. I suppose that made him a commodore, although I don't recall anyone making an issue of it.

"There were also four Romanovan and eight Union ships there, one of which was my ship, the *Emeka Moro.* I was her weapons officer, so I had my eye on the tactical plot almost the whole time. Khalil was better than Admiral Windham, who was the Union commander, or Commodore Polyphonus, who led the Romanovans'. Khalil's tactics were innovative, daring, and unpredictable. Vessel deployment, use of weapons and sensors, management of kinetic energy—all brilliant. What I saw says he's courageous, intelligent, perceptive...and crafty. Looks like you've got yourself a good king. I'd take my ship into battle at his side in a heartbeat." He chuckled. "And here's a coincidence. You look a bit like him."

"That's no coincidence, Captain. Khalil is my brother." He smiled modestly. "My birth name is Khalid al-Saud. I am eleven years older than the king, but we are a warrior people who, particularly in these times, require a warrior king, and I am no warrior, at least not in the sense of leading men into battle. I do, however, have a certain facility and a great deal of experience with matters of intelligence and diplomacy. I am to head both of those ministries. Alas, I shall have to leave management of the shop to my daughter and Giles.

"So, enough polishing the blade. Time to attend to the edge. My brother, quite wisely in my view, has no faith in the Krag and believes that their goal is to eradicate humans from the galaxy. The king made that belief known when he last met with the six emirs—that is, the heads of each of the royal houses—five days ago. Bassam, the Emir of the House of Habib, voiced his disagreement at the time. Our operatives inside his palace inform us that he is in communication with the Krag and, more than that, is in league with them. The Krag have promised, according to our agents, to put him on the throne and install his House as the permanent ruling house of the Kingdom in exchange for keeping Rashid out of the war. Our desire was to meet with Union representatives in secret because we thought an avowed meeting would alert the Krag and allow them to attack us preemptively even before we came to any agreement." He looked at the doctor expectantly.

"First," Sahin responded, "I need to know how I am to address you. Prince? Minister? Your Excellency?"

"'Minister,' will suffice, as I am meeting with you in the capacity of foreign minister."

"Very well, then, Minister. Based on what you have told me, I must tell you that the official position of my government is that what you have described to me is a purely internal power struggle. Out of respect for the independence and sovereignty of the Rashidian Kingdom, and the statement in the Union Constitution that self-determination is a fundamental right of all sentient beings, it would not be appropriate for us to take any action relative to that dispute at this time."

Max shifted visibly in his seat in displeasure. One didn't have to know Max well to see that he thought highly of the Rashidians as warriors and wanted them in the war on the Union's side. Sahin stilled him with a quick kick under the table. Sahin wouldn't presume to tell Max how to deploy his weapons in combat. This, on the other hand, was the doctor's field of battle, and he knew what to pull out of the arsenal and when.

The minister responded amiably. "Perhaps I have not made myself clear. We are not asking the Union's assistance in putting down the emir. We are quite capable of doing that. Quite capable. In fact, I expect the emir to be put down in the most emphatic and permanent manner within the next few minutes. Rather, the king wishes to explore the possibility of the Kingdom going to war against the Krag."

"Ah. That is rather a different situation." The doctor acted as though the minister's statement constituted a revelation rather than a declaration of the glaringly obvious. "My government's position is that the Union would welcome any news that the Kingdom was entering the war against the Krag. I'm certain that your highly capable general staff can find suitable military objectives for your forces. But as I said, the Union's strict adherence to principles of self-determination for all peoples dictates that we allow your government to do what it wishes in its own way, without our interference."

Diplomacy. It was a dance as formal and precise as any Tchaikovsky ballet or Lenzi kineto-somatic poem. Each man knew the steps and took them with precision and skill, staying in time with the music that they both knew by heart. But time was short. The conductor increased the tempo.

The minister picked up his coffee cup, sipped, again did his best to conceal his disapproval, and set it back down. "Ambassador, the position of my government is that, were Rashid to enter the war on the side of the Union, it would be to the advantage of both powers to coordinate our activities to maximize the effect of our actions and to prevent one party's forces from interfering with the operations of another."

"So, you are proposing an *alliance*, then?"

"My government believes that the term 'alliance' connotes a more extensive level of integration of forces and unification of command than we would wish. We are also concerned that, in the past, alliances have been the prelude to annexation. We are adamant that our independence be preserved in all its aspects and attributes."

"You may be assured, minister, that the Union has never 'annexed' any independently governed system. The objectively documented historical record amply documents this fact. Every member joined voluntarily."

"Although that statement may be true, ambassador, in a formal sense, that same objectively documented historical record amply documents that some of these systems 'volunteered' to join after being hemmed in by Union systems on all sides and having their trade strangled by tolls, tariffs, navigation restrictions, and customs rules, none of which the Union applies to its members or was applying to other similarly situated non-Union trading partners at the time."

Touché. "Minister, as we have both read the same diplomatic histories, it would be disingenuous of me to deny that the Union may have employed certain rather punitive economic measures calculated to add to its membership and territory early in its existence. It was then, as you recall, picking up the pieces from the disastrous governance imposed by the Earth Confederation. Current conditions, however, are fundamentally different.

"Now that we are at war, with all the demands thus placed on our economy, manpower, resources, shipping, and manufacturing capacity, the Union desires no members who do not desire us. In accordance with strict enactments of our legislative bodies, and the announced policy of our president, we simply do not employ those kinds of strong-arm tactics on other humans any more." *What, never? Hardly ever.* Briefly, the question and response from *H.M.S. Pinafore* popped into the doctor's head.

"In any event, annexation is a practical impossibility, at least under the present circumstances. Our forces are put to full use defending our space and our worlds from the Krag. We do not have resources to spare for the intimidation, much less the conquest, of any other power, particularly one as well and skillfully defended as the Kingdom.

"Nevertheless, in recognition of the legitimacy of the Kingdom's concerns, the Union is prepared to do the following. First, we offer a looser mode of cooperation than an alliance. I would suggest that the Kingdom consider joining the war effort as an associated power, much as have the Pfelung, a race known for their prudence, highly developed ethics, and staunch independence.

"Second, the Union is prepared to give whatever reasonable formal guarantees the Kingdom may require to respect its independence and territorial integrity. In that regard, I would note that the Union has, from the very day of its establishment, strictly respected the Kingdom's independence, its sovereignty, and its borders. We have been proving our good faith to the Kingdom for decades in the most convincing manner possible, by our actions."

"That is, indeed, true" the Minister acknowledged. "We have never had any complaints about the Union as a neighbor. I believe that such an arrangement might be acceptable to my government, subject to negotiation of the precise terms of the formal guarantees of our independence, and provided certain other appropriate provisions were made."

"Such as?"

"We would require that our forces operate with complete independence and that participation in any given operation be voluntary."

Sahin turned to Max, who understood that it was his place to articulate the Union's position on purely military issues. He did his best to sound diplomatic.

"That's insane," he said without a trace of rancor. "Complete independence has never been the basis of any joint operations since the first human space forces were formed in 2034. In combat, it would be a disaster. Any time your forces and our forces happen to be involved in the same battle, there would be no overall commander. Maybe the two commanders manage to cooperate and work out a joint plan, in which case only a little bit of time will be wasted while they do that.

"Or maybe they won't, in which case the two forces operate at cross purposes, don't provide coordinated fire support, aren't on the same communications frequencies, transmit sensor beams that interfere with one another, and get in the way of each other's battle maneuvers. Who knows, they might even get hit by each other's missiles.

"Mister Krag, who is not stupid by any means, figures that out, uses the lack of coordination to his advantage, and cleans the clocks of both forces. I can tell you as a warship captain and a former tactical officer that unified command, at least at some level, is an absolute military necessity."

"I accede to the captain's bluntly stated but obviously valid observation." The minister gazed longingly at his coffee cup, as though wishing it had coffee in it that he liked, considered taking a sip, and then decided against it.

"My government is not averse to the notion of coordinated commands on certain levels under some circumstances, but is concerned about placing large units on a consistent basis under the authority of Union commanders. We do not wish our divisions and squadrons broken up and, for example, used piecemeal as replacements, thereby losing their cohesion and identity as Rashidian units."

Max nodded, recognizing the validity of the concern. "But at what level? Fleets, task forces, operational groups—they're all assembled from certain building blocks. The sticking point is the size of the blocks. Will your forces always operate together at the task force level, or can the task forces be broken down into operational groups that will be used to help assemble joint task forces, or maybe even divisions that can be put together into joint operational groups? And you can't just decide at the beginning that everything will be integrated at a given level, because operational demands are going to require different levels of integration. We can't do it under those rules."

"Minister, Captain, if I may?"

They both looked at the doctor, both convinced that a man who confused cruisers and corvettes because their names both start with a "C" could have nothing to contribute to this particular aspect of the discussion. The obvious annoyance displayed by

Max and the minister at being interrupted didn't stop the acting ambassador. It didn't even slow him down.

"I do not have in-depth knowledge of this business of 'task groups' and 'operational divisions'"—Max grimaced at the nomenclature errors—"but it seems to me that these issues have already been worked out in detail and even approved at the highest level by both governments. That agreement can be adopted by reference, and this issue would be resolved." The minister and the captain looked at him blankly.

"*Equilateral*, the set of command, communications, and control protocols worked out between our two governments and the Romanovans for a set of joint military exercises not too long ago. I was looking over your shoulder, Captain, when you called up the communications protocols from that exercise in response to the order from that fighter escort. You paged through an index that showed a detailed list of arrangements to determine what units would be integrated at what level, who would command them, when a unit could refuse to participate in an operation, and a whole plethora of similar matters. It was all there in the exercise documentation. I remember it most distinctly."

"There is a lot to be said for this approach, Mr. Ambassador, and my government has indeed thought of it," the minister said after a few moments' reflection. "You may not be aware, however, that there are several ways in which *Equilateral* is an imperfect fit for the current situation. Captain Robichaux could probably set them forth more accurately than I." He looked expectantly at Max.

Max nodded. "Okay. I can see several differences. First, *Equilateral* assumes three players: the Union, Rashid, and Romanova. What we've got now is the Union, Rashid, *and Pfelung*. Second, that exercise was a joint task force operation. What we're doing is much bigger. We'll be coordinating forces at the theater level, maybe higher. Third, both we and the Rashidians have changed our order of battle since then. We've shifted the building blocks around into a different force structure. Fourth, since that time we've put the Talon missile through two upgrades, which will require changes in joint targeting parameters; and fifth, we're in the process of adopting a new fighter, the FS-104 Wildcat, with substantially improved operating characteristics over the FS-101 Banshee it replaces, which will mean some new fighter tactics. So, there are going to be a lot of questions about joint operations and joint command that *Equilateral* isn't going to cover."

"So, there are going to be situations that, until more precise and detailed rules are worked out, will not be covered by the pre-existing framework, is that correct?" the minister asked evenly. "We will not be able to tell in advance how they will be resolved, and we will essentially have to rely on the commanders in the field to come to an accommodation and make the correct decision."

"That's right. I can't see how it could be otherwise. But we need to remember that none of the people in question are idiots: your commanders are damn smart and our commanders are damn smart, as well. You put smart commanders in a battle zone and give them a problem—they're going to find a way to solve it. You don't get to be a commodore or an admiral unless you have a truly outstanding ability to solve complex problems. It's what these guys do."

Max could see that the minister was still wavering. He must have some very, very serious concerns about his people's forces going into battle under Union commanders. The Kingdom had gone its own way for a long time. Max didn't know diplomacy, but he did know people, and he was pretty sure he knew what the minister's sticking point was.

"Minister, I know what you're worried about. I think we both know our military history and the many examples in history of joint operations where a commander of a joint force has used an ally's forces unfairly. You know—he gives the glory missions to his own guys and the grunt work to the others; the low-risk objectives to his own and lets the others take the heavy casualties. I could give you a laundry list of examples, but I think you know them just as well as I do.

"In the end, it all comes down to trust. No agreement that we sign, no assurance that we give you, can take the place of your trust in the good sense and the good will of our commanders, just as we are going to have to trust the good sense and the good will of yours."

Suddenly, Max remembered something his Mother Goose on the *San Jacinto* had told him: "Giving your trust is like handing over your baby: you can't hand a baby to a position or an office. You have to put that baby in the living hands of an actual person."

"Minister, if I'm any judge of men, you've been following the conduct of the war very closely." Wortham-Biggs nodded his agreement. "Then you know the reputation and the combat records of the admirals we've got in the major operational commands: Litvinoff overall, Hornmeyer and Middleton commanding the two major theaters, with Lo, Diem, and Barber running the Attack and Maneuver Groups. Truthfully, sir, can you see *any* of these men turning into a Sir Ian Hamilton? It's almost absurd when I think about it.

"Minister, I know two of these men personally. If Admiral Charles L. Middleton isn't the most honorable man in Known Space, he's the runner-up and the guy ahead of him should be emperor of us all. The other one, old Hit 'em Hard Hornmeyer, may kick you in the ass, and he may curse you to your face, but he's sure as hell not going to stab you in the back. If these guys wind up commanding some of your forces—and remember, there will be times when *your* admirals will command *our* forces—you can be certain that they'll make decisions based on military considerations only.

"This is not the same Navy that fought at the Great Rift. Our admirals aren't politically ambitious, power-seeking, effete headquarters drones and empty heads in pretty uniforms who move icons around in the tactical projector."

"I understand that, Captain. I have no doubt that these are honorable men. I have come to know the ambassador here as an honorable man, and your actions prove you also to be a man of honor. But we would be forming a relationship not just with Admirals Litvinoff and Middleton and Hornmeyer, and with Captain Robichaux and Dr. Sahin, but with dozens of admirals and commodores and thousands of other officers. Trust in this situation does not come easily."

"Sir, this is the Navy I've been a part of since I was eight years old and that I love as much as my life. It's the most effective large military force in the history of the human race. Our admirals are seasoned warriors; our officers, tough and competent professionals; our Navy, an instrument of death. We've been fighting for our lives for thirty years. We, or the Krag, have weeded out everyone—at least everyone at the senior levels—who isn't brave, capable, and aggressive, not to mention honorable and worthy of trust as well. I would trust any one of them with my life. In fact, that's exactly what I do. Every day."

"Minister," Sahin added, "you know what is at stake. If the Union falls, the Kingdom will not be far behind; then the Romanovans, then the Ghiftee, and everyone else. No one will be left behind to pray to Allah, to tend the graves of your ancestors, to carry the flame of learning and achievement and building and exploration handed down to us over the thousands of years from those who have come before. To fail to make common cause against the Krag now is to take the torch that bears that flame and to cast it into the dust. All of mankind's struggles through the ages will have been for nothing."

He paused, drew in his breath, and played what he hoped would be the trump card. "Visualize the holy places on all the worlds defiled, then leveled and covered with the dust of the ages, without so much as a single human eye to shed a single human tear for their passing. Imagine all the cities and homes of man, empty and silent for all time. Think of the Orion-Cygnus arm of the galaxy not as the cradle of man, but as his graveyard."

The man whom Sahin had come to know as Mr. Wortham-Biggs stirred his coffee again, stared at the liquid for a moment, and set his spoon down in the saucer. He touched the handle of the cup but did not pick it up. Again the internal battle: he wanted coffee but resisted subjecting his sophisticated palate to an inferior beverage. With a subtle shake of the head, he decided that the coffee was best left in the cup, eventually to find its way into a drain somewhere.

He withdrew his hand from the cup as he met Max's eyes and then those of the doctor. Clearly, he had made a decision. And not one about coffee. "The King has authorized me to speak for him in these matters. But he also gave me clear instructions. I fear that I have deviated from them slightly by insisting so strongly in securing these guarantees for the Kingdom. The need to strike the best bargain possible is deeply rooted in my nature, and, of more importance, I felt a duty to my people. In a just cause, the blood of our sons may be spent, but must not be squandered. The fathers and mothers and wives and children of the men who serve are worthy of the best assurances in that regard that I could provide."

He stood, his eyes grave. His head turned sharply toward the window that looked into the courtyard containing the broken airplane, the shattered trellis, the broken statues, the crushed roses, and the obliterated ferns. Machine gun fire could be heard in the distance—the king's troops finally arriving to deal with the emir's forces. "We are a warrior people: our culture celebrates and ennobles the warrior virtues of courage, honor, loyalty, and sacrifice. We do not, however, celebrate or glorify the taking of life, the spilling of blood, or the death of our own men. We know that if we enter the war now, many of our brave sons will die, and that they will start dying very soon. Next week. Tomorrow. A few hours from now. How soon will it be when the first names of the dead are made known, the first notices to the families, the first lists on the newswebs with their pages bordered in black?"

A burst of automatic weapons fire echoed down the streets. The minister gestured vaguely in the direction of the sound. "In a manner of speaking, our first casualties are bleeding and dying right now." He sighed heavily.

"The price of doing nothing is too great to contemplate. If there are to be future generations of our people, we must act. Our grandchildren are so precious to us that we must buy their lives with the blood of our sons."

He assumed a formal stance. "Ambassador, Captain, the Unified Kingdom of Rashid, Allied Emirates, and Protected Islamic Worlds will enter the war on the side of the Union as an Associated Power with appropriate Union guarantees of the continued independence of the Kingdom. The *Equilateral* protocols will serve as a framework for the integration of forces, further arrangements to be made by commanders in the field or further negotiations between the representatives of our governments. Are we in agreement, Mr. Ambassador?"

The doctor stood and bowed formally. "We are in agreement, Minister. May our swords shine together."

"And may their edges be a scourge to our enemies," the minister completed the benediction. He touched the comm panel. "Authorization Altair-Mirfak-Deneb."

Less than two seconds later a voice came over the panel's transducer. "Yes?"

"It is done."

The comm clearly picked up a heavy sigh, but it was a sigh of resignation and resolve rather than of sadness. "Good. We will do what we must.

"Ambassador, Captain, this is Khalil." Not "the king," not "King Khalil." Just "Khalil." "All of Rashid, every man, every ship, every drop of blood, every gram of treasure, is now committed to this cause. Humanity will stand together. We will fight beside our Union brothers and let nothing stand between us. Admiral Taniq and a small staff will leave within the hour for the *Halsey* to serve as liaison between your command structure in this theater and ours. Taniq is a fleet admiral, and the fourth most senior officer in our Navy. He has my complete trust and will be empowered to make binding agreements as to the use and deployment of all our forces without recourse to any higher authority.

"Further, at my suggestion, five years ago we elevated the status of the 'military attaché' to our embassy on Earth from a commander's posting to a rear admiral's billet and greatly enlarged his staff. Obviously, this team's true purpose was to be ready to step in as the Kingdom's representative and his staff in any joint command arrangements that we might make were we to enter the war. Orders activating those personnel in that capacity will go out momentarily, as will our notice to your president. Captain, is there any other military step that you suggest we consider taking immediately?"

Max gulped. He wasn't used to being asked for advice by anyone higher than a captain by rank, and here he was being asked for advice on the force disposition of one of Known Space's great powers. By a king. What do you even call a king? The last king to actively rule his forebears was George II of Great Britain, and that didn't end so well—he threw them out of Canada, and they wound up in the territory known as Louisiana. He threw a panicked look at the doctor, who perceptively mouthed "Your Majesty."

Deep breath. Tactical officer. Captain just asked for a recommendation. Done that before. "Yes, Your Majesty, this is Max Robichaux. If the emir is in league with the Krag, and if he knew that you were planning to enter the war on our side, then I think we may safely assume that the Krag know that too.

"Now, I'm just a destroyer captain, sir. I operate on the tactical, not the strategic, level, but if I'm the Krag Horde Master for this theater of operations, I've got to be thinking about making a preemptive attack the minute I suspect that the Kingdom is going to enter the war. Strike now to eliminate the Kingdom's forces before they can be made ready for combat and get integrated into the larger force structure of the Union.

"I don't know the readiness state and disposition of your forces, but if I were you, I would get as much of my fleet as possible—and preferably all of it—fueled, loaded for bear, and deployed. And I would not waste any time doing it either. I'd want my forces in an operational deployment no more than two hours from now. That's the earliest an attack force of fast destroyers could get here if the Krag launched it immediately upon finding out from the emir that you were going to join forces with us."

There was an uncomfortable pause. "One moment." Whereas at the beginning of the conversation, the king's voice sounded determined and confident, there was now a definite note of concern. Max could hear the click followed by deadness that meant the audio pickup on the other end of the comm had been muted. About a minute and a half passed. Another click.

"I have given the orders to dispatch Admiral Taniq and activate our liaison on Earth, and to notify Admiral Hornmeyer and the Union president of what has taken place today. Now,

Captain, to your suggestion: we gave the activation order hours ago. My brother will fill you in on our forces' status. Once you understand the complete situation, if you have any further advice, please convey it to him. Be assured that he has my ear at all times and that, in light of your most interesting combat record, any insights you may have will be welcome. Good day to you both, Captain, Ambassador. My brother, we will speak soon. Khalil out."

Max could not help but notice that he closed the comm link more in the manner of a warship captain than a civilian political leader. A warship captain with a problem.

Max wanted to get to the bottom of this. Quickly. "Minister, I may not know squat about kings, but I've been taking orders from warship captains since I was eight years old, and I know when one of them is worried. That was one worried warship captain. Why?"

The minister retook his seat. He glanced down at his watch, still on the table. The machine gun and assault rifle fire outside were rising to a crescendo, punctuated by the occasional burst of a grenade or mortar round. He turned back to Max and took a deep breath in the manner of a man charged with the delivery of unpleasant news.

"Unlike the Texians and many of the other Independent Powers, our Navy does not have institutional roots in your Navy. Accordingly, our ships are not an extension or branch of the same design lineage as yours. There is no 'family resemblance' between the vessels of the two navies as there is between those of the Union and so many other human powers. We have always gone our own way. That is why our ships look so different from yours and possess radically different strengths and weaknesses. What many people do not understand is that the difference is, as we say, 'more than skin deep.' Indeed, it goes to the very core.

"Your fusion reactors are of the Svavarsdottir, or 'S-Dot,' design in which plasma containment is achieved purely by means of two spherical and concentric reciprocally polarized graviton fields. S-Dot reactors can achieve a cold start in less than five minutes, but at the expense of a comparatively low power-to-weight ratio and less than optimal fuel efficiency."

Oh, shit.

The minister continued. "It is little known outside of the Kingdom's naval circles that our warships are not powered by S-Dot reactors." *Double shit.*

"Don't tell me you are still using tokomaks," Max said anxiously.

"Nothing even remotely so primitive. In fact, our reactors are of an extremely advanced design. As you are probably aware, almost 90 percent of the energy expended in an S-Dot reactor to achieve complete containment is directed to bottling up the most energetic 10 percent of the plasma. We employ a hybrid design in which the plasma is 90 percent graviton contained, and the remaining 10 percent is contained by a more energy-efficient technology—conventional Bussard-Polywell polyhedral electromagnetic coils.

"This design approach is, as far as we know, used only by us and by the Romanovans, with whom we jointly developed it. It has advantages of a more than 20 percent increase in efficiency and accompanying savings in fuel consumption, as well as an almost 30 percent improvement in power-to-weight ratio. The reactors are also smaller per unit of power and have less demanding cooling requirements, resulting in additional savings in power, size, and weight."

"But you have to granny-start them, don't you?" said Max.

"Granny-start?" It seemed that there was no bit of spacer slang of which the doctor was not ignorant.

As usual, Max filled in the gaps in his knowledge. "Slang for 'incremental volumetric ignition.' The way you typically start an S-Dot reactor is you flood the containment vessel with gaseous deuterium up to its rated pressure, then kick in the graviton generators and rapidly compress the gas almost to the point at which it would begin fusing, then kill the field, and in the milliseconds before the compressed gas has enough time to expand much, you squirt in another volume of gas; compress that amount to a slightly larger volume again, almost to the point at which it would begin fusing; and so on, until the whole vessel is full of deuterium just on the cusp of fusing; then you kick in the field for good, and use it to compress the gas that last little bit necessary to initiate the fusion reaction.

"Once you power up the field. it takes only a few minutes to start the reactor, but you have to run the graviton field at very high levels to be able to snap it on and off and on again like that and stabilize rapidly enough to keep compression-heated deuterium confined.

"But in an S-Dot reactor, if your graviton generators are damaged and can't be run at peak output, you do a granny-start. You start the reaction gradually. The first step is the same as a normal start—you fill the vessel to the highest safe pressure and then compress that gas almost to the fusion threshold, but once you get there, things go a lot more slowly. Then you slowly add more gas while gradually increasing the volume of the containment field. The gas has to be kept right on the edge of fusing, without starting the reaction, because it's only at the edges of the containment vessel, close to the emitters, that the field is strong enough to contain fusion plasma. When you finally have the vessel full of deuterium just at the fusion cusp, then you compress it across the fusion threshold and initiate the reaction.

"It takes anywhere from four hours to something like eighteen hours, depending on how much power the generators will take and how big the reaction chamber is. So, Minister, what's the start-up time on your reactor design?"

"Twenty-three hours on most of our ships. They got orders to start their reactors seven hours and..."—he glanced at the watch still on the table—"nineteen minutes ago, when we first had indications that the emir was going to cause trouble. We also have three older destroyers and two frigates that use more conventional reactor designs. They have already powered up and put to space."

"Twenty. Three. Hours." Max slowly came to his feet and paced deliberately to the window, a deadly coldness coalescing in his chest. His percom gave a brief, quiet buzzing sound, the sound it made when its beep had been muted. Max looked at the alphanumeric display, flipped the device open to its main display, and entered a few commands on the soft screen. The doctor surmised that he had programmed some sort of time alarm into the system.

"We accepted that design limitation," the minister continued confidently, "because our enormous investment in the best early warning system in Known Space gives us sufficient lead time. We can detect any attacking force at least twenty-seven hours away, giving us an adequate safety margin."

Max's cold feeling got colder. "And Minister, is any essential part of this early warning system accessible to the emir or individuals who might be loyal to him?

"I am not really familiar with the infrastructure associated with the system. It has never been within my sphere of responsibility. Allow me to check."

He walked over to a side table that held a coffee service, a water carafe and water glasses, an ice bucket, a stack of coasters, and a stack of napkins, all on a tray. He removed the tray, setting it on the conference room table. He then pressed a hidden lever that caused a keyboard on a sliding tray to deploy from the table. He pulled a chair out from the meeting table and positioned it in front of what was now a portable workstation, adjusted the position of the workstation so that it faced a nearby wall, and keyed a sequence on the keyboard.

A portion of the wall changed into a black rectangle that in turn displayed a log-in screen. The minister logged on to the system, supplied what was undoubtedly a very high-level password, and navigated through a series of menus to display a diagram of the infrastructure for the early warning system, which was apparently code-named *al Qasr* ("the Castle").

"Here are the sensor arrays." A sphere of red dots appeared, enclosing Rashidian space. There had to be at least a hundred and fifty of them. "And here are the command posts where the signals are aggregated and turned into warning and tracking data." Ten blue dots appeared, arranged in a sphere, the surface of which was about halfway between Rashid and the arrays. "And here are the limits of the space controlled by the emir. A yellow area, shaped roughly like a lopsided egg, appeared. It enclosed none of the arrays or command posts.

"It does not appear that any of the facilities lies within his territory," said the minister.

"I'm not so sure," said Max. "How do the arrays get their data to the command posts?"

"I would assume by standard high-bandwidth metaspacial tunneling transmission," the minister replied.

"Which means that, unless those emitters have planetary class–power generating capabilities, there have got to be some relay stations along the way, probably every couple of light years or so, right?" Max stood near the screen, a little off to one side.

"Let us see." He entered some more commands on the keyboard. A smattering of green dots appeared, about thirty of them, in two concentric spheres, roughly twenty in the outer and ten in the inner. Each dot bore the label, "RLY STN" and then a number. Number 9, one of the outer group, was in the yellow egg.

"Can we see the lines of communication? Which arrays communicate with Relay Station Nine?" More keystrokes. The station in question sprouted fifteen orange lines leading back to sensor arrays, and a description of the network's operating protocols appeared at the bottom of the screen.

"I know what you are thinking, Captain," said the minister, "but the emir has not sabotaged this relay station. Had he done so, under this set of protocols the system would have notified its operators, and the computer would have automatically rerouted the data transmissions from the affected arrays to unaffected relay stations that can handle the additional signals by reducing bandwidth and, as a result, provide the data, albeit at a lower level of temporal resolution. There has been no such notification."

He clicked some keys, and the *al Qasr* diagram was replaced by a status table. "As you can see from this status report, every aspect of the system is functioning nominally." A few more keystrokes, and the status display was replaced by a series of panels, each apparently representing a section of space surrounding the Kingdom. There were several contacts indicated, but all bore labels showing them to be innocent.

"Can we see the section of space that is scanned by the arrays that use Relay Station Nine?" Max was squinting at one of the panels.

A few more keystrokes, and one of the panels, by apparent coincidence the one that Max was looking at, expanded to fill the screen. There were about forty targets, all friendly freighters and civilian craft. "There do not seem to be any threats in that region of space," said the minister.

"Minister, you mentioned that if this relay station went out, the signals would be routed through other stations. Is there a way you can do that without alerting the station in question?"

"Yes, the command goes to the arrays, not the relay station. The arrays can be commanded to double up on their download cycle and to send the second download to their alternate station. The primary would never know anything."

"Would you humor me by doing so, and then display this section of space as viewed by means of the alternately routed scan data?"

"Of course. Give me a moment." Rather than entering commands that reconfigured the system, the minister sent a message to the system controller who managed such things. A few minutes later, a message appeared on the screen.

"It will take about five minutes for the command to propagate through the system and for the alternately routed signals to reach us, be processed, and then be displayed."

"While we're waiting, could you tell me more about the disposition of your forces right now?"

"We have one carrier and an escort of two frigates deployed in the outer system, and the other ships I mentioned earlier that have gotten their reactors going, as well as two destroyers and a few corvettes on system patrol. The remainder of our fleet is moored."

"Moored? How? Where?"

A flurry of keystrokes. "Here. At the Fleet Harbor Facility in orbit around Rashid V B." He pointed to a schematic of the system. "Here's the gas giant, Rashid V. There's its first moon, Rashid V A, which is inhabited and is a significant mining and industrial world. And here is Rashid V B, a moon with an ocean of largely comet-originated water covered by a layer of ice. The fleet moors here to be close to its fuel source. And here is the mooring facility."

A few more clicks. A schematic showed row after row of ships held in place by automated tugs only a few dozen meters apart from one another, in synchronous orbit around Rashid V B. There did not appear to be any defensive batteries protecting the approaches to the facility.

"What protects these ships?"

"Time, distance, the early warning system, and a few patrol craft to keep saboteurs and unauthorized civilian craft away."

The icy feeling was becoming a dagger-like icicle of certainty stabbing into his heart. He knew what was coming next.

An alert began to flash on the screen. "Our signal reroute is nearly complete." The minister entered the commands to return the display to the area of space in which Max was interested. The screen continued to show ordinary civilian traffic. Then, the data source indicator changed from "VIA RLY STN 09" to "VIA RLY STN 04." A second later, amidst the innocent civilian traffic, appeared twenty-five red dots, neatly arranged in five rows of five. A few seconds later, the computer supplied labels for each: "KRAG DSTR DERVISH CLS" along with range, bearing, and speed.

The minister grew pale. "No. How?"

Max dropped into a nearby chair. "Twenty-five Krag *Dervish* class destroyers," he said, almost to himself. "They must have left Krag space three or four days ago, making the trip on compression drive only."

Then, to the minister. "It's a trick we've theorized about for years, but never seen in practice. The emir hacked the relay station, most likely with Krag technical assistance, and inserted a signal-processing routine that blocked display of the enemy ships, probably by adding characteristics to the target detections that would cause the computer to classify them as noise or natural phenomena or your own side's covert military traffic that you don't want tracked. Anything that the system would not report to its operators."

He turned to the doctor, knowing that further explanation would be required for him to understand. "What you see on the screen is never a real, unprocessed sensor return like they used to get on the old-fashioned radar scopes where they relied on the operator to distinguish between airplanes, icebergs, sea return, ships, clouds, rain, flocks of birds, atmospheric turbulence, and submarine periscopes. Now, what the operator sees is a computer interpretation of the sensor returns, in which not only does the computer identify the targets but it scrubs out anything it judges that the operator doesn't need to see. As you can see, sometimes the computer can be fooled." He paused for a moment before continuing. "Minister, this projection doesn't show the distance from the mooring facility—how long until they reach the fleet?"

The minister tilted his head slightly and looked up and to the left, the way people sometimes do when they are performing mathematical calculations in their head. "Approximately six hours. More than ten hours before the fleet is able to defend itself. Horrible. Just horrible. Of what historical event does this remind me? Some other naval disaster. A saltwater fleet, attacked by surprise, bombed at its moorings. It was a terrible defeat. I can't remember the name."

"None of your ancestors came from the United States, did they?"

"No, Captain, I don't think that any of them did. Why do you ask?"

"Because, if they had, I don't think you would have any problem with being able to remember Pearl Harbor."

CHAPTER 5

00:44Z Hours, 20 March 2315: The Battle of Rashid V B

"Your text message from the *Clover* was a huge surprise," DeCosta said, finding that he liked having a name to hang on the microfreighter. "But when the CO says he needs his ship in the Rashid system ASAP, it's the XO's job to find a way. We were ready to undock and part company from the tender within fifteen minutes. But we ran into a problem with her skipper. Apparently, he believed that Admiral Hornmeyer's replenishment and refit orders took precedence over a CO summoning his own vessel. The man was actually concerned about incurring the admiral's wrath, if you can imagine. I was very happy, at that point, to have Major Kraft's help."

Max turned to the *Cumberland*'s Marine Detachment Commander, Major Gustav Albrecht Kraft who, despite the seriousness of the situation, seemed as always to bring an enthusiasm bordering on mirth to the performance of his duties.

"My Marines and I are always ready to do whatever is necessary for the good of the ship. Think nothing of it," he said to the young XO.

Then, to Max, "It was a simple matter, really. Some of the tender's crew members on board needed some, shall we say, 'encouragement' from my Marines to find their way off the ship."

"What kind of encouragement?" Max was wary. He could just see the Formal Complaint from the tender captain about assaults on his crewmen, trouble that he most decidedly did not need. As it was, he was trying not to think about the admiral's reaction to what was essentially a violation of a direct, written order by pulling his ship away from the tender in the middle of a refit.

The timing, however, was lucky. When DeCosta received the order Max sent from the microfreighter as soon as his sensors spotted the first group of escort fighters, the repair crews had already finished their work on the reactor cooling system and jump drive. Their remaining work (interior bulkhead and fixture repair as well as a fair amount of instrumentation work) could wait.

Kraft smiled and waved his left hand in a dismissive motion. "Not that we weren't prepared to frog march them or even carry them off the ship, but it never came to that. Most left immediately upon a polite request from one of my Marines." Of course, those Marines had their weapons with them. *Always.* Even the most polite request from one of Kraft's heavily armed, highly trained killing machines would feel like an order from a grand admiral. "If anyone was particularly reluctant, I just sent Zamora and Ulmer to have a conversation with them, and we never had to lay a finger on anyone. Of course, they *did* just happen to be carrying battle axes at the time."

Max almost laughed out loud. The Marines on naval vessels tended to run big, and Zamora and Ulmer were big even for Marines. They had to be 210 centimeters tall, easily massed 125 kilos each, had necks the diameter of tree trunks, and looked like grizzly bears with crew cuts. No, come to think of it, Max didn't think that there were many warship repair and refit technicians who would want to argue with Zamora and Ulmer. Their customary disarming grins and boisterous laughs would have been put away in favor of their Marine war faces, which would have given pause to Chesty Puller himself.

"The only other problem was that, since our departure was contrary to the admiral's orders, the tender captain refused to withdraw his accommodation tubes and equipment transfer ramps. We couldn't get underway without causing severe damage to both ships. Lieutenant Brown helped me with that," said DeCosta.

"Wernher, what did you do?" Max wasn't sure he wanted to hear this.

"It's not what you think, Captain. We didn't hack their systems, shut down their computers, override the ramp controls, or anything of the sort that might constitute 'damage or interference with the operation of a naval vessel in a war zone.' They shoot people for that, I hear. Instead, I just had Tomkins make up a few small packages with tiny antennas protruding from them and then attach them to the tubes and ramps."

"Packages? Like packages of Plasti-Blast with antennas for the remote detonators?" Max's voice carried more than a hint of alarm.

"What an astonishing coincidence, Captain! Now that you mention it, the packages did—by pure coincidence mind you—bear a striking resemblance to that very thing. As it is, they were nothing of the kind." Brown practically oozed innocence.

"What, exactly, were they?"

"Ham sandwiches."

"*Ham sandwiches?*"

"Yes, sir," Brown answered in a matter-of-fact tone. "Ham sandwiches. On white bread. With spicy mustard and kosher pickle slices. Chief Boudreaux in the galley made them up just the way you like them. We wrapped each sandwich in brown, opaque flexawrap, attached an antenna with ordinance tape, and then stuck them with adhesive putty right where they would go *if* they had been explosives and *if* we were going to blow the tubes and ramps. And of course, when he was attaching them, Tomkins conspicuously and obviously handled the packages with great delicacy. After all, we didn't want to damage the captain's lunch, did we? Then, we gave them all a once-over with a hand scanner, just to verify that the ham was fresh, you understand.

"And you never know, the more I think about it, the more I believe that those scans will come in very handy if we ever have need—for whatever reason—to prove that those packages contained ham sandwiches instead of something else. In any event, *somehow* the presence of these innocuous offerings of delicious food changed the tender captain's mind. When he agreed to retract his tubes and ramps, we removed the sandwiches, closed the airlocks, powered up the main sublight, and we were on our way. In case you're wondering, sir, the sandwiches are in your day cabin cooler. You'll want to eat them in the next day or so, or the bread will get soggy."

"I'll be sure they don't go to waste, Lieutenant." Max shook his head appreciatively.

"Thank you, gentlemen. For your ingenuity, for your loyalty... well done. Very well done."

The conversation took place in the *Cumberland*'s CIC, Max sitting at the CO's station and DeCosta sitting at the XO's station, with Kraft and Brown standing on the command island at their sides. The doctor sat in his accustomed seat at the Commodore's Station. Clouseau, rather than lying beside him as usual, was curled up on top of the projector for the 3D tactical display, which was just the right size for a cat of his rather considerable size and was always warm.

In a seat near Chin at Comms, sometimes used by a second Comms officer, sat the man whom Max and the doctor still thought of as Mr. Wortham-Biggs, who had talked his way aboard the *Clover* on its redlined journey to return Max and the doctor to their ship in time, Max hoped, to prevent the impending destruction of the bulk of the Rashidian fleet at its moorings around Rashid V B.

"Approaching rendezvous point in thirty seconds. Preparing to go subluminal," announced Chief LeBlanc from Maneuvering. The *Cumberland* had been making the cross-system journey from Rashid IV to the vicinity of Rashid V on compression drive at 10 c. The two planets at the time happened to be at nearly opposite points in their orbits, a nearly 4 AU trip, taking just over three minutes. "Disengaging compression drive in three, two, one, *now*." At the "now," Spacer Fleishman moved the compression drive controller from the .02 setting to the NULL setting. "Ship is subluminal and coasting, sir," announced LeBlanc.

"Very well," said Max. "Lay us alongside the Rashidian carrier, fifty kills off her port beam. Speed and course at your discretion."

After the chief acknowledged the order, Max turned to DeCosta. "So, XO, we have a few hours until twenty-five Krag *Dervish* class destroyers arrive. To combat them, we have one *Khyber* class Union destroyer, that Rashidian carrier over there and its three fighter squadrons, plus a mixed bag of superannuated Rashidian destroyers, frigates, and corvettes. Can we stop them?"

DeCosta didn't need even a second to provide the answer. "No, sir. Not with conventional tactics, anyway. The *Dervish* is the Krag's latest generation of destroyer. Very tough. They'll just brush off those Rashidian destroyers, frigates, and corvettes like gnats. They've got those dinky little 35-gigawatt Bofors-Plasma Dynamics Corporation pulse cannons. Good units, but the Krag's new deflectors just laugh at them. Actually, they're not even worth a laugh. More like a snicker. And because of their antiquated fire control systems, those older Rashidian ships are limited to firing an outdated old missile that's based on our Wolfhound. It's just not fast enough and smart enough to get through the Krag countermeasures and point defense systems. Their new missile—I forget the designation, it's just a string of letters and numbers—would do all right—not great but all right. But those old ships can't fire it."

"The old missile, does it have the same two-and-a-half megaton warhead as the Wolfhound?"

"No, Skipper. They don't have to pay for as many warheads as we do, so they pack a little bit more lithium deuteride into the warhead and get a bigger yield. They get 3.27 megatons out of theirs."

"That's not a Wolfhound," said Max. "That's a Mastiff. Extra big warhead. I think that might be useful. Okay, what about the Rashidian fighters—how are they going to stand up against those destroyers?"

DeCosta had already worked out the answer. "They'll whittle the rat-faces down. But they won't get them all. No way. *Dervish* is both very fast and very hard to kill. What they're going to do is pack those little fu—um... devils into a really tight formation and just punch their way through the fighters. Instead of the fighters having a speed advantage, these destroyers are actually faster than the Rashidian fighters. The fighters won't be able to stay with the targets and make successive attacks, which is how they're most effective. Instead, they get a single attack run and have to fire all their missiles at once. Result is at least a 35 percent decrease in their effectiveness, and probably closer to 50.

"When the fighters are done, applying standard analytical techniques and assuming that they use conventional tactics, it's looking like half, maybe even two-thirds, of the Krag force will survive. That's more than enough to accomplish their objective despite anything we do before, during, or after. If only we had a few of those moored ships or a fraction of their firepower, that could turn the balance, but those ships won't even be able to do anything but creep around on maneuvering thrusters until ten hours after the Krag have already destroyed them. And that makes them totally useless."

"Totally useless? Maybe not *totally.*"

Max's "crafty grin" made an appearance, quickly noticed by most of the CIC crew, some of whom gently elbowed nearby watch standers. "Mad Max is about to do it again," said Petty Officer Ardoin in an undertone to Spacer Sanders.

"Mad Max?" said Sanders just as quietly.

"Yep. Mad Max. That's what I call him. As good a name as any. Man like that's got to have a nickname," Ardoin said emphatically. "I'm telling you, he's a genuine, certified, tactical genius. He's going to be famous, and he's got to have a nickname."

"Well, you'll have to do better than that one, mate. I can't see that name ever catching on as a nickname for a destroyer captain or, for that matter, anywhere else, either."

"Minister," said Max to Wortham-Biggs, "who's in command of the Rashidian forces in this engagement?"

"That would be Admiral Jassir. On the battleship *Saif*, one of the moored ships. A very fine officer. One of his most exceptional qualities is that he is wise enough to know that he does not know everything."

"An uncommon trait in admirals, that's for sure. Chin, do you have all the comm protocols from *Equilateral* ready to go?"

"Affirmative, Skipper. Frequencies, encrypts, data transfer handshaking, everything."

"Outstanding. Please signal Admiral Jassir. Give the admiral my most respectful compliments and inform him that I urgently request the privilege of voice communications with him at the earliest opportunity."

Chin acknowledged the order, entered a few commands, and said a few sentences quietly into his headset. Not thirty seconds later, Chin announced, "Sir, Vice Admiral Jassir is standing by on your primary voice channel."

"I'll take it here." Chin hit a button and flipped a switch. The red AUDIO P/U LIVE light on Max's console came on.

Showtime.

"This is Lieutenant Commander Maxime Robichaux, Union Space Navy, Commanding the destroyer *Cumberland*. Do I have the honor of addressing Vice Admiral Jassir?"

"This is Admiral Jassir. It is a pleasure to speak with you, Captain Robichaux.

"And a pleasure to speak with you, as well, Admiral. You are the first flag officer of your Navy I have ever had the honor of addressing."

"I am sure that we are little different from the flag officers of your Navy. I must say that I have been eager to make your acquaintance after having so enjoyed the tale of your arrival at the Ministry of Trade. Thanks to you, that facility's grounds-keepers need not be concerned with their job security for some time. In any event, how you managed the ambassador's transport will make an interesting tale to add to our Navy's rich body of lore." Long silence. "Provided there is any Navy after today."

"Then," Max quipped, "for the sake of my own status as a legendary figure, we'll just have to make sure that there is."

"Indeed." The admiral didn't sound convinced. He sighed. "Captain, we have projected the likely outcomes of a conventionally fought encounter. They are not favorable. We can expect to impose, at most, losses of 65 percent upon the enemy force."

"Our projections are similar. If anything, they are more pessimistic."

"We have some unconventional tactics in mind that may even the odds somewhat, but our projections show that they are not enough. Given the likely outcome, any suggestions you might have, even if they are the kind of unorthodox methods that we hear you tend to employ, would be well received."

"Unorthodox suggestions are the only kind I make, Admiral. But first, I need a bit of information. May I ask a few questions?"

"Proceed."

"Your ship and the other moored ships... they are on internal power, not on power supplied from the mooring facility, aren't they?"

"That is correct."

"What's the power source?"

"The same as on your vessels, standard auxiliary nuclear power units. They all have G.E.-Westinghouse compact, pressurized, water-cooled fission reactors, built on license by our naval reactor fabrication plant on Rashid V A. I believe that every human power uses the old Rickover-type fission units to provide auxiliary power when the fusion reactors are off-line."

"Will the Rickovers run inertial guidance, attitude control, maneuvering thrusters, and navigation scanners?"

"Certainly. We like to be able to move the ships around the yard, get them in and out of repair hangars, and so on, without having to start the main reactor. But they can creep about at twenty or thirty meters a second at most."

"That's all we'll need. Can they fire missiles?"

"No. As on your ships, the missiles are targeted using the main sensor array, which requires more power than the fission power plant can provide. Further, the missile tubes' acceleration coils are not configured to receive power from the Rickover."

"What about fire control?"

"Fire control runs off of the ship's main power grid, which is tied to the Rickover so one can operate the console, but it is useless without the sensor array to generate the data to compute a firing solution."

"Unless it receives the data from some other source," Max said to himself as much as to the admiral. "Okay. Can power be routed to the launch coils from the main grid? Just enough to get the missiles out of their tubes?"

"What good would that do? They would never get past the Krag point defense batteries without the acceleration from the coils."

"Don't worry about that for now. Sir. Can the power be rerouted?"

"Let me ask one of my engineers." There was a brief discussion in the background. "Affirmative. I am informed that it is a simple matter of operating a manual power shunt."

"One more question. Your fleet's in a Clarke orbit. Are they over the deuterium separation plant?"

"As a matter of fact, they are."

"Then you might want to warn the people in the plant to get to their radiation shelters. In about four and a half hours, things are going to get a little hot."

It had been a busy four hours, but everything that could be done had been done, and the pieces were in place. As usual,

Max made sure that everyone on board had the opportunity to eat before going into combat. This included the captain himself, who ate two of the ham sandwiches in his cooler, sandwiches that were already enshrined in the *Cumberland*'s developing oral tradition as the "exploding" ham sandwiches. The doctor had left CIC to be certain that the Casualty Station was ready to receive battle casualties, if any. As a result, he had been absent when the plan for the coming battle had been formulated. Upon his return to the Commodore's Station, he found himself surrounded by people who refused to enlighten him as to what was in store.

"Tactical data link with all vessels is stable. Refresh rate is six cycles per second, and every ship in the provisional task force has confirmed that it is receiving and compiling data from every other ship," Chin announced.

Max looked around the CIC. No surprises. Every man at his station doing his job. Maybe a bit nervously, but doing it nonetheless. And maybe not with the confident professionalism and calm proficiency that Max had become used to on the *Emeka Moro* and some of the other taut ships on which he had served, but head and shoulders above the brow-beaten, drug-addicted, down-hearted group of misfits who had greeted him when his feet had first touched the *Cumberland*'s deck two months ago. *Admiral Hornmeyer was right when he said that these men have come a long way.* If they could just live through the next hour or two, Max was resolved to take them even further.

"All right, people," Max announced to the CIC at large, "we're the closer. We spend most of the game in the dugout, but come the bottom of the ninth, the manager puts us in, and it's up to us to save the game. Until then, let's stay alert and pay attention to what all the players are doing. We just might learn something."

"As expected, attacking force is forming up into its own version of a Daggett Dagger," Bartoli said. "Enemy formation consists of twenty-five ships, positively identified as *Dervish* class Krag destroyers. Now at bearing two-two-five mark one-two-seven. Heading is one-three-seven mark two-three-five. Continuing to close at point-six-five c. First Rashidian fighter squadron has just gone buster."

The doctor turned to Max. "Buster?"

"More 'impenetrable pilot jargon,' Doctor. It means that the fighters have kicked in their afterfusers. They're injecting highly compressed pure deuterium into the densest part of the plasma stream in their thruster nozzles. That initiates a second-stage inertially confined fusion reaction, increasing thrust by about 50 percent, but cutting their fuel economy roughly in half. It's analogous to going on afterburners in an old air-breathing jet."

Every man in CIC, and many men elsewhere in the *Cumberland* whose duties did not preclude them from doing so, was watching the events on a tactical repeater and could see what was happening. It was like watching another person playing a trideo game while knowing your own life might depend on the outcome.

The first Rashidian fighter squadron, consisting of 12 SF-89 Qibli fighters, bore down on the Krag destroyers, which in turn made no effort to evade or expend precious ordinance on anything but their primary objective—the Rashidian capital ships moored helplessly in orbit around Rashid V B.

Realizing that they would not be fired upon, the Qibli pilots held their fire until they reached the optimum range for their antiship missiles, designated only by the unexciting model number C-57D. Once they reached that point in space, a distance of eighty-five hundred kilometers from their targets, each fighter fired all six of its missiles. In an effort to overwhelm the Krag point defense systems with their somewhat less than state-of-the-art missiles, the Rashidians theorized that an effective tactic might be for each two-fighter element to fire all twelve of its missiles at a single destroyer.

The twelve fighters selected the foremost six enemy destroyers, paired up against them, closed to optimum missile range, and fired. In three cases, the excellent Krag point defense and countermeasures systems engaged the Rashidian missiles and defeated them. In two others, a single missile got through and in another, two reached their mutual target. Each missile carried a 250-kiloton thermonuclear warhead that made quick work of the three unlucky *Dervishes*, swallowing them whole in newborn miniature suns of fiery destruction.

Everyone in CIC knew what would happen next. Everyone was wrong. The first to catch on was Max, whose finely tuned tactical sense told him the exact point at which the fighters should veer off to return to their carrier. When they reached that point and continued to accelerate toward the Krag destroyers, forward deflectors on maximum and drives firewalled, he heard himself say, "Oh, God."

Wortham-Biggs nodded grimly, the only man not surprised. He spoke quietly. "These men know what is at stake, Captain. Their fleet, their Navy, their homes, their families, their whole world. And all mankind besides. I ask you, would you do anything differently?" He met the eyes of Max, DeCosta, Kasparov, Bartoli, Levy, and LeBlanc and saw his answer there.

"I thought not. My brother issued a message to the fleet immediately before we left. He said that Rashid did not join the war just to fight alongside our brothers. We joined the war to turn the tide. And not only that, but that we were *going* to turn the tide. At the Battle of Rashid V B. These men are resolved to do that. At all costs. This is the day. This is the hour. Mankind's victory over the Krag begins now."

Discerning the fighters' unexpected intentions, the destroyers began firing their pulse cannons. The fighters evaded. They opened up their formation to give each other room and to reduce the likelihood that the destruction of one craft would damage another, and then began weaving, dodging, twisting, sliding, jinking in three dimensions as unpredictably as possible to elude the rapid, computer-directed fire.

The Krag pulse cannons quickly eliminated three of the fighters, whose pilots were ever so slightly less skilled and inventive at evasive maneuvers than their fellows. Five more succumbed to pulse cannon fire as the range closed, making hits easier to score. Another was incinerated by a destroyer's point defense batteries, obliterated by a weapon that normally operated as an antimissile missile. The warhead was not, of itself, powerful enough to destroy the tough little fighter, but at a relative closing velocity of more than 90 percent the speed of light, the impact between missile and fighter converted both into a cloud of glowing vapor and molten bits of metal, the eternal laws of kinetic energy rendering the missile's tiny warhead irrelevant.

Three fighters, however, eluded destruction by the Krag defenses. They smashed through the destroyers' deflectors like howitzer shells through plywood, their impact on the hulls of their targets shattering the fighters and nearly obliterating the destroyers as an almost incalculable amount of kinetic energy transferred from one body to the other or was converted into heat and radiation. The fusion plasma that had been contained in the Krag reactors finished the job, leaving behind scarcely a particle of solid matter, consuming the wreckage in spectacular secondary explosions that blossomed in the hearts of, and then overwhelmed, the first set of fireballs.

Chief Tanaka, after Chief Wendt the most senior enlisted man on the ship and a man who had seen more than his share of battles, said in a voice just loud enough to be heard throughout CIC, "Farewell, my brothers."

Several other men, Max included, almost reflexively said, "Amen."

Now it was the turn of the second squadron. The first squadron had approached the destroyers at roughly a 45-degree angle. The second came at the enemy from dead ahead, afterfusers engaged, their drives maxed, as the enemy was now aware that no man had any concern for fuel consumption or prolonging the service life of his craft's engines. Before they got inside the range of the Krag pulse cannon, they spread out and began evasive maneuvers.

Like the first group, they launched their full load of missiles when they reached optimum range from their targets. Unlike the first group, however, the fighters did not launch in pairs. The fighters attacked only six of the destroyers, but in this effort each fighter launched one of its six missiles at each of the target destroyers. In that way, each destroyer was targeted not just by twelve missiles, but by twelve missiles coming in from six different attack vectors, one from each fighter.

As the Rashidian weapons lacked the Cooperative Interactive Logic Mode of the more advanced Union missiles, this was the best tactic for creating the greatest challenge for the Krag defenses. Compared to the first attack, it was more successful. Four of the destroyers targeted met swift thermonuclear ends, brief lightning flashes of death in the endless night.

Like their late comrades, the pilots of the second squadron did not turn aside after firing, but bored in, weaving and dodging to evade and confuse the Krag pulse cannon fire, but otherwise on an unwavering course. Unlike their comrades, however, who had lined up with each fighter aiming for a different destroyer, these fighters lined up on attack vectors that demonstrated that each destroyer under attack was being attacked by two fighters, hoping to divide the destroyer's defensive fire and point defense systems between them and increase the likelihood of one craft getting through. The tactic initially made no difference, as the fighters were still far enough away to be engaged by the pulse cannons of almost the entire destroyer formation, ships that were under attack and ships that were not being attacked alike. Direct hits quickly blew two of the twelve fighters to flaming atoms.

But as the range closed and the fighters moved out of the firing arcs of the ships that were not being engaged, the fighters' attack pattern started to pay off as each destroyer was faced with the difficult choice of focusing its fire on one of the fighters and ignoring the other, or of halving its effective firepower by dividing its attention between the two. Because the defensive fire was computer directed, each ship made the same decision, the statistically sensible but counterintuitive election to focus its fire on one of the two ships and ignore the other until the first was destroyed. In this way, two more fighters quickly met their end, the defiant light of their pilots' courage and resolve snuffed out in an instant.

Eight remained, the eight smartest, quickest, and most skillful of the lot. Not surprisingly, the eight survivors included their squadron leader, a man whose nickname translated into Standard as "the Mirage." In combat exercises, just as an opponent would get him in his sights or get a missile lock, the elusive Mirage would somehow evade, slip out of sight, and manage to reappear on his attacker's tail. The Mirage had more techniques (his opponents called them dirty tricks) for confusing and misdirecting his opponents than any three other squadron commanders combined, and with each new exercise, it seemed he had at least one new trick that no one had ever seen before. Now, he pulled up his fighter's tactical direction display, an interface that allowed him to give nonverbal instructions to the other fighters under his command, and tapped the key that sent a preloaded command.

The Mirage had one last dirty trick to play.

Responding to instructions sent over the TDD from their leader, the fighters lined up in four two-man elements, each consisting of a lead and a wingman, deviating from an arrow-straight path only enough to evade the pulse cannon fire. As soon as it appeared that the fighters had committed to a terminal attack vector, each Krag ship committed its pulse cannon and its point defense systems to defending against those two ships, approaching at that speed, from that vector. This cybernetic decision caused each destroyer's defensive fire to slacken for what Rashidian Intelligence had determined from (covertly intercepted) Union combat data would be exactly 2.2 seconds as weapons and sensors were trained by computer to new azimuths so that the attackers would fly into a region of space already filled with an impenetrable wall of defensive fire.

When their onboard timers indicated that exactly 2.195 seconds had passed and that the Krag defenses had committed, each fighter began a series of maneuvers designed to last only 2.1 seconds and end with the death of its pilot. First, each executed a radical course change, veering away from its putative target through a dizzyingly rapid, curving twist. The tiny ships' new courses crisscrossed and zoomed past one another in a computer-confusing and seemingly chaotic pattern until, at the same instant, they all once again banked hard and turned, two fighters per enemy ship, directly into the destroyers.

Because each destroyer was now under attack by two entirely new and different fighters, approaching from vectors that were not only different from the original attack angles but also at least 90 degrees apart from each other, the Krag computers took the better part of a second to decide that the fighters that had been attacking them were no longer attacking them and that they should interrogate the sensor subprocessors to determine whether any other ships were attacking in their stead, identify which ships were attacking, and then implement new protocols for defending against the new attackers.

This process, in effect, disoriented the computers for a critical instant, allowing the fighters to get closer to their targets without being engaged, and when they were finally engaged, rendered the destroyer's deployment of their point defense weapons hopelessly uncoordinated. The eight Rashidian warriors streaked past the destroyers' ragged defenses, eight fighters slamming into four destroyers, causing all twelve to meet their ends in spectacular mutual immolation.

The *Cumberland*'s CIC was filled with the glare of this orgy of destruction, causing even the men who were not facing one of the displays tied to the forward optical scanners to squint against the brilliance. The light waxed, waned, and then went out. No one spoke.

John Thomas "Jacky" Finnegan, the ebullient, red-headed spacer second class manning the Number Two Environmental Control Station, unconsciously made the sign of the cross in accordance with the rite of Rome: top, bottom, left, right. Immediately to his right, Athanasios "Hats" Hatzidakis, the reserved black-haired spacer second class manning the Number One Point Defense Control Station, unconsciously and simultaneously mirror-imaged the same gesture in accordance with the rite of Constantinople: top, bottom, right, left. Each caught the other's movements out of the corner of his eye, turned to the other, and nodded solemnly. Brothers in Blue, they shared bonds that not even the Great Schism of 1054 could put asunder.

Twelve *Dervishes* remained. They emerged from the roiling plasma and debris resulting from the destruction of the eight fighters and four destroyers, quickly arrayed themselves into a new, more compact version of their previous formation, and continued their advance toward the moored Rashidian fleet. The third and last fighter squadron wheeled into place to meet them, expertly and smoothly shifting formation from a standard holding matrix to their own version of the Hammerschmidt Cone, placing themselves directly in the path of the Krag vessels and engaging their afterfusers.

"The Hammer," as pilots called the formation on voicecom, was a textbook attack and defense formation, used by fighters and rated warships alike, shaped like a cone pointed away from the enemy. Ships using the Hammer place the enemy in the center of the space inside the cone, then turn simultaneously to face their targets and fire. This geometry places all of the targets at roughly equivalent ranges from all the fighters, meaning that their missiles all arrive almost simultaneously, overwhelming the enemy defenses.

Accordingly, the Krag ships prepared themselves to defend, as they had before, against an all-out missile salvo followed by a kamikaze attack. The fighters confirmed this expectation by powering up their missile targeting scanners and arming the missile-seeker heads, actions that showed up plainly to the Krag sensors, making the Krag even more certain of the defenders' tactics. The two formations closed rapidly.

The fighters reached the point at which calculations of geometry, time, acceleration, and distance, equally apparent to both sides, dictated that they launch their missiles.

They did not fire.

Instead, after waiting just long enough for the Krag to start to react to this development, they shifted formation again, this time into a dense, sharply angled flying wedge pointed at the center of the Krag group, the ships scarcely two meters apart from one another, forcing yet another delay in the Krag reaction.

Viewed from the perspective of the Krag warships, the fighters were lined up almost precisely behind one another. As pulse cannon fire picked off one fighter, then another, then another, the next fighter, protected by its armored hull, simply flew through the fireball of its obliterated brother and closed ranks, thereby presenting to the Krag a minimum number of targets, bringing about a huge reduction in the statistical likelihood that any one shot would score a hit.

The Rashidians' narrow chevron reminded Max of the Greek letter lambda (Λ), carried into battle on their shields by the ancient warriors of Sparta. The pilots' iron determination called to mind that of the ancient men who bore those shields into battle under the hot Mediterranean sun. There was no comm chatter from the fighters. Into the near silence in CIC, Max repeated with quiet reverence a line from the *Iliad*: "But silently the Greeks went forward, breathing valor."

In the silence of space, the fighters went forward and, their pilots breathing valor in epic lungfuls, tore into the heart of the Krag formation. Once the fighters were among them, the Krag ceased firing for fear of hitting their own ships. Suddenly, just short of the geometric center of the Krag formation, the tight Rashidian wedge shattered, the seven remaining ships veering into wildly weaving, corkscrewing, unpredictable trajectories that carried them to points more or less equally distributed throughout their enemies. Upon reaching those points, every ship simultaneously detonated all six of its missiles' warheads, the explosions merging into a huge, swirling maelstrom of plasma and debris nearly fifteen kilometers in diameter and so destructive that it seemed nothing could emerge from it but blinding light, heat, and hard radiation.

But something else did emerge. Too many of the fighters had been destroyed before reaching their destinations for the fireball to be hot enough and to exert a high-enough blast pressure to destroy everything within its boundaries. Five of the twelve ships survived: those on the edge of the fireball, whose commanders had deduced the fighters' tactic and protected themselves by shutting down everything but their deflectors and structural integrity fields while veering away from the center of the formation at the last second. They formed their own flying wedge and came on. Undaunted. Relentless.

Max took a deep breath. "All right people, time for us to get to the pitcher's mound. Maneuvering, put us ahead of the Krag formation, range ten thousand kills, and then match our velocity to theirs."

"Ahead of the Krag by ten thousand, then match speed, aye, sir," LeBlanc acknowledged. He had been plotting and replotting that course for the past fifteen minutes, so he required no further computation to give the requisite steering orders to the men at the controls. With a burst of acceleration, the *Cumberland* sprang from her waiting position and nimbly dropped into her planned slot, athwart the oncoming enemy's line of advance, precisely ten thousand kilometers ahead of the lead ship. This series of maneuvers took just under ten minutes. "Sir, we're station keeping with the enemy force, ten thousand kills ahead."

"Very well. Mr. Kasparov, Mr. Bartoli, any indications that our friends with the whiskers are doing anything different?"

They both replied in the negative.

"Countermeasures, initiate maximum jamming of the Krag sensors, all modes, all bands," Max said.

"Aye, sir. Maximum jamming. All modes. All bands," said Lieutenant Sauvé from Countermeasures. He keyed his console, triggering a series of commands he had loaded hours earlier and had checked and rechecked with borderline obsession at least five times since. Probably more like ten. "Maximum jamming implemented, sir. All sensors, all modes, all bands."

"Outstanding, Mr. Sauvé. Let's keep the mice tightly blindfolded so that they don't detect *anything* in their path. Weapons, bring the Stinger to Prefire."

"Aye, sir. Stinger to Prefire," Mr. Levy acknowledged.

The Stinger, officially known as Pulse Cannon 4, was the 75-gigawatt, rear-firing Krupp-BAE Mark XXII pulse cannon, a little brother to the 150-gigawatt Mark XXXIV units, three of which were mounted in the bow. At a range of ten thousand kilometers, the Krag warships were just inside its reach.

Levy keyed the command that powered up the systems that would divert plasma from the fusion reactor, direct it to the Stinger's firing chamber, aim the weapon, and keep the whole system cool so that it wasn't vaporized by the 10,000-degree Kelvin plasma that made the whole thing work. On the Weapons Console, the blue light marked PLS CNN 4-STANDBY winked out, and the orange light marked PLS CNN 4-PREFIRE winked on. "Pulse four at Prefire," Levy announced.

"Pulse Cannon four to Ready. Target Hotel Three," Max ordered. According to the Tactical Display, Bartoli had designated the middle destroyer, the one in the lead, as Hotel Three.

Levy acknowledged the order and keyed the commands that sent the plasma that was effectively the "cannonball" fired by the "cannon" to the firing chamber, locked the cannon's aiming mechanism on the target, and readied the exquisitely engineered but disposable, cryogenically cooled field generator that went inside the plasma bolt, confining it in a tight sphere until it reached its target. The green light on his console, labeled PLS CNN 4-READY illuminated.

"Pulse Cannon four at Ready. Weapon is locked on Hotel Three."

"Set cannon at full power, low rate, with a two-second pause between cycles. Maintain firing until further orders."

"Aye, sir. Full power, low rate, two-second intercycle pause. Maintain firing until further orders." Levy smiled, knowing that it was all part of the show. He keyed in the requisite commands. "System set for full power, low rate, two-second intercycle pause, indefinite sequence."

"Fire."

Levy hit FIRE. Plasma flowed from the firing chamber through a liquid helium–cooled conduit into an acceleration tube where magnetic coils aimed it at its target and accelerated it to seven-tenths of the speed of light. The plasma charge then received its containment field generator, exited the ship, and sped toward its target. This cycle was repeated every seven seconds—five seconds for the system's normal cycle and two seconds of additional pause inserted at Max's order. After each shot, the system would evaluate the trajectory taken by the plasma bolt and, if necessary, adjust its aim to zero in on the target.

"How long do we keep doing this?" Sahin asked. The Stinger had fired at the lead Krag destroyer nine times and scored seven hits.

"Until we get to where the fleet is moored, which will be in just over eight minutes," Max responded

"Our firing on the enemy ships does not seem to be having any effect," Sahin said, his voice tinged with surprise as he scrolled through the Enemy Condition reports available from his console.

"I know. I didn't expect it to."

"Then why are we doing it?"

"Because it's what the Krag expect us to do. From their perspective, now that the fighters are gone, the only way we have of possibly keeping them from destroying the moored ships is to stay ahead of them and hope we get lucky with the Stinger."

"Why not attack them with the pulse cannons in the front of the ship? I seem to recall hearing something to the effect that they are far more powerful than the ones in the back. Or the missiles in the front. I understand that we can fire two at a time of those."

Max didn't wince at the use of "front" and "back" to describe parts of a warship. Much. His reply was patient and even. "If we turn on the Krag ships to use our forward-firing weapons, our rear countermeasures array would lose its lock on the enemy sensors. Before we could bring the forward countermeasures array to bear and reestablish, the Krag would get a firing solution and blow us halfway to the outer galactic arm. Besides, we don't have enough firepower to take on five *Dervish* class cans.

"No, we'll continue as we are, which gives us a plausible reason to stay ahead of the enemy ships and do what we are really here to do, which for sure isn't sitting up here at extreme range trying to pick them off with that little popgun we have in the stern."

"And what, exactly, *are* we here to do?"

"Something else entirely."

"And let me guess. That 'something else entirely' is another one of your borderline insane, elaborately dangerous, made-up-on-the-spur-of-the-moment, labyrinthinely complex, Rube Goldman stratagems."

"Goldberg."

"What?"

"That's Goldberg. Rube Gold*berg*."

"If you are going to be fussy about irrelevant details, I suppose that *is* the name. I could literally draw you a schematic of one of his ludicrously overly complex devices, but I got the name slightly scrambled."

"I see."

"Well, is it?"

"Is what?"

"Your plan. Is it one of your typically wild, dangerously gut-wrenching, nail-biting, death-defying stunts?"

"Most of what we are about to do is no more dangerous than any other set of maneuvers typical for a destroyer in combat. Except for what we are doing right now. And even that isn't something I would describe as being inherently dangerous. It's more that there are very severe consequences if we don't do it exactly right."

"And what is 'most of what we are about to do'?"

"You'll see."

"All right, then," said the doctor after snorting with exasperation, "perhaps you will give me a clue pertaining to what is dangerous about what we are doing right now?"

"Only that if we lose our jamming lock for as little as two seconds, the computers on those Krag ships will automatically generate a firing solution and launch their missiles. About five seconds after we lose the lock, we die."

"Actually, with all due respect, Skipper," interrupted a broadly smiling Bartoli, "allowing for the typical time for Krag to generate a firing solution, the length of their missile firing cycle, and making proper allowance for the range, I calculate that once we lost the lock it would be more like seven point four seconds before we were vaporized."

The doctor heaved a mock sigh of relief. "Oh, *seven point four* seconds. That makes a whole galaxy of difference, doesn't it?" He lowered his voice and spoke confidentially to Max, "You, sir, have corrupted them. These are impressionable young men who very nearly worship the very ground on which you walk, and you have corrupted them utterly. Not only has their brief association with you inured them to extreme danger and reckless exposure to outrageous risk; it has also made them *flippant* about it. They toss off jokes in the face of death. You are a bad influence. What do you have to say for yourself?"

In an equally confidential tone, Max replied, "I would say, Doctor, that I am turning them into real Man of War men: men who can fight the ship and repair damage and put out fires and repel boarders and charge across a boarding tube onto an enemy's deck and cut off a Krag's legs at the knees with a boarding cutlass, all without pissing themselves at the first whiff of danger or the first sight of the enemy. I couldn't be more pleased. I've been working for that since the first minute of the first day."

When Bram harrumphed his condemnation, Max pretended not to notice. He continued at a volume audible throughout CIC. "And then there is also the matter of having to maintain precisely the range to the enemy."

"Why is precise range so important?" The doctor set his criticism aside, for now.

"Because we need to remain within 10,500 kills of the enemy in order to hit him with our pulse cannon, but if we stray within 9,987 kills, we will be within range of *their* pulse cannon, which has a backup optical aiming mode impervious to jamming, and with five destroyers, each armed with four forward pulse cannons, they could pound us to dust in about five seconds."

He looked over his shoulder at Bartoli, who nodded in confirmation that, under those circumstances, the *Cumberland*'s destruction would indeed require roughly five seconds.

"Is that not a rather narrow margin, particularly given velocities at which we are travelling?"

"It is, but we are in the capable hands of Mr. LeBlanc and Mr. Fleishman. I have every confidence."

"From which I am sure I take the most profound reassurance." Sahin's tone of voice said otherwise.

The two men fell into silence. CIC was quiet except for the occasional report from a man at his station, calmly acknowledged by Max. The signs of increasing tension were evident even without the doctor's acute powers of observation. The shuffling of feet, the drumming of fingers, the variety of ways that men had of dealing with sweaty palms and churning stomachs. DeCosta literally found himself unable to sit down, and was prowling CIC, looking over the shoulders of the watch standers, asking them, in the friendliest terms, extremely specific and detailed questions about what they were doing and about their systems and data sources.

As DeCosta was stepping from one station to the other, Max met his eyes and then stared pointedly at the XO station. DeCosta got the point and sat back down in his seat. As soon as the younger officer settled in, Max stood up, moved over until he was standing beside the XO's console, and pointed to one of the tactical displays, leaning in as though to discuss some point of maneuvering or tactics.

Instead, he said softly, "XO, you don't want to bounce around CIC like that. It makes the men think one of two things, both of them bad: that you don't have confidence in them or that you're too nervous to sit down. It's best to stay at your station unless you have a particular reason to get up."

He pointed to a different part of the display, maintaining the charade that he was talking to the XO about something there. "Working as a senior officer rather than someone who is actually operating a system or is analyzing a specific kind of data is hard to get used to. It leaves you feeling like you have nothing to do but worry. Breathe deeply, slowly, regularly, from the diaphragm, to calm your nerves. Always have your coffee or whatever it is you like to drink at your station. Holding a coffee cup or a can of juice gives you something to do with your hands. Sit still and don't fidget. If you need something to do, use your console to pull up the other displays around CIC, see what everyone else is looking at, and then see what control inputs are coming from the various consoles—that tells you whether the folks at those consoles are paying attention and staying on top of things. But do it deliberately and calmly—not like you're in a hurry or in a way that conveys nervousness. Understood?"

The young man nodded. "Yes, sir." Max heard something in the young man's tone that wasn't quite right. He needed a little bit more. Well, that's what skippers do.

"You're a good officer, DeCosta, and you've got the makings of a damn good XO—you've got the tactical, systems, and ship-handling parts of the job down cold. But that's about half the job. The other half is leadership, and two thirds of *that* is exemplifying in your own conduct the qualities you would most wish to see in that of the men. That means more than telling them what to do and more than showing them what you want every now and then. It means living the example. It means *being* what you want them to become, every minute of every day. That make sense to you?"

"Perfect sense, sir. And Skipper?"

"Yes, XO."

"Thanks."

"For what?"

"For taking the time to explain that to me. In the middle of a battle. When you have so much else on your mind."

Max smiled at a pleasant memory. "Commodore Middleton told me that the middle of a battle is one of the best times to learn. He said, 'There's nothing like the prospect of sudden, violent death to focus the mind.' Think nothing of it. It's my job."

"Well, sir, no one has ever taken much of an interest in my development as an officer before."

"Not true. I know for sure that someone else has."

"Who's that?"

"Admiral Hornmeyer. He picked you for this billet personally." Max slapped him on the shoulder. Two quick, sharp pops.

"Skipper," Bartoli called out, "the lead Krag destroyer is powering up his pulse cannon. He's just gone to Prefire. I don't get it. We're out of range. They can't hit us."

"Maybe they don't know that," said the doctor, drawing several barely "what a stupid remark" glares and snorts from various CIC personnel.

"He's gone to Ready." Pause. "Firing."

One of the optical scanners on the hull automatically locked onto the incoming ball of brilliant plasma and followed it as it approached, a tiny speck that slowly grew to the apparent size of a pea before exploding hundreds of kilometers away from the *Cumberland.* Because the coolant that preserved the containment field generator was exhausted, the generator was destroyed by the plasma that surrounded it, and the released plasma violently expanded in a blast very similar to a small thermonuclear explosion. There was a collective breath of relief.

"Uh, sir?" Bartoli didn't sound the way one would want a tactical officer to sound after an enemy weapon has just exploded short.

"Yes, Bartoli?"

"The extreme outer range of Krag pulse cannon is supposed to be 9,987 kills. Well, that one just went 10,298 before detonating. More than two standard deviations beyond the average range."

Shit.

Bartoli continued. "They must have made some sort of modification. If we assume that this bolt was more or less average, and given the standard deviation of range previously observed in Krag pulse cannon bolts, and given our current range, we can expect something like one round in four to have the range to reach us. Given the observed accuracy of their optical targeting system and extrapolating to the current range, and taking both factors into account—range and accuracy—we can expect to be hit by something between one in six and one in fifteen of their shots, depending on the breaks and depending on where that first round falls on the range bell curve. But sir, I have no idea what they did."

"I do," said Levy.

Max spun to face the young weapons officer. "Shoot, son."

"I put my back room on watching the sensor take on the Krag weapons as soon as I thought they might shoot, just to see if I could learn anything. The difference was apparent as soon as they fired—lower color temperature of the plasma. Turns out they reduced the amount of plasma in the bolt without reducing the size of the containment field. So, it's at a lower pressure, meaning lower temperature, meaning the coolant in the field generator lasts longer before it gives out and the generator is vaporized. Buys them more range."

"Good job, Levy. Why did they stop firing?"

"First shot was likely an experiment, sir, to see if the modification worked. Now that they see that it does, they're busy modifying their pulse cannon plasma control software in the other three pulse cannons on the lead ship and in all four tubes on the other ships and, when they get that done in a few minutes, they'll open up on us with all twenty tubes."

"I can hardly wait," Max said. "And there's no helping it because, if we pull out of their range, then the range will be too long for us as well, and then the cat is out of the bag. Looks like we're going to have to take some hits, people. Deflector control, rear deflectors to full. Damage Control, have DC parties stand ready to receive damage from enemy action in frames seven through twelve. Maneuvering, when they start firing again, execute evasive maneuvers at your discretion." Max trusted LeBlanc's judgment in how best to dodge the enemy fire.

As all of those orders were acknowledged, Max turned to Chin. "Mister Chin, One MC." One Main Circuit—since before World War II, the naval name for the main voice channel heard throughout the ship.

"Aye, sir, One MC."

The light went on. "Men, we're about to start receiving enemy fire. We'll have to take it for a few minutes. Stay at your stations. Do your jobs. DC parties, you've been trained for this. Keep your heads and do what the old timers tell you to do and you'll be fine. Men, you are equal to this challenge. Skipper out."

Just over a minute passed without a word spoken in CIC save routine reports and acknowledgments. Then, Max could almost feel Bartoli tense up. "All five hostiles going to Prefire on pulse cannons. All four tubes on each." A few seconds. "All tubes now at Ready . . . firing."

The displays tied into the aft optical scanners picked up the cluster of twenty tiny incandescent pinpricks spat out by the Krag destroyers. The tiny stars slowly grew larger on the screen as every sphincter in the compartment puckered. LeBlanc was watching something on his console intently and muttering to his men in a low voice. Then, when the pinpricks had grown to pea sized, one of them exploded. It had come to the end of its extended range. Then another. Then two more. Then three. Then eight in quick succession, leaving five that were now very close.

His expert eye judging the relative positions and ranges of the five remaining bolts, LeBlanc brought his left hand down smartly onto the right shoulder of the man at Yaw and snapped out, "Port, to the stop," and then brought his right hand in the same manner down on the left shoulder of Pitch, "Up, to the stop." Yaw turned his yoke all the way to the left while pitch pulled his all the way back. The agile ship pulled hard "up" and to the left. Half a second later, his hand landing on Yaw's shoulder, LeBlanc said, "Back off a quarter." Yaw turned his yoke one-fourth of the way between the stop and the center position. The ship straightened out slightly.

Four pulse cannon bolts zoomed past the *Cumberland* and exploded. The fifth, its containment field disrupted by the ship's drive trail, detonated harmlessly in the destroyer's wake. LeBlanc gave the orders to return the ship to its base course. The ship straightened out and steadied on its former course, and Sauvé reestablished the lock his jamming transmitters had on the Krag missile targeting sensors, with about six-tenths of a second to spare before they were able to generate a firing solution.

"They're all at Prefire again," said Bartoli. "All twenty tubes." A pause. "Now at Ready... firing." Again, twenty star points appeared on the optical displays, only instead of all of them simply growing larger, meaning that they were all targeted exactly on the *Cumberland*, most of them seemed to move ever so slowly, down, left, or right against the stellar background, indicating that they were targeted at points slightly offset from the ship's position, in a firing pattern designed to bracket the ship so that in whatever direction it dodged, there would be a pulse cannon bolt in the vicinity.

"Skipper," Levy said, "My optical readings show that these bolts have a significantly lower color temperature than the others, meaning that they have much lower pressures and heat levels. My rough estimate is that they all have the range to reach us, sir, but that there is going to be a major drop in explosive yield. At least 30 percent, maybe more."

"Thank you, Mr. Levy." *Yes, thank you so very, very much Mr. Levy for the wonderful news. Oy vey.*

"Maneuvering, expect little or no attrition on this pattern," said Max.

LeBlanc knew what to do. He gave the orders to his people. Another violent maneuver. The ship headed at Emergency toward the edge of the slowly spreading pattern of glowing plasma spheres. LeBlanc had eyeballed the pattern carefully and found the two bolts at the edge that, due to random variation, were the farthest apart, and headed toward the gap between them.

WHAM! Max felt as though he had been driving in a ground car that was rear ended by a delivery truck. The inertial compensators took out most of the blow, but that didn't keep everyone from feeling as though their eyeballs were bouncing off the bulkheads. Two pulse cannon bolts had detonated within a kilometer of the ship, their plasma shock waves striking the *Cumberland*'s deflectors hard enough to give her a hard kick in the behind.

LeBlanc ordered the ship back to its base course so that sensor jamming could be restored in what should have been, once again, in the nick of time. Unfortunately, the direct path between one of the destroyer's jamming emitters and the targeting sensor arrays on the Krag destroyer at the far left edge of the formation—but only that destroyer—went right through the fireball created by one of the Krag plasma bolts and was disrupted for three additional tenths of a second. This was not long enough for the Krag ship to lay down the lengthy series of polyphasic, polarized, multiplaned, multifrequency scans that would give it a clear picture of what was ahead, but it was good enough to give it a firing solution on a warship only 10,500 kilometers ahead. The same explosion disrupted the *Cumberland*'s passive sensors to such an extent that it was not able to detect this fact.

Accordingly, no one on board the Union destroyer was expecting incoming missiles until Bartoli called out, "Vampire, vampire, vampire! Hotel One has just fired missiles, Foxhound type. Full spread of six. No other launches."

Thank goodness for small favors. Six missiles were quite enough to lend excitement to the day. None of the men said a word, retched, passed out, or otherwise displayed any fear or emotion of any kind. Midshipman Gilbertson, only nine years old, was not quite so stoic. To his credit, his only reaction was to whisper a single word. "Shit."

Max thought, irrelevantly, that some one should put the young man on report. There was no evading the attack; the evasive maneuvers necessary to get away from missiles would not only break the jamming lock that was preventing the Krag from being able to see ahead, which was the entire purpose of their tactics, but would also allow all the other ships to fire *their* missiles. *We don't want to go there, do we?* There was only one thing to do. "Maneuvering, go to Emergency and turn the handle."

"You heard him," LeBlanc said to Fleishman at Drives.

Fleishman shoved the main sublight drive controller all the way to the stop and then grasped the ring just under the knob on the lever, rotating it one-half turn clockwise. That turn sounded a tone and lit a purple light in Engineering, signaling that department to take out all of the safety interlocks and governors on the system and to cause it to generate as much thrust as possible without actually melting down the drive or blowing up the ship.

The purple status light on the Drives console illuminated a second later, showing that Engineering had complied with the signal. The additional speed would not cause the ship to be able to outrun the missiles, but it would decrease their relative speeds, giving the point defense systems more time to respond and therefore a higher probability of destroying the incoming weapons.

The Krag missiles were equipped with a cooperative attack mode similar to that of the Union weapons, but—at least for now—the Union jamming technology was sufficient to prevent the missiles from communicating with each other. Each weapon was on its own.

Accordingly, each sensed the location of its brothers and veered off so that they could all approach from amidships, each from a different direction. At six thousand kilometers, the *Cumberland*'s electronic defense systems engaged the missiles, sweeping them with electromagnetic energy of various frequencies, polarizations, and phases, in order to confuse or disrupt the missiles. Two succumbed to the attack, one detonating and the other losing its target lock and wandering into a useless trajectory.

As soon as the remaining four missiles got within forty-five hundred kilometers, the destroyer's active missile defense system engaged them. A swarm of forty tiny Terrier antimissile missiles issued from a launch bay near the stern. Having already received their targeting instructions, the Terriers divided into four packs of ten, each pack closing rapidly on one of the attacking weapons. The attackers fought back, varying their courses to evade the defenders, broadcasting confusing electronic signals, then going silent and stealthy to evade detection, and finally transmitting high-energy pulses designed to fry the electronics of the tiny hunters.

In this war of missile versus missile, two of the Krag weapons were overwhelmed. Three Terriers penetrated the first Foxhound's defenses and exploded in its path, the shrapnel produced by their demise shredding the Foxhound into useless scrap. The second Foxhound had run at a deceptively slow speed, and when the Terriers committed to an intercept trajectory at that speed, accelerated at the last minute. The Terriers, however, though lacking true Cooperative Interactive Logic Mode attack software, did have a rudimentary communications ability, which caused the missiles to arrive upon distributed solutions to certain kinds of intercept calculations, sending a few missiles ahead and a few missiles behind the most probable enemy trajectory, just in case one of the operative assumptions proved to be wrong. Accordingly, two Terriers were not "fooled" by the Foxhound's deception and were ready and waiting when it accelerated away from the remaining defending weapons. They intercepted it easily, destroying it with a combination of their small warheads and the enormous kinetic energy of projectiles colliding at high sublight velocities.

That left two. At two thousand kilometers, the *Cumberland* automatically engaged the missiles with its rail guns, electromagnetically accelerating tiny projectiles to over half the speed of light in rapid-fire succession, sensors adjusting the aim to try to cause the stream of pebble-sized "bullets" and the incoming missile to intersect, destroying the latter. One missile was quickly obliterated in this fashion, its tiny fusion reactor chamber penetrated by two of the rail gun projectiles and filling the surrounding space with plasma. This plasma, however, so disrupted the rail gun targeting scanners that they were unable to engage the last missile, which aimed itself for the center of the *Cumberland*'s mass.

With only one incoming missile remaining, the whole of the ship's defensive capabilities were able to focus on the single attacking weapon. The deflectors surged and focused their full power on the missile, producing a nearly impenetrable wall of polarized gravitons, which, like gravity in reverse but tens of thousands of times more powerful, repelled the missile and arrested its forward progress nearly a kilometer away from the hull. Sensing that it would get no closer, the missile's computer decided that causing some damage was better than causing no damage at all and detonated the weapon.

"Missile detonation, one hundred and two point eight kilotons, range one kill, epicenter at frame eight, azimuth one-two-five," announced Tufeld at Damage Control in a rich, arresting voice more befitting a tridvid announcer than a Navy petty officer.

"Several systems off-line, either tripped by EMP or damaged physically, impossible to tell at this point. Unavailable Tier One Systems at this time are number two IMU, auxiliary fire control, primary air handling, auxiliary has taken the load. Unavailable Tier Two Systems at this time are all starboard lateral sensor arrays, all starboard lateral comm arrays, all starboard amidships point defense systems, coverage of that area being picked up by starboard forward and starboard aft point defense, starboard deflectors from frame three through frame thirteen.

"Several Tier Three systems as well, will report them if requested. My board shows DC parties responding. I'll update you as soon as I know more. And sir, I would *strongly* advise that we not take another major hit anywhere in that part of the ship. If we do, you won't need to file a report about it, if you take my meaning."

"I do, indeed. Thank you, Tufeld."

Suddenly a loud and seldom heard alarm started hooting.

"Hull breach," Tufeld practically shouted over the too loud alert signal.

"Turn that damn thing off," Max barked. The alarm fell silent.

"Hull breach: Auxiliary Fire Control, nothing further at this time. All my feeds from that compartment are EMP tripped at this time. Reset expected in approximately two minutes." Tufeld hit a few keys. "I've just detailed my Alfa DC team to that location. We should have a report shortly."

"Thank you, Tufeld. Good job."

"Hello? Hello?" Midshipman Park nearly shouted, but there was something funny about the sound. It didn't carry the way it should have. He didn't know what was going on except that it was very dark and very cold and there was a loud whistling sound that he didn't recognize. For some reason, he was lying on the floor. Not floor. Deck. The deck of the ship. His ship. He managed to stand up and the room spun around him. "Hello?" he shouted again into the already noticeably colder darkness.

No answer. Then his thoughts started to reassemble themselves. He had been at his battle station in Auxiliary Fire Control. A missile got through the defenses, and the next thing he knew, he was on the deck in the cold darkness. If only he could see.

Wait a minute. He wasn't just little Park Dong-Soo from a tiny village in Korea that no one had ever heard of, he was *Midshipman* Park Dong-Soo (the Korean custom is for the surname to come first) of the USS *Cumberland*, this vessel's "Will Robinson." And he was dressed for duty. That meant... he reached into the appropriate pocket... it was there. He pulled out his compact hand torch and turned it on, methodically sweeping the compartment with the narrow beam of light. What he saw scared him shitless.

There were five men in the compartment, all unconscious on the deck. What had happened was obvious. The shock wave from the explosion propagated through the hull and into the air of the compartment, knocking the men unconscious. Park, on the other hand, shorter than the men and having a 170-centimeter-tall fire control console between him and the outer hull, had been shielded. The primary shock wave had passed right over his head, leaving only the much weaker reflections off the flat surfaces in the room to strike him, knocking him out briefly.

He found the emergency lights and manually activated them. The automatic trigger had been fried by the warhead's EMP. The only exit was blocked by one of Auxiliary Fire Control's secondary processing units that had gotten torn from the bulkhead. The six-hundred-kilo Auxiliary Fire Control secondary processing unit. Park knew he was not leaving the compartment without help. He looked at his percom. Red light. The unit was not in communication with the network. EMP again. He tried the comm panels on each of the four consoles. All dead. More EMP. He was on his own.

To top it off, there was a hole in the outer hull the size of his fist that was venting atmosphere.

That was why his voice sounded so thin. The air pressure in the compartment had already gone down so much that sound no longer carried well. That was also why it was so cold. When you lower the pressure, you lower the temperature. Gay-Lussac's law.

CLANG! The air vents into the compartment slammed shut. The ship was protecting itself from bleeding all of its air into space by closing off the vents, stopping the flow of air into the compartment. Only when the sensors in the compartment detected that the venting had stopped would the computer repressurize the area.

Even with Park's limited training and experience on board a warship, the situation was absolutely clear to him: if he didn't patch the hull breach, everyone in the compartment would die. In just a few minutes. Six lives now depended on him.

Unbidden, the voice of the now-dead Chief Amborsky, his old Mother Goose, spoke from his memory. "You never know when some of your shipmates' lives, maybe all of them, will depend on you. Maybe never. Maybe next week. Maybe this afternoon. But when that moment comes, you had better be ready."

That moment was now.

He had been trained for this: patch the breach. He knew how to do that. Problem: the breach was near the ceiling, over two and a half meters from the deck, and he was not much more than a meter tall. He would have to climb. On what? He had to be fast. He was starting to feel the hypoxia. He knew what it felt like from training in the hypobaric chamber. He knew what to watch for: euphoria, like being drunk. He had never been drunk. Maybe now, he would never be drunk. How sad. *Think. Get back on track.*

Get going, Park. You don't have much time. First, he located the patch kit. It was where it was supposed to be, in the Emergency Locker for his compartment. There were six portable oxygen units, each consisting of a mask and a small tank. He grabbed one and put it on. It wouldn't save his life if the air pressure in the compartment got too low, but it would buy him a little more time by enriching the thinning air around his nose and mouth with a higher proportion of oxygen molecules. He'd get an extra minute. Maybe two. It might make a difference.

There were also six emergency pressure suits. Far too large for him. He could get into one and it would keep him alive until rescue came, but he was so small and the suits were so large, there was no way he could wear one and get the hull breach patched. He could save his own life, but only by letting five men die. No. Park would either save his shipmates, or he would pay for his failure by dying with them.

Too bad the Navy didn't make a Space Combat Uniform small enough to fit him. If he had been in an SCU like the rest of the crew, he could have just reached in the thigh pockets, pulled out his gloves and soft helmet, zipped them on, activated the oxygen generator in one of the breast pockets, and he would be enclosed in a flimsy but serviceable emergency pressure suit that would keep him alive for hours. He wouldn't have to worry about passing out from hypoxia while he was trying to keep everyone else from dying. If he lived through this, there would be a nasty memo. Maybe not. His hands were already so cold that even if he had been wearing an SCU, he probably couldn't have manipulated the zippers well enough to make them seal. He was certain he couldn't get SCU gloves and helmets on five unconscious men in time.

The only way anyone in the compartment was going to live was if he managed to get to the breach and seal it. First, he shoved a chair under the opening. Then he started piling on the chair whatever he could find. Ration boxes from the Emergency Locker, equipment and tool drawers, even two rectangular light fixtures that had been knocked loose by the shock. It looked like it might be enough, especially since the EMP knocked out most of the gravity generators in the compartment, leaving something like 0.5 G.

He slung the patch kit's strap over his shoulder and started to climb. Already suffering from moderate hypoxia, he grew dizzy from the small exertion and fell to the deck. He lay on his back for a few moments, staring at the ceiling, wondering why he was so dizzy and so cold. The skin under his fingernails was noticeably blue. There was a name for that. Cyano-something. Cyano de Bergerac. He giggled.

Then it all came back to him. He stood up and saw the five men on the deck. He had only been rotated into this station a few days ago, but these men had been nothing but kind and fatherly to him. They had taught him the ropes of the systems in that room, told him interesting stories about Navy life (many of which were wildly improbable), and gave him some sensible advice about how to approach his duties and his training. They amiably referred to him as "Admiral Park," smilingly saluting him when he came into the compartment at the beginning of watch. He always returned the salute, put on a haughty expression, and said, "As you were, gentlemen. Despite my high rank, you know I don't stand on ceremony."

He gritted his teeth with fierce determination. He was not going to let the icy vacuum of space claim their lives.

Not today.

He stood up and slowly climbed his makeshift pyramid. When he reached the top, he was still several centimeters short of the hole. And he knew he had already piled on everything that he could move and lift and that could be stacked on the chair with any kind of reasonable stability. *Think*. He opened the patch kit anyway and sorted through the various sized patches. Some of them were a meter square, and some were only a few millimeters in size. Then he came up with one the right size for that breach, one about the size of a sheet of paper. But he couldn't get it to the hole.

Something was nagging at him. He knew he had the solution in his hand. It was getting so cold. Ice was forming on the inside of his oxygen mask. He had only a minute, maybe two, and that would be it. When they found his body it would be frozen solid, like a tiny Korean icicle. No it wouldn't. When the DC people got into the compartment, he would still be warm and breathing. He had the solution in his hand. Yes! He had the solution in his hand. Literally.

He unrolled the largest patch, a patch large enough that its top portion would reach and cover the hole while he held the bottom from the height he could reach. Park held it flat against the hull by placing his hands to the left and the right of the center. Then he slid it upward toward the breach pushing it as high as he could with the tips of his fingers. It was fairly stiff, so it held its shape well enough not to flop back down as he edged it further upward, shifting his hands closer to the bottom of the patch as he inched it higher and higher. Soon part of the patch was over the breach and held in place by the compartment's diminishing air pressure. A few more shoves managed to get the breach completely covered. The whistling stopped.

Then he pulled out the aerosol can of patch sealant and sprayed it over the edges of the patch to hold it in place. His arm was wobbly and his aim was bad. He got some of the sealant on his uniform sleeve. He hoped it didn't stain. He so liked looking squared away and shipshape. Chief Tanaka would make him run an extra mile on the treadmill for having a soiled uniform. He hated that treadmill. Park tumbled to the deck, the low G impact of his tiny body barely making a sound in the thin air. He couldn't remember how to get back up. The compartment seemed to be getting dark again. And cold. So cold. He needed to go to sleep. Just as he closed his eyes, he heard the whistling of air rushing into the compartment.

"Why are they not firing their cannon?"

"Because, Doctor, they fired missiles and don't want to interfere with them." Max kept himself from shaking his head. Sometimes talking with the doctor was like talking to one of the great minds of the age, and sometimes it was like talking to the newest hatch hanger. Even Mr. Wortham-Biggs, still in CIC because he liked being close to the action and because he was far too important a personage to be shooed away, could barely keep from rolling his eyes. "You use only one weapons system at a time to keep one from damaging or disrupting the other. It's called the fratricide effect. Now that the missiles have run their course and the Krag can't generate a new firing solution for them, I'm certain they will resume firing their pulse cannon. They just need their optical scanners to recover from the flash of that nuclear explosion so that they can aim accurately. Speaking of which, Mr. Levy, can we modify our pulse cannon to increase our range the way the Krag did theirs?"

"Affirmative, Skipper. In fact, I put Pavelka and Healy on it a few minutes ago, and they tell me that the software modifications should be ready to be loaded a minute or so from now. It's a simple matter of reducing the plasma volume and changing the timer on the field generator. Of course, it really cuts into the weapon's explosive yield, which is why we don't do this all the time. I wasn't going to implement it without your approval, sir, but I didn't see the need to bother you with getting a few men started on working the problem."

"Levy, I might just have to put you in for a citation. I'd put you in for a promotion too, but we have a rule in the destroyer service that you can't be made lieutenant until you're old enough to shave." Max smiled at the very young officer. "Good job, Levy. Tell me when it's ready. Maneuvering, I'm not in a mood to be shot at any more. Let's open up the range to..." He looked at Levy.

"Twelve thousand kills, sir."

"You heard the man. Twelve thousand."

"Aye, sir." LeBlanc's relief was audible.

About a minute and a half passed. "We're ready, sir," said Levy.

"Resume firing." From a greater range, the weaker pulse cannon bolts from the Stinger flew toward the Krag, posing less of a threat, but accomplishing exactly what Max wanted to accomplish.

He looked at the tactical display, then at the large CIC chrono. "Now, it's about time for a little payback. Mr. Levy, Mr. Sauvé, have we confirmed the computer's sequencing and timing of the next act of this drama?"

"Aye, sir," they replied in unison, and then looked at each other. Levy, being junior to Sauvé, made a subtle "go ahead" gesture.

"Countermeasures timing is in place, sir. I've consulted with Mr. Bhattacharyya, who informs me that Krag reaction time on average is a bit faster than ours. Intelligence has subjected this problem to intense study based on combat data over the course of the war, and has concluded that mean time from the appearance of an unexpected situation, counting sensor detection, recognition and comprehension, issuance of the appropriate order, execution of the order, and physical response of the ship's systems to that order, is thirteen point four seconds, with a standard deviation of two point one seconds. So, we plan to give Mr. Krag a ten-second look. That should allow ample time for him to see and understand what's about to happen to him while not being long enough for even the most adept Krag crew or a particularly speedy and decisive Krag captain to do anything about it."

"Outstanding," Max said. "Mr. Levy?"

"We have been continually cross-decking our sensor readings and position data on the Krag vessels to our friends. Comms confirms receipt of the data and that the Rashidians have been putting out the welcome mat and turning down the sheets in the spare bedroom for our guests. We've confirmed a clear corridor for our own exit vector three ways—digital file transfer, voice, and text. Mr. LeBlanc has it. We've got an Egg Scrambler loaded in the number-three missile tube. Launch is set to go—synchronized with Mr. Sauvé's play. When Mr. Krag sees what's going on, he won't be able to tell a soul."

The Egg Scrambler was a Talon missile modified to carry a metaspacial disruptor pulse warhead, the detonation of which prevented FTL communications and operation of a compression drive within a radius of about 4 AU for roughly two hours.

"Outstanding. Mister LeBlanc, are you ready to walk that tightrope? One false step and we're going to be *cochon de lait.*" Max and Mr. LeBlanc were both born on planet Nouvelle Acadiana, a world settled mostly by Louisiana Cajuns, for whom a suckling pig communally roasted over a pit of hot coals, known as a *cochon de lait*, is a delicacy.

"*Mais oui, mon Capitain*," he responded.

"*Ça c'est bon*. Mr. Chin, are our friends ready?"

"Affirmative, sir. They signal Ready." Pause. "We've received a signal from Admiral Jassir."

"Read it."

"I'm not sure I understand it all, sir. It says, 'Thank you, Captain, for conceiving this inspired course of action. I look forward to drawing swords with you again.' Now, here's the part I don't understand. Next it says, 'Al-Baqarah two,' then there's a colon, then 'eighty-two.'"

Sahin and the minister looked at each other. The doctor gave the minister a short, deferential nod.

"It is a citation to the Holy Quran," Wortham-Biggs said, reverently.

"What does it mean? I can't even spell it well enough to look it up," Max asked.

"Captain, although it is preferable that the Quran be read and recited only in the original Arabic, I think that providing a translation would be acceptable under the current unusual, nontheological circumstances. The doctor here is far more the linguistic scholar than I, but I believe an approximation in Standard would be, 'Whoever does evil and surrounds himself with sin, those are the inmates of the fire, and there they shall abide forever.'"

A sharp nod from Max. "Doctor, do you people say 'Amen'?"

"Almost. That is a Hebrew word. Hebrew and Arabic are closely related, both being Semitic languages. The word in Arabic is 'amin.'"

"Outstanding. Mr. Chin, send 'Amin' in reply.... Belay that. Just a second." He turned to his console, pulled up a reference menu, and quickly typed a query. "Okay. Chin, send 'Amin' and then Psalm 106, verse 18."

"Aye, sir." He prepared the message and transmitted it.

Max sat up straighter and squared his shoulders. "Mister Chin," said Max, "One MC."

"Aye, sir, One MC."

Chin flipped two switches. Every man on board would hear him. *Deep breath. You're on.*

"Men, this is the skipper. My timer shows we're just over a minute from execution. The Krag have rattled us around a bit, but they haven't put us out of action. We'll still run this according to plan. I have complete and absolute confidence in your abilities, and in each of you. Stay focused, stay alert, and we'll make this a day to remember. What we are about to do together will be something you can look back on with pride every day for the rest of your life. When your children and your grandchildren sit at your feet and ask about your time in the Navy during the Great Krag War, I want you to look them square in the eye and tell them with everlasting pride what you and your shipmates of the USS *Cumberland* did at the Battle of Rashid V B on 20 March 2315. I guarantee, you will forever be a hero to them, as you have been heroes in my eyes from the day we met. Now, let's get the job done. Skipper out."

Dr. Sahin, who had been paying close attention to the discussion, happened to look at the tactical display on his console and almost fainted. "Captain," he managed to sputter, "those objects on my display . . . those *dozens* of objects, fifty-four of them . . . the computer has attached a label to them that I don't understand. What are they?"

"Something we don't want to hit. Chief LeBlanc?"

"Right on track, sir. No worries here."

"Outstanding."

What the doctor saw on his display was that the icon representing the *Cumberland* was a short distance from a large array of blue icons, each of which was labeled PROV RSHD TF and a numeral, starting with 1 and going up to 54. Between the destroyer and the blue icons was a blinking yellow dot labeled EXEC PNT, which the destroyer was rapidly approaching. Before Dr. Sahin could ask what "PROV RSHD TF" and "EXEC PNT" meant, the *Cumberland*'s icon reached the yellow dot and Mr. Bartoli sang out, "Execution Point! Firing tube three!" Bartoli's console showed a status change. "Tube three just fired."

At that same moment, Sahin saw a profusion of tiny dots appear in front of the blue icons that had so alarmed him earlier. There were seventy-four of them, moving very quickly. There were too many for the computer to label, so it placed an asterisk next to each one, with a note at the bottom of the screen explaining what they were. Dr. Sahin, quite naturally, noticed neither the asterisk nor the footnote.

The next step belonged to Countermeasures. Sauvé announced, "Jamming shut down in five, four, three, two, one, NOW."

Responding to the cue, LeBlanc patted Fleischman twice sharply on the shoulder, causing the young spacer to push the controller for the main sublight drive all the way to the stop, kicking the *Cumberland* into the most rapid acceleration she could accomplish in normal space.

"Egg Scrambler just detonated," announced Levy.

Max smiled, and turned to the doctor and the minister. "Nicephorus, thou dog of a Roman, son of an infidel mother, my reply shall not be for thine ears to hear, but for thine eyes to see." Both men nodded in recognition of Max's reasonably accurately paraphrase of the famous letter written in the year 802 by the namesake of both the star system and of its capital city, the brilliant strategist, Caliph Harun al-Rashid. The famous letter that al-Rashid sent to Nicephorus—just ahead of his avenging army.

A few seconds later, in the Command Nest of the Krag Hegemonic Warship 96-11589, the commander of that vessel, and of what was left of the attack force sent to destroy the Rashidian fleet, chuckled to himself when he was told by his sensors specialist that the sensor jamming being transmitted by the humans' destroyer had just ceased. Doubtless, he thought, another failure of their ill-conceived and poorly engineered technology. With a sweeping motion of his left arm, he instructed his central command display to clear itself of the myriad subdisplays arranged on it in a complex matrix of tactical plots, ship performance graphs, and course projections.

Touching a few controls on the input pad, he instructed the large, now-blank panel to devote itself to showing him, at the largest possible scale, the location and arrangement of the inert, moored enemy fleet and of the pitiful tail stump of the enemy force remaining to wage a futile, dying effort to prevent its destruction. He wanted to be able to give, quickly and accurately, the orders that would bring his destroyers in position to deliver the killing blow.

It took a few seconds for his ships' sensors to obtain the information. Finally, when the data was processed, exchanged, reconciled, and reprocessed, it was ready to be presented on the commander's display for view and, truth be told, a moment of self-congratulation, even gloating. It took less than a second for the symbols representing the tactical situation to pop into existence on the display, and only another two seconds or so for the brilliant Krag commander to take it in.

His tail, which had been extending from his rump almost perfectly parallel to the deck and whipping excitedly from side to side, suddenly dropped like a piece of limp rope. He'd been had. At least, however, he would not have to spend painful years burdened by regret for his errors. Instead, he knew he would regret them for the rest of his life—just over five seconds.

It was so simple, now that he saw the end game. The Rashidian fleet was not waiting helplessly to be destroyed at its moorings. Rather, the vessels had crawled out on their auxiliary fission reactors and maneuvering thrusters, arraying themselves like a wall across the destroyers' path: five rows of roughly ten ships each.

Fifty-four Rashidian vessels head on. And each of those ships had somehow managed to fire at least one missile, seventy-four missiles all together, using firing coordinates provided by the humans' destroyer. That same destroyer had run ahead and jammed the Krag sensors, not to keep from being fired upon, but to keep the Krag from sensing the trap into which they were being led.

The Krag commander could only watch impotently as the *Cumberland* streaked under full acceleration through a five-hundred-square-meter gap in the oncoming formation of 74 C57-D and assorted other nuclear-tipped homing missiles, and then through the middle of the Rashidian ships, before sweeping around in a great arc to orient its most sensitive sensors, as well as its forward-firing weapons, back in the direction of the Krag. The Krag commander then began to issue futile orders, all the while watching in stupefied horror as approximately *fifteen* missiles per target started bending their courses to surround his formation.

Given the abundance of nuclear ordinance at their disposal, the Rashidians gave their missiles an attack profile that made the advanced Krag defenses irrelevant. Set for simultaneous circumferential detonation, they converged from all directions on the space containing the five enemy ships and detonated at the same instant just outside the range of the Krag point defense systems, dozens of points of light merging into a blinding but short-lived newborn sun, producing a zone of dazzlingly bright destruction over forty kilometers across in which solid matter simply ceased to be, then fading into blackness. The Krag were gone.

Since 16 July 1945, when mankind first unleashed the immense energies that since the beginnings of the universe had lain tightly coiled in the atomic nucleus, never had human beings simultaneously detonated so many nuclear weapons in one place, nor released so much explosive power in a single instant. Though the men in CIC were combatants in a three-decade-long interstellar war, waged with thermonuclear weapons, between two advanced, star-faring civilizations, what they saw on their displays stunned them to silence.

The doctor finally spoke. "Captain," he said softly. "That biblical citation that you sent to the admiral. What was it?"

"The 106th Psalm, verse 18. 'Fire blazed among their followers; flame consumed the wicked.'"

"Amin," said the doctor, Mecca in accord with Jerusalem.

"Amen," said Finnegan and Hatzidakis together, Rome and Constantinople adding their concurrence.

Back to business. "Comms, contact the Rashidian flagship. Extend our most respectful compliments to Vice Admiral Jassir and inform him that, with his leave, we wish to come alongside. Request traffic control instructions. Maneuvering, follow exactly the instructions Chin relays to you. We don't want to piss off our new friends by dinging one of their ships."

"Why are we putting ourselves so close to the Rashidian flagship?" asked the doctor. "Isn't the battle over?"

Over the background noise in CIC, Max's voice did not carry beyond the command island. "I seriously need to talk to the admiral. We're not out of the woods yet. Not even close. We've still got almost nine hours until this fleet's main reactors are running. That's nine long hours until they can maneuver and fight. Three full Rashidian fighter squadrons have been wiped out to the last man: that's nearly a third of their total fighter force, half of their Navy's active-duty fighter pilots, and nearly all of the really good ones. It will be at least forty-eight hours before the Union can get any kind of a defensive force in here—probably closer to seventy-two—and for all we know there is a second wave of attacking Krag on its way right now.

"In fact, I'd bet on it. I had a few irons in the fire that might have solved this problem, but it doesn't look as though they're going to amount to anything. We may have just delayed the disaster by a few hours. I would seriously like to avoid bringing Rashid into the war and having their Navy blown to flaming atoms in the same day. Not exactly the sort of thing that would look good on my service record."

"Particularly as we would be likely to be vaporized right along with them," added Bram.

"Right. Shame too. It would totally ruin any chance I might have for promotion. And there's one more thing. Think of the message it would send to prospective allies if the Krag can destroy the Rashidian fleet and take over the Rashid system on the very day they join the fight."

"That had not occurred to me," the doctor said, shaking his head. "It would certainly work to discourage other powers from joining our cause."

"You got it, my friend. It would discourage them powerfully. That could lose the war for us right there. And I don't have the first idea of what to do about it. Not one."

Returning to his CIC voice, "Chin, when you're done with getting traffic control directions from the Rashidians, ask if there is any way they can cross deck the scans from their early warning system to us—I'd like to see what's out there and analyze the raw data with our own computers rather than having to rely on reports from the Rashidians."

As soon as Chin repeated the order, Kasparov broke in. "Sir, as you might expect, sensors are a complete mess from all those nukes and won't be very useful for several more minutes, but I'm pretty sure I just picked up a burst of Cherenkov-Heaviside radiation from this system's Charlie jump point."

"The Rashidians have that covered with a very serious battle station. If it's bad guys jumping in, we'll be picking up the fusion flash of their demise any second now," said Max.

"Sir,"—this time it was Chin—"I'm getting heavily encrypted traffic originating in and around that jump point. It's on a Rashidian channel, sir. Transmitter profiles phase discriminate out as two signal sources: some kind of warship and the Rashidian Military High Command transmitter. I've got nutcrackers for almost all of the Rashidian military encrypts, sir. We could probably listen in if you wanted to."

"Mr. Chin, I'm shocked. Absolutely shocked. The Rashidians are an Associated Power with the Union. You know that gentlemen don't intercept each other's encrypted military transmissions. I'm appalled that you would even make that suggestion."

"So am I, sir. Absolutely. In fact, I'm surprised I can live with the shame. And sir, are you going to want to listen to that transmission on your console or on headset?"

"Console, please. Put it on an open channel."

Dr. Sahin merely shook his head. It could have been disapproval. It could have been resignation. It could have been both.

Chin hit a few keys that put the transmission on the audio output on the captain's console and made it available to anyone on the ship whose duties allowed them to listen. In less than thirty seconds, a crackle came over the transducer as the computer's application of the nutcracker, or decryption algorithm, to the data stream caught up in real time and locked in the interpretation matrix.

"—firm your clearance as requested. Set your transponder to squawk Kilo Tango Alfa Galaxy. Proceed to holding point three, at standard acceleration, but do not exceed point two; then go to station keeping and monitor this channel for further instructions. After a short delay, you can... Stand by... um... just a moment." The man suddenly sounded a little flustered. "Please prepare to receive a direct transmission from his Serene and Celestial Majesty, Khalil the First, King of the United Kingdom of Rashid,

Allied Emirates, and Protected Islamic Worlds. . . . Um . . . Your Majesty, you may proceed." A brief silence.

"Khalil here. Identify yourself." *No bullshit. Pure business.*

"Your Majesty, I am Rear Admiral Marcus Quintus Catalus, commanding the Imperial Romanovan Battleship *Ravenna*." His voice was proud. Determined. This man was ready to fight. "We received a back channel communication from a Union naval officer named something like Maximian Romus Cato—I apologize but I believe the name was garbled somewhat in transmission—that you were under attack by the Krag.

"Emperor Adiuvatus dispatched us immediately upon receipt of the message, and before we jumped out, we received confirmation that the Senate just voted a contingent Declaration of War. Your Majesty, it is the will of the Senate and of the people of Romanova that if Rashid is at war with the Krag, then Romanova is at war with the Krag. The rest of the force under my command will be coming through the jump point as fast as they are able and should all be in system within the hour.

"Our battle group consists of the *Ravenna* as well as a carrier, another battleship, two battlecruisers, and six heavy cruisers. Our orders, from the emperor himself, direct us to render any assistance you may require. He also directs that I convey a personal message to the king."

"Proceed."

"The message is: We will fight beside our brothers. The sons of Rome will stand with the sons of Mecca, together in victory or defeat, until the last battle is fought."

"Thank you, Admiral. Your offer of assistance is both welcome and timely. On behalf of the Kingdom, I accept it with gratitude. I am on my way to join the fleet at this moment. I would be honored if you would meet with me on board our flagship."

"It would be my privilege to do so, your Majesty."

"Very well. My staff will transmit traffic control instructions." Short pause. "Oh, and Captain Robichaux, or should I say 'Maximian Romus Cato,' if you can hear me, you may certainly join us. Be aware that, although I *should* take offense at the eavesdropping, I do not begrudge your listening today. A warrior must have sharp eyes and a keen ear. He who leads men into battle must listen to the wind itself."

CHAPTER 6

09:28Z Hours, 20 March 2315

"If the Rashidians and the Romanovans want to go after any reasonably attainable Krag military objective, and they want us to go with them, and if I get a vote, the vote is 'yes.' Actually, that's not true," Max corrected. "My vote is 'hell, yes, what are we waiting for?' Brown here thinks our repairs can be completed before the Rashidians and the Romanovans have got this operation put together. So, I say, let's go and kick some more Krag ass. The rat-faces have it coming. They've had it coming for more than thirty years."

"I can't deny that being part of a truly offensive strike into Krag-held space would be a bracing change of pace. One does so crave variety from time to time, you know." Lieutenant "Wernher" Brown, a native of planet Avalon, settled by the British, sometimes carried the English love of understatement and dry wit too far. There is dry, and then there is desiccated.

"Obliterating a major repair and refueling depot would not come close to satisfying my personal craving for revenge against them for everything they've done to the human race and to people I know," added Major Kraft. His scowl slowly turned to a wolfish smile, "But it would be a very good start. I would certainly be in favor of it."

The XO, chief engineer, Marine detachment commander, chief medical officer, and commanding officer were meeting in Max's day cabin. The commander wanted to bring his little "Kitchen Cabinet" up to speed on what had happened when he met with King Khalil, the senior Rashidian commanders, and Admiral Catalus.

"Since everyone else has seen fit to express an opinion on this subject, Doctor, do you have anything to say?" Max smiled at him warmly.

"Actually," he said, "I rather think that I do not. Certainly, on an emotional level, I would find inflicting widespread destruction upon the works of the Krag and their implements of war to be intensely gratifying. But as Admiral Hornmeyer is fond of saying, I don't know a parsec from a parsnip.

"Actually, as a point of pride I looked up the definitions of both terms. But my newfound ability to differentiate between a unit for measuring astronomical distances and a carrot-like root vegetable is beside the point. I know nothing of naval tactics or strategy. My opinion on such a matter would be of no more value than yours on whether to treat a case of Long's Dementia with psychotropic medication or with neural reconstructive microtherapy. My sense of the matter, however, is that none of the opinions in this room is likely to be particularly determinative in the outcome. One opinion and one opinion only matters here: that of Vice Admiral Hornmeyer."

"I think you've hit the cartridge on the primer with that one, Doctor. I sent a signal to the admiral as soon as I got back from the meeting. You know how he is about things like that. We're likely to get an answer—a very clear, specific, and emphatic one—in about a tenth the time it would take anyone else to make up his mind." He smiled as a thought occurred to him. "You know, I've never seen anyone so decisive. I think the man was born with all the decisions he is ever going to have to make already loaded into his brain. They're all sitting in there, just waiting for the right occasion to arise so he can announce them."

Max enjoyed the general laughter the remark triggered. He could not begin to understand how a man without a sense of humor could ever successfully command a warship.

He let everyone settle down a bit, take a few more sips of their coffee, take a few bites of the truly outstanding cinnamon coffee cake that the galley had prepared for the captain's table, and restore themselves a bit. It was not even mid-morning, but it had already been a long day, a day that included a desperate life-or-death fleet engagement before breakfast.

"You should be aware, Doctor, that I had a very interesting discussion with the Romanovan admiral right after I persuaded the King to give us repair priority in the same shipyard that maintains the royal yacht, which, it seems, is actually a bit larger than the *Cumberland*."

"Indeed? And what might that have to do with me?"

"Once we had finished the substantive meetings, we had what you would call a social gathering on the Romanovan flagship, to start building some bridges—you know how that works. We sat around very amiably drinking their version of espresso. *Poo yai*, let me tell you, that stuff will put stains on your teeth and grow hair on your chest—sort of like coffee with an antimatter chaser. No wonder they serve it in such tiny cups.

"Anyway, Admiral Catalus mentioned to me that he'd heard a rumor that a Union warship officer was impersonating a Romanovan cutter captain for the purpose of boarding purportedly neutral freighters to verify their neutral status and search for contraband."

The doctor had, on two previous occasions, done that very thing, down to wearing the comically ornate uniform associated with that post and speaking the slightly mutated Latin, the language of the Romanovan Imperium. Sahin blanched.

"Don't worry, Doctor, I told him that it was my pleasure to deny the rumor categorically. I told him, 'I can assure you, Admiral, on my honor, that neither I nor, to my knowledge, any *command officer* of any Union warship has ever impersonated the commander of any Romanovan vessel.'"

In response to the accusatory look Sahin gave him, a look that practically screamed "*liar*," Max pointed to the silver star, embossed with the Rod of Asclepius, on the left breast of Sahin's uniform.

"Doctor, the star you bear is silver, not gold. Meaning, my friend, you are assigned to one of the Navy's noncombat branches and are not now and never will be a command officer, irrespective of your rank. My statement to the admiral was perfectly true."

The doctor shook his head. "Literally true, I suppose, but practically misleading. You deliberately led him to a conclusion about the facts that you knew to be untrue. Irrespective of whether a literal parsing of the words does not result in a precise semantic falsehood, it is a dirty lawyer's trick."

Sahin expected Max to take offense at the accusation and to reply sharply. He did not. Instead, he shrugged.

"And a perfectly acceptable expedient according to the centuries-old customs of my profession," Max said. "It was up to the admiral to pay careful attention to my exact words. Even if we are all fighting the Krag, he is still a foreign officer, and we were talking about the tactics employed in a classified military operation. Tactics that, by the way, I might want to use again sometime.

"Custom, which in this case is as binding as any law, holds that as an officer and a gentleman, I had a duty to refrain from telling him a literal falsehood unless required to do so by a direct order or other military necessity. Otherwise, I'm under no duty not to mislead him unless we are on the same side and I am providing him with information material to an upcoming military operation in which lives will be at stake.

"Like it or not, Doctor, lying is a part of warfare: lies to your enemy, lies to your allies, lies to your subordinates, lies to the people back on their homeworlds. You can't fight a war without telling lies, my friend, and telling them by the bushel basket at that. Falsehood is as much a part of war as is killing the enemy. Anyway, my statement had the desired effect. Admiral Catalus was mollified, and goodwill was maintained between allies."

Max's reference to the Romanovans as "allies" failed virtually every test of linguistic precision. Although there were four powers at war with the Krag—the Union, Rashid, Romanova, and Pfelung—the precise legal relationship of those four powers was anything but simple. As a result of a Krag attack that, but for the *Cumberland,* would have had genocidal results, the Pfelung had entered the war months ago as an Associated Power of the Union. Rashid had also just entered the war as an Associated Power with the Union. Rashid's entry and the resulting Krag attack, under the terms of its long-standing mutual defense treaty with the Rashidians, had brought the Romanovan Imperium into the conflict as "an equal and coordinate ally, partner, and cobelligerent" of the Rashidians. Meanwhile, there was no formal military relationship between the Union and Romanova, and virtual no relationship of any kind—even diplomatic relations—between Pfelung and the Rashidians or the Romanovans.

Obviously, if these four independent and, in some cases, scarcely acquainted, powers were going to conduct coordinated military operations against the Krag, something would have to happen to get them all singing out of the same hymnal. And it would have to happen soon or the Krag would take advantage of the absence of coordination. If they didn't hang together, the Krag would be sure to hang them separately.

The comm buzzed. "Chin here. Signal from Admiral Hornmeyer, sir. It's in your box." Max opened it from his workstation. True to form, Admiral Hornmeyer provided responses to both issues—whether the *Cumberland* would participate in the raid on the Krag and the joint command problem—in a single communiqué.

Max got up from the meeting/dining table at which everyone was seated and stepped over to his workstation. As the message was not coded EYES ONLY, Max keyed it for wall display so that everyone in the room could read it. Not only did all of these officers have Top Secret or higher clearance, but he'd need their active help to implement the orders. They might as well see them now.

09:13Z 20 March 2315

TOP SECRET

URGENT: FOR IMMEDIATE IMPLEMENTATION

FROM: HORNMEYER, L.G. VADM USN CDR TF TD

TO: ROBICHAUX MAXIME T., LCDR USN

1. YOUR REQUEST TO PARTICIPATE IN JOINT OPERATION WITH RASHID AND ROMANOVA IS DENIED. CUMBERLAND IS NEEDED FOR OTHER DUTIES.

2. IN RESPONSE TO THIS COMMAND'S URGENT REQUEST FOR A SENIOR NEGOTIATOR TO BE DISPATCHED TO THIS THEATER, BE ADVISED THAT CMRE JOSEPH A. DOLAND IS EN ROUTE TO RASHID TO REPRESENT UNION IN NEGOTIATIONS WITH RASHID, ROMANOVA, AND PFELUNG RE MULTILATERAL THEATER FORCES OPERATIONS ACCORD. AS PER ORDERS OF COMTRANROUT IN NORFOLK CMRE DOLAND IS BEING TRANSPORTED

BY USS WILLIAM GORGAS, FLE 0476, CMDR GERARD DUFLOT COMMANDING.

3. AFTER COMPLETING NECESSARY REPAIRS AT RASHID, USS CUMBERLAND, DPA 0004, UNDER YOUR COMMAND, IS ORDERED TO PROCEED AT BEST PRUDENT SPEED TO COORDINATES 1198753.5116254.0085324, THERE TO RENDEZVOUS WITH FRIGATE-DESTROYER GROUP TD-2008 NOW CONSISTING OF WILLIAM GORGAS AND USS BROADSWORD, DGG 0585. GROUP IS UNDER DUFLOT'S COMMAND. CUMBERLAND IS HEREBY ATTACHED TO FRIGDESGRU TD-2008 FOR DURATION OF PASSAGE TO RASHID OR UNTIL FURTHER ORDERS.

4. DEUTERIUM TANKER/REPAIR TENDER USS PATTILLO HIGGINS, TXA 1912, WILL BE AVAILABLE AT RENDEZVOUS POINT TO REFUEL YOUR VESSEL. ACCORDINGLY, CONSERVATION OF FUEL EN ROUTE TO RENDEZVOUS NOT A FACTOR.

5. N2 EXPECTS KRAG ATTACK ON THIS FRIGDESGRU IN ATTEMPT TO PREVENT DOLAND FROM REACHING DESTINATION. DELIVERY OF ENVOY TO DESTINATION IS VITAL TO CONDUCT OF THE WAR AND IS TO BE GIVEN HIGHEST POSSIBLE PRIORITY. ADDITION OF YOUR VESSEL TO THIS GROUP NECESSARY TO INCREASE STRENGTH OF ESCORT TO MEET PROBABLE ATTACK. YOUR ORDERS AND THOSE OF CMDR DUFLOT ARE THAT IN ORDER TO COMPLETE THIS MISSION YOUR VESSEL AND ITS COMPLEMENT ARE TO BE CONSIDERED EXPENDABLE.

6. AS YOU WILL SEE FROM REVIEW OF HIS BIOSUM, CMDR DUFLOT IS NOT FAMILIAR WITH CONDITIONS THIS AREA. I EXPECT YOU TO

PROVIDE THIS EXPERTISE WITHOUT CHALLENGING HIS AUTHORITY. IT IS CALLED BEING DIPLOMATIC, ROBICHAUX—A HANDY SKILL THAT IT IS ABOUT TIME YOU LEARN.

7. GO TO THE RENDEZVOUS. GO DIRECTLY TO THE RENDEZVOUS. DO NOT PASS 'GO' AND DO NOT DETOUR FOR ANY OF YOUR 'ADVENTURES.'

"These orders came from the admiral himself," said DeCosta with awe. To him, Admiral Hornmeyer was more like a deity from Mount Olympus than a human being. "There's no way some staff drone wrote that."

"It is *so* reassuring to know that the admiral takes a personal interest in us," Brown said with no more than the usual healthy helping of sarcasm.

"Well, men, we might as well look at that homework the admiral just assigned to us," Max said resignedly.

"Homework?" The doctor looked perplexed.

"Sure, Doctor, homework," said DeCosta. "One thing everyone knows about old Hit 'em Hard is that he never wastes a single word in a signal. Ever. Every word means something. If you think that something is just thrown in as filler or to sound good, you're not reading it right. Here, if the admiral wanted only for us to know that this Duflot guy wasn't familiar with conditions in the area, he would have just said so and not a word more."

"But that's just what he did."

"No, it's not," said the XO. "He led in by saying, 'As you will see from review of his Biosum.' With most admirals, that might just be an offhand remark meaning that you can confirm his lack of relevant experience by looking him up."

"But with Vice Admiral Louis G. Hornmeyer," Max continued, "it's a subtle but direct order that we do so because there is something in there that he wants us to see. And we are to do it with *celerity.*" Everyone smiled at the reference to the word that Hornmeyer had used when giving his first standing orders upon taking command of the task force back in January, a word that had become a favorite among the officers and crew that served under him.

Max worked his way through some menus on his workstation to get to the right section of the database. Because no one else in the room was officially cleared for this information, Max called it up on the workstation display instead of on the wall.

"Okay, here we go." Just because they weren't cleared for it didn't mean he couldn't share with them what he thought pertinent, right? "Duflot, Gerard Michel, Commander, USN. Assignment: Commanding Officer, USS *William Gorgas*, registry number blah, blah, blah. Usual time as midshipman and greenie, standard list of assignments as an ensign and junior officer. Basic Qualifications in Combat Logistics, Space Warfare, and Escort Vessel Command." Long pause. "Only... just those three. Date of posting: 5 October *2309*." Dr. Sahin immediately felt a heavy cloak of dismay settle over the compartment.

"Why this sudden gloom? Is 2309 a famously bad year for commanders in much the same way that 2303 was for wine on Terroir?"

Max laughed, "No, Doctor. It's not the vintage. It's that no one wants to drink the wine. You see, Duflot has been commanding the same frigate for six years. That's a bad sign. Think about it. The Navy has suffered millions of casualties. Thousands of officers are killed every year, sometimes every month. And we have *thirty* shipyards devoted 100 percent to building warships and another forty or so that have at least some warship production. They're churning out ships by the hundreds every year. The demand for manpower is always critical, and competent skippers often go up the chain of command like rockets.

Charles Middleton went from being a lieutenant commander skippering a broken-down old Picket destroyer to a rear admiral commanding one of the two primary attack groups at the Battle of Mullinex V in just six years. Until they get to the top of the ladder where there isn't much elsewhere to go, officers with ability don't stay in the same command doing the same thing for more than two or two and a half years at most. If they prove themselves at one level of responsibility, they are left there only long enough to get some seasoning and experience, produce results for a little while, and then are moved up to a higher rank, a posting of greater responsibility, or, more likely, both.

"If I am still commanding the *Cumberland* three years from now, it means that someone has made a decision that I am not worthy of promotion, and more than that, it probably means I'm not very good at the job I've got. It's one of the most reliable principles in the whole Navy.

"It gets worse. Apparently almost that whole time, this Duflot character has been on convoy duty, part of the escort package attached to those huge convoys that move supplies, personnel, and new ships up to Admiral Middleton's primary staging area from the Core Systems. You know, those eighty and ninety ship monstrosities commanded by a rear admiral that take three months each way because of how long it takes to run all those ships through each jump?

"Years ago, those convoys always got pounced on by Krag destroyers that would slip through the sensor nets along the frontier—they managed the range with huge drop tanks. But eventually, they got enough escort protection on those convoys that it's become impossible for the Krag to hurt them. There hasn't been a serious run at any of those convoys for four years now. So, not only is Duflot not in the promotion pool, but neither he nor his crew have seen any combat in years.

"On top of that, he doesn't have a qualification badge in weapons, sensors, tactics, or in multivessel command. I have all those qualifications—all the ones he has, and three others besides—and he is my senior. Either he doesn't have the ambition to seek those credentials, or he has sought them and been denied because the brass think the training would be wasted on him.

"He lacks the practical experience too. I don't see anything in the summary that indicates that he has ever commanded a multiship force before, so he has no practice giving orders to other captains. None of that fills me with a rosy glow of confidence. Of course, you never know. He might be one of those guys who is completely squared away but just doesn't get along with one of those convoy admirals or someone in Norfolk and is getting held back unfairly. I've seen that sort of thing happen before. It doesn't happen that much any more, though—the human race doesn't have the luxury of failing to make the best possible use of good officer material just because someone has a personality conflict."

"But Skipper, on the *Hidalgo* I worked with some guys in Tactical who came out of frigates and destroyers on convoy duty, and they seemed like they were on the way up," the XO said.

"*They* probably were," replied Max. "But you need to remember, XO, all of these men were promoted *out* of escort duty and *in* to duty on a capital ship to get some departmental experience in a big, well-worked-up back room, so they could learn how things are done by a really proficient team. And once they have that, then they get moved up to someplace where they can get some command training. Someplace like... oh, I don't know... a berth as XO of a destroyer."

DeCosta smiled and nodded his understanding.

"But Duflot isn't someone who has just come out of a frigate on escort duty. He's still there, right where he has been for six years. He may surprise me, and I'm going to keep an open mind about him, but this isn't giving me a warm, fuzzy feeling. Let's just hope being stuck in a dead end hasn't made this guy bitter or cynical or lazy."

"Although that might be a normal psychological reaction to those kinds of circumstances," the doctor said in that airy tone of voice that he tended to use when he was even more disconnected from reality than usual, "I would think that a naval officer would understand the military necessity of these kinds of decisions and understand his duty to acquiesce to them cheerfully and without negativity for the greater good not just of the service but also for the very survival of mankind."

Most of the men in the room tried to suppress snickers at the doctor's comment, but Kraft burst into raucous laughter, a hearty effusion of mirth that filled the room. Soon everyone in the room, except for Sahin, was laughing uncontrollably. Initially, Bram scowled with irritation but, after a few seconds, began to smile, recognizing how naïve his statement was. The captain was the first to be able to speak.

"Doctor, if you're surprised that there are men in the Navy who can't rein in their egos merely because something as trivial as the survival of the human race is at stake, then I am afraid you have a great many rude, hard lessons to learn about life in the fleet."

"I do suspect that I have many such lessons in my future, Captain." He lifted his coffee mug in salute. "But I cannot imagine a better set of men in whose company to learn them."

The other men raised their mugs to return the gesture.

DeCosta, however, had not taken his eyes off of Admiral Hornmeyer's orders. "Skipper?" DeCosta said tentatively after a few minutes.

"Yes, XO."

"You know how Hornmeyer's orders never have any wasted words?"

"Yes."

"Take a look at this." He stood up, walked over to the display wall, and pointed at a section of the orders. "*As per orders of COMTRANROUT in Norfolk*.... Maybe it's my imagination, but it looks like Hornmeyer is telling us that it wasn't his idea to put Duflot in command of the group. I think he's saying that the decision was imposed on him by the admiral in charge of Transit Routing. I'm not sure I like the looks of that."

"XO," said Max, nodding, "I bet you're right on that one. COMTRANROUT is Vice Admiral Hoffman. His brother's a senator. I'm sure I don't like the looks of that. Not one bit." He snorted derisively. "Escort duty. Been there. Done that. Paid for the memory wipe. I spent the dullest year of my life doing it one month. Seriously, it's the dullest duty in Known Space. I wish we could get a more interesting assignment."

The doctor looked genuinely horrified. "Perish the thought," he said hurriedly.

"What's wrong with wanting more interesting duty?"

"The problem, Captain, with wishing for more interesting duty, is that—based on the history of your association with this vessel—you are very likely to get your wish." He paused. "And will then wish to God that you had not."

Max interpreted the admiral's remark about not conserving fuel as an implicit directive to head for the rendezvous point in a straight line on compression drive at the *Cumberland*'s maximum safe sustained speed of 1960 c. The system in which the rendezvous was to take place lay roughly in the direction of the Core Systems, the fifty or so star systems at the heart of the Union that were home to 42 percent of its population and 67 percent if its heavy industrial capacity.

Roughly thirty light years separated the *Cumberland*'s current position in the Rashid system and the rendezvous point, six days' travel at 1960 c. A quiet, six-day, high-c run would be nice. Max would see that the crew got in some much-needed training, finished repairing some of the battle damage that the Rashidian shipyard did not get to, and generally tended to the mundane but important business of keeping a warship in fighting trim—or in the case of the *Cumberland*, trying to *get it* into shape in all respects, after having been so badly, abusively, and incompetently commanded for so long by Max's predecessor, the thrice-damned Commander Allen K. Oscar.

After getting a bit of sleep, checking on Park and the injured men in the Casualty Station (all of whom were expected to make a full recovery), and grabbing a sandwich (the last two of the "exploding ham" variety), Max followed a nagging hunch by going to Engineering to check how the compression drive was holding up under the stress of a long high-c run.

The first place Max went was MECC (pronounced "meck"), the Master Engineering Control Center, a compact compartment equipped with consoles from which all key engineering systems could be controlled and monitored. Unless there was a problem, Lieutenant Brown could usually be found here. Every console was manned, but not by Brown.

Not a good sign.

If Brown weren't in MECC, then there was likely a problem, probably with the compression drive. Max knew: find the problem and you find Brown. Max headed for the Compression Drive Equipment Room. He palmed the scanner, punched in his code, and entered.

Brown was at the Compression Drive Main Control Console with two men standing beside him, looking so intently at the systems status displays that they didn't hear Max come in. Max could see from his vantage point at the door that there were several caution and warning indicators blinking yellow and orange on the display. All three men looked worried and perplexed.

"It's looking like a bloody triple failure," Brown said to the other two men.

"But that's impossible," the other two responded in nearly perfect unison. The man closest to Brown, whom Max recognized as Petty Officer Second Class Ravelojaona, went on. "Those units are designed to withstand five times that much load—for thirty years without failing! If it wasn't for the freak deflector feedback caused by that Krag warhead, we wouldn't even be talking about replacing the originals until years after we're all retired. Now that we've got three fresh units in there, I can't believe we're having issues with even one, much less three."

"Somehow we must have gotten a bad set," Brown said reasonably. "Bugger me how three bad units got past quality control, but look at the display. We just swapped them in, and none of the three is performing up to specs—they're not smoothing out the natural particle rate fluctuations from the Randall-Sundrum generator. We're going to have to shut the unit down. I can do a nanomolecular refusion on the old units that will let us run them at normal output until we get to the rendezvous point. The *Patillo Higgins* will have spares for us there. All right lads, start preparing the system for a staged shutdown. I'll notify CIC. The skipper won't like this one bit."

"Bugger what the skipper thinks, old man," Max said in a laughably bad facsimile of Brown's British accent, causing all three heads to swivel in his direction. He went on in his usual unremarkable Standard, "Just get the problem solved. What units are we talking about?"

"The Frasch-Freiburg capacitors," Brown answered.

"The 'French Fries'?" Max said, disbelievingly. "But—"

"Exactly, my good man. But the board doesn't lie."

"This smells fishy to me, Wernher. I've never heard of one of these things going bad until it was old enough to run for a seat in the Assembly. You get ready to take the unit off-line, and I'll let CIC know what to expect." Just as Max touched the comm panel, an alarm started to blare. He snatched his hand back reflexively, as though he had somehow triggered the malfunction.

"Bloody Hell!" Brown exclaimed. "All three units just slagged."

Max didn't know exactly what happened when three Frasch-Freiburg capacitors melted and lost their resistant properties simultaneously. But since the units were responsible for evening out the random variations in the raw tachyo-graviton output from the compression drive's Randall-Sundrum generator, it wasn't likely to be good. He went to the Emergency Actions panel in the compartment, keyed in his access code, manually activated the compartment's blast containment field, switched the fire suppression system from SAFE to READY, engaged the radiation shielding, and isolated the area's atmosphere circulation. These actions showed up immediately on Brown's status panel.

"Good man, Skipper. You're about twenty seconds ahead of me," Brown shouted over the alarm.

Max then keyed the comm panel to speak to CIC. Nelson was in the Big Chair. "Mr. Nelson," he said, "sound general quarters, engineering casualty. Set Condition Two throughout the ship. Have all hands prepare for emergency compression drive shutdown."

Nelson acknowledged the order. Max could hear the GQ alarm sounding in the background. He turned his attention back to Brown, who was going down the Compression Drive Emergency Power Down Checklist. It sounded as though he and his men were pushing to finish the checklist as fast as they could.

"Buffers purged," said Brown.

"Buffers purged, check. Light is blue, gauges read 10 percent or lower," answered Ravelojaona.

"Primary coolant system from RUN to AUTO SCRAM."

"Switching primary coolant system from RUN to AUTO-SCRAM," responded Archer, the other crewman. "Main indicator selected for AUTOSCRAM. Auxiliary toggle switches confirmed disengaged."

"Secondary coolant system from STANDBY to OFF."

"Secondary coolant, STANDBY to OFF," Archer answered. "Main switches thrown, auxiliary switches confirmed disengaged."

"Confirm GO/NO GO for Emergency Compression Drive Shutdown," said Brown. "Primary systems and emitters."

"GO!" shouted Ravelojaona.

"Secondary systems and coolant loops."

"GO!" shouted Archer.

"Shutting down main power to compression drive, NOW." He grasped a large orange-red lever on the main panel and, with obvious relief to be shutting down the system without any serious casualty, moved it decisively to the ZERO position.

Nothing happened.

"Balls!" the engineer proclaimed. "Manual!" He and Archer literally ran to a locker located near the drive unit, from which the two men each extracted an L-shaped lever with a complex-looking set of teeth on one end and a handle on the other. Each man inserted the teeth straight down in a sleeve at the base of the unit, Archer into one nearer the door and Brown into one further away. When both levers were seated, they stood up from their insertion points about chest high, where they bent at a right angle to form a meter-long handle with polymer-grip handles for two men each. When both men had firmly grasped one of the handles, Brown shouted, "Push!" Brown and Archer pushed as hard as they could, veins standing out on their faces and necks, but neither arm budged.

Max and Ravelojaona ran over to help, taking the other set of handles on each bar. This time, Max gave the order, "Give it your all on three. One. Two. Three!" All four men strained mightily for fifteen or twenty seconds, to no effect.

"Bloody, bleeding bollocks!" Brown cursed. "They're fused. Skipper, you and I are going to have to blow the main coupling."

"Shit," was all that Max could say. Blowing the main coupling would disable the compression drive for hours until a new coupling was installed, but the alternative was an almost certain compression shear event that would destroy the ship so thoroughly that even her atoms would be shredded into their constituent particles.

Both men took their positions at the main power coupling, a cluster of conduits, equipment boxes, and a console mounted on the aft bulkhead. Brown palmed a biometric scanner on the console and input his authorization code, followed by Max. The console then generated two large red blocks at opposite ends of its two-meter length, each labeled BLOW COUPLING. They were far enough apart that one man could not touch both at the same time. "This has to be simultaneous," Brown said. "On three."

Max happened to glance over at the compression drive unit and saw that Archer was now standing near the main access panel. Ravelojaona was busy rousting out the heavy fire extinguisher in case the pyros used to blow the unit started any fires, so he wasn't watching what the younger crewman was doing. Just as a ball of liquid nitrogen started to coalesce right behind Max's breastbone at the sight of the man standing in what was, at that moment, the most dangerous place on the ship, he noticed a blue-green glow starting to build behind the observation port in the access panel. He knew what was going to happen.

"Archer," he screamed, "on the deck!"

Just as the young man looked in Max's direction and started to process the command, the glow became a blinding glare as the buildup of excess gravitons became too great for the housing to contain. The latch and hinges on the access panel failed under the extreme pressure, blowing the panel off with an ear-splitting *BLAM,* taking the upper half of Archer's body with it. For a split second, the young man's legs continued to stand upright and then flopped over onto the deck, dribbling blood. The rest of Archer's body was smashed between the shattered access panel and the far bulkhead, turned into an obscenely gelatinous red goo by the extreme force of the impact that reduced his bones to grit and fine powder.

Removed from their generating and containment field, the gravitons passed easily through the hull of the ship and dissipated into space. The shock wave from the explosion, on the other hand, a pressure wave of ordinary air molecules, stayed in the compartment, knocking the three other men to the ground. Bleeding from their ears and noses and barely conscious from internal injuries, Brown and Max struggled to their feet and staggered to the panel. Their eyes met. Max restarted the count, his voice an almost inaudible croak. "One. Two. Three!"

On "Three" both men hit "Blow Coupling." With a *BANG* the pyros detonated and broke the power connection. The compression drive unit and its control consoles shut down. As one, Max and Brown fell unconscious to the deck.

Six hours later, Max, Brown, Dr. Sahin, DeCosta, Major Kraft, and Chief Wendt were seated in the Casualty Station main ward. The treatment beds had been pushed out of the way, and a portable table set up, large enough for all six men. The heavily sedated Ravelojaona was in a patient bed in a subsidiary treatment room. As he had been a few meters closer to the blast than Max and

Brown and had actually been running toward Archer to knock him to the deck, his injuries were more severe.

"I still believe that this meeting is entirely premature," Dr. Sahin said before any of the senior officers could bring the meeting to order. "Both the captain and the chief engineer should be in bed, under light sedation, not sitting upright making decisions that can well be postponed."

Max smiled wanly. "Doctor, I'd love to be horizontal and sedated right now, but I don't think this can wait. I smell a rat bigger and fatter than the fattest Krag, and I want to get the stink out of my ship. Fast." He turned to Major Kraft.

"I know I dumped a big load in your lap, but I didn't see any choice under the circumstances." He looked significantly at the IV line in his arm. "Have you made any progress?"

"Yes, sir," Kraft answered. "At least as to the first stage. Because the initial issues were technical rather than legal or law-enforcement related, I enlisted the help of Chief Wendt, who has informed me that he has some conclusions for us. Other than that, he hasn't told me what his findings are, so I will be learning them at the same time as the rest of you."

"Very well," said Max. "Chief?"

Wendt, a small, fox-faced, precise man in his mid-fifties, was (except for some "ancient mariners" working as cooks and stewards) the oldest on the ship. He was also Chief of the Boat, the senior noncommissioned officer on board, and was deeply experienced in the ways of naval machines and of naval men. He knew as much about the parts and pieces that went into making the *Cumberland* run as any man alive.

"This incident is all about the Frasch-Freiburg capacitors, or the 'French Fries' as the men like to call them. So I started with the capacitors themselves. I recovered the slag remaining from the meltdown of the units in the compression drive and tested twenty samples from various locations to be sure that the material I was testing was representative of the composition of the capacitors before they melted down. The slag was consistent within a few percentage points. It tested out as 76 percent silver, 17 percent tantalum, 3 percent gold, 3 percent platinum, 1 percent various impurities and trace elements."

"*Gott im Himmel*," exclaimed Kraft.

"*Droga, merda, porra*," exclaimed DeCosta.

The doctor said nothing. All eyes turned to him. He made a sound of exasperation. "Oh. I suppose that immemorial naval custom requires that I now adopt a shocked expression and then utter an exclamation of horror in a language other than Standard. Very well. *Allah askina!* Will that suffice, or is a stronger outburst required? Will someone now tell me what has happened? Truly, you people must remember that I am not a member of your secret society. I do not know the clubhouse password. I have never been taught the secret handshake."

Max had paled as soon as Wendt said *76 percent silver*. He began to speak with some difficulty. "Bram, that's the composition of a standard civilian capacitor. For a freighter or a short-run passenger liner. For a drive that is never run at higher than 500 c."

"What, then, is the composition of the military unit?" Dr. Sahin asked.

"Very different," said Wendt between gritted teeth. It's "81 percent gold and 19 percent tantalum, not counting a thin plating of tantalum on the outside."

Dr. Sahin nodded slowly, grimly. "I begin to understand. Am I overly cynical in concluding that the civilian unit is tantalum plated as well?"

"You are not," said Wendt, quietly.

"Which would mean that any cosmetic differences between the civilian and military units are trivial, I take it, and would be fairly easily disguised?" The doctor's voice was grim.

"Correct," said Wendt.

"And how much gold might there be in one of these 'french fries'?"

"Total weight, including the contact points and the main capacitor rod itself, 73.5 kilos. Each." Wendt's voice had a bitter edge.

"What do the civilian units cost on the open market?" asked the doctor.

"Just over 235,000 credits each," Wendt replied.

Dr. Sahin winced at the number and then nodded sadly. "And what is the likelihood that one of these spares would be needed during the lifetime of the vessel?"

"Absent battle damage or sabotage, there is a less than 1 in 850,000 chance of any one of the original units failing and needing replacement," said Wendt. "And if one unit failed and was replaced with one of these lower quality units, the compression drive would still function normally by routing additional graviton flux through the other two units—in practice, they can take nearly three times what they are rated for. It would show up on some of the status displays but might not be noticed for months—at least, not the way Engineering was run when Captain Oscar was in command."

"Would it be correct to say, then, that an enterprising crew member could sell the true replacement units for several million credits, use a tiny fraction of that sum to purchase civilian units altered to look like the real thing, and reasonably expect that no one would be the wiser until the ship was taken out of commission and the culprit retired?"

"Yes. That would be accurate," said Wendt.

"It's a practice as old as the hills," Max added. "They even had a name for the practice back in the Age of Sail. They called it *capabarre*. It was expected that certain people on the ship who had custody of the ship's goods would sell off worn or outdated equipment and matériel for their own account. It was considered an acceptable part of their compensation. Many, however, would take the practice beyond acceptable limits and sell perfectly serviceable equipment and replace it with substandard stuff, to the detriment of their ship. These men could be court martialed, and some received very harsh sentences."

While Max was speaking, Dr. Sahin had been watching Wendt's face closely. "You already know who did this, don't you?"

The other men leaned forward with interest and surprise. "I am almost certain that I do," he said. Five seconds of silence. "Chief Edwin." In response to the looks of frank astonishment he received from the officers, he added, "You officers don't know him the way I do. Yes, he is extremely efficient. Yes, he salutes briskly, shows up for every watch on time, and seems eager to jump to anything any officer ever asks of him. Yes, his trouser creases are knife sharp, his brass shiny, and his boots gleaming black. But he is also the most greedy, mercenary, unscrupulously money-grubbing man ever to go to space.

"He always has some kind of racket going—gambling, hard-core porn vids, semilegal energy drinks—it's always something. Never anything so far over the line that there is ever an official investigation and discipline, but enough so that every several months I have to dial him back and shut down whatever his game is at the time. And not a drop of loyal blood flows through his veins. He'd sell his own mother for the price of a couple of beers.

"He's got shady connections in every station and port, so he would be the man on board most likely to have a partner on the beach somewhere with whom he could conduct this transaction. Add to that he's been an angel these past few months. None of his usual scams. And even though he has always spent his money like water, the absence of a racket doesn't seem to have made him any more frugal. There seems to be no end to his money lately.

"The change was right after we spent a week at T-Gloon III for scheduled compression drive maintenance. Edwin had unrestricted access to the compression drive spares then, and several people saw him rolling a large box out of that area on a dolly one night when no one was supposed to be around. We inventoried the stores and found nothing missing. Now I know why—he substituted the civilian part. Selling out shipmates for money."

"All of that is circumstantial," said Major Kraft. "We need better evidence than that to convict."

"Major, I may not be a lawyer or an officer," said Wendt, "but I've been in this man's Navy for longer than anyone else at this table and I know you don't need any kind of formal evidence to discipline this man. It just takes a 'reasonable basis' for the captain to find him guilty of misconduct, bust him to greenie, and put him on the beach the next chance he gets, based on what we know today."

Kraft smiled slowly. "Chief, my plan is that this man not ever see the beach again. His actions resulted in 'damage or interference with the operation of a naval vessel in a war zone.' Resulting in death. A man died. No enemy within twenty light years. Unless the captain has something different to say,"—he looked at Max, who gave no sign of opposition—"I aim to see this man shot."

"Where are you going to get evidence of the kind necessary to put a man before a firing squad?" Wendt's question was more curious than accusatory. "I don't think that you'll find Edwin cooperative at all, given that he may be facing a bullet. Are you going to talk to his friends, find out who his connections are, and then find the man with whom he did the deal and get him to give you a sworn statement? You won't find his friends very talkative either. And it might be months before we can get back to T-Gloon III. Even sending a message to their planetary law enforcement and getting them to bring the guy in and question him might take weeks."

"To the contrary," said Kraft. "Before I confront Edwin, there is only one man with whom I need to speak, and I expect him to be the very soul of cooperation."

Less than an hour later, PFCs Zamora and Ulmer, who were not only the two largest Marines on the *Cumberland* but also two of the largest examples of *Homo sapiens* Max had ever seen, hustled Chief Petty Officer Third Class Ferrell K. Edwin into the destroyer's wardroom, the ship's tiny interrogation room being too small for the number of people assembled for the questioning. After shoving their charge none too gently into the chair at the foot of the wardroom table, the two Marines stood menacingly on either side of the hatch, right hands resting on the butts of their sidearms, looking for all the worlds like pissed-off Sequoias.

Edwin quickly scanned the room, looking for allies, but saw that every chair around the table was occupied by an officer appointed to the ship since the change in command: Max, DeCosta, Brown, Sahin, and Kraft. Every chair but one. His eyes lighted on the COB, Chief Petty Officer First Class Heinz Wendt. The two men had served together through the purgatory of being under Captain Oscar's command and had shared thousands of bull sessions in the Goat Locker, as well as untold gallons of beer and other strong drink in the Enlisted Mess and various ports all around the Union. His eyes took on a pleading quality. "Heinz? What...?"

The crusty old COB cut him off before he could get the third word out. "Shut up, Edwin." His voice was low and cold. Like a beautiful rose dipped in liquid helium and flung to the floor, those treasured shipmate memories were now shattered forever. "I'm not 'Heinz' to you any more."

The COB pointedly turned away from Edwin and focused on Ulmer's immaculately maintained 11.43-millimeter (some still said *.45-caliber*) Model 1911 sidearm. He imagined using it to blow Edwin's head off. He imagined it in every detail: the weight of the pistol in his hands, the resistance of the recoil spring as he pulled back the slide, the distinctive *clack* as he released the slide and it slid forward to chamber the round, the pressure of the trigger under his index finger, the *blang* of the weapon firing, the sharp upward and backward pressure of the recoil, the explosion of living tissue from the back of Edwin's head. But no. It would be enough to watch him stand before the firing squad.

Maybe not.

"Skipper," Wendt said, "when we shoot this bastard, I want to be one of the men holding a rifle. For Archer. For every man in Engineering he could have killed."

Max nodded. The request was unusual, but within his power to grant. "Okay, COB. If we shoot him."

Edwin turned white. Even his lips lost all color. Dr. Sahin opened a briefcase-sized medical bag, took out what looked to be a largish wallet, set it on the table, and unzipped it to reveal an array of preloaded pressure syringes, each a different color and each carefully labeled. He pulled out the white one and set it on the table to the right of the rest. To Max he said, "Vasodilator. We don't want the bastard passing out, do we?"

"Quite right," grunted Brown.

Max turned to Kraft. "Major?"

There was a distinct *slap* as Kraft dropped a thick folder on the table. He slowly opened it and looked in Edwin's eyes. "Chief Edwin. Since 29 September 2314, you have made a series of transfers to your ship's cash account from your shore account on Alphacen, in amounts ranging from five hundred to three thousand credits, isn't that correct?"

Edwin smiled slightly. A *That's all this is about* smile. "Yep. That's right. Nuttin' wrong with that. For *incidentals*, like." He used the word "incidentals" like it was a recent acquisition, a new piece of verbal furniture to be showed off to company.

"Incidentals. Right." Kraft's tone said he didn't believe a word of it. "The account on Alphacen is in your name, correct?"

"Yep. That's right. I got nuttin' to hide."

"Of course, you don't," said Kraft. "That's why there are dozens of other transfers out of that account, ordered by you, each in excess of 150,000 credits, and totaling more than three million credits, apparently to purchase beachfront property and negotiable securities on New Polynesia."

"Why not?" Edwin was starting to squirm a little. "It's my money. I've been saving my salary since I was a mid so I could retire in style."

"I'm sure you have," Kraft said, like an good attorney on cross examination, his tone becoming more sarcastic by almost imperceptible increments. "And Edwin, it appears you've been saving your money in the most interesting of places. Including a very large account at Credit Suisse in Zurich, from which you have transferred 5.43 million credits to your shore account."

"Hey, wait a minute!" Edwin became more indignant than terrified. "Bank accounts in Switzerland are secret. There isn't supposed to even be a name on that account, just a number. And everywhere else in the Union, my bank records are private by law. You can't see them without a court order. And no matter how you played this scenario," he pronounced it *skenario*, "you haven't had time to get one."

Kraft smiled indulgently. "Edwin, you are absolutely right. Your bank *records* are absolutely private. And the communications that any of your banks send to you are also strictly confidential. *Your* communications *to the bank*, however, are a particle with a different polarity. When your funds transfer order is transmitted from a Union warship, in a war zone, in time of war, it is recorded in the ship's database and may be retrieved on order of the captain if he reasonably believes it affects the safety of the ship."

"And I've got a dead crewman that says it is," said Max.

"D-d-d-dead?" Without a full corpse to roll through the corridors, the transfer of Archer's pitifully meager remains to the Casualty Station in a discrete cargo container had not alerted the ship's brilliantly efficient rumor mill.

"That's right, Edwin." Dr. Sahin surprised everyone by speaking. "Ordinary Spacer Second Class D. L. Archer. Quite dead. Everything from a centimeter above the knees up is gone. The rest is what you people like to call *strawberry jam*. I've collected it in two specimen containers. When we're done here, you can see them in the Casualty Station. And the legs."

Kraft continued, "Once I got the captain's okay, it took Ensign Bales only about twenty minutes to access the records, find the relevant transactions, and pull together the sequence. We've got you dead to rights. Emphasis on *dead*. What do you have to say for yourself?"

Edwin got pale again and swayed in his seat. Dr. Sahin administered the vasodilator injection, the syringe making a quiet hiss in the otherwise silent room. The accused chief managed to gather his thoughts, put his palms on the table, and opened his mouth to speak.

"Shut it." Max barked, making everyone in the room jump. "Not a fucking word. I don't want to pollute my memory of the valuable service you gave to this vessel with any disgusting justifications you might offer for your actions, or any greasy, nauseating pleas for mercy. Your guilt is there." He pointed to Kraft's folder.

"And there." He pointed to Edwin's face. "So. Just shut the fuck up. I don't need to hear another word." His voice became formal. "Major Kraft?"

"Yes, Captain?"

"Draw up the necessary documents immediately. Time of execution is three hours from now."

"Yes, sir. I'll have them for your signature in less than two."

"And Major?"

"Sir?"

"No firing squad. He betrayed every man on this ship. Naval tradition tells us what to do with his kind."

"Aye, sir. My pleasure."

A loud thump at the foot of the table caused heads to turn in that direction as Chief Edwin landed unconscious on the deck.

Two hours and fifty-eight minutes later, the group from the wardroom, as well as a few more senior officers and enlisted men were gathered at the main boarding hatch—the hatch through which every man boards the ship from any station or other space facility. Every new midshipman is first brought aboard through the hatch, even if it means docking a shuttlepod or launch there rather than landing it on the hangar deck. Traditions die hard in the Navy.

Held up by Zamora and Ulmer, and fortified by pharmaceuticals injected but not described to anyone by Dr. Sahin, Edwin listened to the charges against him, the formal finding of guilt, and the recitations of various certifications by various officers that he was, in fact, ready to die and that it was, in fact, legal to kill him. He was wearing a plain jane—a version of the Working Uniform that had no name tag, no rank or seniority insignia, no specialty or certification badges, no ship's patches, nor anything else to identify its wearer by name, rank, ship, skill, or specialization.

A man wearing a plain jane was already stripped of his identity. There was, however, a small aluminum plate in one of the pockets, inscribed with his name, rank, and serial number.

Then came the part of the procedure that was contained in none of the execution documents, was printed in no regulation, and could not be found in any book. Yet, it was known to every man who made the black sky his home and was as much the law of deep space as any regulation from Norfolk.

"Ferrell Kent Edwin," said Max, "it was through this hatch or one very like it that you were brought into the brotherhood of the men who serve this ship and the others like her. With them, you have breathed the same air, drunk the same water, shared their joys and sorrows, endured the same hardships, and faced the same dangers. You owe your life to them many times over. Yet, you betrayed them. You. Betrayed. Them. There is no more base treachery than this. So, it is fitting that, in front of your former brothers, you be cast out of their sight, out of their fellowship, and out of their lives, into the eternal darkness from which, for you, there shall be no return until the end of days."

At Max's gesture, Zamora and Ulmer shoved an openly weeping Edwin through a hatch into a small enclosure that had a similar hatch on the other side. Ulmer hit a switch and the inner door closed. Max walked up to the door and keyed a few controls on the panel. A chime sounded. "Airlock pressurization is at 150 percent of standard. It is recommended that excess pressure be relieved immediately." The computer warning purred in its cybernetic sex-kitten voice.

Max dug his fingernail under a protective switch cover and flipped the cover up. He pressed the button.

Another chime sounded. "Warning!" the computer intoned. "Airlock pressure safety override engaged. It is now possible to open outer airlock door when airlock is under pressure."

Max dug his fingernail under a second cover and flipped it up. He pressed the button.

"Warning!" the computer interjected. "Airlock personnel safety override engaged. It is now possible to open outer airlock door with non-pressure-suited personnel in airlock. This procedure is not recommended. Warning! Sensors indicate non-pressure-suited personnel inside airlock. Opening outer airlock under present conditions is a violation of Union Naval Safety Regulations and is likely to result in severe injury or death."

He flipped open a third protective cover, exposing an innocuous, square black button simply labeled OPEN. Max reached for it. A strong hand, fingers cold as ice, suddenly gripped his wrist. Max turned to glare at the man who had dared to lay hands on him.

It was Wendt. Eyes as gray as the North Sea in winter met Max's. "Skipper. He was an enlisted man. A chief. He was my responsibility."

Max nodded and stood aside. Wendt stepped up to the control and looked through the window in the hatch at Edwin, beating on the hatch with his fists. His voice was inaudible, but his lips were moving quickly, obviously begging that his life be spared. Wendt looked the condemned man in the eyes and, seeing nothing worth saving, pressed the button.

The outer door snapped open revealing a rectangle—the depths of interstellar space as framed by the outer bulkhead. In the brightly lit compartment, the men's eyes could not see any stars. The overpressure in the airlock quickly and efficiently shoved Edwin out into the void where he rapidly shrank to a white dot that drifted out of view. Max closed the hatch, put the safety covers back in place, and turned to face the men.

"Dismissed."

CHAPTER 7

18:11Z Hours, 20 March 2315

Max was looking at one of the training schedules prepared by the XO. The frantic edge needed to go, and there was too much time spent on taking the people who were already competent and getting them up to a higher level, and not enough on reaching down to the people who were at the lowest levels of proficiency and bringing them up to competency. Where one arm was strong and the other weak, the strong arm does the hard work. Max needed to find a way to strengthen the weak arm. Tie the strong arm behind the man's back? How do you do that on a destroyer?

The coffee in his mug had gone cold. Max didn't mind cold coffee so much. He had pulled many hundreds of Middle Watches in forgotten corners of large warships, where at 02:53 the only coffee that could be had without committing the unpardonable (not to mention court martial–worthy) offense of abandoning one's station was burned, stale, and cold. Drinking coffee that was merely cold was scarcely an inconvenience, much less a hardship.

He tossed the dregs of the cup down the hatch like a shot of cheap liquor and was reaching for the comm button to call for some more when the panel buzzed, making him drop the mug. It shattered into hundreds of pieces on the metal bezel that marked the boundary between the comm panel and the captain's desk. "Crap," he muttered as he punched to answer. "Skipper."

"Captain, this is Dr. Sahin. I was wondering if you might be available to meet with me. A matter of some importance relative to the welfare of the crew has arisen, and I would like to discuss it with you."

"Absolutely." No questions asked. Well, there was *one* question. "Doctor, is there anyone else whose presence might be beneficial?"

"Not initially. Ordinarily, I would think that having the XO sit in would be advisable. Given what he is doing at the moment, though, I would be reluctant to interrupt him." The XO, Brown, and Chief Wendt were trying to work out some way to determine whether Chief Edwin had sold any other valuable matériel out of the ship.

"Sensible. I'm available now if you would like to come to my day cabin."

"I'm on my way. Sahin out."

Max debated asking his steward or whoever had gash duty to clean up the mess, but decided against it. He was still picking up the pieces of the shattered coffee mug when the doctor arrived. Max waived his visitor to a chair, dropped the mug shards into a waste receptacle, and sat down.

"I see your exaggerated startle response is still causing you problems," Sahin said matter-of-factly.

Damn. The man might be a babe in the woods on a starship, but his ability to observe minute details and fit them together into hypotheses about what other people were doing and thinking bordered on the uncanny. In this case, however, Max had little difficulty following the chain of deduction; after all, he was pretty good at reading "tells" himself. He caught it when the doctor glanced at the comm panel. A few errant drops of coffee were splashed where the mug had shattered, and two tiny specks of the mug itself were resting between some of the buttons. If a person were observant enough to spot the coffee and the mug pieces, and knowing that the panel had buzzed unexpectedly only a few moments before, it would be a simple matter to figure out what happened. *If* you noticed, that is.

"Yes, I know better than to lie to you. I hide it pretty well when the men can see me, but I still jump pretty bad when I'm alone."

"You have come to understand the root of that response now, haven't you?"

"Yes, Bram, we have been through this many times."

Max had undergone two major childhood traumas. First, when he was eight years old, he watched his mother and infant sisters die in a Krag biological warfare attack, after which his father almost immediately shuffled him off to the Navy. Max's father died in an accident a few months later, and Max never saw him again. Only a year and a half after that, the cruiser on which Max served as a midshipman was boarded and taken by the Krag who killed, or tortured and killed, almost the entire crew. Max, however, survived, managing to avoid being killed or captured by hiding out for twenty-six days while the Krag relentlessly hunted him through the air ducts, access crawlways, and cable conduits.

"You tell me, Bram, that my childhood experiences were all traumatic stresses triggering post-traumatic stress disorder, which, at its root, is an anxiety disorder. Although I am generally handling it well, part of my mind fears recurrence of these experiences and seeks to protect me from them by being constantly on guard with the fight-or-flight response set to a hair trigger. You call this 'hypervigilance,' which you described to me as the mind's effort to keep me alive in a dangerous environment by monitoring every aspect of that environment very carefully. But it's a strain on the mind and the body, like keeping a ship at General Quarters indefinitely."

"Generally correct," said Sahin. "But you state that I am the one who says that these events were traumatic. You don't admit it to yourself. Your refusal to admit the severity of these traumas is the foremost impediment to your progress in addressing your anxiety issues."

"Doctor, while I admit that these things were bad experiences, they were not as bad as you make out. We're at war and these things are part of war. People experience horrible things. They live through them. They bear up. They go on with their lives."

"And some of them are horribly traumatized and become crippled by fears and neuroses and psychiatric disabilities requiring extensive treatment. You, my friend, are in denial. But we have spent too many hours on this subject for me to believe I am going to make progress on that issue any time soon. You will move forward when you are ready, and not before. Something will happen; sudden learning will take place, and the door will open. Until you are ready to open the door, it is useless for me to keep knocking. So, since I cannot get to the root of the poisonous plant, I am relegated to trimming the leaves. We have talked about some of the cognitive strategies for combating hypervigilance. Have you been applying those?"

"Bram, that stuff is a lot more easily said than done. I'm supposed to work to convince myself that in this particular environment I am safe and can let down my guard. I have to tell you, though, that's a lot easier when you're sitting in a nice medical office on Earth or Bravo than when you're in the Captain's day cabin on a *war*ship, in time of *war*, in a *war* zone, in which not only is my ship *theoretically* an object of sneak attack by the enemy, it *actually was* the subject of total surprise attack just a few days ago."

"I can see how that might be an issue, Max, but there is a critical distinction that you are missing. Although *the ship* is subject to being sprung upon unawares, crept up upon from behind, and fired upon when we are not looking, you—I mean you, personally—are not. As captain, you need to be certain that Officers DeCosta, Kasparov, Bartoli, Levy, and Bhattacharyya, as well as men like Chief Wendt and Chief LeBlanc, are ready for anything and can spring into action at a moment's notice. You, on the other hand, do not have to keep your reflexes spring-loaded to deal with an attacker in the same room. You need not worry about some stealthy assassin tiptoeing up and blindsiding you from your *eighteen hundred hour position*." Impressed by his own eloquence in the use of naval argot, the doctor allowed his face to take on a slightly smug expression.

The smugness was short-lived. "That's *six o'clock* position. Six. O'clock."

The doctor was crestfallen. "But I thought that 'eighteen hundred hours' and 'six o'clock in the evening' were equivalent expressions."

"They are when you're telling time. But 'six o'clock position' is a way of giving a rough bearing to a target. It lets you give the angle of something you see with the Mark One Eyeball without having to calculate degrees. The numbers are based on the angles of the numbers on an old twelve-hour analog clock. Ever seen one?"

"Oh, yes. I had never made the connection. Now it makes sense. Had that fact been explained to me in the first instance, I am certain that I would have understood it perfectly from the outset."

"I'm sure. Bram, as fascinating as this is, you told me that there was a matter affecting the welfare of the crew."

"Indeed I did. You are aware of your standing order requiring that any man who falls asleep at his post when we are running on a regular watch schedule be examined by me to determine whether there is a medical cause for his inappropriate choice of naptimes."

"That's a standard standing order on most warships. I've always thought it should be a regulation. The watch schedule is set up so that every man gets enough rest. If a man is falling asleep on duty, chances are he's got some sort of problem: medical, psychiatric, personal, whatever."

"You should be aware that four men have been referred to me pursuant to this regulation."

"Well, we're almost three weeks into the month. I admit that four would be a bit unusual, but it's not cause for alarm."

"Not four men this month. Four men in the last two days."

"Oh. That's different. Okay. You have my attention. What's the reason?"

"The purely medical diagnosis in all four cases is identical. Exhaustion. They are not getting enough sleep. The computer keeps a wake/sleep log on all ship's personnel based on biometric monitoring. Don't worry—it is deeply confidential, CMO Eyes Only. But it shows them being awakened at all hours, usually for duty-related matters."

"Duty related? That's not supposed to happen. Regulations prohibit a superior officer from waking a man during his sleep period absent a ship's emergency or other compelling necessity, and if he does so, he is required to log who he woke, the date and time, and his reason."

"This was not superiors waking inferiors, but the other way around."

"Oh. That's very different. Who are these men?"

"If you order me to tell you, I will. This is not one of those confidences protected under the Navy's atom-sized notion of physician–patient privilege, but I would prefer not to say. I believe we can discuss the problem and you can provide a solution without knowing which specific men came to me."

"All right. I'll go along. For now. I know you well enough to be able to tell that you think you have put this whole thing together and can explain the whole problem to me. You have that self-satisfied look on your face."

"I wouldn't know about 'self-satisfied,' but yes, I do believe I have an understanding of what is going on. I talked to these men about the specific circumstances under which they were awakened—who woke them up and what for. I then looked at the wake/sleep logs for several other men similarly situated and they showed a similar, although not quite as severe pattern of disruption. Many of these men are also showing stress-related symptoms. I have identified seventeen men who are affected. If something is not done soon, they will all begin to suffer serious medical problems from sleep deprivation and nervous exhaustion."

"Why? I don't understand. We've tossed Captain Oscar's obsessive cleaning routines and insane reporting requirements out the airlock. We've arranged the training schedule so that it is reasonable and places only sensible demands on every department. Each section on each watch is being given only a small number of exercises to build proficiency. The scores are going up, the ratings are improving, and we're making progress. Why should seventeen men be about to drop in the traces?"

"Because they are pulling almost the whole load. They are carrying the ship."

The two sat together in silence. Then it clicked. That is what Max had been seeing. That's what was wrong. As the proficiency demands became higher and higher, the crew was responding by relying more and more on the small number of men who either had a high level of proficiency and expertise to begin with or who were very fast learners. And as the supposed proficiency level of the section or department got higher and higher, and the exercises and the work took that higher level into account, they got further and further above the heads of most of the rest of the crew, who had to rely ever more heavily on that same small number of highly proficient men.

The weak arm was letting the strong do all the work. And the work was now so hard that the strong arm was breaking. The strong needed the help of the weak. How do you strengthen the weak arm?

Or the weak *eye*.

"Doctor, isn't there a disease called 'lazy eye' that children get sometimes?"

"There are several conditions that receive that imprecise layman's label. I presume that you are referring to strabismic amblyopia, a condition in which there is a misalignment of the eyes that results in the highly neuroplastic brain of the child essentially learning to not see or to reject the image from one of the eyes. It is often treated by realigning the eyes with surgery and then taking some sort of action to teach the brain to accept and process the signals from the disfavored eye."

"Exactly. Didn't they used to put a patch over the strong eye to force the child to see through the weak one?"

"A crude way to say it, but yes. When the brain was presented with only one image, the child's brain quickly learned to accept the only available visual input. As soon as the brain is using both eyes with rough equality, the patch comes off and the problem is cured. But that is not the modern treatment."

"Why not?"

"Children don't like wearing the eye patch. The other children tease them. So, we pharmacologically penalize the good eye."

"You what?"

"Pharmacologically penalize. Essentially, we put in eye drops that make the vision in the good eye blurry, so the brain will start relying on the weak eye."

"Then that is what we're going to have to do. To make the weak eye strong, we're going to have to make the strong eye weak."

"How do you plan to do that?"

"First, I'm going to have to trouble you for those seventeen names."

"I understand." He reached into a pocket of his tunic and pulled out a folded sheet of paper. "Here they are. I thought something like this might be necessary. And next? Are you going to tell the men that they have become too dependent upon these seventeen individuals and take them off duty, requiring the other men to shoulder the weight?"

Max recoiled in abject horror. "Oh, no, Doctor. That would never do. If I take those seventeen men out of service completely, the ship would go to pieces. We can't do without them entirely, or even most of the time. Plus, the reaction of the men to something like that would be a disaster. The seventeen would feel as though they were being punished for performing their jobs too well, which they would resent, and the remainder of the men would interpret the action as an implication that they are incompetent, which *they* would resent. We mustn't foster resentment when we can avoid it. We're going to have to do something else entirely."

"Captain, I very much fear that you are about to unveil one of your ruses."

"Doctor, I very much fear that you are right."

USS *Cumberland* DPA-0004: Ship's Standing Order #15-14
20 March 2315
Effective immediately:

1. Starting tomorrow and on every third day thereafter (Day 2 of every watch cycle) the persons listed on Attachment A will attend Special Leadership Development Training from 08:00 to 16:00 hours, with appropriate breaks for coffee, lunch, and so on, as determined by the person(s) conducting said training.
2. So that the listed personnel may devote full attention to their studies and be appropriately rested, they are not to be disturbed by any person for any reason without the explicit permission of the CO or XO for the entire 24-hour period of the training day.
3. As this training program imposes substantial additional work requirements, the listed personnel are to be exempt from any duty-related requirements on Days 1 and 3 of the watch cycle except when they are on watch. They are not to be disturbed by any person for any reason when they are off watch, without the explicit permission of the CO or XO.
4. The listed personnel are similarly prohibited from engaging in any activities related to their regular duties on Day 2 of the watch cycle or when they are off watch without explicit permission of the CO or XO.
5. The provisions of this standing order are automatically suspended when the ship is at general quarters.

■

Having written and posted the general order, Max spent a few hours at his workstation, slogging through the endless bureaucratic minutiae that seemed to be one of the primary burdens of command. He had his supper brought to him. It was outstanding. The *Cumberland* was still eating high on the hog with provisions purchased on Rashid IV and given to the ship by Mr. Wortham-Biggs in exchange for information that he had been unknowingly selling supplies to the Krag through intermediaries.

Max dined on fruit cocktail, shrimp and crab gumbo (alas, the Rashidians did not cultivate oysters, which would have been a delightful addition), Cajun potato salad (potatoes, eggs, mayonnaise, and some mild seasonings, without all the chopped vegetables that usually go into potato salad), fresh French bread, and strawberry pie.

Between the Rashidian supplies and having a couple of Cajuns and a few more men of Southern descent in the galley, Max was starting to worry about gaining weight and being assigned mandatory workouts with the Chub Club, crew members found to be overweight and under medical orders for exercise over and above normal requirements. He hadn't eaten so well since the four months he had attended the Navy's Covert Operations and Unconventional Warfare School on his homeworld of Nouvelle Acadiana five years ago. Max ate at the keyboard, reading a series of newly issued intelligence estimates on Krag intentions and capabilities in the *Cumberland*'s current operational area. According to Intel, the Krag were about to begin a considerable push in this sector.

Unless, of course, they decided to consolidate their previous conquests and adopt a defensive stance for the time being, before initiating a major push sometime in the future.

Unless, of course, this sector had been indefinitely downgraded to a secondary theater in favor of major operations to take place against Task Force Sierra Bravo (Admiral Middleton's force).

Take your pick.

Intel. Useless. No, that wasn't true. When you got an Intel guy in the same room with you, you could usually get some decent answers out of him, and if you could get your hands on the intermediate level reports prepared by the Intel officers attached to the task forces, you could learn a lot. But the top level reports out of Norfolk were so full of caveats and weasel words that they meant virtually nothing. If the top Intel brass put as much effort into being right as they did into not saying anything that could later turn out to be wrong, they might get somewhere. If those guys played poker, they would try to raise, call, and fold at the same time.

Older, more tired, but no wiser, Max turned his attention to a series of projections from NAVSUP, more fully known as the Naval Supply Systems Command, estimating the quantities of fuel, foodstuffs, ordinance, replacement parts, and other supplies that would be delivered to Task Force Tango Delta and other forces under Admiral Hornmeyer's command over the next forty-five days.

The Pfelung contribution to the war effort was starting to make itself felt. As an Associated Power, the Pfelung brought one considerable asset to the table in addition to their not inconsiderable Navy: deuterium. Not only were they a prime producer of the vital fuel, they were a prime producer located close to where the fighting was going on, meaning that the fleet now had a significant source of fuel that didn't have to be hauled almost a thousand light years from the Core Systems or produced in newly constructed separation plants or portable units. As a result, total tonnage was up by almost 25 percent, as shipping capacity freed up by the Pfelung's fuel production was used for other transport.

NAVSUP estimated that the increase would eventually reach 40 percent, when production from the Pfelung system's Europa-like ice moon Pfelung VII C, known locally as Strulp, was fully ramped up. The logistics bean counters hadn't even begun to put together figures on how much difference Rashid's contribution was going to make, particularly given that Rashid also had a substantial deuterium production facility as well as industrial capacity on Rashid V A that came close to matching some of the second or upper third tier of industrial worlds in the Core Systems.

Then there were the Romanovans. Were they even going to be allies? Their enormous potential contributions weren't even a gleam in NAVSUP's eyes.

The shipping increase resulting from in-sector fuel production meant fewer ships sitting idly in rear areas waiting for repair and replacement parts to arrive, fewer ships being sent into combat without a complete loadout of missiles in their racks; more and better food on the men's plates; better inventories in the ships' spare equipment bays; more rapid issuance and installation of improved and upgraded sensors, computers, fire control systems, point defense batteries, and weapons; and a subtle but measurable increase in the fleet's combat effectiveness and ability to inflict death and destruction upon the enemy.

Good news for everyone. Except the Krag.

As hopeful as this news was in terms of the impact on the war (even so, Max's rough calculations told him that it was not enough to overcome Krag advantages in production capacity and population, but it did narrow the margin), the reports themselves were deadly dull, even in comparison to other naval reports. Max had several hours' worth of material through which he had to wade, much of which consisted of tables listing the tonnage of various commodities projected to be made available in the sector month by month. There was no way that his brain was going to assimilate any of that stuff unless he gave it a break.

He decided to go to the wardroom to see what the galley had put out for midrats. Max had been serving as a midshipman on warships for three years before he learned that "midrats" stood for "midnight rations" and not for "midshipmen eat rats" or something to that effect. Starting at 00:00 and lasting until the culinary staff needed to clear for breakfast, the galley crew set food out in the wardroom and the enlisted mess. It wasn't anything fancy, just dinner leftovers, sandwich makings, dinner rolls, sweet rolls, and a rotating variety of donuts, gelatin, fruit, cakes, pies, and cookies, and other simple but sustaining food on a self-serve, all-you-care-to-eat basis.

There were a lot of things the Navy did that just made good sense, and this was one of them. On a warship, there were men doing hard physical work and standing watches around the clock. The very least the Navy could do for these men was to make sure that they didn't go hungry as they worked through the night, and no man had to go to his rack with an empty stomach after a long day's duty.

Max made himself a salami and pastrami sandwich, and snagged a couple of kosher pickles, a handful of chips, three (or was it four) chocolate brownies, and two tall iced glassfuls of the reconstituted-from-powder, artificially flavored fruit beverage that, dating back to the days of the saltwater navies, has been known as "bug juice." According to a rumor that Max had never verified, the powder from which bug juice was made also served the galley staff as an abrasive cleanser. Sometimes, Max wanted to know whether the rumor was true. Most of the time, he didn't. There were things that men, even captains, simply should not know.

Thus fortified, Max was ready to spend some more time trying to keep up to date in the larger picture of what was happening in the war. He was walking from the wardroom to his quarters when Midshipman Hewlett overtook and passed him in the corridor, moving as fast as his little legs could carry him without running. Hewlett was the second smallest of the "squeakers," "deck dodgers, "panel puppies," or "hatch hangers," the youngest group of midshipmen, the boys taken on the ship to be inducted into the satisfactions, the adventure, the dangers, and the hardships of naval service.

As the cream of the Navy's future, all 1025 millimeters of him, whizzed past, Max noticed that the young man had around his waist a web belt, the kind made for holding hand grenades, and that in the web belt were sixteen or seventeen ping-pong balls painted in an altogether festive but distinctly non-naval array of pastels that looked as though they would be more at home at a bridal shower than on a destroyer in a war zone. Max chuckled to himself. He hadn't seen an Easter Egg Hunt in years.

Mr. Hewlett's miniature legs could carry him only so fast, so Max didn't have to exert much effort to fall in behind the diminutive hatch hanger who, according to the time-sanctified rules of the Easter Egg Hunt, was prohibited from running. The midshipman rounded a corner and opened a hatch that admitted him to a room full of equipment storage lockers.

Max peeked in the door and saw Hewlett pull a padcomp out of his web belt, consult it hurriedly, and then go straight to the fifth locker on the aft wall, deftly operate the latch, reach inside, and pull out another ping-pong ball. This ball was a color that Max recognized as being called "sea-foam," a word that he knew only by virtue of having seen, on what was still called "movie night" although the last conventional motion picture was filmed in 2023, a tridvid comedy about the mayhem, hijinks, and hilarity that ensued when identical twin brides married identical twin husbands and insisted that all the bridesmaids and groomsmen also be twins. Max remembered not getting most of the jokes.

Hewlett stuck the ball in his web belt with the others, closed the locker, and engaged the latches. Max quickly ducked out of sight into an access crawlway alcove until the boy had emerged and was going down the corridor again. If this hunt held to form, the next "egg" would be on another deck, in an entirely different part of the ship. Max knew that the boy was nearly done with the hunt because it looked as though his web belt held close to eighteen of the ping-pong balls. Easter Egg Hunts always contained eighteen "eggs."

An Easter Egg Hunt was an old naval training exercise for midshipmen. A midshipman was issued a padcomp with the locations of eighteen "eggs" located throughout the ship. The locations were given only by the official name of the location, such as "Main Engineering Emergency Equipment Locker #4." The locations were all places to which midshipmen have authorized access, and other than being put in those locations, the eggs were not hidden in any way. They were painted in festive pastels, to stand out on a warship. Mids were to retrieve the eggs in the order listed on their padcomps, not run at any time, and not ask for help unless in some sort of trouble. A mid could ask the ship's computer for help, but only to show him the location of the egg, and then only with a thirty-second time penalty. He couldn't ask the computer how to get to the location, on pain of spending twenty-four hours in the brig.

Max had no desire to chase after the midshipman to whatever far corner of the *Cumberland* held the final ping-pong ball or two, particularly since the path to the last "egg" usually involved crawling through an air handling shaft, worming through one of the more circuitous of the cable conduits, or traversing a narrow catwalk over a crackling, snapping, fully charged polaron differentiation grid. Instead, Max headed for where Easter Egg Hunts always end, the junior midshipmen's lounge.

Because junior midshipmen are subject to orders by almost everyone else on the ship, not to mention being the objects of a fair amount of good-natured teasing, mostly from the senior midshipmen, they were provided with a sanctuary from all that. The junior midshipman's lounge was off limits to all personnel except the midshipmen's trainer, a few of the ship's most senior officers (who, by tradition, entered rarely and only for a specific purpose), and the junior midshipmen themselves.

Max keyed in his entry code, palmed the lock, and stepped through the hatch. As always, one middie was posted just inside the door against just this contingency. When the boy saw that the man coming through the hatch was the captain, his eyes went wide. But to his credit, he did not freeze at all but performed his function without any appreciable delay.

He sprang from a sitting position to ruler-straight attention so abruptly that Max swore he could hear joints cracking, and barked out, "Captain on deck!" with as much authority as he could muster, doing a creditable job, notwithstanding the pitch of his voice falling in the frequency range depicted by the treble rather than the bass clef.

The other five deck dodgers all snapped to attention. Chief Petty Officer Tanaka, the midshipmen's trainer who stepped into the position upon the death of the beloved "Mother Goose" Chief Amborsky, gazed pointedly at a line formed by the joinder of two deck plates, resulting in the boys' quickly shuffling a few centimeters forward or back until the toes of their boots exactly met the line. He then walked down the line, directing the boys silently with his eyes, subtle gestures, and an occasional touch to nudge a shoulder a bit further back or a chin a bit higher.

When his charges had come to attention in a manner that met his truly exacting standards, Tanaka turned with precision that could be bested only by a mechanical device, snapped out a perfect drill manual salute, and announced, "Captain, Chief Petty Officer Tanaka reporting five squeakers, cords cut but still damp, plus one in the Casualty Station and one on an Easter Egg Hunt, sir."

Max returned the salute. "Very well. Chief, I saw Mr. Hewlett retrieving one of your eggs from the firefighting equipment lockers. I believe you will be seeing him very shortly. With your permission, I would like to stay for the Basket Lesson."

By custom, this was the chief's turf and the training of the mids, his responsibility. Even as august a person as the captain entered, watched, or participated only at the midshipmen's trainer's invitation. Tanaka nodded his acceptance.

"Thank you. Carry on, Chief."

"Thank you, sir." He turned to his charges. "Midshipmen, as you were." The boys returned to the seats they had occupied before Max came in. The compartment was small, but comfortable, with a few couches; tables that could serve equally well as dining, studying, or game tables surrounded by chairs; plus a few lounge-type chairs; a tridvid unit; and—glaring down at the proceedings as they did in every junior midshipmen's lounge in every ship in the fleet—two icons of military virtue, presented to the boys as models worthy of emulation: Patton and Litvinoff.

As he always did when entering the lounge, Max took a moment to examine the images. General George Smith Patton, Jr., "Old Blood and Guts," was shown in a photograph taken circa 1943 when he was a lieutenant general commanding the United States Army's Second Corps fighting Rommel's forces in North Africa. Patton was in a field uniform, wearing a three-starred helmet,with binoculars hanging from his neck, standing outside what looked to be a North African village, using his riding crop to indicate something in the distance to the men standing around him, his eyes and his mind clearly focused on that faraway objective and how to take or destroy it.

From the set of his mouth, he was clearly saying something, perhaps giving an order, his words now lost to history. Here was Patton in his element—in the field with his troops, radiating confidence and authority, leading his men. It occurred to Max that if Old Blood and Guts had been given an opportunity to select which of the thousands of photographs taken of him in World War II would be hanging on this wall in this time in this place, he might well have picked that very picture.

Admiral Vladimir Nickolai Litvinoff, "the Fighting Czar," was shown in a two-dimensional capture from the famous tridvid documentary shot in the CIC of the Battleship *Actium* at the Battle of Rackham III on 2 November 2305. Litvinoff, then a rear admiral, was in the Working Uniform with Arms, the simple blue jumpsuit worn day to day on most warships, carrying his M-1911 sidearm and boarding cutlass, the latter looking more like a broadsword on his diminutive frame.

The image was taken at the pivotal moment of that crucial battle. Thanks to the documentary, those few minutes were engraved indelibly in the collective memory of virtually the entire human race: the task force under Litvinoff's command seemed on the verge of being wiped out by a numerically superior Krag force. The fleet carrier *James A. Lovell* had just jumped in and could not launch its fighters until its systems were restored from the jump, a process that would require five critical minutes. The four officers seen in the image, staring grimly into the 3D tactical plot with Litvinoff, had just unanimously advised the admiral that his task force faced almost certain destruction unless he withdrew it immediately, abandoning the *Lovell* and its four squadrons of Valkyrie fighters to certain annihilation. The senior of them, Captain Fouché, had just said "Admiral, we must preserve this fleet. We must withdraw."

Of all the men in that CIC, only Litvinoff believed that he could hold off the Krag until the fighters launched, and that he could then concentrate them and his reserve against the two battleships anchoring the Krag line, break the enemy formation, and turn defeat into victory. The image froze history at that moment: the admiral's chin jutting out defiantly, his right hand pointing to where his force was plotted, as he said, "Withdraw? Not today. Not one meter. We *will* hold this line."

And as everyone knows, it went just as the Admiral envisioned: line held, fighters deployed, forces concentrated, and Krag formation broken. A famous victory won. Litvinoff, whose reputation as a great fighting commander was secured on that day, was now a grand admiral, in overall command of all the Navy's forces fielded against the Krag.

Max saluted first the admiral and then the general. It was the custom. Navy men saluted heroes even if, as in Patton's case, they had been dead for centuries and were part of a service only distantly related to the modern space-faring Navy.

At that moment, the lock on the hatch cycled, and Midshipman Hewlett burst into the compartment, flew across the room (running *was* allowed in the lounge), and emphatically slapped the STOP button on the large timer mounted on the far bulkhead, halting the clock at 1:32:17. The boy then turned around and, for the first time, noticed that both Chief Tanaka and Max were in the room. Hewlett knew he was supposed to salute and report, but he didn't know the rule to apply in this situation.

Salute and report to the senior officer present? Salute and report to the person whose orders he was executing? Salute them both and then give his report? He froze.

Tanaka instantly deduced what the problem was. "Mr. Hewlett," he said, his pronunciation exceptionally precise, his tone patient, "while the captain is the senior officer present, you have just executed my order. In that case, military courtesy dictates that you salute and report to me, then salute the senior officer."

"Aye, aye, Chief." The boy turned to face straight at Tanaka, pulled himself up to the limits of what little height he possessed, raised his hand to a salute, and rattled out, "Midshipman Hewlett, reporting all eighteen eggs retrieved. No problems to report."

Tanaka returned the salute. "Very well, Midshipman." Hewlett snapped his hand back down, pivoted to face Max, and raised his hand to another salute, just as smart as the first.

"Captain," he said simply.

Max returned the salute. "Midshipman. Carry on."

The boy turned back to Tanaka, who said, "At ease, Midshipman. Let's see what you've got."

Hewlett then emptied the contents of his web belt into a plastic bin sitting on one of the tables and stood beside the table at parade rest. Tanaka quickly sorted the ping-pong balls, each of which bore a tiny numeral, written with a marker in Tanaka's own handwriting. After verifying that all eighteen "eggs" were present and genuine, Tanaka turned to Hewlett.

"That's all eighteen. As for the time, Mr. Hewlett, I've seen better. I've seen a lot better." And then, just as bitter disappointment started to write itself across the boy's miniature features, the chief let just a hint of a smile show as he added, "But on a first hunt, I have also seen much, much worse. The official ship's record for the worst hunt by a midshipman is four hours, twenty-three minutes, and two seconds. But that's not all. Every now and then I run into some poor, bedraggled boy who got sent out last year. He's still crawling through the ship somewhere looking for that last egg. He hasn't a clue where the port EM sensor array signal accumulation and initial processing unit is located." Hewlett's face brightened.

"I know where. It's on B Deck, amidships, *starboard* side, in that little equipment bay just aft of CIC. It has 'port' in the name, not because it's on the port side of the ship, but because it takes in sensor inputs from the port-side arrays."

Damn. Max bet that the XO hadn't learned the location of that unit yet.

"Correct. Now I know not to put any eggs there until the next batch of squeakers arrives. Now, Mr. Hewlett," Tanaka continued, "as you are the first of this group to complete a hunt, and as each of your classmates will embark on one either today or tomorrow, could you please tell your shipmates *why* you did it?"

That seemed to stump him. "Because I was ordered to do it by Chief Petty Officer First Class Tanaka?" he said lamely.

"That is a literally correct and responsive answer, but not what I was looking for, Mr. Hewlett." The chief's voice sounded infinitely patient and understanding, yet somehow managed to convey the slightest flavor of disappointment. "What I want to know is if you can tell me the *purpose* of the exercise. And make no mistake, my little tadpoles, although we may call it an Easter Egg Hunt and treat it like a game, it is absolutely not a game. Not in the slightest. Does anyone else have an idea?"

One boy stood up. He was a few millimeters taller than Hewlett, but probably weighed half again as much. Hewlett, with his blond hair, fair skin, blue eyes, and pink ears blushing from the attention, looked like a tiny elf who should be making toys in Santa's workshop, not being trained to be a deadly warrior in a desperate battle for the survival of his species. This other boy was just as fair as Hewlett, but much stockier. He looked as though he would be a natural wrestler or weight lifter. He was going to grow into a big man.

"Yes, Mr. Gunderson?"

"To teach us the ship, sir."

"What about the ship?"

"Where things are. How to find places."

"Very good. That is the primary reason, the most important one. There are others. Can you tell me what they are?"

"I don't know, sir."

"I think I do, sir." It was Hewlett again. Now that he knew the kind of answer the chief was looking for, maybe he could look back at what he had just done and see what it had taught him.

"Go ahead," said Tanaka.

"It's more than just where things are, sir. You also learn . . . you learn the fastest way to get from one part of the ship to another." He stopped talking. Obviously, he thought he had hit upon the complete answer. But Tanaka kept looking at him expectantly, silently urging him to dig deeper. Hewlett's face became scrunched with concentration, and then suddenly lit up.

"Oh, oh, I see now. I get it. There's *a lot* more. It makes you see all of the access crawlways and cable conduits and pipes and tunnels from the inside, so you get to know them just as well as you get to know the parts of the ship you see every day." He started talking faster.

"And . . . and . . . you learn how to get into things, the crawlways and lockers and storage bins—how to work the locks and the latches and open the access panels and covers and remove the safety grills and work loose the vent bezels. How to get into them in a hurry, when you're nervous and in a rush. And you have to do it over and over for all the different kinds so that I'm betting after you've done several of these Hunts, it will be like, you know, automatic. You won't have to think about how to get into something. Your hands and fingers will just know how and go ahead and do it."

"That's called 'muscle memory,' Mr. Hewlett and, yes, that's very good. It is a refreshing surprise for a still wet squeaker to spend an hour and a half doing something and to actually get the point of why he was doing it. Don't worry. I will not expect it to happen again any time soon." Then he smiled. A brief, reserved smile that said that he really didn't expect it to happen any time soon, but that he wasn't angry about it.

"We do many things to teach you about the ship when you are a midshipman. That is one reason you are given so many assignments in so many parts of the ship on such a rapidly changing basis, so you get to see every part of the ship and get an introduction to what every department does, how it works, who is in it, and what they do. And that is why each of you is assigned to one of the repair and maintenance teams for two watches a week: not just to hand them tools and shine a hand torch where they are working and retrieve dropped screws, but so you follow them around and crawl through the cable conduits and burrow into the nooks and crannies of this vessel. You see what's beneath the surface, deep under the skin.

"So, we want you to know the ship like the back of your hand, and we do many things to make that happen. Which of you gentlemen can tell me why? Why do we want you to know every little hole and burrow, every locker and latch, every panel and console?"

Another boy stood up. Tanaka motioned for Hewlett and Gunderson to sit down. The new boy was a handsome lad, a head taller than the others, with the darkest skin Max had ever seen on a human. "Mr. Koyamba, do you have some light to shed on this subject?"

"Sir, my father is a Marine, and he always talks about how a Marine knows everything about his rifle. He can take it apart, clean it, oil it, and put it back together in the dark really, really fast. He also used to talk about how important it is for a fighting man to know the ground he is fighting over. Isn't the ship kind of both, sir? It's what we fight with, but it can also be where we fight."

"Excellent, Mr. Koyamba. That is truly a perceptive observation. There are many full-fledged spacers who don't have that figured out. You are absolutely right. This ship, for all practical purposes, is your entire universe. Right now, you could go ten billion kilometers from here in any direction and not find a rock bigger than Mr. Hewlett, much less something with water and an atmosphere to keep you alive.

"Your ship and your shipmates are everything to you. The ship is your world that sustains you with air and water and shelter. Your shipmates are your family that provides you with care and support and companionship and even love. Together, ship and crew are your hometown that contains your restaurants and entertainment and school and even your hospital as well as the people who make all those places work.

"When we encounter the Krag, it is your weapon. If we are ever boarded, it is your battleground. In order to do your jobs you will be required to have intimate knowledge of this ship. Intimate knowledge of this ship, or of any other ship on which you serve, may save your life and the lives of your shipmates. In a boarding action, knowing all the hidden places and paths can give you ways to outflank your enemy, to sneak up on him from behind, to surround him, to escape him and, if things go badly for you, to hide out, perhaps for days at a time."

"Chief?" It was Mr. Hewlett, again. He always seemed to be asking questions. He was almost as bad as Park.

"Yes, Mr. Hewlett."

"I heard a story from one of the senior mids that once a midshipman hid out from the Krag for weeks and weeks on a ship that got taken, outsmarting them day after day. That's just a legend, isn't it? No one could hide for that long, right?"

Tanaka was in a difficult spot. On one hand, he didn't know his captain well enough to know whether his experience on the *San Jacinto* was a proper subject for discussion with the squeakers. On the other, there was the near sacred naval tradition that a midshipman trainer must always be truthful with his mids. Not just that he not affirmatively lie to them, but that he must be *truthful*: he must not mislead them, in any way, ever. He could choose to be silent on a subject, as one might expect in a military organization where much information was distributed on a need-to-know basis, but if he spoke, every word, every implication, every nuance had to be as perfectly truthful as he knew how to make it. Young people needed to have at least one adult authority figure in their lives in whom they could have unqualified trust. The Navy understood that and provided them with one. The mids knew that from their trainer they would hear only truth.

There was only one thing to do in this situation. American football was still played on several dozen worlds; hence, mankind had not forgotten the meaning of the word "punt."

"Captain, this might be something that you can answer better than I."

Well, Bram *did* say that he was supposed to talk about his experiences, right? He mentally sprayed a few gallons of insecticide on the butterflies in his stomach and stepped carefully into the breach.

"It's no rumor, Mr. Hewlett." *Deep breath. Do this the Navy way. Just the facts, man.* "The cruiser USS *San Jacinto* was boarded and taken by the Krag. The logs record that active resistance ceased at 13:42 hours on 10 September 2296. She had a complement of 446. Of those, 421 gave their lives defending the ship. Twenty-four were taken captive. Most of those were killed later. All of them were tortured. That left one, a midshipman second class who, on the orders of his Mother Goose, hid himself as the ship was being taken.

"After that, he continued to evade capture, eluding the Krag in the access crawlways, the cable conduits, the spaces between the false ceilings and the pressure bulkheads, empty food lockers, voids left by equipment upgrades, and all the other nooks and crannies and hidden ways inside a ship that you learn about as a midshipman but that a Krag wouldn't know about.

"He got water from the water reclamation condensers. He stole food, even going so far as to trigger alerts that would send the Krag running out of the mess to action stations, so he could grab the rations off their plates. For twenty-six days. On October 6, at 17:57 hours, *San Jacinto* was lured into a trap by a small task force under the command of Commodore, now Fleet Admiral, Charles L. Middleton. The midshipman and two other survivors—the chief medical officer and the communications officer—were rescued. Oh, and the ship's cat, wily old Sam Houston. The Krag never caught him either. He lived for several more years without once leaving the ship."

"But sir," it was Hewlett again. He asked enough questions for a whole class of hatch hangers. "What about the midshipman? Almost all his shipmates were killed. All his friends. His bunkies. His Mother Goose. His CO. And then he had the rat-faces chasing him for almost a whole month. Wouldn't he still feel guilty for living when they died? Wouldn't he still feel afraid? What happened to him? How's he doing? Is he okay?"

From the mouths of babes. That's the heart of the matter, isn't it? How is he doing? Is he okay?

Max looked at those faces, all etched with concern, anxiety, and worry for a little boy whom, as far as they knew, they had never met. Yet, to these midshipmen, this boy was a brother—someone like them who wore the Blue, slung his hammock in a small compartment with his six bunkies, went on Easter Egg Hunts, surreptitiously turned off the artificial gravity generators in the cargo holds and played zero-G tag, breakfasted on "spam, spam, eggs, and spam," and was drilled by Mother Goose on how to use his dirk and put out fires and patch hull breaches and operate an escape pod. Max remembered the utter horror that had galloped across those young faces when he had described what he had been through, even though he had done it in the most clinical and bloodless terms. Those mids had taken a brief glimpse at what he had endured for twenty-six days and found it unimaginably terrifying.

Max had spent nearly twenty years telling himself that what he had gone through wasn't so bad, that it was little more than an unpleasant memory not to be dwelt on. He had consoled himself again and again with the rationalization that it was well within the range of normal experiences of the millions of human beings who had gone into battle with the Krag during the long course of this horrible, deadly, destructive war.

All lies.

The edifice of self-deception that Max had been carefully building and repairing for the better part of his life collapsed in an instant. For years he had been telling himself one thing, but those faces—*those faces*—told him another. Those faces told him instantly, and with a power that could never be conveyed in words, that it *had* been so bad.

They convinced him in a second of what Ibrahim Sahin had been trying to get him to believe for months: that he was in denial about just how utterly, soul-breakingly terrifying those twenty-six days had actually been. The midshipmen's faces were like a mirror, allowing him to see the experience of those twenty-six days reflected back to him, not from the perspective of the man he was today, but from the perspective of the young boy who'd actually gone through the ordeal. To those boys, what he'd survived was a thing of such unimaginable horror that they couldn't conceive of enduring it without some sort of crippling consequences.

And they were right. Now he knew. He really knew.

With that knowledge, came power. Commodore Middleton never tired of quoting Sun Tzu. One of his favorites: "Know the enemy and know yourself, and in a thousand battles you will never be in peril." All this time, he had not known the enemy he was fighting within himself. He had thought his foe to be weak and inconsequential. Wrong. His enemy was strong and terrible—a horrible, traumatic fear that had left scars that he had ignored for all these years. Now he knew. And now that he knew, he could fight effectively. Now that he knew, he could win.

All of this went through his mind in less than five seconds. The mids wanted to know about the boy. How is he doing? Is he okay? Well, *is* he? *Let's find out.* "Gentlemen, let me ask you. How does it look like I'm doing? Do I seem okay to you?"

It took a full second for the boys to reason through the implication of their captain's questions. When they got there, the shock in the room was palpable. The boys' faces were an amalgam of wonder, amazement, surprise, and awe. It was Hewlett who managed to say what they were all thinking, "Sir, that... it... the midshipman... was *you*?"

"Yes, Mr. Hewlett. It was."

Silence sat heavy in the room while the midshipmen's minds processed what they had learned, connecting what they had heard about the famously elusive midshipman with what they had heard and observed about their captain. At first, it seemed that the man who had been their commanding officer for these past few months could not possibly be that boy grown to manhood. But then the traits of the boy of legend and the traits that marked this captain, traits that were already legendary on board the *Cumberland*, started to fit together. The tenacity. The courage. The resourcefulness. The defiance. The refusal to be beaten. They all made sense now. Not only was it possible that this man was that boy grown to manhood, it was impossible that he be anyone else.

Hewlett, the only one of the mids who was already standing, almost as a reflex or an instinctive response, drew himself up to attention. And saluted. When he looked back on that moment, he could never identify quite what it was that moved him on that day. Whatever the cause, whatever he felt, the other boys felt it too. As one, they came to their feet, brought themselves to the most prefect attention Tanaka had ever seen them manage, and saluted. Trying to ignore the lump that had just formed in his throat, Max returned the salute with solemn precision.

"Thank you, gentlemen." He managed to keep the strong emotion from showing in his voice. Most of it anyway. "I must be doing all right then." He smiled at the boys warmly. There was nothing he could do or say that would add to what had taken place, which—to any wise leader—means that there is only one thing to do. "Carry on, gentlemen. Chief." He started to turn toward the hatch.

Before Max could complete the turn, Tanaka said, "Thank you, Captain." He saluted as well. Max returned the salute and left. Both men knew that military courtesy did not call for a salute in that situation. Neither gave it a second thought.

Max walked back to his quarters. Those logistics reports were still waiting for him. He shook his head unconsciously. Something important had just happened. Something had changed. He felt different. Some part of the turmoil that for years had raged deep in his innermost self had quieted. Not all of it. Not even most of it. But some of it. In one corner of his being, where there had been anguish and pain and fear, there was now peace.

It felt good. It felt very good.

CHAPTER 8

00:37Z Hours, 21 March 2315

"Middle Watch," also known as "Graveyard Watch" (a term that the Navy, understandably, discouraged), was the least-loved watch of the day. It ran from midnight (00:00, often referred to as "four balls") to 04:00, the period of the human diurnal cycle when intellect, strength, stamina, and alertness are at their lowest ebb. It was a well-known naval statistic that of the seven watches stood during any twenty-four-hour period, it was the Middle Watch that consumed the most coffee and high-sugar snacks.

It was also the Middle Watch in which the crew committed the most Mandatory Logging Discrepancies, the term the Navy uses for errors and omissions of sufficient magnitude to require that they be logged by the head of the offending department. And not coincidentally, it was the watch in which the largest number of noncombat-related deaths occurred.

Space was dangerous, the high-energy systems and toxic materials needed for its conquest even more so; accordingly, there were hundreds of ways to die on a warship, many of which did not involve contact with the enemy, but required only a moment's inattention or an apparently trivial error to invite a visit from the Grim Reaper.

And this Middle Watch was to prove more difficult than most. Today was the first day of the "Leadership Training" ordered by the captain for the men he privately called the "Sweet Seventeen." When First Watch ended thirty-seven minutes ago, and the five of those seventeen who stood that watch went off duty, none of the seven assigned to stand the Middle Watch came on. Further, under the terms of the new standing order, none of the seventeen was available to answer any questions, solve any problems, or explain how to repair the minor malfunctions that were supposed to be fixed "in department" rather than by Engineering staff.

The captain's theory was simple and, at least in the opinion of Dr. Sahin, ingenious. For one day in three, the other 198 officers, men, and boys would have to figure out how to operate the ship without the aid of the Sweet Seventeen. And on the other two, the seventeen's contributions to the running of the ship would be limited to what they could do during their regular watches, which would force the rest of the ship's complement, if not to stand on their own two feet, then to use the seventeen as a walking stick rather than a wheelchair.

No one in the Sensors back room (or Staff Support Room as it was referred to formally) had any inkling of what the captain was doing or why. It was in that compartment that twenty or so men monitored the input from the arrays of sensitive instruments that *Cumberland* used to monitor its environment, locate its enemies in order to evade or flee or destroy them, manage those instruments and systems, and see that the sensors officer in CIC had on demand whatever sensor information was needed by the man in the Big Chair. It was also in that compartment where the rubber of the captain's plan first met the road of reality.

"Chief Klesh, the computer is telling me I've got a twitch on the LCDA," announced Able Spacer First Class James Smith, referred to by everyone as "Greenlee" (from the name of his homeworld) to distinguish him from the other two James Smiths on board. The Chief Klesh to whom he made the announcement was Chief Petty Officer First Class Tadeusz Kleszczynska, of Swiatzpols, the senior man in the compartment now that Ensign Harbaugh, one of the Sweet Seventeen, was unavailable. Klesh was the fourth most senior noncom on the ship.

The chief got up from his station and stepped over to Greenlee's console. Looking over the spacer's shoulder he could see on the Alerts and Messages display a flashing notification stating "Local Compression Detection Algorithm analysis of fluctuations in this vessel's compressed space to normal space interface indicates the likely presence of another compression field within a three-light year radius."

When another ship was using a compression drive within a few light years, residual superluminal distortion propagated through the space-time continuum to exert a minute effect on the *Cumberland*'s own compression field. Although these effects were not visible on any display given the large amount of random fluctuation that was always present, the computer had an algorithm that could detect whether a systematic component was present in the random noise. In this case, the computer had just made such a detection.

"Can you localize it?"

"Negative, Chief. I've asked the computer for bearing information and it comes up blank."

"And what does that mean?"

"I don't know, Chief. There's never been an algorithm detection on my watch that Lieutenant Goldman or Ensign Harbaugh didn't handle."

"Okay, when you don't have experience to rely on, you fall back on theory. Think about how the system works. How does the algorithm derive bearing information? Under what conditions would it not be able to make that kind of computation?" The chief's area of expertise was mainly in repairing, maintaining, and calibrating the sensor systems, not in interpreting the readings, but he hadn't had his fingers stuffed in his ears for the twenty-two years he had been in the Sensors back room of eight different ships.

"An initial detection is of the distortion only. Bearings are derived from phase shifts in our own field over time. There are distinctive patterns associated with different bearing changes, and the computer uses those changes to do a target motion analysis, first to derive a bearing and then to derive a range."

"Right. Now, when would that system not give any useful information?"

"Oh, I get it—there has to be a bearing change for there to be a bearing detection."

"Good. Now think back on your basic tactical geometry. What are the three conditions under which a moving ship will observe no bearing change on a contact?"

"One, the contact is dead ahead. Two, the contact is dead astern. Three, the contact is on a congruent course with your ship: identical course, identical speed."

"Exactly. Now, we need to make a call: notify our officer in CIC what we've detected, and provide him with a recommendation. You tell me, Spacer Greenlee, what exactly have we detected?"

"We have a local compression algorithm detection of a superluminal target under compression drive, no bearing change, indeterminate distance."

"Right. What's the recommendation we make?"

"Sorry, Chief, I don't know."

"Anyone else know? We're not talking *n*-space topological mechanics here, people. You're the guys who can read the emission lines in a drive spectrum—it's just a bunch of decorator toothpicks to me. You should be able to figure this out based on the simple geometry of the thing."

An ordinary spacer third class raised his hand.

"We don't raise our hands in here, Onizuka. Just speak up."

"Just speaking up" wasn't the easiest thing in the worlds for Onizuka, but he cleared his throat and spat it out. "Resolve the ambiguity, sir."

Klesh kept himself from smiling and nodding. "How do we do that?"

"Pick a new course, ninety degrees from our current one on any axis. No matter whether the target is ahead, astern, or on a congruent course, unless he can match our course change immediately, even if by chance we head directly toward him, there will be an immediate bearing change."

"Bull's-eye. Now, Greenlee, you watch your console closely because CIC is going to want to know pretty damn quick what happens when we change course, if that's what they decide to do back there. Okay, I suppose I'm supposed to make the notification."

The chief went back to his console, pulled up the display at which Greenlee was looking, referred it to the Sensors Station in CIC, and then hit a button in a row of three, each of which was over a colored light: one red, one amber, one green. The one he pressed was over the amber.

On the CIC Sensors console at which Ensign Hobbs had the watch at this moment, the SSR STATUS light went from green, indicating all is well, to amber, indicating that the sensors officer needed to do two things. First, he should look at the SSR ATTN display, which always showed what the back room thought the

CIC officer needed to be looking at—at the moment, the LCDA detection screen and some related graphs and information.

Second, the man in CIC should communicate with his back room. There were lots of ways to do that, but when the amber light went on, the usual method was by voice link. It was up to the man in CIC to initiate the communication, because when the light went on, he could easily have been involved in a discussion with the captain or another CIC officer that the back room would not want to interrupt.

Hobbs opened the link and spoke quietly into his headset. "SSR Sensors, CIC Sensors." State who you are calling, then identify yourself. Otherwise, if there were some kind of glitch somewhere or you punched up the wrong channel, you might wind up trying to discuss a sensor contact with the Breads, Rolls, and Biscuits Chef.

"SSR Sensors, Klesh here."

"What's up, Klesh?"

"We show a local compression algorithm detection of a superluminal target under compression drive, no bearing change, indeterminate distance. Recommending course change, delta niner-zero degrees on any axis, to resolve ambiguity."

"Understood. Why don't you go ahead and monitor the main CIC voice pickup so you hear what we're doing. If we change course, you'll want to watch that detector closely. We'll want to localize him Alfa Sierra Alfa Papa. We don't want to run into the guy."

"Affirmative. We'll keep an eye out for you."

"Thanks. CIC out."

Hobbs then examined the SSR ATTN display, spent a few seconds scanning the raw data, ran a few cross checks and decided that the call checked out. A good CIC officer wasn't just a parrot for the calls made by his back room. He used his independent judgment and experience to verify the call before he announced it in CIC because, according to the old saying, "Once you say it, you own it." It would be his responsibility. "Blaming the back room" was not only a cardinal sin and a good way to lose the loyalty of the people whose loyalty you need most, it was also something that skippers frequently criticized in FITREPS.

"Officer of the Deck," he said.

In the middle of the night, with the ship on compression drive, deep in interstellar space and light years from any star system, neither the skipper nor the XO was in CIC. The ship's nerve center was instead presided over by the "Officer of the Deck," a duty that rotated among all the ship's officers save the CO, XO, the chief engineer, the chief medical officer, and the Marine detachment commander (the first three being too busy and the last two lacking the necessary training and experience to con a warship).

For the duration of this watch, the Officer of the Deck was Ensign Levy. As it happened, this was Levy's first time performing that duty. Accordingly, when Hobbs asked for his attention, Mr. Levy had exactly forty-one minutes and nineteen seconds of experience in the Big Chair.

"Yes, Mr. Hobbs."

"We have a local compression algorithm detection of a superluminal target under compression drive, no bearing change, indeterminate range. I recommend a ninety-degree course change, any axis, to resolve the ambiguity."

"Very well. Intel, have we been notified of any possible superluminal friendlies within a three–light year radius?"

Intel was supposed to know what the good guys were doing as well as the bad. In fact, it would be best if Intel knew everything about everyone. No one was holding his breath.

"Negative, sir. This is supposed to be an empty subsector except for us," said Petty Officer Second Rhinelander, who was standing watch at that post tonight.

Crap. The captain had left orders to maintain the current course and speed. But he hadn't anticipated running into a possible enemy contact. Fortunately, the book covered this one.

"Maneuvering, reduce speed to 800 c. Alter course, negative z, niner-zero degrees. Make it a sharp delta, but don't strain anything."

Chief Lugatsch at Maneuvering acknowledged the order and then gave the command to his man on Drives to reduce speed and to his man on Pitch to turn the ship sharply "downward" 90 degrees.

Now for the fun part. He selected a voicecom channel and pushed the comm button. A few seconds later a voice emerged from the comm panel. "Skipper." Somehow, the captain managed in that one word to convey the additional meaning, "I'm listening, but it had better be good."

"Skipper, this is Levy in CIC. We picked up a superluminal target, no bearing change, with the local compression algorithm. Pending further orders from you, I reduced speed to eight hundred c and ordered a negative z of ninety degrees. We're on the new course now and should have more from Sensors in a few minutes. Orders, sir?"

"Well done, Levy. Steady as she goes. I'm on my way. Skipper out."

Mr. Levy was curious. He noted the time on the Chrono. It took the skipper exactly one minute and forty-seven seconds between saying, "Skipper out" and when he cycled through the CIC security door. As soon as the skipper entered, Levy stood, vacating the Big Chair and moving to the left to stand in the space between the CO's and the Commodore's Stations. When Max reached the CO's station and sat down, he said, "I have CIC."

"You have CIC," Levy repeated. He turned in the direction of the nearest CIC omnisound pickup and announced, "Computer, log that the Officer of the Deck transferred CIC Con to the CO at zero hours, forty-six minutes."

"CIC Con transfer to commanding officer logged at zero hours, forty-six minutes," announced the computer, its voice sounding perversely like a cross between an inhuman mechanism and a nymphomaniac sex kitten. The regulations were clear: only one man was in charge in CIC at any given time, and there was never, ever the slightest doubt as to who that was. Every change was announced and the time logged. After all, the joke went, if anything happened to the ship, and the man who had the con survived, he would be shot. And the Navy wanted to be sure to shoot the right man.

"Status."

"Sir, course is zero-four-three mark two-five-eight, speed 800 c," Levy reported. "Still awaiting report from Sensors on data acquired from course change. Ship is at Condition Blue. All systems nominal."

Condition Blue was the second lowest readiness state. The lowest was Green. Max never set Condition Green unless the ship was in a well-guarded rear area, preferably in the vicinity of at least a carrier and a couple of battleships, and even then only if he really trusted the captains of the carrier and the battleships. When you command a warship, the question is never whether you are being paranoid, but whether you are being paranoid enough.

"Very well." Now, Max was in a quandary. Because of his orders regarding the Sweet Seventeen, every department in the ship other than CIC was working without the benefit of its best men. Not only that, under the watch rotation system, Second Watch on Day Two of the cycle was stood by the White Watch, the weakest of the three. Max could solve both problems by going to general quarters, which would bring the Sweet Seventeen out of hibernation and would put everyone at battle stations, meaning that every position would be stood by its best man, usually with the second best right at his elbow.

But that would defeat the whole purpose of the exercise. These men, even the least skilled of them, would have to be brought up to a standard of reasonable proficiency. They would have to start walking without crutches.

They would have to start walking right now.

Levy started to move toward his accustomed post at Intel to relieve Rhinelander.

"And where do you think you are going, Mr. Levy?"

"Um, the Intel Station, Captain."

"*Mais, non*. I'm not letting you off the hook that easily, young man. You're the Officer of the Deck, which means for the duration of this watch you are a command level officer for this vessel. Unless and until I summon Mr. DeCosta to CIC, you are my acting XO. Now, take your station, mister."

"Aye, sir." Levy stepped over to the XO's station, sat down, and fired up the console, which had been left on STANDBY, his hands moving deftly over the controls. Apparently, Mr. Levy had spent some time on the Command console simulator preparing for his big night in the Big Chair. Good man.

Max cast a glance over at Hobbs at Sensors. He was deep in a discussion with his back room, rapidly pulling up graphs that looked like various computer-generated hypotheses of the target's motion and the compression readings that would result, trying to find a fit. This was typically done by the computer without much human intervention.

If Mr. Kasparov were sitting in that chair and Mr. Harbaugh running the back room, Max wouldn't even think of intervening, but with Kasparov off watch and Harbaugh sequestered with the Sweet Seventeen, anything could happen. Max should have heard some sort of call from Sensors by now—at least a bearing to the target and a recommendation of what to do to localize it. He looked over at Hobbs again. Nothing.

So, Max did something he had not done since he assumed command of the *Cumberland*. He eavesdropped. The CO's station had the capability of monitoring every data and voice channel on the ship. Max's predecessor apparently spent most of his time doing just that, either from the CO's station or from the workstation in his day cabin, and had configured both consoles to do it easily and efficiently. Max hated micromanagement, but he had a feeling that that his sensors guys might be stuck on something.

He pulled up the data channels that the Sensors back room was sharing with Hobbs. He could see that they were digging into the raw data rather than looking at what the computer was doing with it. The raw data, and even the partially processed raw data, were too complex and too full of random variations for human beings to interpret. It took lots of computer processing to tease out the patterns. This made no sense. Then he looked at what the computer was generating and saw why the Sensors people were having trouble.

The computer was putting out nonsense. Pure garbage. One minute, it was hypothesizing that the target was impossibly wide—272.53 kilometers wide, the size of a not inconsiderable moon—and the next postulating that it was following a zigzag course at unheard-of velocities, making course changes that would tear any ship into ragged shreds, with the points of the zigs on one side and of the zags on the other forming two parallel lines 272.53 kilometers apart that tracked the *Cumberland*'s former course. This was crap. The computer has gotten confused.

No. That's wrong. Computers don't "get confused." *People confuse them*. The oldest adage of computer use, probably articulated about twelve minutes and nineteen seconds after the first computer was turned on, is: GIGO—garbage in, garbage out. *Okay. Find the garbage.*

He pulled up some diagnostic screens. The sensors that read the compressed space–normal space boundary tested as nominal. But that data went lots of places before hitting the computer. He quickly ran the signal path and the intermediate processors—no loss in signal strength from one end to the other on the signal path, and the processors all passed a basic diagnostic check. He was missing something.

The computer's conclusions were derived from what? There were the data from the sensors. That had to be good. There was the algorithm that processed the data. That had been checked by NAVCOMPSYSCOM half a million times under every conceivable data state. That had to be good as well. That left the comparatively trivial few bits of data and limiting assumptions that sometimes got input by the operator. That had to be it. But what did the operator input? It had been four years since Max had worked in Sensors, and this version of the system was newer than that. He didn't know.

Time to 'fess up. "Hobbs. I could see you were having problems, so I was looking over your shoulder. Trying to help out." He shrugged slightly, to acknowledge that he was admitting a kind of transgression, if even a minor one. Just because the skipper was the closest thing to God on his ship didn't mean he should be high-handed. Hobbs nodded quickly, as if to admit that he was a bit over his head and was glad to have the help.

"Look, I see what you guys are doing, but you're on the wrong track. You're not going to interpret this contact by looking at the data yourselves. We've got to figure out what the issue is in the system, so it will give us meaningful output. Maybe it's something wrong with an operator input. The operating system has changed since I was last at that console. What gets supplied by the operator?"

Max read the blank look on the man's face before he could work up the courage to say that he didn't know. Max saved him the trouble. At least he knew that the man would never even dream of bullshitting him.

"Okay. You can't know everything, Hobbs." Max punched himself into the circuit to the Sensors back room. "This is the skipper. Who's on the compression detector?"

"Greenlee here, sir."

"Greenlee? Oh, right. You're the only one of my three James Smiths who's not James Edwin Smith—you're from Greenlee something or other. Okay, Mr. Greenlee, we've got to figure this thing out before this target gets out from under us. What are the operator inputs on this thing? That's got to be where the problem lies."

"Sir, I can't see where," Greenlee said. "There's not much to input. The system mainly relies on the data from the sensors. I input the calibration values from the last diagnostic. I triple checked those. Our speed gets read in automatically. I checked it anyway. It was 1960 c; now it's 800 c. For some reason, it makes me manually input the compression field gradient. I checked that twice and had Chief Klesh verify it. It's right.

"This isn't like the old Mark XXIV system, where you had to supply the number of contacts. The system solves by iterative calculation and finds a number of contacts that fit the data. The operator inputs are really too easy to screw up, sir, even by someone as green as me."

"I just ran a few system checks and everything checked out," Max said. "You guys did too, right?" Both Greenlee and Klesh said they did. "Is this system capable of generating its own visual plot of the contact in addition to feeding the plotted coordinates to Tactical?"

"Yes, sir," said Greenlee. "We don't use the routine much, though. The Tactical display has a lot more capabilities."

"I understand. Pull it up anyway. It might give us a better idea of what the system is doing and why the interpretation algorithm is so confused."

Greenlee keyed in a few commands and the main 3D plotting display in the back room and the secondary tactical display in CIC went dark. After a few seconds, they started to display the new data. First came the plotting grid, faint blue lines dividing the cube into hundreds of smaller cubes. Then came the blue dot in the center of the plot, representing the *Cumberland*. Finally, the system projected a fuzzy green dot representing the contact.

"Mr. Greenlee, why is the system projecting the target as being indistinct or fuzzy?" asked Max.

"Sir, the system's projection is a probability determination," Greenlee answered. "The target is somewhere in that area, with the area of highest probability in the darkest green and fading out as the probability decreases near the edges of the area."

"Very good. Now, let's see it at larger scale. Don't worry about keeping the *Cumberland* in the projection. The folks in Navigation have a general idea where we are." That got a few chuckles. Even though the ship was travelling at high multiples of lightspeed through the vastness of interstellar space, the "folks in Navigation" prided themselves in knowing the *Cumberland*'s location within a few meters.

The scale changed and now the target projection occupied a blurry sphere about two centimeters in diameter. Klesh glanced at the display without much interest and then turned back quickly. He stood and walked over to the display. Max in CIC was looking at it intently as well.

"That's odd," said Klesh.

"It sure is," said Max.

"It's not supposed to be that indistinct," observed Greenlee.

"Wait a minute," said Max excitedly, "that projection's not a sphere. It's elongated—along the *x* axis. It's an ellipsoid. No target projection is supposed to be an ellipsoid. Unless..."

"But sir," Greenlee said, "the computer is trying to solve for one target, two targets, and for more than two, but still can't get a valid solution."

Suddenly, an idea hit Max. *Could it be that simple?* "Gentlemen, when we ran our tests on the data transmission path, did you do what I did and test only for signal strength?" Max asked.

They both said they had. It was, after all, the standard procedure.

"How about if we test for signal *resolution*?" said Max. "I know that there isn't a common fault that affects the res, but what if we're getting garbage out of the computer because the data for two targets is getting blurred together into the data for one, but the computer is too smart to assume that one superluminal spacecraft is more than a hundred kilometers wide or is zigzagging back and forth across that distance on a microsecond time scale? Initiate a high-resolution multitarget test signal right where the signal comes into the ship from the sensor array, and read it at every signal node."

Greenlee looked at Klesh anxiously. The older noncom sat down beside the young man and smiled. "Not something we do every day. Let me show you how." The test took about a minute and a half of rapid keystrokes to set up. "All right. Let's let 'er rip."

A green box labeled INITIATE TEST was flashing on the display. Klesh touched it decisively. A few seconds later, he chuckled. "Lookee here what I found." His display was showing a schematic of the sensor signal path from its beginning in the sensor array to its end in the main sensor data processer. One spot was blinking orange.

"It's the signal conditioning processor," he said, his voice conveying both relief and irritation. "It takes the initial data stream from the array, amplifies it to something strong enough to be sent through the ship's systems without being corrupted, strips out the noise and artifacts, and then sends it down the line. It's got some minor fault that's causing it to blur or degrade the signal. That box is deeply buried in the bowels of the ship, though. It takes a few hours to swap out."

"I don't have a few hours, Chief. I need reliable contact data right now." Max was the captain. Making impossible demands went with the job.

"Well . . ." The chief pondered the problem. "Skipper, the unit has an auxiliary setting where it runs on a backup processor—it's not as sensitive as the main, but we've got a strong contact here, so it should read it just fine. Normally, it switches over only when the main fails, but I think there's a way to send a manual command that will make the box disregard the main and run on the auxiliary until we can get it swapped out."

A broad smile spread over Max's face. "Try SCE to AUX."

Klesh and Greenlee looked at each other blankly. "Um, sir, that's not a valid command."

"It used to be, gentlemen. This just reminded me of something from Jurassic Space. Just keep doing what you're doing, Chief."

"I think I've got it, Skipper. I just sent what should be a valid command to switch to the auxiliary processor. Let's give the system a few seconds with a cleaner data stream."

Max turned his attention from the 3D display back to the Sensors console's SSR ATTN data channel that he had earlier pulled up for display on his own console. In a few seconds, the nonsensical conclusions reached by the computer resolved into usable data. Yep. Two contacts. Solid bearings, ranges, speeds.

"Contact!" said Hobbs, nearly shouting. Max turned to him sharply and made a downward patting motion with his right hand to signal him to lower his voice. Hobbs got the point, rattling off his designation of the contacts as Uniform One and Uniform Two, their speeds, bearings, and ranges, in something approaching a normal tone of voice.

"Maneuvering, get us back on our former course and speed. Match our former course track exactly and put us at the point in space where we would be if we had not changed course. As fast as possible without compromising stealth." Lugatsch acknowledged the order.

"Hobbs, keep a close eye on those two contacts. Don't blink. Don't even fantasize about blinking. If they so much as swerve to run over a rattlesnake, I want to know. Understood?"

"Understood." Max could hear the compression drive increasing the ship's speed and the cooling system for the fusion reactor working harder as the power plant increased its output to supply the staggering amount of energy needed to trick the space–time continuum into propelling the ship at more than two thousand times the speed of light. About ten minutes later, he heard the notes of both power plant and cooling plant drop as the speed dropped to 1960 c. Lugatsch announced that the ship was back on its former track at its former speed, where it would have been had nothing happened.

Max asked the mid stationed in CIC to assist the captain to get him some coffee, pointed at the pot, and raised an inquiring eyebrow at Levy, who nodded. Getting coffee was part of the job description, and the boy who happened to have that duty for this watch—a nine-year-old named Gilbertson, one of the second or third youngest class of squeakers—almost skipped over to the coffeepot to fetch for both officers. *Oh, to have that kind of energy at about one in the morning.*

While he was doing that, Max punched in the voice loop for the Sensors back room. The USS *Cumberland* College of Advanced Space Warfare and Keeping Your Ass from Being Nuked by Some Rat-Faced Krag Bastard was now, once again, in session.

"Gentlemen, this is the skipper. I want to thank you for your hard work just now. I know that because of the new training schedule, you are short a few people who might have made things run a little smoother, and I understand that. I'm on your loop to remind you that just because you are constantly hearing that Mr. Krag doesn't do very well at thinking outside the box is no excuse to keep *your* thinking inside the box.

"Why? Because we're talking two different boxes, people. Don't make limiting assumptions. Always know what your assumptions are and if, when you apply them, you turn up nonsense, go back to them and try a different set. Never assume that your equipment is working properly until you have tested for and eliminated every conceivable malfunction. Keep trying until you get something that explains the data. Men, never forget, the job of the Sensors section is to find truthful interpretations that fit the sensor data, not to find data that fit your interpretations. It's likely to be an exciting watch, folks, so stay alert. Keep your eyes peeled and your minds open. Skipper out."

The coffee arrived. Both men took a few sips.

School wasn't over. He had dismissed the big lecture class of freshmen and sophomores. Now for the senior seminar. "Well, Mr. Levy, a good weapons officer doesn't have his head stuck in the Fire Control console. He needs to know something about what is going on with the targets he's shooting at. So what's going on here?" Seeing a bit of a blank look, Max prompted, "Start with the basics and work up from there."

Max could almost hear him gulp. “Well, sir, there are two targets, Uniform One and Uniform Two, currently unidentified. Uniform One is right on our six, matching our velocity at 1960 c at a range of 1.116 AU. Uniform Two is 272 kills off his port beam. I don’t think they know we’ve spotted them back there.”

“Why do you think that?”

“We just got an upgrade to our local compression detection system. That gave us about a 40 percent increase in its range. As far as we can tell, the Krag are still at their old level of technology. There’s no way they just blundered into us way out here in interstellar space dozens of light years from the FEBA. The only theory that makes sense is that they somehow knew we were coming through, lay in wait along our flight path, picked us up, and then fell in behind us, beyond what they thought was our detection radius. When we did our localization maneuver, we never entered their detection radius, so they should be ignorant of what we did. They aren’t really interested in tracking us. They’re acting like they know where we’re going. They just want to get there right behind us.”

“Exactly what I had concluded. All right. Now, who are they?”

“Well, sir, we’ve got to presume they’re Krag.”

“Can we do more than that? Do we have any evidence of who they are?”

“No, sir. At this range and at superluminal velocities, all we can do is to detect bearing, range, and speed. We don’t have any of the phenomenologies that give us an identification.”

“Don’t we? What’s the range to Uniform One again?”

“One-point-one-one-six AU.”

“Anything about that number sound familiar to you?”

“Come to think of it, it does ring a bell, but I can’t remember what it is.”

"That's because the contexts are too different for your brain to make the connection easily. Fortunately, you've got a memory aid." He pointed at the keyboard.

"Riiiiight. Sir." Levy typed in a query, asking the computer to find other distances, ranges, and sizes that were 1.116 AU. There were fourteen matches. He started down the list: the mean diameter of the Hoffman Nebula, the periastron of a periodic comet in the Alphacen system, the length of the first experimental compression drive flight undertaken by the Pfelung, and... "That's the mean distance of the Krag homeworld from their sun. It's basically their AU."

"You got it. That's a nice comfy distance for them. When they want to stand off a safe distance from something, that's a distance they often pick. Not always, not even most of the time, but often enough that when you see something at that range you know it's a Krag ship. In some ways, they're a lot like us. Haven't you heard skippers say, 'Maneuvering, put us one AU behind Hotel Three'—things like that?"

"Yes, sir."

"And there's a clincher. What's the range between the two ships?"

"It's 272—no, 273 kills."

"No. The exact distance. Take it to two decimal points. I'm betting that it's exactly 272.53 kills."

Levy input the query. "That's right, sir. How did you know?"

"The fundamental Krag unit of linear measurement is .27253 meters. I think it was the length of the first Hegemon's foot, or something like that. Lots of the things they do come out to a nice round power of ten of that distance. Like the maximum range of their Foxhound missile, which is...?"

"It's 27,253 kills. I get it."

"Again, they're a lot like us that way. Can't you just hear the big cheese back there telling the smaller cheese, 'Position yourself a thousand Kragometers,' or whatever they call their unit, 'off my port beam'? That's just the sort of thing we'd do. That's why I often give orders to stand off at odd ranges."

"So, sir, that pretty much makes them Krag."

"I wouldn't bet against it, Levy. Not even if I were betting with your money. Now, let's get a little speculative. What does that mean for us?"

"Well, Skipper, I suppose it would have to mean that the Krag had in their possession sufficient information for an intercept."

"Which is?"

"It's what you need to determine a velocity vector in time and space. Departure point, departure time, either course or destination, and speed."

"Right, Levy. Now, if they had our departure point and time, course or destination, and speed, what does that imply?"

"There has to be some sort of leak, or spy, or Krag ability to intercept and decrypt at least certain critical tactical communications, or they somehow observed our departure."

"Observation wouldn't have helped them. You weren't on watch, so you wouldn't know this. I departed the system nearly 90 degrees off the lubber line on two axes and ran at 1580 c for an hour and a half, then turned toward the rendezvous point and increased speed to 1960 c. So anyone taking a read on our departure or tracking us for the first ninety minutes would have been completely misled as to direction and velocity. So, we're back to the first set of possibilities. How do we narrow that down? Any ideas?"

"Sir, I'm not much on Intel. Too much guessing. I'm better at concrete stuff, like what my warhead is going to do against a Krag deflector."

"Bullshit, Levy. I've been a weapons officer and I've worked in Intel and I can tell you that the two have more in common than you suppose. A great deal of Intel is just as precise and concrete and logical as the data you deal with as a weapons officer. There's lots of hard data involved in both. It's something you need to get a handle on. To be a well-rounded officer, you've got to understand at least the fundamentals of every one of the warship combat disciplines: Tactical, Weapons, Sensors, Intel, Countermeasures, and Stealth. And it doesn't hurt to know a thing or two about Logistics, Engineering, Damage Control, Environmental Systems, and Personnel, either. If you want to rise to command rank, you've got to be a well-rounded officer."

The young man raised an inquiring eyebrow, as if to ask if he had a chance at command rank. Max nodded and shrugged at the same time, as if to say, "You have the potential, as far as I can tell, but whether you make it is going to be up to you." Just because a lot of important things went *unsaid* between Navy men did not mean that those important things went *uncommunicated.*

"Okay," Max continued. "How do we narrow down where the Krag are getting their information? I'm not asking you to recite an Intel maxim. I'm asking you to go at it logically. You're a logical man. You can figure it out."

"Well...where I would want to start is to know the source of their information. We would get a good start on that by identifying which communication or report or filing or data entry, exactly, they got their paws on."

"Bull's-eye. Okay then, where would the Krag get the data points they need to intercept us in the vastness of space? Work it out. Use elimination if you have to."

"Well, it's not our orders because the admiral didn't give us a specific c multiple or even dictate that we use compression drive instead of jumping. It doesn't have our time of departure or our exact starting point in the Rashid system. Without those, you'd have a hard time finding us with twenty ships, much less two. And then, your deceptive departure course would put us on a slightly different track.

"No signals have left this ship since we left for us to be tracked with. So, that leaves . . . our cruise plan? Did the cruise plan include your deceptive maneuver?"

"It did."

"That has to be it, then. The Krag got their paws on our cruise plan."

Max smiled. "See, Mr. Levy, you may be able to get a handle on Intel after all. That makes a pretty little puzzle for Intel, doesn't it? How did they get it? Send a message to the XO that, on my order, I want you and Bhattacharyya to have your administrative periods today at the same time. You and he are going to trace what happens to a cruise plan when it gets filed, and come up with your best hypothesis about how the Krag got it.

"Look at it from their perspective. If you wanted to get a cruise plan, how would you go about doing it? Route your report—nothing fancy, two pages or so—to me. I'll put my spin on it and send it to Admiral Hornmeyer's N-2 section—see what the Intel/Security boys have to say when they learn they've got a major leak somewhere. Meanwhile, I'll get off a signal directly to the admiral right away to let him know there's a leak and that any compartmentalization he was counting on for this mission has been blown."

"But sir, with all due respect, the leak isn't the biggest problem we've got."

"Don't worry, Ensign, I haven't forgotten about our friends back there with the whiskers and tails. I just haven't figured out what to do about them yet."

■

"Hey! Cho!" Recruit Spacer Second Class Antonio "Doozie" Balduzzi yelled down 37.9 meters of access crawlway to his partner, Able Spacer Third Class Cho Jintao. Fortunately, he had a powerful set of lungs to carry his voice over the distance, particularly with the profusion of humming, buzzing, chirping, clicking, whizzing, whumping, and even, occasionally, banging equipment between the two men in the confined space.

"Yeah, what?" Cho's powers of projection, though not quite on par with Balduzzi's, were still quite impressive. Neither man had any difficulty hearing the other. It never occurred to either to use their percoms to open a voice channel.

"This one's running at 73 percent, and the one before was running at 77."

"Damn, Doozie, I'm seeing the same thing. The last one I checked was at seventy-five, and the one before that at seventy-two." Doozie crawled aft to the gravity generator regulator that controlled the gravity generators the two men had just checked. Cho was running a diagnostic routine on the mechanism and was getting nothing but green lights.

"I bet every one in this series is doing something similar."

"I've got the same feeling, but I'll be a Pfelung's grandmother if I can tell you why," said Cho. "I've just run two diagnostics on the regulator. It checks out across the board. The machine is clean and green."

"What do you do in this situation?" Because he fell below the ship's proficiency average in his specialty, Doozie had never been sent to work on an equipment problem that wasn't instantly diagnosed by the computer or that turned out to be a straightforward fix involving swapping out a board or a module.

"Well, babe, what I normally do in this situation is I call Petty Officer Liebergot. Him or Aaron. They're the "hottie Scottys" on all the electrical/environmental subsystems, and the gravity generators are right down Liebergot's alley, but they're both off limits today because of the skipper's new training thing."

"Is there anyone else we can call?"

"At 02:27? Any man not on the White Watch is in his rack inspecting his eyelids for photon leaks. So, my friend, you and I are the White Watch experts on this system. For better or worse, it's you and me, babe." Doozie was starting to get annoyed at Cho's habit of calling him "babe," but he did his best to overlook it.

"Can we leave it to the next watch? You and I and everybody else know that the Blue Watch has got a lot more on the ball than we do in White. I'm sure there's someone in that bunch that can straighten this out."

"Invalid input, babe. Two reasons. One, the work order came from Lieutenant Brown himself and he marked it 'Resolve this Watch,' which means it gets done before end of watch or we die trying. We don't get to hand it off to someone else. And two, there's a real safety issue. Think about it, Dooze: a man steps from one G nominal through a gradient that's only a millimeter or two wide into a zone that's point seven three Gs, and then skips down the corridor literally light on his feet for about forty meters and then hits one G again without warning. You think he might have a chance of tripping, especially if he's carrying something?

"And not just any schmo either, but a shipmate. You want some guy you bunk or eat chow with laid up with a broken ankle or a concussion because you passed the buck on a work order? For me that's at least a forty, light year guilt trip and I'm not up for it. You?"

"Nope. Don't want to make that trip. I don't even want the T-shirt. I've had enough of that to last me at least till the end of this war and probably well into the next." He sighed heavily. "Well, Cho, what do we do then?"

"You got your padcomp on you, Dooze?"

"You think I'm crazy? Of course, I do. It's a regulation, isn't it? Besides, I don't want Lieutenant Brown to catch me without it after the way he skinned 'Wacky' Waechter the other day."

"I heard about that. Everyone said it was an ass chewing of truly legendary magnitude, babe. Well, you've got yours and I've got mine. Let's put 'em to use. How about we sit right here, I hit the repair and maintenance database, and you hit the maintenance board archives and help boards. Someone, somewhere, has either had this problem before or thought it might come up. I bet if we follow in their footsteps, we can figure this out, babe, you and me."

"Cho, that sounds like a plan."

At the stroke of 09:00, about six hours after Cho and Doozie started to get the upper hand in their epic struggle with the gravity generators, the patients and staff in the Casualty Station witnessed an event unprecedented in the history of the *Cumberland*. First, Zamora, Ulmer, and four other enormous Marines almost their equal in size marched into the compartment in their emerald-green dress uniforms, complete with drawn ceremonial sabers in their right hands and resting on their right shoulders, followed by Major Kraft, also in his dress greens and also carrying his saber.

Kraft led the detail along the equipment lockers that lined the left side of the compartment as viewed from the patient beds. "Company, HALT," Kraft ordered, his parade-ground voice dialed back eight or nine notches in deference to the presence of wounded. The Marines all halted on the same step, their brilliantly shining boots snapping to the deck in unison with a satisfying stomp.

"Left HACE!"

They pivoted like separate parts of a single machine to face the center of the room.

"Atten-HUT!"

Boot heels snapped together. The Marines were now rigidly erect and perfectly immobile, more like robots awaiting orders than human beings.

As though cued by the snap of those heels, Captain Robichaux led the senior officers, DeCosta, Brown, Dr. Sahin, Kasparov, and Sauvé, into the compartment. Wearing their dress whites and carrying their dress sabers, they lined up across from the Marines, also at attention. The only one with his blade sheathed was Max.

He scanned the room, seeing first the five men from Auxiliary Fire Control in patient beds to his left. They were being treated for internal bleeding and other injuries caused by the shock wave that had breached the hull in that compartment, as well as for exposure to near vacuum and cold before Midshipman Park had sealed the hull breach. Five more men were in other beds, all being treated for various wounds, none serious, sustained at the Battle of Rashid V B. They would all be returning to duty within the week. Four more were resting out of sight nearby with sheets pulled over their faces. Their duties were done.

Near an empty patient bed was Midshipman Park, who had on some pretext just been helped into a wheelchair by a nurse. Park was wearing the blue standard-issue Navy pajamas that, but for the thinness of the fabric and the presence of slippers rather than boots on his feet, would look very much like a uniform. Park had some ugly bruises and the whites of his eyes were spidered with burst blood vessels from exposure to near vacuum. Cotton protruded from one ear canal to protect a ruptured eardrum. Ointment covered his nose and ears where he had been frostbitten by the cold of space. He looked as though he had been roughly handled. But he sat up straight in the wheelchair and watched the ceremony taking place in front of him with enthusiasm and wonder. Park Dong-Soo was bloody but unbowed.

Max looked at the small boy, who practically vanished in the wheelchair made for a fully grown man five or six times his bulk, and barely managed to repress a smile. With all the gravity he could summon, he announced, "Midshipman Park, front and center." Nurse Church wheeled Park to the center of the space between the line of Navy men and the line of Marines as Max marched to stand just in front of the same spot. Park's face wore a look of bewilderment.

Max continued in his "official" voice. "As you all know, almost every aspect of what we do in the Navy is governed by a great many rules and regulations. The same is true for the awarding of medals and citations. Most citations can be awarded only on the authority of flag-rank officers, Norfolk, or the Commissioners of the Admiralty, and only to personnel who have attained at least the rank of able spacer. There are, however, a very few awards that can be given on the authority of a warship commander to individuals under his command, irrespective of rank.

"Because the temptation to give awards to men with whom one serves closely is very great, most warship commanders make such awards very sparingly and only for conduct of the most conspicuously outstanding nature. It is my honor, and my pleasure, to recognize such conduct today." He reached into his tunic and produced a small box that he opened with gentle reverence.

"'For meritorious service and superlative achievement, performed at grave risk to his own life, exemplifying resourcefulness and courage in the highest tradition of the Service above and beyond the call of duty, Midshipman Third Class Park Dong-Soo is awarded the Navy and Marine Achievement Medal, Combat Grade.'"

Max extracted the medal: a twelve-pointed bronze star, embossed with the silhouette of a battleship from the First Interstellar War superimposed on a silver-rayed sun, hanging from a blue ribbon bearing seven tiny gold stars. A large gold-plated letter "V" was pinned to the ribbon, symbolizing that the award had been earned in combat.

Max bent down, pinned the medal to Park's chest, and came back to attention. The rather modest medal looked almost absurdly large on the boy's tiny torso. "Company. Sa-LUTE!" Max brought his right hand to his right eyebrow in a standard salute, while the rest of the company flashed their sabers to the salute position, hilts held in front of them just below their chins, blades held vertically in front of each man's right eye, cutting edge to the left, elbow tucked close to the body. The gleaming blades sent reflections of the bright Casualty Station lights chasing each other over the equipment lockers and banks of medical equipment.

A stunned Park returned the salute. Max snapped his hand down. The men with sabers whipped them down by their right sides, the twelve keen blades making a faint but distinct swish.

Max did a precise about face and marched out of the compartment. "Shoulder ARMS," ordered Kraft. Each man brought his saber back to his shoulder.

"First detail. Right HACE!"

The naval officers performed a reasonably good turn.

"Detail, MARCH."

They marched from the compartment.

"Second detail. Left HACE."

The Marines pivoted perfectly to face the hatch.

"Detail, MARCH."

They marched out, followed by Kraft, who closed the hatch behind him.

For ten seconds or so, the Casualty Station was silent except for the sounds of the ship itself and the quiet beeps of the monitoring equipment connected to some of the casualties.

"Here, let's get you back in bed, young man," said Nurse Church who had suddenly appeared at Park's side. "I think that's enough excitement for you this morning. In a few hours, when the captain's steward brings us the box, we'll put your medal away for you and have someone put it in your space chest where it will be nice and safe."

The boy quickly clapped his hands over the medal and shook his head vigorously, a determined smile on his face. He wasn't giving it up without a fight.

CHAPTER 9

06:06Z Hours, 21 March 2315

The senior officers group was gathered in Max's day cabin. Although these gatherings were not scheduled and did not occur at stated times on stated days, they were becoming a fixture in the ship's routine and in day-to-day management of the *Cumberland*'s affairs. Not only was having these five men—Max, DeCosta, Kraft, Brown, and Sahin—in the same room at the same time once every few days a good mechanism with which to make sure that the right hand knew what the left was doing, but Max was convinced that he owed a great deal of his effectiveness as a commander thus far to the advice and assistance of these men.

Admiral Hornmeyer had, to a large degree, made up for assigning Max to a problem ship with a troubled history and crew by giving him this truly exceptional command team. Max knew very well how lucky he was to be surrounded by officers of this level of ability. The more he thought about it, the more he expected every man in the room, including Dr. Sahin, to achieve very high rank someday. He was coming to count on them, as they were coming to trust him.

Max usually brought them together early in the day, saw that an inexhaustible river of coffee flowed into their mugs, and fed them all a hearty breakfast of their choice. It didn't exactly make them happy to be there, but it did tend to put them in a better frame of mind.

"Well, gentlemen," said Max when everyone had eaten and was sipping their coffee, "we've had the Sweet Seventeen out of the mix for six hours or so now. Any effect yet?"

"The hull hasn't come apart at the nanowelds, if that's what you mean," said Brown. "It's been too short a time to see much of an effect. There are, however, some signs that may be harbingers of good things to come. Two men who I thought were probably not up to the job managed to diagnose and repair subnominal output from a string of gravity generators on C deck. The malfunction was a pretty oddball one too. When I read the summary of the problem in their log I was surprised they managed to figure it out."

In response to DeCosta's questioning look, he explained, "A sensor emitter—a completely separate system—had a graviton leak that was interfering with one of the generators, which then amplified the spurious output, throwing the whole string out of calibration. There were three similar incidents, with results somewhat less surprising but equally felicitous, elsewhere in my department. In each case, crewmen who normally would be calling for assistance were rolling up their sleeves and solving the problem themselves. Of course, it's taking them from three to ten times as long to do the job as it would take one of our seventeen, but they *are* getting it done, and they're having to dig in and learn the systems better besides. Hits on the ship's engineering, maintenance, and repair database so far today are nearly double the average for those watches."

"Out. Stand. Ing. And here are two other things they're learning," said Max. "Number one: how to figure out how to solve problems on their own when they don't know the answer off the top of their heads. It's a process, you see. All of you know how to do it, but a lot of these men have yet to master it—how to dig for answers and put them together from bits and pieces and hints and guesses. That's one of the most important parts of knowing how to be a crewman of a Navy fighting ship, who can improvise in a pinch, adapt to new conditions, and overcome obstacles.

"And number two: confidence. Without confidence, all the competence in the world is useless because you don't think you are competent *enough*. You're not up to the challenge until you *believe* you are up to the challenge. These men need that. And I think they're about to find it." He took his napkin out of his lap, folded it, and placed it on the table with a gesture of finality. "Well, gentlemen, unless you have anything more we need to discuss, that's all I have."

"Captain?"

"Yes, Doctor."

"Aren't you forgetting something, sir?"

"Such as…?"

"Such as those two Krag warships about one astronomical unit behind us."

"What to do about our pink-eared friends is not our call. As of our receipt of Admiral Hornmeyer's order, we're not on detached service any more. We're attached to Frigate/Destroyer Group TD-2008, Gerard Duflot, Commander. I don't have discretion to engage targets of opportunity any more. Instead, regulations require that I communicate with Duflot and get instructions.

So, as soon as we get past this supernova remnant that's blocking the line of sight so I can get a direct comm signal through to Commander Duflot, that's exactly what I'm going to do."

07:02Z HOURS 21 MARCH 2315
URGENT: IMMEDIATE RESPONSE REQUESTED
TO: DUFLOT, GERARD, CMDR USN, CO FRIGDESGRU TD-2008
FROM: ROBICHAUX, MAXIME, LCDR USN, CO USS CUMBERLAND
RE: PROBABLE ENEMY TARGETS

1. THIS SHIP HAS MADE COMPRESSION PROXIMITY DETECTIONS OF TWO VESSELS, IDENTIFIED AS PROBABLE KRAG WARSHIPS, UNKNOWN TYPE, BASED ON SPECIES-SPECIFIC TACTICS EMPLOYED BY CONTACTS.

2. CONTACTS ARE TRAILING THIS SHIP MATCHING COURSE AND SPEED AT A RANGE OF 1.116 AU.

3. ETA THIS SHIP AT RENDEZVOUS COORDINATES 19:34Z HOURS 25 MARCH 2315.

4. RECOMMEND THAT WE ENTRAP, ENGAGE, AND DESTROY ENEMY VESSELS USING KUIPER HYPER DIAPER RUSE.

5. REQUEST ORDERS RE THESE VESSELS.

11:49Z HOURS 21 MARCH 2315
URGENT: FOR IMMEDIATE IMPLEMENTATION
TO: ROBICHAUX, MAXIME, LCDR USN, CO USS CUMBERLAND
FROM: DUFLOT, GERARD, CMDR USN, CO FRIGDESGRU TD-2008
RE: PROBABLE ENEMY TARGETS

1. RECEIPT OF YOUR COMMUNICATION 07:02Z HOURS THIS DATE ACKNOWLEDGED.

2. THIS COMMAND DOES NOT CONCUR IN PURPORTED IDENTIFICATION OF TARGETS AS KRAG WARSHIPS. REGULATIONS SPECIFICALLY PRECLUDE SUCH AN IDENTIFICATON BASED ON A SINGLE PHENOMENOLOGY.

3. ACCORDINGLY, KUIPER HYPER DIAPER RUSE INAPPROPRIATE IN THAT IT CALLS FOR ATTACK ON TARGETS BEFORE AMBUSH FORCE COULD POSIDENT THEM. ATTACK WITHOUT POSIDENT IS VIOLATION OF SPECIFIC ROE SET DOWN BY NORFOLK FOR THIS THEATER OF OPERATIONS.

4. YOU ARE ORDERED TO PROCEED AT BEST PRUDENT SPEED TO RENDEZVOUS COORDINATES. IF TARGETS FOLLOW YOU TO RENDEZVOUS AND IF THEY ARE POSIDENT AS HOSTILES, I WILL EVALUATE TACTICAL SITUATION AND GROUP UNDER MY COMMAND WILL EITHER ENGAGE USING CONVENTIONAL TACTICS OR WITHDRAW, DEPENDING UPON CORRELATION OF FORCES.

5. YOU ARE FURTHER ORDERED, ONCE YOU ARE WITHIN 80 AU OF RENDEZVOUS COORDINATES, TO NOTIFY ME ON CHANNEL 70609 AND TO MONITOR THAT CHANNEL FOR FURTHER INSTRUCTIONS.

6. GIVEN THE OBVIOUS DEFICIENCIES IN YOUR SUGGESTION, YOU ARE ADVISED THAT, IN THE UNLIKELY EVENT THAT THIS COMMAND DESIRES SUGGESTIONS FROM A SUBORDINATE COMMANDER, WE WILL REQUEST THEM EXPRESSLY. YOU SHOULD NOT EXPECT TO RECEIVE SUCH A REQUEST AT ANY TIME IN THE NEAR FUTURE.

14:18Z HOURS 21 MARCH 2315
URGENT: IMMEDIATE RESPONSE REQUESTED
TO: DUFLOT, GERARD, CMDR USN, CO
FRIGDESGRU TD-2008
FROM: ROBICHAUX, MAXIME, LCDR USN, CO
USS CUMBERLAND
RE: PROBABLE ENEMY TARGETS

1. MY ORDERS FROM ADMIRAL HORNMEYER SPECIFICALLY DIRECT ME TO ACQUAINT YOU WITH CONDITIONS IN THIS SECTOR. TO THAT END, WITH ALL DUE RESPECT, SIR, I AM CONSTRAINED TO POINT OUT THAT CONDITIONS IN THIS SECTOR ARE DIFFERENT FROM THOSE UNDER WHICH YOU ARE ACCUSTOMED TO OPERATE. WARSHIPS IN TASK FORCE TANGO DELTA ROUTINELY CLASSIFY VESSELS AS HOSTILE BASED ON A SINGLE PHENOMENOLOGY WHEN OTHER CIRCUMSTANCES STRONGLY INDICATE THAT THE CONTACT IS KRAG. SEE AFTER ACTION REPORTS ## 86407, 89114, 90437, AND 92225.

2. I AM FURTHER CONSTRAINED TO POINT OUT THAT THE OPERATIONAL PATTERNS OF THE TARGETS THAT WERE THE SUBJECT OF MY EARLIER SIGNAL THIS DATE ARE CONSISTENT WITH THE KRAG TACTIC OF FOLLOWING ONE SHIP TO A RENDEZVOUS, AVOIDING DETECTION BY STAYING IN THE LEAD SHIP'S COMPRESSION WAKE, THEN LURKING OUTSIDE OF SENSOR RANGE AND STALKING THE GROUP WHEN IT LEAVES THE RENDEZVOUS, AND ATTACKING IT WHEN CONDITIONS ARE MOST FAVORABLE TO THE ATTACKERS. SHIPS EMPLOYING THIS TACTIC WILL NOT BLUNDER BLINDLY INTO AN ENGAGEMENT AT THE RENDEZVOUS POINT BUT

WILL BIDE THEIR TIME AND ATTACK WHEN AND WHERE THE ODDS ARE MOST IN THEIR FAVOR. SEE, FOR EXAMPLE, AFTER ACTION REPORTS ## 65888, 67950, 99582, AND 100224.

3. TO FAIL TO TURN THE TABLES ON THESE VESSELS BY DICTATING THE CIRCUMSTANCES OF THE ENGAGEMENT IS TO CONCEDE TO THEM THE TACTICAL ADVANTAGES OF INITIATIVE AND ABILITY TO CONTROL THE TIME, PLACE, AND CONDITIONS OF BATTLE, AND, VERY LIKELY, ALSO CONCEDING TO THEM THE ADVANTAGE OF TACTICAL SURPRISE. SO MANY CONCESSIONS OF SUCH ENORMOUS TACTICAL MAGNITUDE COULD VERY WELL COST THIS GROUP AT LEAST ONE OF ITS SHIPS, IF NOT ALL.

4. ACCORDINGLY, I URGE IN THE STRONGEST POSSIBLE TERMS THAT WE CONTROL THE TIME, PLACE, AND CIRCUMSTANCES OF BATTLE BY HAVING THIS VESSEL LEAD ENEMY INTO TRAP SET BY TWO REMAINING VESSELS CONCEALED IN SYSTEM'S KUIPER BELT AS I SUGGESTED IN MY FIRST SIGNAL TO YOU THIS DATE, OR UNDER OTHER CIRCUMSTANCES DIRECTED BY YOU. ANYTHING WOULD BE BETTER THAN HAVING TO FEND OFF THESE SHIPS AS THEY STALK US AND ATTACK US AT THEIR LEISURE.

16:25Z HOURS 21 MARCH 2315
URGENT: FOR IMMEDIATE IMPLEMENTATION
TO: ROBICHAUX, MAXIME, LCDR USN, CO
USS CUMBERLAND

DUFLOT, GERARD, CMDR USN,
CO FRIGDESGRU TD-2008
RE: PROBABLE ENEMY TARGETS

1. RECEIPT OF YOUR COMMUNICATON OF 14:18Z HOURS THIS DATE IS ACKNOWLEDGED.

2. YOU ARE BOTH IMPERTINENT AND INSUBORDINATE, AS MY REPORT TO ADMIRAL HORNMEYER AT CONCLUSION OF THIS MISSION WILL REFLECT.

3. YOUR ORDERS ARE UNCHANGED. DO NOT WASTE YOUR TIME RENDERING FURTHER TACTICAL ADVICE TO THIS COMMAND. ADDITIONAL SUGGESTIONS OF THIS KIND ARE NOT WELCOME AND ARE HEREBY FORBIDDEN.

4. MY INFORMATION IS THAT YOU HAVE ENOUGH PROBLEMS JUST TRYING TO RUN A SINGLE, VERY SMALL DESTROYER WITHOUT GETTING IT OR TOO MANY OF YOUR CREW BLOWN TO BITS. CLEARLY, TAKING ON THE ADDED TASK OF DEVISING TACTICS FOR AN ENTIRE OPERATIONAL GROUP IS BEYOND YOUR ABILITIES. DEVOTE YOUR ATTENTION TO IMPOSING SOME REMOTE SEMBLANCE OF ORDER AND REGULARITY ON YOUR SHIP, WHICH IS SORELY IN NEED OF THE SAME, AND LEAVE TACTICAL PLANNING TO THOSE OF US WHO HAVE THE CAPACITY, SKILLS, AND TRAINING TO DO IT COMPETENTLY.

5. YOU ARE DIRECTED TO ACKNOWLEDGE RECEIPT OF THIS MESSAGE AND ADVISE BY IMMEDIATE RETURN SIGNAL YOUR INTENTION TO COMPLY WITH THE FOREGOING ORDERS.

18:11Z HOURS 21 MARCH 2315
TO: DUFLOT, GERARD, CMDR USN, CO FRIGDESGRU TD-2008
FROM: ROBICHAUX, MAXIME, LCDR USN, CO USS CUMBERLAND
RE: PROBABLE ENEMY TARGETS

1. RECEIPT OF YOUR COMMUNICATION 16:25Z HOURS THIS DATE IS HEREBY ACKNOWLEDGED.

2. THIS OFFICER AND ALL PERSONNEL UNDER THIS OFFICER'S AUTHORITY WILL COMPLY WITH NAVAL REGULATIONS REGARDING OBEDIENCE TO SUPERIOR OFFICERS AND OFFICERS PLACED OVER THEM BY ORDER IN OPERATIONAL COMMANDS. IN SHORT, THIS VESSEL AND I WILL FOLLOW YOUR ORDERS.

"I have already taken an extremely strong dislike for this Commander Duflot," Sahin said. "He is an unnecessarily sarcastic and condescending individual who has a compulsive need to exercise power over others. Further, he demonstrates a strong predilection to use the power that comes with his position as a means of demonstrating his personal superiority. He exalts himself by demeaning others. He is a bully in uniform. I should like very much to punch him in the nose." Sahin pointedly turned his back on the exchange of signals that he had just read from the monitor/display wall of Max's day cabin, his body language an emphatic rejection of Duflot's message.

"I've never met the man," said Max, "and I generally make a point of not forming a negative opinion of anyone in my chain of command, above or below, until we have met face to face, or at least operated in the same formation for a while. There are just too many people who look great on paper and turn out to be arrogant assholes, or who send you a snippy signal or write a sarcastic order but in person turn out to be totally stellar individuals. They were just having a bad day, or something they said comes off as sarcastic when it wasn't meant that way; you know how that goes."

"I do know how that goes." Bram sat down and folded his hands in his lap. "Something that is meant in a joking manner can sound sarcastic or condescending when reduced to a terse electronic communication. And as difficult as it may be to believe, I have personally had situations in which my communications were mistakenly interpreted as being sarcastic when they were not so intended."

"I find that difficult to believe."

"I assure you, it is true. People are very ready to find sarcasm in what they read."

"Bram, you're not understanding me. I'm not saying that I don't believe that someone thought something you wrote was sarcastic. I'm saying I don't believe that they thought so in error."

The doctor snorted. "I suppose I should be offended, but you have isolated one of my most pernicious and deep-seated character flaws. It has cost me many friends and alienated more than one colleague whose favor would have been advantageous to have. I have often wondered why it has not alienated you, as well."

"Because I know enough psychology to recognize a defense mechanism designed to keep people at a distance when I see one. Because I know the difference between sarcasm and true insult. Because I view everything you say through the lens of my knowledge that you are my loyal friend and would never willingly hurt me. Because I understand that your nature is to look at everything around you and analyze it objectively, the good and the bad, and then tell me what you think, without pulling any punches to spare my feelings. Because I know how tone deaf you are about how your objective, clinical observations about the situation will affect people's feelings and, when those feelings are bruised, I know it's not because you meant to bruise them.

"And because I'm not some thin-skinned military hospital administrator running his antiseptic little fiefdom in a safe rear area, but an experienced combat officer who is accustomed to the company of other men who have been in battle and who are some of the most sarcastic beings that the galaxy has ever spawned. Because you are my friend, and friends overlook small slights and minor injuries: when two people walk closely together down the same narrow path, sometimes they can't help stepping on each other's feet or jabbing each others ribs with their elbows. When they arrive at their destination covered with bruises, it doesn't mean they've been in a fight."

The doctor nodded his understanding, smiled, and looked at the tabletop. Not since his parents had died had anyone ever come right out and said that they recognized one of his faults and accepted him in spite of it. Ibrahim Sahin had always felt like a square peg in a round hole. Now, for the first time in his life, he had the sense that, although the hole was not quite square, neither was it completely round, and that his friend was making it more square for him every day. He didn't quite know what to make of the feeling. All he knew was that he liked it. "I don't know what to say, except 'thank you.'"

Max made a dismissive gesture with his right hand, something looking vaguely as if he were encouraging a fly to leave the vicinity. "Think nothing of it. You are a tremendous asset to me, both personally and professionally. If that doesn't entitle you to a few allowances, I don't know what does."

"So, my friend, back to this west end of an east-bound camel, Duflot. You were saying that you don't like to come to any kind of negative assessment of a man whom you have never met. I may sometimes be a bit 'tone deaf' as you say, but I could swear that I heard the distinct sounds of a 'but' approaching."

"But"—Max smiled at Bram—"I'm afraid you're right. I may have to make an exception for this guy. He's not only arrogant and condescending, but stupid as well."

The two men were having a light supper in Max's day cabin. Thanks to the supplies obtained from the art dealer turned Foreign Minister of Rashid IV, both men ate well. Max was having a shrimp po-boy sandwich: French bread loaf segment, still anachronistically referred to as a "foot-long," sliced submarine style, filled with fried shrimp, and dressed with mayonnaise and just a bit of spicy mustard (no lettuce and tomato this far out, alas), along with French fries, and cherry pie. The shrimp were good, having been frozen shortly after being caught on seas of Rashid IV, which teemed with transplanted Earth marine life, and the bread—the foundation of a good po-boy—was excellent, with a light but crispy crust and tender fluffy insides.

Good bread was one of the compensations of life on board a warship in deep space. No matter how long a warship had been out and how scarce the vegetables and milk and eggs and meat became, there was nearly always fresh bread because the ingredients for bread occupied little space and could be stored for years.

The doctor was having a sandwich as well, an open-faced roast beef affair covered in savory brown gravy and made to be eaten with knife and fork rather than held in the hand. The roast was excellent as well and fork-tender, Chief Boudreaux in the galley acting in accordance with the traditional Cajun wisdom that a roast is ready to be made into sandwiches only when it "falls apart with a hard look."

"Why do you say that Duflot is stupid, other than that he lacks the wisdom to avoid unnecessarily belittling and alienating someone with whom he is about to be working closely in a matter of life and death directly affecting the lives of hundreds of people and indirectly affecting the course of the war and, as a result, the fate of more than two hundred billion people?"

Max chuckled ruefully. "When you put it like that, it makes him sound even more stupid that I was thinking he was. I suppose that getting this envoy to the negotiations *is* pretty damn important."

"Pretty damn important? We are talking about forging a strong military relationship among the four powers now at war against the Krag and therefore changing the balance of power in a war that our species is fighting for its very survival. I believe you told me at one point that the absence of a coordinated military effort by these four powers could cost us the war. 'Pretty damn important' understates the situation somewhat, don't you think? That's rather like saying that the human heart is a 'relatively significant organ.'" Max nodded his acquiescence.

"What I do not understand is why, if it is so important, is Norfolk attempting to accomplish it with only these three ships? Why not put Commodore Doland on one of those huge battleships that's as big as a reasonably sized city, escorted by a huge fleet carrier and a bunch of cruisers so that it would take the entire Krag Navy to do him ill?"

"That strategy sounds good but is likely to lead to disaster. Here's why." Max was secretly impressed by the doctor's having uncharacteristically gotten the names of the ship types and other naval concepts and nomenclature correct in his question.

"First, a force comprised of capital ships is going to be slow. The energy requirements of pushing a ship that big through compressed space are too high to make sustained runs at high c factors, so for anything longer than a crossing from one star system to the next system over they need to jump. A trip that would take only a week in a light force would take more than a month in a force of that size—it takes hours just to get all the ships through one jump point. I'm sure we need a theater forces agreement as soon as possible. We can't wait a month.

"This brings us to the second disadvantage: that you can't move a force like that in secret. You start moving that many big ships through inhabited systems or even systems that have any civilian traffic in them—and if a system has got jump points, it almost always has at least some civvy poking through it somewhere almost all the time—then, in a day or so, the blabby freighter captain has told all his buddies about the huge task force that he just saw on his sensors, and everyone in the sector knows that something is afoot. Then, you've got problems. Since your huge protective convoy is so damn slow, once the Krag know what's going on, it's a lot easier for them to get a force in there to attack you.

"Remember, they don't have to defeat the force—just destroy the ship carrying the envoy, which they would have a high probability of doing if they got in there with four or five destroyers. They come in fast and catch the group by surprise. The carrier doesn't have time to launch fighters, so the only cover is the Combat Area Patrol and your escorts. The destroyers converge from all around in all three dimensions so that the defenders have to cover the entire sphere. The CAP is almost guaranteed to be in the wrong place or headed in the wrong direction, so the destroyers just blow past them; then they ignore the escorts—the attackers take some attrition, but they're moving so fast that most get through—and bore right in on the envoy's ship.

"Then, they all fire their missiles, break off, and run like smoke and oakum. At least one of those Krag Foxhound missiles gets through, and *POOF*—no more envoy."

"Smoke and oakum?"

"Old nautical expression. Used a lot in some wonderful old novels I'm reading. You'd like them. There's one series where one of the heroes is a doctor."

"I'm sure I would find the portrayal of my fictional brother perfectly odious and that I would feel for him not the slightest trace of kinship. What, by the way, is 'oakum'?"

"I'm not exactly sure, but it sounds good with 'smoke.' Anyway, when you look at their options, I can't criticize Norfolk on their basic tactical decision. The odds are better if you use a small number of very fast ships. They can use their compression drives to cross through interstellar space straight to their destination at high c factors, making them hard to locate and even harder to catch. They are stealthy enough to hide from most attackers and fast enough to evade most of the rest."

"All right. Now that you explain it that way, it makes sense. It is a very counterintuitive idea though, that one can actually be safer with a smaller, less formidable force. But you still haven't explained why you think that Commander Duflot is stupid."

"It's simple. Just like I explained in that signal I sent him, those Krag ships on our tail will follow us into the system, hidden from planet-based sensors by staying in our compression trail. Then they go subluminal and kick in their stealth systems, hiding out until our little group pulls out. Then they follow us out of the system and tail us by following our base course until they see a good opportunity to attack. Something tells me that Duflot isn't going to have us follow a deceptive course or do anything tricky like randomly varying our speed, so we'll be damn easy to locate and intercept.

"Then, somewhere far enough from any of our forces that help cannot reach us fast enough to do any good, they attack out of the black, by surprise, when we least expect it. And if the attack is not successful, they try again and again and again until we either succeed in destroying them or they obtain their objective. So, I called Commander Duflot stupid because his narrow-minded, ignorant stubbornness is not only likely to cause our mission to fail but also to bring about one more bad result."

"And what might that be?"

"It's likely to get us all killed."

CHAPTER 10

19:52Z Hours, 25 March 2315

"CAPTAIN REPORT TO FLAG STOP MESSAGE ENDS." This was the signal communicated by the near-ancient expedient of flashing lights and Morse code from the USS *William Gorgas* to the USS *Cumberland.* Commander Duflot's orders from Norfolk required him to make every effort to avoid being detected by enemy forces, hence his use of lights rather than conventional radio.

He could have established a laserlink, but Duflot was apparently not interested in efficient two-way communication and information sharing with the destroyer; he just wanted to order Max to come on board, and to do so in the most imperious fashion possible. Accordingly, wearing dress blues and a sidearm (Chin blinkered his counterpart on the frigate and found out what the Uniform of the Day was on board the pennant ship), Max was on board his ship's launch, making the 1800-meter crossing between the two vessels.

It was with some chagrin that Max saw that the docking director lights on the starboard side of the *William Gorgas* were blinking red, indicating that the launch was being directed to dock on the frigate's port side. It was the third snub in just a few minutes. The first was in not establishing a laserlink between the two ships, as though the *Cumberland* were in possession of no information in which the *William Gorgas* could conceivably have any interest.

The second was in the wording of the signal. Although Duflot outranked Max by a single step, both men commanded rated warships. Accordingly, a communication from one captain to another was supposed to be more or less between equals. A senior captain possessed authority to give orders to the others, but was restrained by a measure of deference and recognition of the other captains' independent authority.

Typically, the signal would have been worded something like, "CAPT DUFLOT SENDS REGARDS STOP REQUESTS HONOR OF CAPT ROBICHAUX ON BOARD THIS VESSEL AT HIS EARLIEST CONVENIENCE STOP MESSAGE ENDS." Duflot was also, Max thought, overstepping a bit with "report to flag" when Duflot was not a commodore or an admiral and therefore not of "flag" rank. The lead ship of a group of vessels commanded by someone not of flag rank was technically the pennant ship of the group, not its flagship.

But the third, and worst of the snubs was being directed to dock on the port side. Starboard was the side of honor. Docking to port meant that the *William Gorgas* would receive him without ceremony: no boatswain would pipe him aboard with the announcement "*Cumberland* arriving"; no side boys would be present; the ship's Marines and Officer of the Deck would not salute him or render him any other honors; and he would not be treated as a member of the never formally recognized, but still very real Brotherhood of Exalted Warship Captains, a status accorded him by Admiral Hornmeyer, who was a full-blown vice admiral with three gold stars on each shoulder and hundreds of ships under his command. Rather, Duflot's whole attitude toward Max was that of a superior dealing with a subordinate, nothing more.

When the red lights started blinking on the frigate's port side, the man piloting the launch, Ensign Mori, made an inarticulate snort of disgust and turned to Max. With an annoyed gesture at the docking director lights, he said, "I can still dock us on the starboard side, sir."

"Thank you, Mister Mori. I'm sure you're good enough to get snugged up there without the grappling field to slip us into place, but that doesn't engage the docking clamps or open the airlock."

"Well, sir, you're not supposed to know this officially, but when the frigate didn't initiate a laserlink, Sparks and Gates hacked their ENAP, so we could pull a download and do a one-way update on our database."

Max sat up and took notice at that one. This statement was an interesting revelation in four ways. One, the *Cumberland* now had covert access to the frigate's computers through the latter's external network access portal, or ENAP, the same portal through which the ships would be communicating if Duflot had permitted a conventional laserlink. Two, hacking a warship's ENAP was supposed to be well-nigh impossible, but these two men had accomplished it in a matter of minutes. Maybe they acquired a good nutcracker for that system from some of their friends in low places or even managed to crib the passwords from someone. The latter, in fact, was by far the more likely explanation given how popular a prick like Duflot was likely to be with his men. It was not as though Duflot had to be worried about the Krag pulling the same trick.

Three, at some point Chin and Bales had sufficiently impressed their shipmates to be awarded the traditional and honorific nicknames for their posts: Sparks, for communications officer and Gates, for the computer and information systems officer. Four, Chin and Bales, who had been at loggerheads going back to when they were midshipmen together on the battlecruiser *Aeglos*, apparently had worked together on what was likely an off-watch project, meaning that they had probably resolved their long-standing differences.

"So, if you want, I can let Sparks know by blinker and Gates can remote activate the grap field, pull us in, and open the airlock, with all the tell-tales and alarms deactivated. We could be drinking coffee and eating pound cake in the wardroom before anyone even knew we were there. It would be squeaker work, sir, as easy as kiss my hand." Mori seemed eager to try it, especially given the obvious snub to his captain.

"Not today, Mr. Mori, not today. Those two Krag ships dropped off our tail as soon as we went subluminal, and they're lurking out there somewhere, so I'm not really enthusiastic about hacking into the operating system of this group's most powerful ship. Not to mention that I don't think it would be a good idea for Commander Duflot to know that we hacked his systems. He seems the type who would take offense. I'm not eager to go before a court martial right now. I'd rather fight Krag, if it's all the same to you."

"Aye, aye, sir. I just wanted you to know that the option was available."

"Thank you for that, Mori. As they used to say back in the Age of Sail, larboard side, Mr. Mori. Handsomely now, row dry.'"

Mori laughed, as much at the idea of rowing a spacecraft as at the skipper's low-budget tridvid drama version of an English accent. Something of a buff about such things, Mori did, however, recognize that the skipper correctly used "larboard," the term used for "port" in the British Royal Navy until 22 November 1844.

"Larboard side it is, sir," he answered in an English accent considerably more authentic than Max's. He had an ear for accents.

Max took a good look at the frigate through the front view port—one actually piloted a tiny auxiliary vessel such as a launch, at least in part, by looking out a window with the Mark One Eyeball. He smiled at the sight of her familiar lines. The *William Gorgas* was a frigate of the *Edward Jenner* class, of the same design and even from the same yard as Max's last ship, the *Emeka Moro*, on which he served as weapons officer.

He found himself enviously contemplating her four forward missile tubes that allowed her to launch a far more effective salvo than he could fire from the *Cumberland*'s two forward launchers—her single rear tube being useless against forward targets. So many of the tactical situations in which Max had found himself since taking command of the destroyer would have been made simpler by the availability of another pair of missile tubes. For that matter, he sure wouldn't turn his nose up at those big pulse cannon turrets that let the ship train her main batteries in any direction.

His wistful contemplation of augmented firepower was brought to an abrupt halt when he noticed that, although the green "Dock here" ring around the port main docking hatch was illuminated, another small vessel was only about twenty meters away from docking with it. Another green "Dock here" was signaling, this one around the number four port hatch, the opening into the Engineering spaces usually used for loading equipment and supplies bound for that part of the ship that were not so large that they had to come in through the hangar bay. Almost every rated warship had a hatch in roughly that location. It was generally called the "Servants' Entrance."

Make that four snubs.

As the launch headed to the designated hatch, it passed within a hundred meters of the other docking vessel—close enough for

Max to read the registry number: GCRU-8481. Out of idle curiosity, Max punched the number into the SVR database. The vessel was attached to the Union Naval Logistics Service base in the system, a waste retrieval and disposal transport. But no one ever called the type by that name except when filling out official documents. In common conversation, those vessels had another name dating back to the Age of Sail. The commanding officer of the *Cumberland* was being compelled to yield docking precedence to what everyone called a garbage scow.

Make that five snubs.

Mori docked the launch at the Servant's Entrance with his customary deftness. Within a few seconds, the larger ship's artificial gravity took hold by induction through the deck plating, and the computer announced, "Initiating artificial gravity." As if it took a computer announcement to be able to tell the difference between microgravity and being held in your seat by 1 G.

"This shouldn't be long, Mori, and I'd like to be able to leave quickly when I'm done. Just wait right here, and leave everything powered up." Max expected a short, unpleasant meeting with Duflot and didn't want to be forced to endure an uncomfortable wait around a docking hatch.

"Aye, sir. No worries, I'll be right here with the thrusters hot. We'll be able to undock and be on our way five seconds from when you give the word."

"Outstanding, Mori."

Max heard the series of hisses, thumps, and clangs that told him that the hatches of the two craft were being precisely aligned, the docking clamps locking, and the inner doors on both vessels opening. He stood and stepped over to the hatch, waiting for the red light labeled STATUS: DO NOT OPERATE HATCH to go out and the green one labeled STATUS: HATCH MAY BE OPERATED to illuminate.

It took four seconds, giving Max four more seconds to contemplate how much fun he was about to have. The red light went out and the green one came on. Both sets of hatches opened, and Max stepped into a nondescript compartment usually used for unloading spare parts, barrels of coolant and lubricant, and buckets of paint. In fact, a few examples of each were present in the small space, looking as though they had just been carried in for the occasion to emphasize Max's importance in the scheme of things.

He pivoted to the right, where the quarterdeck had been located on sailing ships and where the Union and naval flags would be standing if anyone had bothered to set them up, which they had not. Instead, Max found himself saluting a tall crate on which was stenciled: MODEL WPPCP-25878-11929-4 WASTE TREATMENT PLANT CIRCULATING PUMP, AUXILIARY.

Not only was Max saluting a replacement shit and piss pump, but he was also saluting a *secondary* replacement shit and piss pump. Snub number six. Hell, maybe six and a half.

Max then pivoted 90 degrees to face and salute the man Captain Duflot had sent to greet him. "Permission to come aboard, sir."

"Permission granted," replied the man who returned the salute. Well, not a man, actually. The person sent to meet Max and escort him to wherever he was meeting Duflot was a boy of about ten.

Snub number seven.

"This way, sir, if you please," he piped in his child's voice. "The captain is expecting you."

"Thank you, Mister…" The boy said nothing but started to lead Max to the exit. He didn't know what was wrong with the young man, but he was not going to be walking in the company of another Navy man without knowing his name, even if he *was* only 140 centimeters tall and would not be making the acquaintance of a razor for three years, if not four or five.

"Midshipman," Max said gently, "when I said that, it was an implied request that you tell me your name."

The boy stopped dead in his tracks and turned to Max, genuinely mortified. "Oh, sir! I didn't know, sir! It's Füchtenschnieder, sir, Midshipman Second Class."

The boy seemed frightened by the minor miscommunication, a reaction similar in kind, if not in severity, to what Max had seen instilled in his own crew by his abusive and incompetent predecessor, Captain Oscar.

"Don't worry, son, I'm not in your chain of command, and I wouldn't dream of mentioning something so minor to anyone who is. So, what does everyone call you, Midshipman?"

Although he tried to cover it up, the boy seemed surprised and confused by the question. After a moment's consideration, he said, "They call me Füchtenschnieder, sir."

"No nickname?"

"Oh, no, *sir*," he answered, as if the mere possibility of such a thing was unthinkable. "No nicknames on *this* ship, sir."

No nicknames. Then Duflot was an idiot of galactic proportions. There were whole books written about the individual psychological and shipwide morale benefits of crewman nicknames. They helped spacers establish individual identity in a service that tended to reduce human beings to uniforms, grades, and ratings.

Spacers wore their Navy nicknames with pride and often carried them through retirement right into the grave. Max had known many a long-retired old space dog whose friends could not have told you the man's given name for a million credits but who was well known to hundreds of men on forty ships and a dozen worlds by a nickname he had earned as a squeaker or a greenie half a century ago. Max managed to keep from shaking his head.

"Very well, then, Füchtenschnieder," said Max, giving the "ch" the correct Germanic guttural and the "sch" the slightly different sound it had in German than in Standard. Just because he *liked* to use nicknames for long, difficult to pronounce surnames didn't mean he actually *needed* to use them. "Take me to your leader." The boy showed no signs that he was even tempted to smile at Max's slight joke as he led Max out the hatch and toward the bow.

"Mister Füchtenschnieder?" said Max, looking down almost onto the top of the lad's head.

"Yes, sir?"

"Is there any particular reason why you didn't want to tell me your name a moment ago?"

"Oh, no, sir," he replied with defensive abruptness. "I just didn't think anyone who commanded a rated warship would want to know the name of a midshipman second class."

"Füchtenschnieder, does Captain Duflot know your name?"

"Oh, no, sir. At least I *hope* not, sir." Max, of course, knew the names of all of his midshipmen, as well as what planets they were from; what other ships they had served on, if any; how they were doing in their studies and training; and what their current duty assignments were. Max had never met Duflot, yet he was getting the distinct feeling that when he did, he wasn't going to like the man. No, it was more than a feeling. Max was sure he wasn't going to like Captain Duflot at all.

Max was surprised that the midshipman was not leading him to the wardroom where one captain typically met with another over a cup of coffee, generally with some of the other ship's officers present so that they all could get acquainted. Instead, Max was shown to Duflot's day cabin. After Max was kept standing in the corridor for more than ten minutes, the Marine guarding the hatch showed him in.

Assuming none of the customary informality between ship captains, Max marched in perfect regulation form to Duflot's desk, brought his hand up into a perfect salute, and snapped out, "Lieutenant Commander Maxime Robichaux, USS *Cumberland*, reporting as ordered, sir."

Duflot, who had been looking at his computer screen when Max entered, continued to do so for about ten seconds before slowly turning to face Max and scrutinizing every aspect of Max's uniform and posture.

He still had not returned the salute, which Max continued to hold. Duflot finally met Max's eyes. "You're out of uniform. I will be forced to note that fact in my report to Admiral Hornmeyer, mister." Not "Captain." Not "Commander." "Mister." Max had lost count of the snubs.

"Begging the Commander's pardon, sir, what is the precise nature of the uniform infraction?" Max's tone of voice was the epitome of reasonableness and control, an astonishing feat given that he already wanted to break Duflot's head open like an overripe melon.

"Sidearm. The Uniform of the day on this ship is dress blues. Not dress blues with arms. You are not permitted a sidearm, mister."

Continuing to hold his salute, Max said, "With all due respect sir, if the Commander would examine my uniform more carefully, particularly the first citation ribbon on the top row, I suggest that he might come to a different conclusion."

Duflot squinted at the ribbon in question and visibly deflated. "Very well." He returned the salute, allowing Max to snap his hand back to his side. "Stand at ease, Robichaux."

Stand at ease? Not, "Be seated?" This is beyond insulting.

"I see that you have had all manner of, shall we say, difficulties since taking command," Duflot said. "Hornmeyer is known for promoting people whom he regards as promising young officers to posts that are above their heads, only for them to fail in spectacular fashion. Don't be surprised to find yourself relieved of command at the end of this mission and reassigned as a weapons officer or XO of some well-run ship so that you can learn the art of command from someone who knows what he's doing. Until then, do try not to wreck your vessel any further than you already have, and attend to orders from the flag. I will endeavor to make them simple enough for you to understand and carry out."

Max took all of these insults, standing at parade rest, without so much as a twitch. He was certain that his face was red with anger, but there was no helping that. Duflot favored Max with a few more remarks about the deficiencies in Max's command, including an observation that no one he knew of ever needed to replace even one set of Frasch-Freiburg capacitors in a ship that hadn't been in commission long enough to need its thrusters realigned, much less two sets.

During all of this, Max carefully watched Duflot. He was of average height, slightly on the heavy side for a Navy man, with thinning, graying hair and a reddish complexion. His small, pointed nose seemed out of proportion with his large, round head and definitely did not match his thick, protruding lips, which looked rock hard from forming clipped, sarcastic sentences. Duflot moved his head a great deal when he spoke, while keeping the rest of his body uncannily immobile, as though he were one of those dolls with the large, heavy head that bobbled and rolled randomly on a spring.

Having, in his mind at least, put Max in his place, Duflot explained his plan for delivering the envoy to Rashid. "The details are on this data chip for you to bring back to your ship, as I certainly don't expect you to be able to remember all of this. The overall theory, though, is simple enough for you to understand: move the group in a safe series of orderly jumps along a well-protected route, through secure and well-scanned star systems, taking advantage of local forces in place where available. This provides maximum protection for the envoy and the greatest likelihood of delivering him to the conference without incident."

Max had listened to the commander's plan with growing disbelief. "Sir, do I understand the Commander correctly that we are going to *jump* from inhabited system to inhabited system, and then make the crossing from one jump point to the next on pure circumferential courses with no evasion, in convoy formation, broadcasting our location by using active sensors?"

"That's correct. How is that difficult to understand? All of those systems are listed by their various sector commands as having been cleared of enemy forces, and most have planet-based sensor coverage and some sort of defensive forces in place to give us additional protection. When in those systems, we will be safe from attack *by definition*. I can't imagine any safer and more prudent course of action."

Max was almost dizzy with the staggering imbecility of the plan. "Sir, with all due respect, why not just go straight to Rashid? Straight shot across interstellar space with a few deceptive zigs and zags thrown in. This ship's an *Edward Jenner* class frigate—she can sustain 1865 c. If your engineer is on the ball, 1885 or even 1890. The destroyers attached to the group can keep up with that easily. If the enemy were searching with a hundred ships, she wouldn't be able to find us absent the wildest stroke of luck. And if they found us, they'd have a hard time catching us at those speeds, much less being able to manage any sort of attack.

"They can't attack us if they can't find us. We don't need planet-based sensor coverage and forces in place. Let the infinity of interstellar space be our coverage! Let speed and elusiveness be our defense! We'll have the envoy on Rashid drinking the best coffee in the galaxy before the rat-faces even know we've set out. It's foolproof. I'll even tell Admiral Hornmeyer that it was your idea. Didn't Napoleon say *When you set out to take Vienna, take Vienna*? When you set out to go to Rashid, go to Rashid." Max looked at Duflot hopefully. He thought he had made a compelling, logical case.

Instead, Duflot looked at him with unconcealed horror, even fear, which soon turned to rage. "Are you out of your mind? Take an irreplaceable negotiator, on the most important diplomatic mission of the past fifty years, practically *naked* through open, unprotected space? No sensor coverage? No forces in place? No certification from sector command that the area has been cleared of enemy forces? Who knows what forces the enemy has lurking out there? And if we're attacked, we'd be days away from any help.

"No. Absolutely not. That course of action would be impulsive. Rash. Full of unwarranted risk. I'm surprised that you have the temerity even to suggest it."

"But sir, it is a very common tactic in Admiral Hornmeyer's command, and also under Admiral Bushinko. The probability of success is very high."

Duflot slammed his hand, palm down, onto the desk. "Probability! I can't deal in probability. This is warfare, not the gaming tables on Nouvelle Monaco! I have to *guarantee* the safe delivery of the envoy, and that means layering on as many different kinds of security, defense, and protection as possible. I must take every conceivable measure, not roll the dice in some daredevil speed run across the void."

"Sir, with all due respect, warfare is full of gambles and calculated risks. Admiral Hornmeyer constantly refers to his most critical decisions as *bets*. I must insist that the course of action I suggest is far less risky and far more likely to result—"

"You *insist?* You *dare* to *insist* to a superior officer? You are insubordinate, mister. Your remarks have been recorded. If you are not strictly obedient to my orders in this regard, I will be certain that Admiral Hornmeyer receives a copy of the recording. And if you attempt to go over my head on this, I will see you court martialed. You have your orders. Now go back to your ship and carry them out, to the letter. You are dismissed."

He sent Max away with a sketchy, imprecise salute. As Max was marching to the door, Duflot called out, "Oh, Robichaux, one more thing. The envoy would like to see you while you are on board. He's in the VIP quarters. I'm sure you can find your way."

Max assured Duflot that he could and made his exit. With years of service on this class of vessel, Max was able to go straight to his destination, one deck "up" and aft about twenty meters. He gave his name and rank to the Marine at the door.

"The envoy's expecting you, sir," said the Marine, with genuine respect. "Go right in." He shouldered his pulse rifle, entered the access code, palmed the scanner, and the hatch opened.

Max went in. On this class of frigate, the VIP quarters were divided into three compartments, an office-like day cabin, a small but comfortable sitting room jokingly called the "parlor," and a berth cabin. The day cabin was empty, but Max heard a voice booming out of the parlor. "In here, Robichaux. I'm sure you're tired of standing in front of a desk!"

Max stepped through the open door into the next compartment. Lounging in a comfortable chair, with his feet on a stool, was the envoy. He was taller than Max. A LOT taller than Max, and thinner. Whereas Max was built like a quarterback from American football, Commodore Doland looked to be built for basketball. He had dark hair, brown eyes, and a brownish complexion with high cheekbones that spoke of some Native American ancestry along with the predominating European, and he could have been anywhere between forty and sixty years of age. His smile was warm.

Doland held in his left hand a glass containing about an inch and a half of an amber liquid and a few pieces of ice. Max started to draw himself up to salute.

"Lose the salute, son. Don't you know that there's a regulation that says you never salute a seated man with a glass of whisky in his hand?" He extended his right hand. Max shook it. "Joseph A. Doland, Commodore, Envoy, Instigator, and Negotiator, at your service."

"Max Robichaux, pleased to meet you, sir."

"You too, son. Build yourself a drink and have a seat. After twenty minutes with Duflot, you've earned it." Max wondered how the envoy knew that the meeting had lasted almost exactly twenty minutes. "I need a drink every time I have to talk to that narrow-minded, little...let's just leave the noun out, shall we? You deserve a reward for not pulling out that sidearm of yours and shooting Emperor Duflot the First back there."

Max poured himself some of Kentucky's best and sat in the chair indicated by the envoy. He took a sip. "Emperor?"

"Yep. That's what his men call him. I've never seen anyone so high and mighty, and I've met with the president—this one and the last one—more than a dozen times. Apparently the last subordinate to sit in his presence was the ship's cat who has, by the way, jumped ship and is now on a repair tender."

"I'm sure that did wonders for morale."

"I'm told it did, Max. You don't mind if I call you Max, do you?"

"No, sir, not at all." Max found himself warming to the envoy, who had a disarming, natural charisma and personal warmth, mixed somehow with a cool, calculating intellect that understood people very, very well. Doland, Max thought, might have done very well centuries ago as a riverboat gambler.

"And when we're in here, drop the 'sir.' Everyone calls me 'Ollie,' and I'd be grateful if you would as well." Max nodded his acceptance. "Now, Max, that you've met with our friend, the Emperor, what do you think of him, and more importantly, what do you think of his plan to get me to the conference?"

"Well, s— . . . Ollie, if I may speak freely about both—"

"Max, I don't ask questions unless I expect straightforward, honest answers. So, shoot straight and we'll let the medics sort them out."

"Then, I have to tell you that I don't think much of either."

"Go on."

"Any man who is so insecure that he has to come up with a dozen or so ways to snub a newly frocked destroyer skipper has got problems that an extra rotation through command school won't cure. If his lack of confidence is that fundamental, and if his handling of a key subordinate is so incompetent, the man has no business commanding a warship. Sorry, but that's how I see it."

"I'm not going to disagree with you. Unfortunately, he's got friends, or should I say a brother, in high places. What about the plan?"

"I haven't heard anything as stupid since I was a squeaker listening to other squeakers refight the last battle the way they would do it if they were in command. He's likely to screw the mission."

"More than likely."

"Can't you do something about it? You're a commodore."

"Afraid not. I rank him but I'm not in his chain of command. The only orders I can give around here that get followed have to do with the dinner menu and who gets let into my quarters. I'm not even assigned to the Tactical Command any more. You know how that happened, right?"

Max shook his head.

"Nav error. I was a battleship captain—USS *Gary Tyler*. Officer of the Deck jumped her through the Charlie jump point in the Divisio-Bilbon system instead of the Bravo, and we wound up in the middle of a border skirmish between the Themp-Ra and the Ghrinn that was just about to graduate to being a full-grown war. The only way I could save my ship was to broker a ceasefire between them, which I did, followed by a peace treaty. So now, instead of leading men into battle, at which—I might add—I was not too shabby, I'm now the Union's new 'gifted negotiator.' All things being equal, I'd much rather fight. Bottom line, though, is I have no authority over Duflot and no chance of having my operational orders followed on this ship."

"Then we're pretty well screwed."

"Now, don't jump to conclusions, Max. I'm sure some sort of *creative* solution will occur to you."

"You're not suggesting that I—"

"No, son, not at all. I'm not suggesting *anything* except that you keep an open mind and that you take advantage of any opportunity to save the mission that might happen to present itself. I'll help you any way that I can." He drained his glass and set it down.

"I do, however, hope that your creativity manifests itself in its usual way, because this mission has *got* to succeed. I'm not talking about saving my hide either. I mean that this envoy has got to get to the conference and that the conference has got to come up with a four-way framework for conducting this war. Because if we don't," he gestured toward the bottle on the bar, "there's a lot of whisky aging in a lot of barrels up on the mountains of Tennessee and Kentucky, not to mention Scotland and

Ireland, that will go to waste because there won't be any people left to drink it."

"What an appalling breach of military courtesy, not to mention the kind of affront that an officer and a gentleman never inflicts upon another. It's an insult to the honor of this ship and every man aboard her. I won't stand for it."

Kraft was boiling over, and he had actually cooled down a little over the past few minutes. His first responses had been so profane, in both German and Standard, that Max was genuinely embarrassed. Apparently, on Kraft's homeworld, all the best insults were in German and involved ascribing to the insulted man's ancestors a propensity to engage in sexual relations with various species of farm animals.

"Major, we know the man is an asshole," Max soothed. "The days of settling affronts to a man's personal honor by beginning the day with pistols for two and coffee for one are long past. He's a superior officer and he commands this group. I take his shit and we follow his orders. It's that simple. His insults were either subtle snubs that he can plausibly say were all inadvertent and not meant to offend, or else they took place in his day cabin with no witnesses. The best I can say about the whole thing is that he was not able to provoke me into an outburst of anger—which for all I knew he was trying to do—and that I managed to avoid being put on report."

"What would he have put you on report for?" DeCosta was incredulous.

"Being out of uniform. He didn't like that I was wearing my sidearm when the Uniform of the Day on the *William Gorgas* was dress blues, not dress blues with arms."

"That's . . . that's . . . that's . . . just *chickenshit*. Sorry, sir, but that's the only word for it." DeCosta was inarticulate with anger at first, but once he got pointed where he wanted, he steadied his helm on the new heading.

"It's a purely chickenshit thing to put someone on report for. Never in a million years would I put a man on report for something like that, unless it was some sort of willfully defiant repeat offense. I'd point out the error, tell him not to do it again, and be done with the matter. Life's too short for that kind of picayune bullshit."

Kraft smiled ever so slightly, his first display of any emotion other than rage since Max had described his encounter with the group commander. "Not only was the commander being 'chickenshit,' but he was also technically incorrect."

"How? 'With arms' was not the UOD on the *William Gorgas*, and without that additional specification, a sidearm doesn't go with dress blues."

"True, XO, but you are forgetting about that." Kraft pointed to a small, blue ribbon at the left of the top row in Max's three-row "fruit salad" array of decorations and awards over his right breast. The light blue ribbon with seven tiny white stars arrayed in the shape of an "M," one star for each of the *Orion* class gunships of humanity's first tiny space armada that rode into space on the backs of thermonuclear fireballs that desperate July day in 2034 to take the Moon back from the Ning-Braha and save the human race from slavery or extinction. The ribbon that graced no other chest on board. Except the doctor's.

"His CMH?"

"Yes, Mr. DeCosta, his Commissioners' Medal of Honor, an award that is the highest military decoration conferred by the Union and that by statute, regulation, and custom carries with it a fairly lengthy list of privileges." Kraft lapsed into the tone of voice he tended to use when reciting law and regulations: a tone somewhere between the one used by pastors when citing scripture and the one used by secondary school science teachers when they explain a particularly arcane law of nature.

"Some of these privileges are well known, such as the right to wear the uniform after retirement or discharge whenever one pleases, to stand or march in the first rank of any parade or review of naval personnel in which the recipient participates, a lifelong right to have passage on any naval vessel wherever it may be going, a lifelong right to receive food and lodging at any naval base or station in the galaxy, to meet with one of the Navy's senators more or less when one wishes, and so on. And some are more obscure. Such as—"

The skipper drew his sidearm from its holster and placed it on the table. "Such as," he finished for the major, "the right to bear at any time any small arm or edged weapon with which I have personally killed any enemy of the Union. It has to be that actual weapon, mind you, not just the same model."

He picked up the M-62 10 mm Beretta-Browning pistol and fixed his eyes on it. Every eye in the room followed his. "This qualifies. Many times over." He reflexively press checked the chamber to be sure it was empty, holstered it, and closed the holster with a loud snap. "Enough of this bitching. Duflot is running this show, and that's all there is to it. We're in the Navy. We follow orders. Even stupid ones." The comm buzzed. Max leaned over to the panel and hit the button. "Skipper."

"Skipper, this is Chin."

"Go ahead."

"Sir, I sent that signal you ordered. I positioned the transceiver arrays so that I can guarantee that the pennant got none of the leakage."

Metaspacial signals had no directionality and could not be traced. But metaspacial transmitters were not perfectly efficient. When they sent a signal, part of the energy was radiated as ordinary electromagnetic radiation, known in the fleet as "leakage," mostly in the long wave radio band. Chin had made sure that the directionality of the leakage had been away from Duflot's ship.

"And I'm such a sloppy comms officer there is every chance that the transmission won't make it into my comm log. Oops. But in case anyone checks the records, they will find that we had not yet logged the order from the pennant imposing EMCON when the signal went out. It took a few minutes longer to log that order than it should have, sir. Oops, again. I suppose we need to do these things with greater *celerity* in the future."

"See that you do, Mr. Chin. Be aware that this kind of slapdash, devil-may-care, nonchalant, and…"—he rooted around in the attic of his mind for another suitable adjective—"and lackadaisical attitude toward your duties is not going to be tolerated on my ship. Consider yourself firmly rebuked on that point." Max almost managed to sound stern. Almost.

"Oh yes, sir. I do, sir. *Firmly* rebuked, sir. Anything else the comms section can do for you, Captain? Anything at all?"

"No, thank you, Mr. Chin. That's fine for the present. Skipper out." In response to the inquiring looks, Max made a dismissive wave of the hand—a wave serving as the signal for "It's better that you not know right now."

"And you heard right, we're on full EMCON. Here's what's up." He hit a key on the control pad for the wardroom 3D tactical projector. A black cube sprang into being, salted with the tiny, white dots of stars, each labeled with the name or catalog number of the system.

"Here's this sector. We're here, in the Svenskanorsk system." He hit a key, and one of the stars started blinking red. "Our destination is the Four Power Conference in Harun on Rashid IV, here." He hit another key, and another star, about sixty centimeters away in the projection, also started blinking.

"We're crossing this system at .45 c to the Bravo jump point that will take us to this system." He hit a key and a second star, very near the first, started blinking red. "Once we get there, we begin—"

At that moment, the blonde head and conspicuously pink ears of Midshipman Hewlett inserted themselves into the wardroom, followed—quite boldly given the circumstances—by his small form.

"By your leave, sir," he said to the captain, saluting, "I simply need to retrieve a tool and then I'll be out of your way."

Slight smiles appeared around the room, despite the irritation of enduring a second interruption in the middle of an important briefing. A midshipman appearing in the wardroom during a senior officer briefing to "retrieve a tool" could mean only one thing.

Max returned the salute and eyed Midshipman Oliver R. Hewlett. Unlike Duflot's ignorance of even Füchtenschnieder's name, Max knew more about Hewlett than did some of his bunkmates: that the boy came from planet Archopin, that he excelled in physical sciences and mathematics to such a prodigious degree that turning the boy into a naval officer (for that is the direction in which he clearly was already headed) instead of the brilliant scientist he so obviously could become might be a waste of material, and that he loved the writings of Homer and J. R. R. Tolkien of Earth, as well as Graknar-Toth 242 of Pfelung, whose writing was influenced by both. Max wondered if Captain Duflot knew as much about his weapons officer or his chief engineer as Max knew about this child who was almost certainly one of the four or five least important persons on the ship. But "least important" didn't mean "not important."

"Mr. Hewlett, what tool are you to retrieve, and who sent you to retrieve it?" Max's asked.

"Chief Farnell sent me to get the gimbal alignment tool for the port auxiliary guidance platform. He said that the platform went into gimbal lock a little while ago and needs to be realigned, so he needs the alignment tool." The child smiled at the captain, proud of himself for delivering the recitation in letter-perfect fashion without scrambling the unfamiliar technical terms.

The smiles in the room grew broad.

Max sat so that he could be at eye level with the boy. "Hewlett," he said, nothing but interest and patience showing on his face, "do you remember your basic lesson on the ship's inertial guidance system? You would have gotten it... let's see... 'round about your fourth or fifth day on board."

"Yes, sir," he said enthusiastically. "Well, most of it anyway."

"Outstanding. Now, tell me what you remember about the *Cumberland*'s inertial measuring units?"

"Sir, this ship has three fully independent and redundant inertial measuring units, or IMUs, at widely separated locations in the ship, each of which is individually capable of performing all inertial measurement functions. They measure changes in the ship's attitude along the *x*, *y*, and *z* axes by means of three orthogonally mounted ring laser gyroscopes," he said, reciting words painstakingly memorized, "which use the Sagnac Effect to detect rotation by the use of two circular beam path lasers in coincident counterdirectional modes. These lasers, which have no moving parts to wear out or become misaligned, replace..." It finally hit him, and his tiny form seemed to deflate, "Oh, no. Sir, this is *terrible.*"

"Go on, Midshipman, take your medicine."

The young man went on, deeply embarrassed. His ears went from pink to bright red, with the blush spreading to his pale, cherubic cheeks. "Um... replace mechanical guidance platforms, not used since the early twenty-first century, *which employed rapidly rotating motor-driven gyroscopes mounted on gimbals* to maintain a stable frame of reference from which vehicle attitude was measured." He reverted to a more normal tone of voice. A dejected tone of voice.

"So, we don't have a tool to align the gimbals on the guidance platform. Our IMUs don't have platforms. No platforms means no gimbals. No gimbals means no gimbal lock." The boy had it exactly right, and despite his embarrassment, it hadn't taken him long to put it together. Smart. Can think on his feet. Doesn't go to pieces when he learns he's made a mistake. *Who knows, the kid might be sitting in the Big Chair someday.*

The boy's embarrassment became slightly tinged with anger. "Chief Farnell 'practiced on my credulous simplicity.'" Max and the doctor shared a surprised glance at the last phrase but said nothing.

"That's exactly right, son. No one has had to worry about gimbal lock in a manned space vehicle since the last Apollo Command Module flew in 1975."

"I'm sorry, sir." Hewlett came to attention. "Request to be dismissed, sir."

"Negative, Midshipman. Not quite yet." Hewlett suddenly looked apprehensive. "No, son, nothing to be afraid of." Max picked up one of the teaspoons on the coffee service tray and handed it to Hewlett.

"Here. You bring this back to Chief Farnell and tell him that the captain has presented him with his very own 'gimbal alignment tool' so that he need not embarrass any more midshipmen or interrupt any more important meetings. Kindly tell Chief Farnell that I wish to see him in my day cabin at the end of watch. Oh, and Hewlett, just a few words to the wise."

"Yes, sir."

"With the demands being made on the *Cumberland* at this time, I need my midshipmen learning how to operate, maintain, and fight this ship rather than running their legs off being pranked by crewmen. So, here are some lessons for you to remember and pass on to your bunkies. Listen carefully. There is no such thing as a length of asteroid mooring line or a three-dimensional space sextant or a left-handed dome wrench for tightening missile nose cones in their racks. It is impossible to bail out the atmosphere condenser sump—the water you take from the sump and dump into the humidifier module is immediately evaporated and recondensed and runs right back in, so you could bail for a year and never run out of water."

He looked at the other men present. "Gentlemen, what are some of the others?"

"An RT is a reactor technician, you see?" said Brown. "So, if someone sends you to Engineering with instructions to ask one of the men at the reactor for an 'RT punch,' one of the RTs will punch you in the arm, usually hard enough to hurt. Or someone might send you to the spares bay for a 'long weight.' The spares clerk will then get up from his station and say he's going to go get it for you. He comes back in fifteen or twenty minutes or maybe even half an hour, empty handed. When you ask where your part is, he'll say something like, 'I guess the *wait* wasn't *long* enough.'"

The XO started speaking. He was a few years younger than the other men, so his recollection was fresher. "There is no such thing as a 'star hook,' 'relative bearing lubricant,' a tube of 'docking port sealant,' a 'pair of twenty-megawatt hydrogen fuses,' or a 'micrometeoroid dust filter.' There is never any need to find naval jelly for the captain's biscuits or a 'centrifuge motor for the zero G coffeepot.'"

The men all had a good laugh, with their bass and baritone and tenor guffaws joined by Hewlett's soprano/alto giggles. Max slapped the boy on the back.

"So, Hewlett, bring that 'gimbal alignment tool' to Chief Farnell with my compliments, and don't forget that I want to see him in my day cabin at the end of watch. You are dismissed." The boy came to attention and saluted. Max returned the salute, and Hewlett left.

"To be his age again! Warship service an unending wonder, nothing but adventure and the prospect of more adventure stretched out in front of you as far as the eye can see," Kraft said, gazing after the boy wistfully.

DeCosta and Brown smiled too, happy memories that had been deeply submerged in an ocean of present cares buoyed to the surface by the irresistible convection of nostalgia. The smile on the doctor's face showed that, although he spent his boyhood someplace other than a warship, childhood had been a happy time for him as well. Max, however, did his best to keep the others from seeing that the only emotion he experienced at the thought of being Hewlett's age again was undiluted horror.

Max shook it off. Or tried to. Out of the corner of his eye, he thought he caught Dr. Sahin catching him in the act of being appalled before he managed to hide it.

"I do hope, Captain, that you are not too hard on Chief Farnell," Brown said. "Although he is remarkably inept in his dealings with subordinates, he is one of my best men at diagnosing quirks in the guidance and attitude control systems. I would hate to see him take such a verbal drubbing that he ceased to be effective."

"Don't worry, Wernher," Max responded. "I am well aware of his contributions to the ship. I wasn't planning on doing anything more than telling him that I want him to lay off the mids for a while and to pass the word that I don't want them being pranked for the next month or so. We've got too many other things to do."

The engineer nodded his assent.

"Okay, folks, now that we've solved the problems of the junior midshipmen's berth, we've got our own problems to solve. Tougher problems." He gestured to the red blinking star in the projection he had started to talk about earlier. "Once we jump to this system—no name, just a catalog number—you would think that our little group would engage and destroy our two pursuers and then, since we're a light, fast frigate/destroyer group, we'd take off under compression drives at high c multiples and head across interstellar space for Rashid. Maybe not following the lubber line, you know—put a few zigs and zags in to make us hard to find in all that immensity, but otherwise we'd just strike out for our destination. The enemy would never be able to find us, much less catch us."

The illumination element went on over DeCosta's head first. "You mean, sir, that's not the plan?"

"No, XO. Not even close."

"Bloody hell," said Brown, his aristocratic Avalon accent giving the imprecation an impressive ring.

"You got that right, mate," Kraft replied in a rather feeble imitation Cockney, imperfectly picked up from watching tridvid dramatizations of Charles Dickens and Collette Farrar novels.

Max gave the group an overview of Duflot's plan and then showed them the jumps system by system. "That will take us through nine, that's right folks, a total of *nine* systems until we jump into the Rashid system. The supposed benefit of this course of action is that in each of these systems, we will have the benefit of some kind of planet-based or other high-level sensor cover, and in most of them, there are forces in place—a fighter squadron, a few system patrol craft, an older escort vessel—something of that kind."

"That's insane!" DeCosta wasn't pounding his fist on the table, but he was about as close to that as he could come in a senior officers' meeting. "Out there in all those light years, it would take a one-in-a-million stroke of wild-assed luck to get close enough just to detect us, much less get in firing position, much less be able to do all of the difficult things you have to do to be able to hit a superluminal target with subluminal weapons. You don't need planet-based sensor coverage and in-system forces to defend the group when you have light years to hide in and your speed to defend you."

"I couldn't agree with you more, XO," said Max. "And I made my point of view abundantly clear to our new group commander. So clear, in fact, that he threatened to charge me with insubordination.

"He also made clear that he had recorded the entire interview to show to Admiral Hornmeyer if he needed to show how insubordinate I am."

"Recorded it, did he?" The engineer smiled knowingly.

"So he said. Not that it matters. Recording or not, he's got us on EMCON, so I couldn't send a signal to anyone. In-group comms are by lights and lasercom. External comms are restricted to the pennant ship. Oh, and we will be setting up three-way lasercom as soon as we get into formation after going through jump, so we'll be networked with the pennant ship and the *Broadsword*."

"Formation?" DeCosta didn't bother to hide his surprise.

"That's right, XO, formation." Max didn't bother to hide his sarcasm. "We will be in line ahead formation, 250-kill interval, with the *Broadsword* on point and us as Tail End Charlie. And yes, I know that with that interval our passive sensor coverage is going to be in the shitter. Commander Duflot has, however, devised a *brilliant* solution to that problem."

"You don't mean—"

"Indeed I do, XO. Active sensors. Yankee search omni the whole way."

"Queen Bess's bleeding bottom!" It was Brown's turn, and he was moved to employ an oath he rarely used. The old Earth nation-states still mattered, even if they had long been subordinated first to the United Earth and then to the various political associations that had united humans across the stars. The ancient throne of the United Kingdom of Great Britain, Northern Ireland, and British Worlds was sat upon by the much-beloved (and splendidly beautiful) Queen Elizabeth VIII, affectionately known to her billions of subjects as "Queen Bess."

"Why not just turn on the ID transponder to the main Krag squawk frequency and broadcast in the clear in the Krag language, 'Here we bleeding are; now come blow us to flaming atoms'? It's basic inverse square law physics—given equally sensitive sensors, they can detect our active sensor transmissions and get a bearing on us at more than double the range at which we can even begin to get a detectable sensor return."

"You know, Wernher, you're actually not that far off. With what we're going to do, a transponder signal couldn't do a much better job of letting Mr. Krag know where we are. Because, you see, gentlemen, the route from jump in to jump out in each system is going to be a *pure circumferential trajectory*, three hundred AU radius, oriented exactly ninety degrees negative z to the system ecliptic."

"Okay," said DeCosta, not getting it. "That's the base course. What kind of zigzag or drunkard's walk or randomized spiral or other variation is he going to use?"

"None. The only reason it's an arc instead of a line is to get us out of the civilian traffic pattern."

That one took a moment to sink in. "None? Zero?" DeCosta was flabbergasted. "You mean that we are just going to be following a perfect geometric arc—part of a circle with a three hundred AU radius oriented exactly ninety degrees 'below' each system's ecliptic—from beginning to end: a course that any mid could plot with a compass, a protractor, a ruler, and a sheet of graph paper? Please tell me we're going to vary our acceleration at least."

"Nope. AC/DC profile Bravo. We'll use the standard acceleration for the slowest vessel in the group, which is the frigate, until we get to .455 c, and then standard deceleration as we near the jump point. The only deviation from perfect predictability is going to be in the Murban system. Duflot wants to rendezvous with NAVCOMNET relay 8677. He intends to do a laserlink with the relay so he can transmit and receive messages on the fleet network without breaking EMCON."

"But—but—but," DeCosta sputtered, stunned into inarticulacy. "The first law of destroyer and frigate combat is—"

Max nodded and made a mollifying gesture with his hand, something like a patting motion, palm facing DeCosta. "'Stealth Is Life.' If the enemy can't find you, he can't kill you. I feel your pain, XO."

"That means that anyone who wants to intercept and attack us need only plot us for an hour or two and can then extrapolate our position for the whole system crossing, get ahead of us, lie in wait, and already have a nearly perfect firing solution." The XO was really starting to get agitated. "He doesn't have to detect us on sensors. He just keeps an eye on the clock to know when to shoot. We're conceding to the enemy almost every possible advantage. Is this man on the Krag payroll?"

Max bristled. "Hold it right there, XO. It's one thing to question the competence of a brother officer. It's quite another to question his loyalty. I have no doubt that this man is as loyal to the Union and the Navy as you or I. He's simply the prisoner of rather limited abilities and of his experience. He's spent so long attached to those great convoys that are so easy to locate that he has no practical understanding at all of the tactical benefits of remaining undetected. His idea of how to defend something is to surround it with a net of sensors and layers of firepower, not to hide it in the immensity of interstellar space and then cross the void so quickly that even if the enemy localizes you, he has to run flat out to catch you, giving himself away in the process. I'll have no more of that kind of talk on my ship, even in the privacy of these meetings. Understood?"

"Understood, sir. Sorry, Captain."

"No harm done. Anyway, I made all of these tactical points to Duflot. Almost the exact words. Hell, I might as well have been trying to teach compression drive field dynamics to a gerbil."

He shook his head. "Idiot. The only thing that I can think to do is follow orders and then take a hard look to see if there is anything we can do within the scope of those orders that will make the failure of this mission a little less than inevitable. I've done one thing that might do some good, and I was wondering if—" He was interrupted by the buzz of the comm.

He hit the button. "Skipper."

"We just had a request by lights from the *Broadsword*, sir. Her skipper wants to come aboard to see the doctor. Says he needs a shot of Vanchiere-Unkel serum for his Lavoy's Syndrome and that his Casualty Station's batch of the serum is no longer usable. It got accidentally put in the ambient temperature pharmaceuticals locker instead of the refrigerated one."

Max looked at the doctor, who nodded.

"Reply that we await the honor of his visit at his convenience. Skipper out." Max shook his head before returning to his briefing.

Anyway, we've got a few more hours in this system, and with the fighter squadron from the *Wasp* flying escort, we don't have anything to worry about until we jump. In that time, maybe we can figure something that will increase the chances of the envoy meeting with the other envoys instead of with a thermonuclear warhead. Anything further? Then, we're adjourned."

They all stood and left the compartment. In the corridor, Brown pulled the XO aside and spoke in a confidential tone, too low, he knew, to be recorded by the monitoring system.

"XO, I know that things are a bit different on battleships, but out here in the destroyer and frigate Navy, we take a dim view of any affront to the honor of our ship, or to that of our captain. A very dim view indeed."

"Battleships are the same. As far as I know, that's a universal. Been that way in the whole Navy for centuries," DeCosta replied.

"Tell me then. On a battleship, would Commander Duflot's treatment of Captain Robichaux call for the taking of corrective measures?" Brown inquired.

"Absolutely. Serious ones."

"Jolly good, because it does on a destroyer as well. I would do something right now, but…"

DeCosta nodded his understanding. "But the job of vindicating the ship's honor in such a case customarily falls to the XO, doesn't it?" Brown nodded.

DeCosta stood in the corridor for a moment. What to do? On one hand, there was the possible damage to his career from taking retribution in some unknown form against Commander Duflot, a man who must have some sort of powerful connections or he would not have been given this important mission, notwithstanding his obviously limited abilities. On the other, there were the eternal and immutable naval laws. Stand for the honor of your shipmates. Stand for the honor of your captain. Stand for the honor of your ship. What to do?

It wasn't even close.

"Well, 'Wernher,' if I may be so bold as to call you that, I would like very much to even the score and am open to any suggestions you might have."

"You may, any time, sir. Now, my friend, I do have an idea that might do very nicely. We just need to enlist the help of a few more co-conspirators."

"Whoever you need. But remember, the fewer the better."

"Oh, yes. 'A slip of the lip will nuke a ship,' and all that. Just Sparks and Gates. With the four of us, we'll have everything we need to refresh Commander Duflot's understanding of historical military nomenclature."

"Historical military nomenclature?"

The engineer gave the XO a solid thump on the shoulder. "Vocabulary, my good man. We're going to give the commander an unforgettable lesson on what it means to 'hoist with one's own petard.'"

As Commander Kim Yong-Soo, skipper of the USS *Broadsword*, the second escort warship, was piped aboard and rendered honors, Max had time to get a good look at his counterpart. Captain Kim was of smallish stature and lightly built. Max had checked his Biosum and knew Kim to be four years his senior and roughly his equal in combat experience, with a reputation for being a tenacious and resourceful commander.

The "fruit salad" on his dress blue uniform (Duflot had decreed that dress blues were the Uniform of the Day throughout the group) had half a row more than Max's and included a Navy Cross and several decorations that reflected achievements in combat. He moved with the fluid efficiency of an athlete; had the beginnings of smile lines around his mouth and his dark, intelligent eyes; and looked like he was born wearing the uniform and walking the deck of a warship. Max very much liked the cut of his jib.

Honors rendered and senior officers introduced, Max caught the subtle jerk of Kim's head that indicated he wished Max, rather than the mid whom Max would ordinarily detail for the task, to walk him to the Casualty Station. During the short walk, they exchanged small talk, mainly inquiries about men with whom they had both served. Although the two men had never met, they had both been serving in combat commands in the same theater of operations for years, and so had a store of mutual friends, acquaintances, and shipmates. Kim seemed amiable enough, but studiously avoided saying anything of consequence and gave no hint why he wanted Max with him.

The two men entered the Casualty Station and were shown into one of the small treatment rooms by Dr. Sahin's head nurse, a large, burly man named Church, with immense biceps and incongruously soft hands. Kim inclined his head almost invisibly in the direction of the tiny black dome in the ceiling that held the camera for that compartment's surveillance system. Church, a fourteen-year veteran who had served eleven and a half of those years on warships in or near the FEBA, caught the motion and its significance.

"No monitoring in here, sir. Dr. Sahin hadn't been on board two hours before he asked me where 'all the bloody, damned, contemptible spy eyes' were. I showed him, and he started snipping wires himself. Naturally, that brought Major Kraft and Lieutenant Brown down here practically at a run, and there was something of a row, with the doctor yelling about patient confidentiality and the Hippocratic Oath and with the other two men going on about safety of the vessel, security of its personnel, tracking enemy boarders, and all that.

"They compromised—the doctor can be a very stubborn man as you may know—and now there is no monitoring in any patient area, but there is in the doctor's administrative office, my office, the pharmacy, and all the storage areas. If we yell 'help' in here, it will get picked up by one of those, and we'll have Marines in here in less than a minute. But otherwise, whatever goes on in this room is neither seen nor heard by anyone other than the people present."

"Thank you, Nurse Church," said Max. Church reached for the topical disinfectant applicator to prep the injection site.

"Nurse, that won't be necessary," said Kim. "I don't need the injection. It was just an excuse to get me over here to see Captain Robichaux for an informal conference. Now, I'd be grateful if you'd excuse us, but remain in a nonmonitored area so it won't look as though you left us alone." Church looked at Max to see if the request was to be honored. Max nodded his approval and Church left.

"Sorry for all the cloak-and-dagger bullshit, Max. May I call you Max?" Max nodded. "Great. My friends call me Sue." In response to Max's questioning expression, he added. "Long story. Involves a very old American country-western song. Anyway, my friends do call me Sue, and I'd be grateful if you would as well."

"It would be my pleasure, Sue." The two shook hands. "Now, what can I do for you?"

Despite having what was apparently a highly direct nature, Kim seemed to be having a hard time getting started. Apparently, he was uncomfortable with what he'd come here to say, so he attacked the subject from the flank.

"Thank you for the honors when I came aboard. Not every skipper has shown me that level of courtesy."

"As in when you went on board the pennant?"

"You might say that," said Kim.

"Let me guess: you came aboard on the port side, through the servants' entrance, and found yourself saluting the auxiliary shit pump?"

"Exactly. We watched him do the same thing to you, although we couldn't see what happened when you went aboard."

"And when you met with him, I suppose he treated you like deck grunge from one of the enlisted head areas that he'd just scraped off the sole of his shoe, right?"

"That's about the size of it," Kim agreed. "I couldn't believe it. He and I are the same rank. Of course, he's still my senior by virtue of time in grade and being appointed commander of the group, but that just means I have to follow his orders, not that he can treat me like an inferior. I wouldn't even talk to a mid the way he talked to me. It was beyond outrageous. Of course, I know why."

"I wish you'd clue me in."

"Jealousy. Pure, bitter jealousy. The man has been stuck on convoy duty almost his entire career, hasn't been within ten AU of a Krag, and feels that he's been unfairly robbed of his opportunity for glory, honor, and promotion. He resents officers like us with combat records who are on the promotion ladder. He knows that unless something very improbable happens, he'll die a commander at the con of a frigate or behind a desk, either at the grade he holds today or with a courtesy promotion to captain on the eve of retirement so he can draw a higher pension and spend the rest of his life being introduced as 'Captain Duflot' at cocktail parties.

"Between you and me, having him con a Compaq-MAC class workstation would be a favor to everyone because the man's a menace in a CIC. What he doesn't get is that it's not lack of combat experience that is giving the brass the false sense that he can't cut it in battle; it's the absolute certainty on the part of the brass that he can't cut it in battle that has prevented him from accumulating combat experience. I was in his CIC when he was working a contact. Took him and his people more than half an hour to get it localized and classified. Turns out it was a merchie with a malfunctioning squawk box. No big deal. Thing is, though, she was at intermediate range, no stealth, no tricks, following a lubber line course. Your people or mine would have had her localized and classified with a firing solution computed, have run the registration, and would have known the size of her skipper's pecker to millimeter precision in six or seven minutes."

Well, on the Cumberland, maybe twelve or thirteen. Max nodded slowly. Based on what he had seen and what he knew about human nature, it made sense. He understood it. He had even seen it before. But he had no clue what could be done about it. He met Kim's eyes. Kim shook his head.

"Nope. Knowing why doesn't help, except to let you know that you, personally, didn't do anything to earn all the crap the man is shoving in your direction."

"That is good to know, but getting shit on by Commander Duflot is the least of my worries."

"I know," said Kim. "We've got some big ones. One you know about. One you don't. The one you don't know about is that Duflot doesn't believe that the flag stops at the hull."

Max looked at Kim incredulously. "Where does the flag stop, then?"

"It doesn't."

This was an important revelation. Although the *formal* authority of an officer in overall command of a group of ships (a "flag") was as complete as the authority of a captain over his own ship, tradition and custom imposed substantial limitations on that power. One of the most important of these was the long-standing practice that the flag's *actual* authority over other skippers' ships under his command extended only to their deployment and tactics, but not to how they were administered.

The flag would tell the captains in more or less detail, depending on the circumstances, where to go, what formations to assume, when to attack or withdraw, what weapons to fire, and when to fire them. What custom and tradition said they must *not* do is to tell a captain how to run his ship: setting procedures, decreeing the Uniform of the Day, imposing discipline on anyone but the captain, managing personnel, and making maintenance and repair decisions.

After giving Max a moment to process the news, Kim continued. "We caught him trying to pull a dump of all our internal surveillance data, logs, my personal logs, internal text messages, basically everything that you and I regard as sacrosanct."

"How did you catch him? You shouldn't have been able to detect it since his command of the group gives him the necessary clearances. He's just not supposed to use them absent a good reason."

"Normally, it would have gone undetected. I don't suppose I'm revealing any dark secret if I tell you that some of us—I mean ships of the *Longbow* class, especially my ship and the *Rapier*—have been on some rather stimulating intel gathering missions.

"After all, until you guys came along in the *Khyber* class, we were the stealthiest thing going. We've got a blacker than black dedicated processor and gateway infrastructure that's specifically designed to 'hack, nutcrack, and sack,' that is, worm our way into the Krag data networks, break their encryption protocols, and pull dumps on their data. One time when the *Rapier* tried it, the Krag network was set up to reverse hack any intruder, and they almost lost the ship—had to pull the plug on the main computer core and come home in the auxiliary.

"So we've got all sorts of reverse firewalls that other ships don't have, including a really robust set that locks out all non-public files from any external access of any kind, including access by an authorized user, even one who has all the right passwords, without specific biometrically verified approval of a command level officer physically located on my ship. As soon as he got into our system, the firewalls shut him out of all the data and alerted us. Other than the public files he would have access to anyway, he got bupkis. We've been pretending that nothing happened and so has he, but I wanted you to know."

He reached into a pocket of his tunic and pulled out a data chip. "Here's the firewall software. We know it will run on your hardware because it was written to run on *Khybers* as well as *Longbows*. In fact, I'm pretty sure it's already on your system somewhere, hidden behind a password that the brass will give you if they ever decide you need it.

"By the way, that processor and gateway infrastructure we use to break into the Krag computers—you've got the hardware on board right now. Check your spares bay for a crate marked 'ATAD HUNTING GEAR.' Very clever. 'ATAD' is 'DATA' spelled backward. You don't need the hardware to keep Duflot out, but you'll want to install the software right away. That way it will have time to propagate through all your gateways and distributed processor architecture. Then when we laserlink after the jump, he'll be locked out of all the high-level stuff. Duflot will just assume that, since *Khyber* is basically an updated *Longbow* with a few more sacrifices made in the name of stealth, you've got the same sort of software protections as we do. He won't suspect that I gave this to you on the sly."

Installing software on the ship's main computer without the explicit direction or approval of the Office of the Deputy Chief of Naval Operations for Information Processing and Electronic Dominance violated half a dozen regulations. Further, installing a modification to the ship's operating system without review by his own data processing department on the word of a destroyer captain he'd met less than an hour before was both a great leap of faith and an enormous declaration of trust. Both men knew these things. Nevertheless, Max immediately took the chip and walked over to the mini-workstation in the exam room that the doctor typically used to input his exam notes.

Kim continued, "I was worried you wouldn't want to install it. That's why I went to all these pains not to be recorded telling you this. I don't mind what I say going into your system, but I do mind this asshole Duflot being able to find out about it just because he feels like it. He'd probably bring me up on charges."

"Well, we can't have that, can we?" Max pushed a button that caused a dust cover to slide out of place, revealing a socket for the data chip. He inserted it, hit READ, and then walked through all the steps necessary to convince the computer that he was a user authorized to make changes to the firewall and operating system. He then flagged the changes for the attention of his Ensign Bales, and left a short note explaining the reason.

"Okay, that's done," said Max. "We can say what we want without being eavesdropped on by Commander Duflot. What a sad and sorry state of affairs that is. Now, what do we do about our bigger problem? I've got a few ideas."

"Glad to hear it. I've got one or two of my own as well," said Kim. "Max, Commander Duflot's orders for the group are very specific. It's going to be impossible to do anything that will do any good without violating them, at least to some degree. What I have in mind certainly does."

"Same here. All other things being equal, I'd rather not have to go through a court martial. But if that's what it takes to keep Commander Duflot's stupidity from getting the envoy killed, not to mention ourselves and our men... We do what we have to do. If they court martial us for it, we can freeze our asses off on Europa or dig tunnels in asteroids with a clean conscience."

"I thought you'd see it that way. Between you and me, let's see if we can cook up a few surprises for the rat-faces. To that end, I've brought you a small present in my launch."

"What are you going to do about this cretin Duflot's imbecilic directives? Surely, you're not just going to say that *yours is not to reason why.*"

The doctor asked his question over dinner in the skipper's day cabin. Max and Bram had gotten into the habit of having dinner together two or three times a week, depending on demands of duty. Max had also gotten in the habit of notifying Chief Boudreaux in the galley when he would be dining with the doctor. The chief tended to rise above his generally high level of culinary achievement in the preparation of those meals, knowing that they were not likely, as was sometimes the case with other dinners, to be allowed to get cold and be nibbled on half-heartedly later because the person for whom they were prepared was absorbed in untangling some shipboard administrative problem or in treating some crewman's accidental injury.

Tonight the men were dining on a dish that Dr. Sahin had never eaten previously, Southern fried chicken. Not that he hadn't been offered it before, but he had an aversion to the concept of *frying* chicken. Chicken is fatty to start with, and the idea of cooking it by immersion in hot oil seemed a procedure guaranteed to produce a dish that was inedibly greasy. The actual dish proved to be utterly at variance from his expectations.

He never imagined that so prosaic a victual as the humble chicken could be covered with such exquisite, light, crispy, flavorful crust that would—with just the right amount of resistance, like an eager but shy virgin on her wedding night—yield to admit the suitor to the sensual delights within. And what delights!

It was one of the best things he had ever tasted. Bram had marched steadily through a drumstick and a thigh before he even noticed the other dishes on the table: rice with rich cream gravy flavored with crispy pan leavings from the chicken, corn on the cob (previously frozen but still tasty), and a fruit salad made from a variety of canned and frozen fruits.

Max was washing his dinner down with ship's beer, a staple on warships. Beer had a limited shelf life, and warships, often operating without resupply for many months, had to either make their own or do without. The quality of the brew varied wildly from ship to ship, ranging from frothy nectar sung into being by luminous angels to foaming swill passed from the bladders of diabetic water buffalos.

The *Cumberland*'s beer, like that of most ships, fell somewhere in the broad middle of that scale, perhaps a little better than most, and slowly improving in the opinion of the more discerning beer drinkers in the crew. The current brewer had started with no previous knowledge but was learning rapidly from experience and was even finding that he was blessed with a fair amount of aptitude in the art.

Since the ship's previous "brewmaster" had been transferred off the ship after the Battle of Pfelung, and as the replacement draft had not supplied a man who had ever brewed so much as a single barrel, Chief Boudreaux had picked a culinary specialist out of the group of new men, pointed him in the direction of the ship's compact but capable brewery, and told him that everything he needed to know was in the database. When the man asked why he had been picked for this duty over the other three galley crewmen in that draft, Boudreaux had replied that there was something about his name that inspired confidence. And so far, the men were reasonably satisfied with the work of Ordinary Spacer Second Class Bodo "Bud" Schlitz.

"As I was saying, you're not going to just blindly do what you are told under these circumstances. I know you. You've come up with some sort of devious way of turning these things around. You and this Captain Kim fellow seem to be cut from the same cloth. I'm sure you and he have an idea or two."

"Now, Doctor, are you accusing Captain Kim and me of conspiring to circumvent the orders of a superior officer? I'm shocked. Aghast. Dismayed."

"None of which, I hasten to point out, is anything remotely in the way of a denial."

Max shrugged. The comm buzzed. "Skipper."

"Skipper, this is Marconi on comms." Chin had gone off watch. Marconi was the number two man in that department, an eager and conscientious recruit spacer first who, in a few weeks, was likely to be minted as an ensign, the *Cumberland*'s first "homegrown nugget" since Max assumed command. He had chosen to specialize in Communications, notwithstanding that any "Marconi" in the Communications Section was going to be ribbed mercilessly for the rest of his career and, most likely, well into retirement.

"We just got a signal by lights from the *Broadsword*. It's for you and the doctor from Captain Kim. It's in your box."

"Thank you, Marconi. Skipper out." Max got up from the table, walked over to his workstation, accessed the message, and put it up on the display wall.

It read: "BE ADVISED THAT WHILE VISITING THIS VESSEL ENVOY SUFFERED OPEN MULTIPLE FRACTURE OF TIBIA AND FIBULA REQUIRING SURGICAL IMMOBILIZATION STOP HE WANTED TO SHOW THAT HE COULD STILL SLIDE DOWN ACCESS LADDER QUOTE JUST LIKE A MID UNQUOTE STOP ON ORDERS OF DOCTOR SINGH AND WITH CONCURRENCE OF CMO ON PENNANT ENVOY IS NOT TO BE MOVED AND WILL REMAIN ON THIS VESSEL FOR REMAINDER OF PASSAGE STOP MESSAGE ENDS."

"I suppose that this is part of your little scheme, right?"

"I have no idea what you are talking about. I'm certain that Captain Kim would never make a false communication of that sort. And I'm upset that this would happen to the envoy. He seemed such a decent fellow."

"Of course, you are. But why would you and Kim do such a thing?"

The comm buzzed. It was Marconi, again notifying Max of another signal by lights, this one from the pennant. Max displayed it as he had the other. "AS ENVOY IS ABOARD BROADSWORD THAT VESSEL IS DESIGNATED PIGEON AND PENNANT WILL ASSUME THE LEAD IN FORMATION TO BE ASSUMED AFTER JUMP STOP ALL OTHER ORDERS UNCHANGED STOP DUFLOT SENDS STOP MESSAGE ENDS."

The doctor smiled knowingly. "Aha. It now becomes clearer. You wanted to get the envoy on the *Broadsword* and get her put in the middle of the formation. Again, I do not understand the reasons, and I know better than to ask you about them because you will only deny that anything is afoot, or if you admit that you are up to something, you won't tell me, either to keep me out of trouble or to heighten the suspense. One day you will learn that I do not care to be kept out of trouble and that I do care very much about avoiding suspense, but our friendship is not yet sufficiently mature for you to have derived those lessons."

"Maybe I will. Or maybe I enjoy hearing your theories and speculation too much to replace them with specific information. In any event, we're jumping in a few minutes, and I want to be in CIC for some things I plan to do immediately thereafter. Feel free to join me. My steward has told me that there will be Wortham-Biggs Four Planet Coffee in CIC for the next few hours."

"That's all the incentive I need. I'll meet you there."

CHAPTER 11

10:02Z Hours, 26 March 2315

"Initiating standard acceleration profile." Chief LeBlanc was not entirely successful in eliminating from his voice all signs of his disapproval of following a standard acceleration profile under the current circumstances. The *Cumberland* had just jumped into the Kalkaz system after the *William Gorgas* and the *Broadsword.* The other two ships had begun their acceleration through the system along the mathematically perfect arc prescribed by Commander Duflot's orders, and the *Cumberland* fell into its place at the end of the line ahead formation, exactly 250 kilometers behind *Broadsword*, its sensors nearly blinded by proximity to the other ship's drive emissions even if "behind" meant offset just enough so that the ship was not actually swimming in the gases emitted from the other destroyer.

"Sensor efficiency down across the board," noted Kasparov.

"Well, we know what to do about that, now, don't we," said Max. "Deploy the towed array. Let's start off with a hundred kilometers."

"Deploy the towed array, aye, one hundred kills." Kasparov activated the sequence, and one of his displays that had been showing an overly noisy output from an EM detector switched over to a screen entitled "TOWED ARRAY STATUS" and immediately began to show a grid of numbers.

After a few minutes of pulling up various displays on his console, with increasing frustration, Dr. Sahin, who had wandered into CIC with Clouseau at his heels, leaned over toward Max and said confidentially, "Max, I took your advice and was doing some reading on this ship's systems, and I distinctly remember reading something to the effect that the *Khyber* class vessels are equipped with the stowage spool and the deployment arm for the towed array as contingency equipage but are not provided with the array itself or the dedicated processor for interpreting the towed array's output because a ship with a deployed array gives up a great deal of the maneuverability that is one of the class's assets. Did I read that incorrectly?"

"No, you got it right," Max said blandly.

"What am I missing, then?"

"Towed array deployed to one hundred kills," interrupted Kasparov. "Moving it forty kills plus z. Mr. Chin and I have convinced the computers to reroute the data as we discussed. Implementing reroute now." About ten seconds later, a new display popped up on Kasparov's console, this one labeled "TOWED ARRAY CONTACTS OVERVIEW."

"Receiving data from the towed array, sir. It looks like we're getting a clean read too. Only issue is that having to route the data through the laserlink two ways cuts into the refresh rate, but thirty times a minute is plenty for what we're doing."

"Very well, Mr. Kasparov. Have your people keep a close watch on the data stream. They're not used to the way the data from a tail looks, so it's probably a good idea to bring in a few extra men from off watch to back up the ones you've got, in case they miss something."

"*Outstanding* idea, sir. I'll do that." Kasparov spoke into his headset, suppressing a smile while giving orders to Ensign Harbaugh to implement the captain's suggestion.

Max turned his attention back to the doctor and spoke softly. "What you're missing is that it's not *our* towed array. We borrowed it."

"*Borrowed* it?"

"Yep. From the *Broadsword*. She can't use it in this formation without creating a risk that the trailing vessel—which is us—might collide with it. So, Kim brought it with him in his launch when he came over yesterday. Actually, he brought his spare. His main is still installed—just not deployed. We're putting the raw data on the laserlink, running it through his towed array signal processor, and he's sending us back the processed data for tactical resolution and display on our consoles."

"And pray tell, does Commander Duflot know about this?"

Max stared into his coffee mug. "It's such a minor matter that we just handled it between the skippers. We saw no need to trouble him with something so unimportant, what with all the weighty things the man has on his mind right now." While he was talking, Max had pulled up the readouts from the array and was squinting at them with an eye honed by years as a sensor officer. "Mister Kasparov, kindly extend the array to 250 kills, and stabilize the terminus forty kills plus z."

While Kasparov was acknowledging and implementing the order, Bram thought about what Max had done, and it made sense. Contrary to Max's constant snide comments, the doctor had been diligently plowing through the enormous volume of study materials that Max had recommended to him.

From these studies, he knew that a towed array, an idea borrowed from the saltwater navy, was a heavily stealthed passive sensor antenna towed behind the ship at the end of an almost microscopically thin carbon nanotube filament. A guidance package at the end contained an inertial stabilization system, a fuel supply, and thrusters to keep the cable taut and to allow the operator to control the location of the array relative to the drive stream, usually offset from it by about forty kilometers in one direction or another. The towed array allowed the *Cumberland* to have clear sensor reception notwithstanding that it was in *Broadsword*'s wake, particularly given that all three ships were blasting the area with active sensor sweeps, the returns from which were received with exquisite sensitivity by the array's kilometer-and-a-half-long sensor filaments.

"Oh, Mr. Kasparov, you did tell your people what I said about those contacts we talked about, right?"

"Yes, sir. Absolutely. It's all taken care of."

"Outstanding." Max didn't catch the slight smirk that wriggled its way across many of the faces in CIC at the word "outstanding."

"And Mr. Chin, you and the Comms man on the *Broadsword*... you've set up that direct comms override right to the skipper's console over there?"

"Affirmative, sir," Chin answered. "The SUMMON STEWARD—COFFEE button on your console has been reprogrammed to tie you into the override. We thought it best to use a hard key—you know, a physical button instead of a soft key. More positive. Just hit that button and everything you say will come straight out of the comm on the skipper's console over on the *Broadsword*."

"But what if I want coffee?"

"The Control Input Logs show that you've never touched that button since you've come on board, sir. You always have a mid pour you some from the CIC coffeepot."

"I guess that is what I do, isn't it? Outstanding job, Mr. Chin."

"Thank you, sir."

Max looked around CIC. Funny, how he had not taken many slow, careful looks around this compartment in the two months and four days he had been in command. It was the same compartment, and mostly the same men, who had greeted him on 21 January, at which time he'd surprised them all by stepping onto the command island wearing his Space Combat Uniform, a sidearm, and a boarding cutlass, when everyone else was in dress blues. It looked pretty much the same. It felt very different.

Those men in January were losers. Verbally and psychologically abused by a borderline psychotic CO, exhausted and distracted by his obsessions with cleanliness and control, humiliated in encounters with the enemy and in exercises, they hadn't been fit to do battle with a troop of Junior Wilderness Girls, much less the best the Krag had to throw at them. Now, these men were winners. They had met the enemy in battle, had even taken on multiple vessels of superior force, seen their enemies consumed by nuclear fire, and lived to tell the tale. They were confident. Some of them even had a bit of a swagger to their step.

They had been through danger and hardship together and emerged, not only still alive but triumphant. Sure, they still had a long way to go in terms of competence and training and teamwork, but they believed in their skipper and themselves. That made all the difference. They had come so far. But they still had so far to go. Max knew that, somehow, he would get them there. He felt deep in his heart that his destiny and the destiny of these men were bound together for some great purpose, two metals hammer-forged into a single weapon stronger and more resilient than either alone. If only they could live through the next several days.

It was beginning to look like Commander Duflot had been right, and the tactic of crossing through systems with sensor nets and defense forces in place was paying off. At each jump in, the pennant vessel would communicate with jump control, and the tiny "convoy" would wait for whatever forces were available—a few fighters, an SPC or two, one or two superannuated reserve-force destroyers—to rendezvous. They would then move out, crossing the system in the rigorously geometric course Duflot prescribed.

In this manner, they crossed the Kalkaz system and the Murban system, where they also rendezvoused with a Union Naval Comm relay. Doing so allowed the pennant vessel to establish a laserlink with the buoy and thereby tie directly into the Naval Communications Network without breaking EMCON. The pennant received mail for the entire group, as well as sent and received several messages, including one message that Duflot did not command be sent and that, had he known about it, he would have moved heaven and earth to stop.

CHAPTER 12

04:18Z Hours, 30 March 2315

After Murban, it was on to the Madoom system, thence to Schewe 23, and thereafter to Edmonton B. That system had the weakest sensor coverage of any system along the route, there being no planet with a solid surface on which to lay the grids of 146-kilometer-long superconducting cables that are the most efficient means of transmitting the powerful phase- and polarization-modulated pulses of tachyo-gravitons and tachyo-photons that were the best way to scan an entire solar system for hostile ships.

Sensor coverage in the Edmonton B system was provided by two SWACS-equipped frigates, which was good, in theory, but no matter where one positioned the ships, there would be sensor shadows from the one molten, one ocean-covered, and three gaseous planets the system boasted, as well as interference fringes created by the interaction of the sensor transmissions from the two ships. Taken together, these phenomena created huge blind areas in which ships could hide as well as lots of paths a stealthy ship could take through the system without being detected.

"Wouldn't we have seen the Krag jumping into these systems after us? There is that burst of Cherenkov-Heaviside radiation that you tell me is highly distinctive." Despite the early hour, the doctor was in CIC. He liked to be there when something interesting was happening. The ship was at Condition Orange, which was one readiness state higher than the Blue where Max kept the ship most of the time. Above that, there was Amber and, finally, Red, or general quarters. There were no identified threats in the system, but this was where Max expected to be hit.

"No, we wouldn't because the Krag ships aren't jumping after us. They would have watched us jump out of that first system, then run to the next system on their compression drives, getting there while we were still crossing from jump in to jump out. It wouldn't take many jumps for them to figure out what we're doing and to predict our route. Then they just get a few jumps ahead of us and lie in wait, which is what they're doing somewhere. I'm betting it's here. Somewhere."

Max turned to DeCosta who was at his station. "XO, put yourself in the shoes, or should I say 'footwear,' of the Krag who want to ambush our little *convoy*." Max heaped the word with all the scorn that born hunters had for the idea of plodding through space along a predictable path while waiting for the enemy to come to them. It was the contempt that a wolf might have for a ewe.

"Well, sir," he answered, making it clear that he had given some thought to the matter, "there are four places I regard as likely." He gestured toward the tactical projection, which at the moment displayed only a 1 AU radius around the ship. Max nodded. DeCosta touched a few soft keys, and the display changed to an overview of the *Cumberland*'s trajectory from jump in to jump out.

The geometrically perfect curve of the group's projected course, traced in green, gracefully arced through the back cube of the projection. A tiny yellow dot near the top of the display represented the system's primary, Edmonton B. None of the planets were visible at this scale. DeCosta touched another key, and four short segments of the green curve turned red.

"The two SWACS ships are flying ovals at opposite ends of the system. These first three segments are places where one of the shadows cast by one planet or another from some point in one of these ovals intersects our trajectory. Coverage is going to be weaker along those segments for at least part of each SWACS ship's patrol cycle. The fourth is an area where our path passes near where a Krag frigate was destroyed by compression shear two days ago when it was running from the USS *Battleax*. There's still a lot of residual interference. In any of those areas, our warning horizon isn't going to be much more than it would be with just our own active sensors, which, against a highly stealthed ship, isn't going to be much. Even with the tail deployed, we'd get only a few seconds before they were in missile range."

"Outstanding, XO. Absolutely outstanding. Let's see how it matches up with my analysis." Max's voice was genuinely enthusiastic and was loud enough for everyone in CIC to know that he was praising the XO about something. Max touched a soft key on his own display, and the four red segments turned orange as yellow segments, almost perfectly congruent, were superimposed on them. A very close match.

Except for one tiny spot.

There was a tiny speck of yellow almost in the middle of the long curve: a segment of the curve so short that it was almost indistinguishable from a point in space. The XO pointed to it. "What's that one?"

"I didn't expect you to identify that one, XO. It's dynamic and not static. When the first SWACS frigate, the *Sicily*, is at the point of its oval most distant from Edmonton B, and the second one, the *Cypress*, is 69 percent of the way through its oval, there is a temporary interference zone created here, lasting for just under thirty minutes. One of the times that zone comes into existence is when we are right here." Max touched a key, and a pale, yellow, blinking spot came into existence, right beside the tiny yellow segment.

"And what's worse, is that the interference pattern created is going to be fractal/chaotic, meaning that it will destroy the coherence of our own active sensor transmissions. Except for passive EM and mass detection, we'll be blind."

"But that shouldn't be a problem," DeCosta said. "Just signal the pennant to increase or decrease speed, and sensor coverage in that area will be normal when we go through."

"Absolutely correct, XO. It *shouldn't* be a problem. But Commander Duflot will not alter speed so much as a meter per second. So, the sensor gap will absolutely be there right when we get there. And that's where they're going to hit us. I'd bet our last ton of deuterium on it."

The doctor had been watching the proceedings with intense interest, without saying anything until now. "What makes you so sure? Why not in those other places?" Max looked at DeCosta, whose inquiring look communicated the same question.

"Remember what Sun Tzu said about knowing your enemy?" Both men answered in the affirmative. "Well, one thing that is essential to know about the Krag is that they are the galaxy's greatest experts on stealth, evasion, and any kind of hiding. Maybe it's because of their rodent ancestry, or maybe it's just a talent that they have evolved as they became sentient. In either event, they are far more attuned than most of us to the nuances of detection and perception, and are experts at exploiting weaknesses in both."

The *Cumberland* had passed without incident through the first three of the danger zones jointly predicted by the CO and XO. The fourth jointly predicted zone was only five hours ahead, but the area where Max expected to be attacked was ten minutes ahead. *Cumberland* and *Broadsword* were at general quarters: all hands at battle stations, all weapons and defenses ready, engines standing by for rapid maneuvering.

Max had dutifully informed Commander Duflot of his expectation. Ignoring the warning, Duflot had the *William Gorgas* at Condition Green. Duflot's signal, informing Max of his decision not to bring his ship to a higher alert status, included the statement: "I SEE NO NEED TO PUT MY CREW THROUGH THE INCONVENIENCE OF STANDING TO GENERAL QUARTERS WHEN THE ONLY EVIDENCE OF HEIGHTENED DANGER IS THE QUESTIONABLE JUDGMENT OF AN INFERIOR OFFICER."

There was no doubt in Max's mind that Duflot meant the word "inferior" in both senses of the word.

Max hoped that Commander Duflot, and indeed the whole group, didn't pay too dearly for his arrogance.

"Mr. Chin, you did signal 'Mike Victor' using the aft omni light?"

"Aye, Skipper, just over three minutes ago. There's no way the pennant saw it."

"Outstanding." He turned to Kasparov. "Everyone in your section needs to be sharp, but I want particular vigilance on the sensor bands the enemy uses for his shipboard targeting scanners.

Not the general sensors they use to localize other ships, but the ones they activate to get a target lock for their missiles. You detect anything that even smells like that, I want to know about it. Don't wait for a confirmation or a second phenomenology or to take a closer look at it. Understood? We're not going to get much warning. With the tail, we're going to get just a few more seconds than Mr. Krag thinks, and we need to take full advantage of them."

"Understood, sir. We're ready. I've got two extra men on that console in my back room, and Goldman is going to be here in about a minute to back me up on this console."

"Goldman?"

"Yes, Skipper. I know he was busted, and I'm not presuming to promote him back to CIC status, but he is the sharpest man I've got on that kind of detection. I'd feel better with him at my side, sir."

"Kasparov, it's your department and you'll be making the call, so if you want to dig up Sir John Jellicoe and put him in that chair, you won't have any complaints from me. Just tell Goldman not to get too comfortable up here. He's still got time to serve down in the waste treatment plant."

"Aye, sir."

Max sat down at his station, unconsciously rubbing his palms on the legs of his uniform to wipe off the sweat. This one was going to be hairy. Just then, Goldman cycled through the CIC security door, followed by a Marine who took up station inside the door. Goldman had lost his general CIC clearance, which meant that if he were in CIC, the Marine would be there too.

A moment later, the doctor cycled through the door. Clouseau came in with him, scampering around his feet while somehow managing not to trip him or get stepped on. Cats do that somehow. The doctor sat at the Commodore's Station, while Clouseau curled up on top of the signal condition equipment box for the Sensors station. The extra signal-processing load from the towed array was making the unit run about 10 degrees warmer than usual, making the box a nice toasty, pre-warmed cat perch, with the added benefit of putting the cat within easy reach of both Goldman and Finnegan, should either have a mind to pet a cat while on watch.

Clouseau stretched invitingly, which resulted in a brief scratch behind the ears and under the chin from Finnegan. Goldman was too wrapped up in his console to notice. Clouseau looked at him with obvious irritation. Goldman was now on the cat's shit list. Anyone who does not believe cats have shit lists has never lived with a cat.

Seconds ticked by, tension gripping all of CIC like a vise. Max found himself having to make a distinct expenditure of attention and effort to keep from sitting on the edge of his seat or fidgeting or standing at the Sensors station watching the take from the towed array. He willed himself to sit back, hands on the arms of the chair or holding his coffee, radiating calm. He wasn't fooling anyone.

He kept glancing over at Kasparov and Goldman, intent upon their console, scrutinizing each of the apparently random dots representing signals processed out of the towed array. Max gave in to temptation and pulled up the same displays Kasparov and Goldman were watching.

To the untrained eye, they were nothing more than two screens, each consisting of a black background covered with a few dozen tiny dots in assorted colors. Each dot represented some kind of signal detection. The location of the dots on the screen, left or right, indicated relative bearing. One screen displayed the bearing on a horizontal plane level with the decks of the ship, with dead ahead in the center, and the two edges each representing dead astern; the other displayed the bearing to the same contacts on a vertical plane, perpendicular to the decks, with "above" the ship in the center, and "below" at the two edges of the display. To help the operator correlate the two representations of each contact, the system would highlight the dot representing a contact on one screen when the operator would touch the corresponding dot on the other with his finger or a stylus.

Each screen's vertical axis represented time, with the newest signals at the top, a new line painting itself across the top of the screen once every two seconds, causing the previous lines to move slowly downward, leading to this data output mode being known as a "waterfall display." The size of the dots showed strength of the signal, and color showed the frequency. If several different frequencies were detected at the same bearing, the computer would display the dots very closely together, surround them with a set of brackets, and place a bright orange vertical line at the actual bearing. A strong detection would show up as a series of large dots, of many colors, accumulating one atop the other in a column, either straight or slanting to one side as the source and the receiver moved relative to one another.

Max pondered the situation. If he was a Krag trying to pounce on this group, where would he lurking? Not dead ahead, because that's where the group-leading *William Gorgas*'s active sensor scans would be the strongest. And not dead astern, because Señor El-Krag can see that there are destroyers in the group and many destroyers are equipped with towed arrays that would provide sensitive coverage in that direction. And not dead abeam, because those bearings represent the flanks that we mammals with vital organs in our rib cages instinctively protect.

No, they're rodents and we're primates. When we're on the ground, we tend to see the threats as coming from around and above us, not below. But underground and in the underbrush is where the rodent goes when he feels threatened. Given his druthers, a rodent comes from underneath and goes for the belly or the throat or the genitalia, which is the last place a primate expects to be attacked.

"Mr. Kasparov, let's shift the towed array negative z to the drive trail, forty-five kills."

"Aye, sir, shift the tail negative z to the wake, zero-four-five kills. And sir, Goldman suggested the same thing about two seconds before you did."

"Outstanding. Good to see that Mr. Goldman is back to his old self. We're going to need everyone's best today, I think." Goldman was one of the crew members who had been taking illegal drugs made on board by the now imprisoned Spacer Green, using an illegally obtained MediMax pharmaceutical synthesizer. Goldman had been taking stims, whereas most of the other drug abusers were taking an antianxiety medication called the "Chill."

"And Mr. Chin, blinker the Piranhas that they might want to focus their attention in our forward, ventral zone, offset twenty-five to thirty-five degrees from our base course on both axes."

Although the group was on EMCON, when the fighters stationed in this system showed up to escort the group, Max had Chin blinker them on the sly, filling them in on the situation and asking them to watch for blinkered Morse code "suggestions" from the *Cumberland*'s aft signal light, positioned where it was invisible from the pennant ship. Max's growing reputation nearly guaranteed that the fighter pilots would be receptive to those suggestions. The four fighters that joined the group, twenty-year-old but still serviceable FS-51 Piranhas, ducked their finger-four formation under the group, divided into two-ship elements, and diverged to accelerate ahead in order to sanitize the area Max was concerned about, blasting it with active sensor transmissions.

Max focused his attention again on the feed from the towed array on his console. He turned his eye to the area of the screen representing the bearings from which he thought the Krag vessels most likely to appear. Just a few random dots. Nothing yet. He picked up a dry-erase marker, commonly used in CIC for indicating or highlighting information on displays, and drew brackets around the bearings where he expected the Krag to be hiding. And just to be sure of himself, he instructed the computer to show him on an adjacent display dots of the colors associated with the most likely Krag missile targeting frequencies. Yep. Those were just the shades of garish pinkish-purple and coffee-with-too-much-cream-in-it tan that he remembered.

His eyes went back to the two waterfall displays, and he looked again at the bracketed areas of the top lines. Nothing. Just a random speck or two of the wrong colors. He saw the men fidgeting. These men were smart, and like spacers going back to the beginning of the space services and the saltwater sailors before them, they were good at reading the mood of their captain. The captain was expecting trouble, and so were they.

Five minutes passed. Ten. The fighters moved from one area to another, systematically searching with eyes and sensors. The group would be out of the danger area in just four more minutes. Max could almost feel Commander Duflot gloating.

But they weren't out of the woods yet. This is just when people start to think they've got it made. Just where their vigilance starts to slacken. Max could feel it around him: stances more relaxed, people taking a second or two to look away from their displays every now and then. They needed to be reminded.

"Just because we're *almost* out doesn't mean we *are* out, people. If I had a tail and whiskers, this is just when I'd hit us." He felt the men's vigilance tighten.

He turned his own eyes back to the two waterfall displays in front of him, focusing on the two areas he had bracketed. Maybe he was being too clever. As the *Cumberland* approached the edge of the interference zone, there was less and less space inside the zone at those bearings relative to the ship. Maybe they would come from the flanks or from the dorsal direction. His eyes ran along the tops of the displays along every line of bearing. He couldn't watch them all at once. That was what he had Sensors people for, but he just couldn't keep himself from looking, even if Kasparov and Goldman might take it as a sign that he didn't trust them to spot a threat as rapidly as he could.

Couldn't keep himself from looking? Bullshit. He switched the displays from the towed array data channels to the fusion reactor efficiency/performance plots. He would trust his people.

To make a point of it, he turned away from Sensors to Weapons. "Mr. Levy, when we have well cleared the danger area, I'm going to stand down from general quarters. This time, when you take the pulse cannons from Ready back down to Prefire, I want to do a purge of the cryoconduits and get someone from GM to verify—"

Out of the corner of his eye, Max saw Goldman stiffen, then point to one of the waterfall displays. Kasparov shifted his gaze to where Goldman was pointing. In the half-second or so that these two actions took, Max turned back to face his console and was reaching for the reconfigured "SUMMON STEWARD—COFFEE" button when Kasparov called out, "Contact! Likely Krag missile targeting scanners, two sources close together, bearing one-zero-seven mark one-eight-five. Signal strength indicates close range."

The rodents came from underneath and a little behind, right for the primate's genitals.

Max felt every inch of skin on his body shrink as a torrent of adrenalin poured into him. The hand that he had shifted to be near the coffee button slammed down with unintended force, shattering the plastic and impressing its shape on Max's palm in a bruise that he would carry for more than a month. Over the now-open voice channel that connected him directly to the CO's console on the *Broadsword*, he nearly shouted: "Dynamo! Dynamo! Dynamo! Dynamo!"

For a while, Max needed to give no more orders. Knowing that seconds, even fractions of seconds, would count when the Krag attack was detected, he and Captain Kim had worked out a complex series of orders to be implemented instantly as soon as he gave the "Dynamo!" call.

First and most important, Max and Kim had agreed that they had to achieve the mission's objective—getting the envoy alive to the conference, even if it meant violating Commander Duflot's idiotic orders and even if it meant a court martial for both of them.

On board the *Broadsword*, even before the second "Dynamo!" came over the speaker, Captain Kim snapped out, "Go, McDaniel, *go*!"

Able Spacer First Class Jackson McDaniel, Drives on the *Broadsword*, shoved the sublight drive controller all the way to the stop as Pitch and Yaw executed the well-planned course change, steering the destroyer through a violent evasive maneuver designed to throw the Krag firing solutions into whatever their species used for wastebaskets and get the ship as far away from the formation as fast as possible.

Once *Broadsword* had pulled far enough away from the other Union ships, she kicked her compression drive to the maximum setting, cracked through Einstein's Wall, and vanished from sight. Bearing the envoy to safety at more than two thousand times the speed of light, the USS *Broadsword*, her captain suppressing a strong personal affinity for combat, ran like a scalded dog.

Prompted by the same call, this time broadcast over standard radio, the four fighters of the 3242nd Reserve Fighter Squadron assigned to escort the group reversed course and pointed their threat receivers back in the general direction of the *Cumberland*. Now that the Krag had activated their missile targeting scanners, the fighters had no problem detecting them. All four went to afterfusers, accelerating rapidly in the direction of the Krag vessels. It would, however, be minutes before they were in missile range.

As they neared, Chin keyed a preprogrammed command to notify the *William Gorgas* on the emergency alert channel via laserlink of what the *Cumberland* had detected and what it was going to do. The only immediate response from the pennant was Duflot angrily demanding that Max tell him where the *Broadsword* went. No help there.

Max knew that the Krag would immediately conclude from the rapid disappearance of one ship that the envoy had gotten away from them. They could never catch, much less successfully engage, a *Longbow* class destroyer running at high compression across interstellar space. With the envoy gone, Krag doctrine dictated that the two cruisers (it had to be cruisers at this range on this kind of mission) would take advantage of a bad situation by engaging and destroying the remaining, inferior force.

He also knew that when two cruisers are engaging a frigate and a destroyer, Krag doctrine said both ships are jointly to take out the more nimble destroyer first, then turn their attention to dealing with the more powerful but less elusive frigate.

That meant that the two Krag ships would now turn from their original target, close on his position, and as soon as they could generate a firing solution for their Foxhound missiles, they would each launch a full salvo. *Adieu Cumberland*.

Pas aujourd'hui.

Time for some fancy footwork. Max looked over at Chief LeBlanc, who was watching a timer. Nine seconds had to elapse from the *Broadsword*'s departure for the fabric of space–time to restore itself to its previous shape. It had been seven. Eight. Nine. Chief LeBlanc simply said to his men, "Go, boys."

Drives ran the sublight drive to Emergency, while the men on the Yaw and Pitch controls suddenly put the ship through a radical turn away from its previous course and out of line with the *William Gorgas*, a maneuver that would delay the Krag from getting missile firing solutions for another four or five seconds. After two seconds, when the range between the two Union ships had opened up sufficiently, LeBlanc slapped Spacer Fleishman on the shoulder, adding, "Switch 'em, son."

Fleishman pulled the main sublight drive controller to zero and flipped the drive actuator to Standby, then flipped the compression drive actuator to Engage and gave its controller the barest nudge, the smallest movement that could be applied to it and still push it out of the zero detent.

"Main sublight nulled and on Standby. Compression drive engaged. Compression field forming," announced LeBlanc. "Field going propulsive."

The ship started to accelerate as the space behind it expanded and the space in front of it contracted, carrying the ship forward. "Speed is point six, point seven, point eight, point nine, point nine-eight-five. Holding at point nine-eight-five." LeBlanc said the last sentence in a tone that clearly conveyed that "holding at point nine-eight-five" was not a common state of affairs.

Eleven seconds elapsed, the shortest period of time that the compression drive could be engaged and then disengaged without triggering an uncontrolled field collapse that would destroy the ship, and also a period too short for deadly compression shear to arise even at a fractional c multiple. LeBlanc slapped Fleischman on the shoulder once more. "Kill it."

Fleischman pulled the controller back to zero, triggering a computer-controlled dissipation of the compression field, a process that took another second.

Max had taken the almost unheard-of step (prohibited by a least three distinct naval regulations and strongly discouraged by seven others) of using a superluminal drive for subluminal propulsion, dashing outside of the Krag firing solution far faster than otherwise possible, avoiding the time-dilation effect that occurs when travelling near the speed of light in normal space, and getting "behind" the Krag warships, forcing them either to divide their attention or to both turn their more vulnerable sterns toward one of the two Union ships.

"Now," Max said, grinning, "time to turn and attack. Mr. LeBlanc, make for the closest Krag ship. Ahead Flank." As LeBlanc acknowledged and carried out the order, Max turned to Kasparov and threw him a questioning look.

"Just getting an ID now, sir, Hotel One is posident as Krag cruiser, *Crayfish* class. Hotel Two..." He was listening to his back room and looking at something on a display to which Goldman was pointing, and then said over his headset, "Yea, okay, same type, we're go."

Then to Max, "Both contacts are *Crayfish* class. Bearing two-four-two mark one-six-seven for Hotel One and two-three-nine mark one-six-three for Hotel Two. Hotel One is continuing to accelerate, altering course from heading toward our former position to heading for the frigate. Hotel Two is turning, likely to engage us, range to both targets 3.27 million kills. Distance between Hotel One and Hotel Two is opening up." A few seconds. "Okay, Hotel Two is at constant bearing decreasing range. Right for us, sir."

"That's *Craw*fish. I keep telling those idiots at Intel. They ought to listen to a Cajun on this stuff, or at least a Southerner. Right, LeBlanc?"

"*Mais, oui, mon Capitain*," said Leblanc.

"Right, Bartoli?"

"Damn straight, sir." Bartoli hit the Alabama extra hard, making sure it came out "*day-umm* straight."

"It's unanimous. Bartoli, what's the frigate doing?" The question was both a request for information and a reminder to Bartoli that it was his responsibility to see that the main tactical display in CIC presented a usable tactical picture of the situation. When the destroyer had run about three million kilometers from the cruisers, the other three ships in the engagement had vanished off the edge of the display. Bartoli needed to change the scale so that all four ships showed up. He did so.

"Sir, the frigate has gone to Flank. He's presenting his starboard beam to Hotel One, while angling away, trying to stay outside missile range. Why hasn't he . . . Okay, there he goes—he's finally got his pulse cannon into action. He's got his starboard batteries plus his ventral and dorsal turrets laying down barrage fire. There, he got off a salvo of missiles too . . . at least two got through, two hits with Talons. I can't tell at this range what kind of damage he did."

Duflot was implementing standard fleet doctrine for a convoy frigate under attack with no pigeon to protect: crack on as much speed as you can to complicate interception and missile targeting, maneuver for a better tactical position, present your beam to the enemy so you can use your amidships pulse cannon plus your ventral and dorsal turrets to lay down a barrage of pulse cannon fire to reduce the effectiveness of any missile attack, and try to do some damage of your own with missile fire. Not terribly imaginative, but a very long way from the worst thing he could do. He might be a tactically obtuse, condescending asshole, but it did look as though Duflot had some grit in his gizzard.

"Weapons, abbreviated missile firing procedure. Make missiles in tubes one and two ready for firing in all respects, target on Hotel Two, set warheads for maximum yield, open missile doors."

"Sir," Bartoli said, "frigate just fired an Egg Scrambler." No FTL comms or compression drive use in the vicinity for a while. *Would have been nice to have been warned.*

"Saves us the trouble, then. Weapons, pull the Egg Scrambler from the aft tube. Reload with a Talon." Max glanced at a timer on his console, a timer that had been counting up from when the *Broadsword* had started maneuvering. It was at 00:01:27.

"Aye, sir, pulling Egg Scrambler from tube three, reloading with Talon. Sir, tubes one and two are loaded with Talons." Levy carried out the order with his usual efficiency. "I'm sure you know, sir, two Talons aren't going to scratch that Crawfish if he's ready for them."

"I know that, Mr. Levy." Max glanced at the timer again. It was now at 00:01:35. "Our two Talons aren't going to be the only guests at the party."

As the timer hit 00:01:40, Mr. Chin called out, "Skipper, receiving encrypted text on one of the JOINTOPS channels. The encrypt is MUDBATH. The decrypt is coming up now. I'm putting it on the Commandcoms channel."

Max hit the bright orange hard key over one of the main displays on his console that punched up the Command Officer's Incoming Communications or "Commandcoms" data channel. The screen displayed "GREETINGS DRY CRUSTY HUMANS STOP THIS IS BRAKMOR-ENT 198 COMMANDING THE 16TH ELEMENT 332ND FIGHTER GROUP PFELUNGIAN SPACE DEFENSE FORCE REPORTING IN ACCORDANCE WITH YOUR REQUEST STOP IF YOU ARE ABOUT TO DO BATTLE WITH THE KRAG AND MAKE OF THEM A MEAL FOR THE LESSER FISH WE WOULD EAGERLY

JOIN YOU STOP QUERY MAY WE JOIN THE FUN STOP MESSAGE ENDS."

"Mr. Chin, please send, "We welcome your assistance and believe there is enough fun for everyone. Form up on me and await instructions."

DeCosta looked puzzled. "Why does this message look like it's transcribed from tachyon Morse or blinker? We've got a high bandwidth data channel."

"XO, there are all kinds of issues translating from written Pfelung to Standard. Don't you know that they have over a hundred different punctuation marks? You get a lot fewer mistranslations if you simplify."

"Understood. But that doesn't sound like the Pfelung communications I've read. Why are they here, anyway?"

"Because, XO, what you've seen are communications from the enormous, lumbering adults, who are halfway between a grown alligator and a hippo in size and about as nimble as an elephant with arthritis. They don't fly fighters. The fighters are flown by the adolescent Pfelung. They're a lot like dolphins, with the personality to match. Very fast, very nimble, genetically designed to defend the baby Pfelung in the water, braver than a lion on stims, with brains specifically evolved for rapid life-and-death combat in three dimensions. Reflexes that make lightning look slow. Best fighter pilots in the galaxy, bar none.

"This is one of the groups I was training right after the Battle of Pfelung. I signaled them back before we went on EMCON and told them to meet us in this system, wait for us to jump in, and track us at three and a half million kills on this bearing. And here they are. Now that we've got that nailed down, XO, don't you have something to do?"

Max jerked his head in the direction of the fighter coordination console, the one that Petty Officer Carlson was firing up.

The one that the XO was supposed to run when a *Khyber* class or other SWACS ship too small to have a separate air coordination officer (generally known as a "Bird Herder") was working with fighters.

"Yes, sir. I'm on it." DeCosta stepped over to the console. Carlson had already pulled up the protocols for JOINTOPS with the Pfelung and had plugged in the transponder frequencies and encrypts, the comm procedures, all the crypto information, and the standard Pfelung fighter maneuvers. By the time DeCosta sat down at the station, everything was ready for him. He turned to the petty officer. "Thanks, Carlson. Good job." Carlson sat down at his station nearby, and the two got to work.

DeCosta put on his headset and looked at the displays that, with the aid of the fighter's transponders, showed him their exact location and what they were doing. The fighters were in two groups of seven, each in a formation that was essentially a three-dimensional version of the classic "finger-four" formation, the three additional ships stacked in the same arrangement as the other flankers but perpendicular to them, the seven ships making the shape of a cross when viewed from the front or behind. Both groups were approaching the *Cumberland* rapidly from aft, both on the port side.

With human pilots, DeCosta would simply speak to the leader. Things were a little more complicated when the language barrier was as high as it was between humans and the Pfelung, whose spoken language sounded like (and was, in fact, derived from) bubbles being blown in soupy mud. The system was set up so that DeCosta could speak orders into the headset, which the computer would translate into Pfelungian text and transmit to the fighter group leader. The leader, in turn, could speak to his system and have his speech translated by his computer into simplified form Standard text and then transmitted to DeCosta's console.

The system, combined with the advanced sensor capabilities with which the destroyer was equipped, enabled *Cumberland* to control the Pfelungian fighters in combat, vectoring them to targets and coordinating their tactics.

DeCosta had even put in a few sessions on the console directing simulated fighters, both Union and Pfelung, in simulated battles. He knew the protocol, which first required that he verify communication between his console and the group leader. He pulled up the screen that provided the automatically generated ID protocols for this engagement. He was Starfish. The first element was Halibut; the second was Tuna. Max was Starfish Actual. Each element had a leader, to be called Halibut One or Tuna One. Halibut One was the overall commander. "Halibut One, this is Starfish, comm test."

A second and a half later, text appeared on the FTRCOM MAIN display: "STARFISH THIS IS HALIBUT ONE STOP COMMUNICATION RECEIVED SIGNAL STRENGTH AND CLARITY WITHIN NORMS STOP QUERY HOW LONG UNTIL WE GET TO START SHOOTING AT THE KRAG STOP MESSAGE ENDS."

"Skipper, comms with the Pfelung fighters verified. They seem a little impatient, sir."

"They're like that, XO. Intellectually brilliant, fantastic sense of humor, very fun-loving. Occasionally a little immature, though. Nothing like the studiously mature adults. Tell them to form up on this vessel, one group finbone star formation port, the other finbone star formation starboard."

"Finbone star, sir?"

"That's what they call that crossed finger four that they use. The angles are like the bones in their fins, just like our fingers, and 'star' is because the drives of the two crossed lines look like a bright star when viewed from a distance. Something like that anyway."

"Roger, sir." DeCosta confirmed the order and passed it on to the Pfelung, who promptly took up station to the left and right of the destroyer that was rapidly accelerating toward one of the cruisers, which in turn was rapidly accelerating toward the destroyer and the fighters. They would be within missile range of each other in seconds.

DeCosta's console beeped. New message from the Pfelung: "STARFISH THIS IS HALIBUT ONE STOP QUERY ARE WE THERE YET STOP MESSAGE ENDS." DeCosta relayed the message to Max.

"I told you they were a bit immature," Max said. "Tell them Wing Attack Plan Romeo. Execute on two red."

DeCosta confirmed and passed on the order. "The Pfelung acknowledge the order, Skipper."

"Very well." Max watched the range tick down. This had better work, because a *Khyber* class destroyer wasn't even a good first course for a *Crayfish* class cruiser. More of an appetizer, like a nice shrimp cocktail with lots of horseradish in the cocktail sauce. A few more seconds. Right. About. Now.

"Mr. Chin, blink two red on the port and starboard signal lamps, if you please."

"Aye, sir. Two red. Port and starboard."

Before Chin could confirm that the signal had been sent, DeCosta saw the two Pfelung formations spring faster than any Union fighter could, their fusion-based sublight drives augmented by a gravity-polarizing technology that was the first step on the long, steep, difficult road to a pure reactionless drive. As they neared the Krag cruiser, it appeared to DeCosta that the Pfelung adolescents had abandoned their formation in favor of clumping together in some sort of random, swirling, chaotic aggregation.

On closer examination, however, he saw that the fighters' movements were not random at all, but resembled those of a school of fish. Although the individual craft were always in motion relative to one another, and fighters kept changing places, creating a visual impression of constant movement and absence of structure, at any given moment in time the formation was the same "finbone star" formation the fighters had originally adopted. But with all the shifts, and the continual rotation of the formation itself, its structure was not apparent. It would certainly be difficult for an enemy to select one fighter, engage it, and target it with weapons.

Both groups approached the cruiser from roughly amidships, continuing to accelerate. As soon as they got near the range at which the Krag point defense systems would engage them, each formation adopted an evasive pattern that again resembled the movements of a fast-moving school of fish, deviating from its base course by darting unexpectedly in one direction and then another at seemingly random intervals, each individual fighter flying perfectly in formation with the rest as they made their abrupt jigs and jags, too fast for any weapons battery to follow.

The combination of the swirling movements within the group and the evasive darting of the formations as a whole seemed to be doing an excellent job of confusing or staying ahead of the cruiser's defensive weapons, as the pulse cannon blasts all seemed to be missing their targets.

At the last moment, both formations dispersed, and the fighters veered away from the Krag ship, fanning out in all directions more or less at right angles to their original bearing, like a stream of water spreading out when it strikes the pavement, until they surrounded the cruiser. They then swerved violently to point their noses at the flank of the vessel, perfectly aligned for an attack that would launch their missiles at the ship's "waistline" to go for a classic simultaneous circumferential detonation.

The computer that controlled the Krag defensive systems recognized the maneuver and threw itself into reorienting pulse cannons, transferring deflector power, and focusing the ship's point defensive systems to respond to such an attack. Following twisting, elusive, corkscrewing, erratic paths, the Pfelung fighters bored in toward the cruiser's midline in their uniquely evasive, fishlike way.

Just as the Krag systems fully committed to defending against this tactic, the Pfelung fighters, as though controlled by a single mind, veered again, catching the Krag systems flat-footed. Still tracing elusive, impossible-to-follow, corkscrewing paths, they all made for one target, an unimportant looking bulbous protrusion at the nose of the cruiser. All of the Pfelung fighters maintained almost exactly the same range from the cruiser—between 4.885 and 5.033 kilometers, a narrow seam between the ship's area defense perimeter defended by pulse cannon and the point defense perimeter defended by rail guns, short range particle beams, and interceptor missiles.

In theory, there was no gap, but extensive testing of captured Krag ships showed that, in practice, the Krag computers' efforts to avoid the duplication of defending any particular zone of space with more than one system created a thin layer where, under the computational challenges posed by actual combat, neither defense layer would energetically engage the attacking fighters.

As the Pfelung fighters were mounting their attack, the *Cumberland* had continued to accelerate, her main sublight drive firewalled. Knowing that the cruiser was busy dealing with fourteen dazzlingly evasive fighters, Max ordered that the destroyer get as close to the cruiser as possible as fast as possible.

Ordinarily, the destroyer would fire its pulse cannons, helping to confuse the targeting scanners for the cruiser's pulse cannons. As it was, Krag weapons were attempting to engage the Pfelung fighters skimming between the cruiser's primary defense zones. It would only be a matter of a few more seconds, though, before some smart Krag figured out that the destroyer was a major threat and manually redirected the fire of at least one of the pulse cannon batteries from futile efforts to keep up with the fighters to firing on the far less elusive destroyer.

"Threat receiver just started going wild, Skipper," Bartoli declared. "Looks like pulse cannon and missile targeting scanners trying to get a lock." So much for a few seconds.

"Countermeasures?" Max probed, turning his head in the direction of that console.

That officer was already furiously working with his back room to defeat the Krag scanners and buy a little more time for his shipmates. Sauvé said, "I can give you ten seconds, maybe twelve; then they'll get burn-through and have us like a bug on a pin."

"Carry on, then. That's all I'm going to need. Weapons, set missiles in tubes one and two for simultaneous detonation, nostril attack."

"Simultaneous detonation, nostril profile, aye."

Having so far evaded the Krag defense systems, all fourteen Pfelung fighters fired two missiles each. Their minutely staggered firing intervals were chosen in conjunction with the slightly differing ranges of the fighters to result in all twenty-eight missiles arriving and detonating within microseconds of each other.

All scored direct hits. The Pfelung missiles were small, elusive, and agile. All but three penetrated the Krag point defense grid and exploded their comparatively small 31.3-kiloton, fusion-boosted fission warheads. Greatly attenuated by the Krag deflectors, the explosions were not sufficient to destroy the cruiser. In fact, they were not enough to inflict any structural damage on it at all.

But they *were* enough to create an electromagnetic pulse (EMP) of sufficient intensity to trip the protective circuitry designed to prevent nearby nuclear explosions from causing EMP damage to the sensor array used by zone and point defense systems for the cruiser's forward section. These were the sensors that told the ship's computer the location of incoming ships and missiles near the forward area of the ship, as well as let it know when a warhead was detonating near the ship, so the system could surge power to the deflectors to counteract the force of the explosion.

No one, least of all the humans who had been fighting them for more than three decades, would accuse the Krag of being fools. Accordingly, the EMP protection system was not designed to trip when a nuclear weapon detonated in the vicinity of the ship, in which case it would leave the vessel vulnerable, but only when hit by extremely powerful EMP from very close.

In addition, the system was designed to reset itself automatically and to do so in the shortest time possible while still allowing for multistage detonations, residual and reflected radiation effects, and similar events—just over five seconds. For those seconds, the defenses for the forward one-third of the Krag cruiser would be blind. In most contexts, five seconds isn't very long.

In space warfare, five seconds is a lifetime.

As the fighters were pulling screaming, hard G turns through the now inert defenses of the forward section of the cruiser and clearing its vicinity as fast as possible, the *Cumberland* had continued to close on the cruiser at the best speed it could make.

Countermeasures yelled, "Cruiser's targeting scanners just achieved burn-through." Those scanners were mounted on retractable masts all around the ship and had not been damaged by the fighters. "They'll have a lock in about four seconds."

Not today.

"Weapons, fire tubes one and two and reload with Ravens. Maneuvering, execute evasive Hotel Papa."

The destroyer fired two Talon missiles toward the cruiser, then made a hard, swooping turn to carry it away from the missiles' target and bear it toward the Union frigate, still in a desperate battle with the other cruiser. The Talons were programmed for a "nostril attack," so named because they were aimed to fly "right up her nose," their aiming points twenty meters apart just on either side of the point of the Krag vessel's bow.

Three-tenths of a second before the Krag EMP protection circuits reset themselves, both 150-kiloton thermonuclear warheads exploded, easily ripping through deflectors and overcoming explosion dampeners running at their standard battle settings instead of being surged to counteract the effects of the two hydrogen bombs. Together, the bombs' total explosive yield was nearly nineteen times that of the primitive fission weapon that had killed seventy thousand human beings 370 years before and forever inscribed in the collective memory of humankind the name "Hiroshima."

Initially, the cruiser's deflectors and blast suppression systems, powered by the still-operating threat sensors in those sections of the ship shielded the aft two-thirds of the vessel from the explosions, but as the forward section dissolved into dissociated highly energetic atomic nuclei and wildly careening electrons, the fireball flowed around the ship's shielded hull, through the area previously occupied by the forward section, and into the ship's interior, the glowing plasma consuming everything it touched and gutting the vessel.

For seven-tenths of a second, the vessel's tough hull held together. But then, the greedy fireball ingested the intricate systems that chained and harnessed the fusion inferno at the ship's heart, causing the cruiser's reactor to lose containment. Union plasma met Krag plasma and, finding themselves kindred, unleashed a détente of destruction that vaporized the rest of the ship in a second explosion nearly as brilliant as the first.

There was no time to celebrate. The *William Gorgas* needed help and needed it immediately.

"XO," Max said, "signal the fighters; tell them to go buster and give that other Crawfish something else to worry about. Attack Plan Papa."

DeCosta passed on the message. The tactical display showed the icons representing the two fighter elements pulling ahead of the destroyer and making for the enemy cruiser.

"Skipper, message from the Pfelung, on Commandcom," Said the XO.

Max looked down at the display, which was already punched into that channel: "MESSAGE ACKNOWLEDGED STOP THAT WAS REALLY FUN STOP WE ESPECIALLY LIKED THE NUCLEAR WEAPONS PART STOP LOOKING FORWARD TO FEEDING THESE OTHER KRAG TO THE WORMS STOP MESSAGE ENDS."

"Pfelung fighter elements accelerating hard toward Hotel One." Bartoli stated the obvious, in accordance with the age-old Navy philosophy of always announcing every material event, including those that would be evident to a reasonably intelligent toddler, lest something, someday, that required attention somehow escape notice.

The Pfelung fighters rapidly accelerated to 0.5 c and closed in on Hotel One, which emptied its missile tubes at the pennant. The frigate unleashed its point defense systems, which destroyed the Krag missiles. Then the ship fired all four of its forward missile tubes, scoring one hit that appeared to damage the enemy cruiser's missile tubes and amidships deflector array. The Krag cruiser was, however, still able to pummel the frigate with withering pulse cannon fire at an ever-decreasing range as the cruiser's speed advantage over the frigate began to tell.

"Pennant is taking some damage," Bartoli announced. "I think she just lost two of her missile tubes and one of her cannon batteries. Sir, I don't think she can take much more. A few more good hits and the pennant is history."

"Mr. Chin, signal the pennant. Let Captain Duflot know that help is on the way. Fighters in less than thirty seconds, us about two minutes after that."

Chin acknowledged the order and went to work. Less than ten seconds later: "Signal from the pennant, sir. It reads 'For God's sake, hurry.'"

Any man in CIC could follow the course of the battle simply by watching the main tactical projection. The Krag vessel closed to administer the *coup de grâce*. Just as its main pulse cannon batteries were ready to open up on the *William Gorgas* at close range, the Pfelung fighters swooped in to engage the cruiser. Looking like piranha in a feeding frenzy, they came at the enemy from apparently random bearings, approaching from all directions at high speeds and following elusive, deceptive trajectories, getting within close missile range, firing, and then dodging away only to return and fire again from another direction.

By presenting the Krag with constantly shifting multiple threat vectors, the Pfelung kept the Krag point defense systems spread thin, unable to concentrate on any single ship or any single direction. And although the relatively small warheads of the Pfelung missiles did not penetrate the Krag deflectors, each detonation sapped the Krag deflector power reserves. Eventually, the reserves would be depleted and the Krag left open to destruction.

"How many missiles do those fighters carry?" DeCosta's question echoed the one in the minds of many in CIC.

Max gave the XO a look that said that this is one of the things he was supposed to know, but he answered the question. "Twenty, each. In an internal bay to preserve stealth. *Very* advanced design. Those fighters with those pilots are going to make a serious difference in this war, and you can take that to the bank."

"Skipper," said Bartoli, "Hotel One has kicked its sublight drive up to Emergency and is trying to get away from the Pfelung fighters. Looks as though he's . . . right . . . He's going for the edge of the area disrupted by the Egg Scrambler, either to get away or to send an FTL transmission to his friends."

"I guarantee it's to get away," said Kasparov.

"*Guarantee?*" Max's question was asked in genuine curiosity, without a trace of the sarcasm that many skippers who used to be sensor officers would have loaded into those same words.

"Yes, sir. *Guarantee.* I've got a clear optical scan of his metaspacial transceiver array. It's twelve thousand eight hundred and nineteen kills away from him. In six pieces. Looks like one of those missile hits stripped everything mounted on a good portion of his outer hull. If he's going to talk to anyone, it's going to be on an Einstein line. No FTL chit-chat for him until he gets back to a Krag shipyard."

"Outstanding work, Mr. Kasparov. That's the kind of information I can use. Maneuvering, get me within missile range of the cruiser."

"Not an intercept course, sir?"

"Negative, Mr. LeBlanc. I've already eyeballed that we won't get an intercept before he kicks in his compression drive. I need to get a couple of hits on him before he gets away."

"Aye, sir, missile range it is." He gave immediate orders to his men to change course in the direction he estimated would put the destroyer within missile range, then interrogated his console to produce a more precise calculation. The result was a few degrees different in both axes, and he implemented the course change.

"The fighters are keeping up with the cruiser, no problem, continuing to reduce his deflector power," Bartoli said. "He's down to just under 50 percent now. Sir, I know what you're going to ask, and the answer is no. His deflectors will not be knocked down far enough for either the Pfelung or us, or both in combination, to finish him before he can engage his c drive. He's about three minutes away from the boundary."

"Bartoli, ninety seconds before the cruiser reaches the boundary, notify the XO. XO, when you get that notification, pass it on to the fighters with orders that they break off their attack immediately and fall back to a range of at least five hundred kills. I don't want any of them caught in the compression field."

Being in an area where the space–time continuum was being radically expanded or compressed could be hazardous to one's health—that is, if one's health required that the atomic nuclei in one's body and in one's ship not undergo spontaneous nuclear fission and detonate like an A-bomb.

A minute passed. The icons in the tactical display gradually changed relative position as the destroyer slowly caught up with the cruiser, proving once again the age old maxim about stern chases being long.

"Ninety seconds to boundary, sir," Bartoli announced.

"Very well. XO, add to the warning we talked about earlier a warning that we are about to fire missiles and that they should stay clear of the attack vector. Tell them to take the usual precautions to avoid the blast. Be sure they know we're firing Ravens, not Talons."

The 1.5-megaton warhead of the Raven missile packed ten times the punch of the highest yield of which the Talon was capable. When a Raven was coming, you gave the blast a bit more room.

"Weapons, abbreviated firing procedure. Make weapons in tubes one and two ready in all respects and open missile doors. Your target is the Krag cruiser dead ahead. Program missiles for common point, time on target, simultaneous detonation."

"Sir, you know that—"

"Yes, Mr. Levy," the captain interrupted, "I know that detonating the missiles at the same time at the same place does not place the level of drain on the Krag systems that you get with two blasts in two different locations. I also know, though, that by concentrating the explosions we will get a very slight deflector penetration and cause some minimal damage to the ship. It's very, very important that we—I mean this ship—cause some damage, no matter how slight. Understand?"

"Aye, sir." Levy acknowledged and implemented the order, not understanding at all. A few seconds later, "Missile range."

"Fire one and two."

"Firing," said Levy. "One and two away."

"Pfelung fighters are clearing the area," said Bartoli, demonstrating once again the firm grasp of the obvious required by his job description.

But this was mainly Levy's show, now. "Both missiles hot, straight, and normal. Tracking target. Missiles are in Cooperative Attack Mode and electing to penetrate the Krag point defense systems along separate vectors. Now they're converging. Point defense penetration. Hit! Direct hit amidships. We got some deflector penetration too—they've lost one of their sensor arrays, and . . . okay." He was listening to his back room.

"I think we might have gotten a small hull breach. My back room is talking to the Sensors back room, and they're coming up with a consensus that there is probably a small hull breach—just a couple of millimeters, but we're getting what looks like some atmosphere leakage."

"Maneuvering, make for the point where the cruiser is going to engage his compression drive. Bartoli, Kasparov, put your heads and your people together. When we get to that point, I want to know where the cruiser is going."

"Aye, sir," they replied in near unison.

"I finally got through to the pennant, sir!" Chin's voice was pitched a bit high, and his delivery was altogether too urgent. Not surprising. Until now, *Cumberland* had fought alone. Chin had never managed comms in the middle of a battle. First time for everything. Max was certain it would not be the last.

Accordingly, a little education was in order. "Mr. Chin, we're getting all the excitement we really need from being in a life-and-death struggle using nuclear weapons." Max spoke in a calm, level voice. "You don't need to add to the mix. In CIC, we make all announcements in a calm voice, even the exciting ones, even in the middle of battle. Especially in the middle of battle. Understood?"

"Understood, sir. Communications with the pennant reestablished." Max did not know that they had been lost, something else on which Chin needed to be schooled, but that could come later. Sensing his error, Chin added, "We lost them for a few minutes. Comms damage to the frigate." He took a deep breath, "Decrypt will be on Commandcom."

Max turned to the display. "PLEASE ACCEPT GRATITUDE FOR YOUR ASSISTANCE AND THAT OF YOUR LITTLE FRIENDS. PLEASE BE MY GUEST FOR DINNER IN A FEW DAYS. I WILL BE DINING ON CROW. I AM AWARE OF YOUR SITUATION. BE ADVISED THAT KRAG CRUISER HAS DAMAGE TO MISSILE TUBES WITH AT LEAST THREE INOPERABLE PERHAPS FOUR AS WELL AS AMIDSHIPS

DEFLECTOR DAMAGE AT LEAST 50 PERCENT AND SOME IMPAIRMENT OF SUBLIGHT DRIVE EXTENT UNKNOWN. YOU ARE ORDERED TO PURSUE AND DESTROY CRUISER TO PREVENT COMMUNICATING TO SUPERIORS OUTCOME OF ATTACK ON THIS GROUP. ACTION NECESSARY FOR SAFETY OF ENVOY. GOOD HUNTING, DUFLOT SENDS. END MESSAGE."

"Safety of the envoy?" The doctor had not spoken a word during the battle for the simple reason that he had nothing useful to say.

"Sure," Max responded. "If the Krag know that the attack failed and that the envoy was spirited away on a destroyer, they might try again. Their chances of finding the destroyer in interstellar space are vanishingly small, but there are lots of ways to kill a man, and we know that the Krag have spies in lots of places. It would not be unusual for them to go after him using an assassin or a bomb or even to try to hit a whole city with nerve gas. We need to keep them from knowing what happened here."

Max turned to DeCosta. "XO, tell the Pfelung fighters that I want them flying combat area patrol and escort for the frigate until it gets back to the fleet or until Commander Duflot releases them. Chin, let the pennant know that they are getting Pfelung fighter CAP and escort, and be sure that his comms guy knows the comm protocols. They'll have a hard time working together if they can't talk to one another."

A few seconds later, "Signal from the Pfelung. On Commandcom." Max read the display: "MESSAGE ACKNOWLEDGED STOP WILL COMPLY STOP QUERY STARFISH ACTUAL DO YOU NOT KNOW THAT FLYING COMBAT AREA PATROL IS BORING REPEAT BORING STOP DESPITE BOREDOM WE WILL KEEP THE WATERS CLEAR OF PREDATORS STOP PERHAPS IF WE ARE LUCKY WE WILL

BE ATTACKED AND WE WILL GET TO HAVE MORE NUCLEAR WEAPONS FUN STOP WE LOOK FORWARD TO SWIMMING WITH YOU IN THE FUTURE ROBICHAUX STOP UNTIL WE ARE IN THE SAME WATERS AGAIN WE WISH THAT THE CURRENT ALWAYS BE WITH YOU STOP MESSAGE ENDS."

"I must say," said Bram, "these Pfelung adolescents have a strange outlook on warfare if they perceive deployment of nuclear weapons as 'fun.'"

"I don't know, Doctor, I always rather liked it," said Max. "How about you, Levy? Do you like firing nukes?"

"Well, sir, I know I'm supposed to say that I am greatly weighed down by the solemnity and mighty responsibility of setting free into the universe the awesome destructive power that lies dormant in the core of the humble atom," Levy intoned with all the gravity he could muster, "But yes, sir, I do get a rush from nuking the Krag, I must admit."

The doctor could only shake his head and look at Max accusingly. It was Sahin's "You are corrupting these young men" look that Max had come to know so well. Max smiled and gazed back innocently in return. It was his "I know. Isn't it great?" look with which the doctor had become very familiar. The idea simultaneously occurred to both men that these kinds of exchanges were becoming common and that their frequency was likely a sign that the men were becoming extraordinarily good friends, notwithstanding their comparatively short acquaintance. It was an idea that they both welcomed.

Bartoli interrupted the wordless conversation. "Cruiser just engaged her compression drive." He looked over at Kasparov and Goldman, both of whom were rapidly scrolling through several data channels, talking with each other and the Sensors back room.

After about twenty seconds, Kasparov turned to Max. "Skipper, we've done a series of active tachyo-graviton scans in six polarization planes and at a dozen phase modulations, and we're getting a definite compression trail. A good, straight heading, zero-five-one mark zero-zero-eight, and from the amount of residual continuum disruption, he must be pulling at least nineteen hundred c, maybe more than two thousand."

"And sir—" Bartoli started to add.

"You don't need to tell me, Bartoli. A good captain always has his bearings. That's straight into Vaaach space."

CHAPTER 13

17:44Z Hours, 30 March 2315

"No response on any of the Vaaach channels, Skipper," Chin reported for at least the twentieth time. The *Cumberland*, back on Condition Blue, had crossed through the several light years of disputed space that might be Vaaach or might be Union and had for the last four hours or so been in space that undoubtedly belonged to the Vaaach.

The Vaaach. The Vaaach who possessed technology centuries in advance of the best that humanity could field, were highly aggressive carnivores and tended to deal with territorial incursions by vaporizing the interloper first and asking questions later.

But Max consoled himself that if they were powerful and dangerous, the Vaaach were also scrupulously honorable. They applied their code of honor to other species to the same degree as they applied it to themselves (a Vaaach would rather slit his throat with his own claws than apply a double standard or engage in the slightest hypocrisy) and honored Customary Interstellar Law, including, Max hoped fervently, the Right of Hot Pursuit.

To preserve the *Cumberland*'s claim that it was hunting the Krag cruiser and to preclude any conclusion by the Vaaach that it was entering their space covertly, the destroyer had been broadcasting a message on the standard interspecies attention channels, stating that the ship was entering Vaaach space without any effort at concealment, in pursuit of a Krag vessel that had fled from honorable combat. That should mollify the Vaaach.

Under Interstellar Law, a warship of one power had the right to enter the space of another when it was engaged in combat with an enemy warship and to continue that pursuit for a reasonable time, reasonableness being a highly elastic concept depending on the kind and quality of the most recent sensor detection, whether the enemy vessel was leaving some kind of trail, and other factors. The Hot Pursuit Doctrine denied to combatants the ability to avoid destruction through the cowardly expedient of slipping just over a neutral border. Surely, the Vaaach would respect such a reasonable and honorable principle, Max hoped.

"We're still on their trail, sir," Kasparov announced. "And we're gaining on them slightly." The ship had dropped into normal space to scan for the aftereffects of the passage of a ship under compression drive. The Krag ship was relying on speed rather than stealth, and was taking the shortest route across Vaaach space toward home. Having verified that the Krag were still ahead of them, Max ordered the *Cumberland* back to 1960 c, which was as fast as he dared maintain for what might be a chase of several days.

Max was drinking hot, black ship's coffee and munching on an "exploding" ham sandwich when Kasparov announced, "Skipper, I've just lost the Krag's compression signature."

"How far behind him were we?" Max asked.

"Six minutes and nineteen seconds, sir."

"Maneuvering, take us subluminal 437,000 kills short of Mr. Kasparov's estimate of where the Krag dropped out of compression. Alerts, general quarters, ship versus ship." As the klaxons and announcements sounded, Max turned to the Stealth console.

"Mr. Nelson, I want the ship at maximum stealth, all modes, as soon as we hit normal space. If Monsieur Visage de Rat is having problems with his compression drive, maybe we catch him with his guard down."

"Aye, sir. Maximum stealth, all modes."

About three minutes after GQ was sounded, Alerts announced, "All decks and all stations at general quarters, ship versus ship, sir."

"Very well."

The hatch cycled to admit Dr. Sahin and Clouseau. As frequently as the two came into CIC together, Max wondered whether they were together in another part of the ship, whether Clouseau had been waiting along Sahin's route to CIC and fell in behind him en route, or whether they both came in response to the klaxons and simply tended to arrive at the same time. One of these days, he would ask.

The doctor sat down at the Commodore's Station and punched up various displays to tell him what was going on. Clouseau scampered over to Gilbertson, who was near the coffeepot and who slipped him a cat treat produced seemingly from nowhere. Once he had convinced himself that one treat was all he was going to get from the midshipman, the ever-larger feline sashayed over to Dr. Sahin's feet, curled around his right ankle, and promptly went to sleep. Several of the older spacers looked at each other and nodded.

"Disengaging compression drive in thirty seconds," announced LeBlanc.

"Very well," Max responded. "Gentlemen, we don't know what the target is up to here. His compression drive might have failed from battle damage, or maybe he's turning to fight, or maybe something completely different. Stay sharp. We need to be ready for anything."

"Ten seconds," said LeBlanc. "Seven. Six. Five. Four. Three. Two. One. NOW." Fleishman brought the compression drive contol lever to zero. The compression drive returned the space around the ship to its normal configuration, and the *Cumberland* rejoined the Einsteinian universe. Max looked at Kasparov for his first indication of what was going on outside the ship. He didn't have long to wait.

"Contact... *two* contacts. Intermediate range. Massive energy signatures. Lots of maneuvering... Weapons fire... Targets are exchanging weapons fire. First contact is consistent with Hotel One, bearing zero-five-three mark one-eight-eight, range based on apparent angular size 1.4 million kilometers. Second contact—second contact, designating as Uniform One, bearing zero-five-five mark one-eight-seven, range roughly equivalent to Hotel One. Hotel One is firing dorsal and ventral turret pulse cannon batteries. His rate of fire is subnominal—he must have sustained some kind of damage, plus he's not firing the starboard battery, which is bearing on the target. Uniform One is returning fire with a weapon that I can't identify at this time. He doesn't seem to be doing much damage, though."

Max saw both Bartoli and Levy get very busy bringing their departments to bear on developing a clear picture of the situation.

"Maneuvering, let's close the contacts," Max said, squinting at the tactical display. "Make for the midpoint between them. Ahead one third." He turned to DeCosta. "XO, speculation. Who is Uniform One?"

"He's got to be Vaaach, doesn't he? I can't think of anyone who's stupid enough to go barging into Vaaach space and start shooting at a Krag ship without their permission." Pause. "Present company excepted."

A smile flickered across Max's face. "I'd agree that Uniform One is Vaaach but for one thing," said Max.

"What's that?," DeCosta replied.

"The Krag ship. *It's still there.* That Vaaach ship that we encountered would have obliterated that cruiser faster than you can say 'mousetrap.' But not only did Uniform One not obliterate Hotel One in an instant; these two ships appear to be in a running battle."

"Skipper," Kasparov interrupted, "the Krag weapons fire has been illuminating portions of Uniform One. We've been assembling a composite image. It's on VC-2."

Max immediately punched Visual Circuit 2 up on his console's primary display. Outlined in blue-white plasma explosions against its deflectors was a long, narrow arrowhead shape, sleek and deadly looking.

"It's Vaaach all right," said Max. "Kasparov, what's the scale?"

Max said the last part without any harshness, even though standard procedure requires that the image include scale markers. No rebuke was necessary. "Sorry, Skipper." Bartoli's voice dripped with remorse. He spoke into his headset. A few seconds later, a set of scale calibrations appeared on the screen.

"Oh, that explains it!" Max said. "That thing's tiny, or at least tiny for a Vaaach ship. It's smaller than we are."

"Skipper," interrupted Bartoli.

Max turned to face the Tactical Station.

"The size and silhouette is a match for a Vaaach *Vernier* class scout vessel. But sir, that doesn't make sense. A *Vernier* shouldn't be engaging a *Crayfish* class. Even given the extent of Vaaach technological superiority over the Krag, those little scout ships don't have the firepower to tackle something as powerful as a cruiser. These little guys are designed only to take on pirates and turn away the foolhardy. When they run into something like that *Crayfish* out there, they are supposed to stay stealthed, transmit their position, and shadow it until a more powerful vessel arrives. If they are detected and attacked, they're faster than anything in this part of the galaxy, so they can just run away."

He stopped to listen to something coming over his headset, then turned to his console for a few seconds. "One more thing, Skipper. The Vaaach ship has taken a lot of damage. He's managed to break away from the Krag and put on a burst of speed that opened up the range and bought him a few minutes, but he just lost one of his reactors. He can't run away now, and his deflectors have taken a real beating. When that Krag ship closes the range enough to use its pulse cannon, it will destroy him."

"Not if I can help it," said Max. "It's a young one, probably on his first mission. When a young Vaaach spies prey, the rapture of the hunt can overpower his better judgment. Mr. Chin, get a narrow focus comm laser tracking the Vaaach ship, and see if he'll answer a hail. Be sure the Krag ship never enters the laser's visibility cone." Chin acknowledged the order.

"Maneuvering, increase to maximum stealthy speed and bring us around in a wide arc so that we end up with the Vaaach ship between us and the Krag."

LeBlanc had just finished repeating the order when Chin spoke up. "Captain, I've got visual from the Vaaach ship on Lasercom."

"Let's have it."

In a few seconds, Max found himself face to face with the image of the Vaaach scout ship commander. Like all Vaaach, he was shaped like a giant koala bear, but with fangs and teeth that were more than a match for the most ferocious Earth predator. Although the typical Vaaach's fur was an assortment of tawny browns, tans, burnt oranges, and light reddish-grays, this Vaaach's fur was several different shades of light and medium green shot through with irregular dark-green blotches the shape of forest shadows. His coat looked like, and probably was, exquisitely effective forest camouflage.

Several speakers around CIC began to emit a series of roars and growls, higher pitched than Max was used to hearing from the Vaaach. The computer provided a written translation on the screen.

"Speak quickly, fruit eater [a term that the purely carnivorous Vaaach use to disparage any species that consumes plants even to the smallest degree]. I am engaged with my prey. Do not interfere unless you wish to become prey as well."

"Bravely spoken, young one," Max said calmly. If the Vaaach weren't attuned to human tones of voice, maybe his computer was. "But according to my sensors, it is the vermin Krag and not the Vaaach who are the hunters here. Before many breaths have passed, you are to be their meat. I have hunted the Krag. I have made them my prey. I have stalked and taken them with the Hunters of Vermin. Allow me to lead this hunt, and it is *you* who will taste *their* meat."

The responsive roaring was shrill and discordant. "You lie! You have never been with the Hunters of Vermin!"

Max drew his boarding cutlass, made two slashing motions in the shape of an "X," and bared his teeth in anger. "Were you not so young," he said in his best drill instructor voice, "your actions would have brought great dishonor upon your sire and all those who hunt with him. You did not offer proper greetings to me and didn't tell me your name, your rank, or what honors you have earned. You did not challenge the sharpness of my teeth and claws, doing me dishonor by depriving me of the opportunity to tell you my name and recite my honors. You are engaged with prey that you can neither kill nor escape without aid. And now, *you* accuse *me* of a dishonorable act." He resheathed his cutlass and sat down, shaking his head in disbelief. When he continued, he sounded more like a disappointed parent than an enraged chief petty officer or sergeant.

"You have much to learn about being a hunter, nameless youngling. But together, we can turn this vermin into meat and add honor to our names."

The Vaaach looked briefly at the ceiling, which Max knew to be a gesture of concession. "I am Vgglarwarrr, Forest Follower of the Third Order [an adolescent who will shortly become an adult], Master of Patrol Vessel 22-2356. I have done nothing to bring honor to my name."

"You have done nothing *yet*. I am Lieutenant Commander Maxime Tindall Robichaux, Captain of the destroyer USS *Cumberland*. We can talk about who and what I've killed, how, with what, when, and where later. Right now, we've got a Krag *Crayfish* class cruiser to handle, and if we don't kill it, it's almost certainly going to kill us." He eyed the tactical display closely. "Are you familiar with the 'my claws from your shadow' maneuver?"

"I am." Vgglarwarrr bared his upper and lower fangs in approval. Because he was an adolescent, they were shorter than an adult's. His were only three-quarters of the length of a man's forearm.

"Will your ship stand up to enemy fire for that long?"

"Yes and longer. Very little longer."

"Has the maneuver been changed in any way recently?"

"Not since it was added to the list of standard combat maneuvers more than seventeen turns ago."

"Very well. We will use the standard distances, signals, and timings. Do not exceed my maximum acceleration profile—do you have it?" The Vaaach bared his fangs twice in quick succession: the equivalent of a nod.

"Good. Execute when you are ready. May you taste blood today!"

"I will begin in a tenbreath [approximately 1.2 minutes]. May your claws and fangs strike true!" the Vaaach replied. "This communication ends." The screen went blank.

"Skipper," Kasparov said, "the Vaaach has dropped his stealth and sensor jamming fields and is transferring power to his drive and deflectors. Check that. He's dropped his stealth and sensor jamming fields in all directions except directly forward. He is still blocking any scans originating from directly ahead. He may also have diverted power to his weapons, but I wouldn't be able to detect that until he fires them."

"I guarantee you that he's diverted power to his weapons," Max said, smiling while he retrieved some data from his console. "Maneuvering, in a little less than a minute, the Vaaach ship is going to turn and head directly for the Krag cruiser. As soon as he does, we will fall in behind him, right on his six o'clock, and keep the Vaaach vessel between us and the Krag at all times. Mr. Nelson, as soon as the Vaaach ship is screening us, discontinue stealth and extend the radiator fins. Let's get that heat sink back in the green."

"How much separation between us and the Vaaach?" LeBlanc asked as soon as those orders were acknowledged.

"I'm getting that information right now. It's in an interspecies contact report I wrote years ago." He entered a few commands on his console. "Here it is. Put us 27.83 kilometers behind the Vaaach. Weapons, make the missiles in tube one and in tube two ready for firing in all respects, except I want the missile doors closed. Target the Krag ship. Direct attack pattern."

LeBlanc and Levy repeated their orders. "He's making his move, sir," said Bartoli. "Engaging his reactionless drive and bearing for the Krag ship."

"Gentlemen, execute your orders," said Max.

LeBlanc had his men steer the *Cumberland* on a course that put the Vaaach ship between it and the Krag vessel. With the Vaaach's stealth and sensor jamming fields blocking scans from forward of the ship, the Cumberland was hidden from the Krag. Accordingly, Nelson put the ship's stealth systems on STANDBY and extended the radiator fins, allowing the ship to start shedding the thermal energy stored in its heat sink.

The Vaaach charged toward the Krag vessel like an enraged bull, steering a straight course without any evasive maneuvers. It turned only to follow course changes by the Krag, apparently angling to bring its most powerful and least damaged weapons batteries to bear. Within a few minutes, several displays around CIC began to show the Vaaach ship, outlined in the coruscating flashes of Krag pulse cannon bolts detonating against its deflectors, shedding currents of incandescent plasma that flowed and swirled over the ship like an unworldly substance created by the merger of smoke, flame, and St. Elmo's fire.

As the Vaaach ship closed on the Krag vessel, the pulse cannon hits become more frequent, and the glow became ever brighter. Max hoped earnestly that the young Vaaach's calculations of his ship's ability to withstand the Krag weapons fire were accurate, because if the Vaaach ship succumbed, he knew the *Cumberland* wouldn't last two minutes against the cruiser's blistering salvos.

"Mr. Kasparov, be sure to monitor the Vaaach's aft signal light. Notify us when you see it blink three times," Max ordered.

"Mr. Nelson, when Mr. Kasparov gives us that notification, engage all stealth modes.

"Weapons, at that same signal, you are to open the missile doors on tubes one and two and verify that both missiles are ready for firing in all respects."

Once those orders were repeated, there was nothing further to say. Men nervously glanced at the image of the Vaaach ship, the nimbus of plasma from the Krag weapons now a brilliant yellow-white, enclosing the vessel and trailing behind like a scale model of a comet, tiny but impossibly brilliant.

Barely visible in the light show surrounding the Vaaach, a tiny lamp blinked three times. "Sir, it's the lamp signal," said Kasparov.

"Very well," said Max as he saw Nelson put the ship back in stealth mode and Levy open the missile doors, and heard them announce doing so. "In about ten seconds, the Vaaach ship is going to veer off. We will maintain course and speed until I order otherwise."

A chorus of "Aye, sir" resounded.

As Max predicted, the Vaaach vessel suddenly turned violently to starboard and pitched down, almost as though it were trying to get around to the Krag ship's flank and/or its belly. The Krag cruiser, surprisingly maneuverable for a vessel of its size and mass, turned to keep up. The bow of the powerful ship was its most heavily armored section and contained its most powerful weapons batteries, strongest deflectors, and most acute sensors; accordingly, the Krag commander wanted that part of his ship pointed at his enemy.

Focusing on the Vaaach vessel, with its most acute sensor arrays pointing in the wrong direction and other arrays damaged in battle with the Union convoy and the Vaaach scout, the Krag failed to detect the heavily stealthed Union vessel now closing from the starboard beam.

"Maneuvering, reduce engines to one-half," Max said. "Put us on the Krag's six o'clock. Weapons, target the exhaust aperture."

"Is there one?" asked Levy.

The business end of a fusion drive is a lot like a rocket engine, except that the exhaust is five times hotter. Which creates a problem. Deflectors work in both directions. A warship's deflectors not only repel incoming weapons fire if activated while the fusion drive is running, but they also bottle up the plasma exhaust near the ship, incinerating it. Accordingly, when the drive is running, the ship leaves gaps in the rear deflectors to allow the hot gas to escape. In combat conditions, the ship generates—at great energy cost because of the increased distance—an "outer deflector," a second deflector layer behind the gaps, to prevent an enemy from firing a weapon through the opening. But when a ship is facing only a single opponent that is safely positioned off the bow, many ship captains will not energize the outer deflector, saving the power for other purposes.

"He's not shielding the aperture," Kasparov said.

Max smiled. "Outstanding. Maneuvering, keep closing. I intend to fire on this target from just outside the weapons' minimum range.

"Mr. Levy, set the weapons for simultaneous detonation. Target missile number one for the inside of the port engine bell, and number two for the center." The Krag ship had three engine "bells," or exhaust nozzles, arranged in a line from left to right.

"We'll be at the designated firing range in 15 seconds, Skipper," Levy said. "Missile in tube one targeted for interior of the Krag port engine bell. Missile in tube two targeted for interior of the center engine bell. Missiles set for simultaneous detonation."

"Very well."

Max heard a gasp from Kasparov. He turned to face the Sensor officer. "Phase and polarization modulated tachyo-photon pulse, high power, far above detection threshold. Skipper, it will take five or six more sweeps before they have a firing solution, but they know we're here."

"*Merde.*"

"Sir," DeCosta said quickly, "that means they'll energize the outer deflector. It takes several seconds before it's at full power, but it will be enough to stop a missile almost immediately."

Max was already coming to his feet. "Maneuvering, ahead Emergency. Make for the center exhaust aperture.

"Weapons, retarget weapon in tube one for the center exhaust bell. Set both tubes for minimum launch velocity. Resynchronize the warheads and set for proximity detonation. Fuse them for twenty meters. And Levy, do the synchronization yourself. Detonation needs to be truly simultaneous. Disengage homing on both weapons—fire on generated bearing.

"Maneuvering, as soon as we fire, I need a hard turn—ninety-degree delta in z.

"Alerts, notify all hands to brace for contact with Krag ship's outer deflector. My intention, gentlemen, is to break the ship through the outer deflector as it powers up, steer for the center engine bell, and fire into the center engine bell through the exhaust aperture from just outside the warhead blast radius. Since the missile seekers won't have time to lock on, we will fire from generated bearing only—they'll just fly straight in and detonate. Any questions?" *Like, "Skipper, are you out of your fucking mind?"* "None? Very well."

The impact klaxon sounded. Alerts intoned over 1MC: "Brace for ship impact on enemy deflector. All hands, brace for ship impact on enemy deflector."

"I'm detecting the outer deflector starting to power up," Kasparov said. "Impact in four seconds. Three. Two. One." *WHAM!*

Even with the inertial compensators at maximum, it felt as though the ship hit a brick wall. It didn't, of course. Instead, it just underwent rapid deceleration as it passed through an area of polarized tachyo-gravitons exerting force opposite to the direction in which the ship was travelling, penetrating the deflectors by virtue of its mass and heavily armored hull where a more lightly built missile would have been destroyed. Max started to fly out of his seat until he was stopped by his station harness and yanked back into place. He saw several red lights pop up on status panels, but it looked as though most of the lights were still green.

"Damage?" asked Max.

"All Tier One systems available at this time," reported Tufeld from the Damage Control 1 Station. "Some of the more delicate Tier Three and Four systems are in reset mode due to the shock. I expect most of them to restore in two minutes or less. I've routed the list to the CO and XO consoles."

"Thank you, Tufeld."

"Firing tubes one and two in three seconds," Levy said. "Two. One. Firing."

The instant the missiles left their tubes, the *Cumberland* pitched "up," making a 90-degree turn, which, combined with the forward motion of the Krag ship, served to create maximum distance between the *Cumberland* and the target in minimum time.

At such short range, the missiles' flight time was 1.7 seconds, not enough time for them to be acquired by any of the Krag point defense systems. Before Levy could announce that they were "hot, straight, and normal," both weapons lanced into the center engine bell and detonated. Mr. Levy had done his job well, and the detonations were in fact precisely simultaneous. Because the warheads went off inside the Krag ship's deflectors and only twenty meters from her hull, the effect of the two 1.5-megaton warheads was truly devastating.

The twin fireballs vaporized nearly 90 percent of the ship, turning the remaining 10 percent into a spray of liquid metal droplets that quickly cooled to form countless hard, spherical metal bullets zipping at high speeds through interstellar space and doomed to never strike a target.

"Maneuvering, lay us alongside the Vaaach ship. Distance 100 kilometers. Mr. Chin, hail the Vaaach."

"Skipper," said Chin, "the Vaaach are hailing us."

"Outstanding. Let's see it."

The young Vaaach appeared again and began to speak. His growls and roars, however, sounded subdued. "I have been in contact with the commander for this sector, who instructs me to direct that you remain at this location until he arrives, which will be in approximately one hundred breaths [roughly twelve minutes]. He says that if you leave this location, you will be hunted down and destroyed. May the commander be less angry with you than he was with me. I am ordered to return for repairs now. Farewell, most warlike fruit eater. I hope to hunt with you again. This transmission ends now."

About eight minutes later, Kasparov announced "Unidentified sensor contact, designated as Uniform Two, bearing three-four-six mark two-five-five, range zero-point-five-two AU. Contact is at constant bearing decreasing range, speed point niner-four. Depending on his decel profile, he'll be on us in about four minutes. Contact is based on Uniform Two's active sensor emissions only. No other readings, mass, EM, or otherwise. It's looking as though they have an incredibly effective stealth suite, and they just decided to turn on an active scan so that we could detect them. If I didn't know better, I'd say that it was almost like they were giving us a buzz on voicecom before dropping in for a visit. Being polite by letting us know they were coming, if you know what I mean."

"I know exactly what you mean, Mr. Kasparov, and I think that is exactly what they're doing. The Vaaach have very strict rules of conduct and honor, and they always follow them."

Then, to the entire compartment, Max said, "Since we're dealing with the greatest known hunters and warriors in the galaxy, we need to look the part, people. Weapons, we want them to find us loaded for bear. Reload with Ravens in all three tubes, bring pulse cannon to Prefire."

Listening to the acknowledgment and implementation of these orders with half an ear, he punched in the voice channel for the Marine detachment.

"Kraft here," came the answer right away, tinged with just a trace of a Germanic accent.

"Major, this is the skipper. I need you and your six biggest men geared up to do battle with anything on two legs in CIC in about three minutes. Possible?"

Max could almost hear the man smiling. Even for a Marine, Major Kraft's gung came with an unusually large dose of ho.

"Sir, as the ship is at GQ, all of my men are already geared up to do battle with anything on two legs and just about anything that runs around on four, six, eight, or ten. Do you want us in camo face paint or carrying any particular kind of heavy weapon?"

"The standard M-88s and M-72s will do fine, but I think the face paint is a good touch."

"On our way."

"Thank you, Major. Skipper out." He punched the channel closed.

"Mr. Nelson, confirm that all stealth systems are off-line. Maneuvering, put us on an intercept course for the target."

As Nelson and LeBlanc were carrying out those orders, DeCosta leaned in Max's direction. "Sir, I'm not sure I understand those last two orders."

"Vaaach psychology," said Max, without a trace of condescension. He knew that what he was doing was anything but obvious.

"The Vaaach have detected us, apparently without difficulty. Stealth, trying to hide, looks like cowardice. Understand that the Vaaach divide all animal life into two categories: predators and prey. Then there are different categories of predator, but let's skip that for now.

"If you don't want to be treated like prey, you act like a predator. So that's what we're doing. We make ourselves plainly detectable and steer an intercept course. In hunting terms, we're going to step out from behind the bushes and face them like equals, not cower in the underbrush like frightened rabbits. That make sense?"

"Yes, sir. It does. What are the categories of predator?"

"Pertinent question. There are two. The Vaaach are sort of a black and white species, so they tend to divide lots of things into two, and only two, groups. The categories of predator are 'Hunters with Honor' and 'Hunters without Honor.' Do you know what 'Vaaach' means in their language?"

"Sorry, sir, but I never bothered to look it up."

"Curiosity about things like that might serve you well, XO. You learn lots of interesting things when you take the time to find the answers to the questions your mind generates because some part of your mind has decided that those are the questions that you need to have answered.

"But to the point in question: it's a compound word made from three parts. 'Ach,' meaning 'hunters'; 'a' meaning 'having,' 'possessing,' or 'being endowed with'; and 'va' meaning 'honor.' Of course their syntax is different from Standard. They put the object of the preposition first, so 'Va-a-ach,' their own name for their race, means 'hunters with honor.' Says a lot about them, don't you think?"

"Sure does, Skipper. Let's hope that they honor us by not blowing us to flaming atoms."

"Amen to that."

"After reading your report from the last encounter, I always wondered…" DeCosta's curiosity remained unsatisfied, because at that moment the ship gave a sudden lurch.

"Grap field," announced Kasparov. "Two-point-three-five million Hawkings."

"Maneuvering, null the drive. Take maneuvering thrusters to standby and inertial attitude control off-line." The orders came quickly, but without any evident emotion. "Not even a battleship could make headway against a field that strong. And they've probably got the damn thing set on 'low.'"

As soon as LeBlanc acknowledged those orders, Kasparov spoke up. "Sir, it's déjà vu all over again. Based on visually observed ship configuration and spectrum of the light from her view ports, Uniform Two is posident as Vaaach, same type of ship as our last encounter. Intel has code named that type *Boron* class. And sir, based on what little trickle of sensor data I'm getting from her, we're thinking it might be the same ship."

"Wouldn't that be an interesting coincidence," Max said, hoping he sounded a lot calmer than he felt. Several CIC displays showed an image of the Vaaach vessel, a gigantic, black spear point, bristling with technologically advanced means of killing other thinking beings. The warships of most known species looked like nonthreatening elongated boxes or elongated cylinders. But when the Vaaach built a warship, the ship itself looked like a deadly weapon.

Suddenly Chin stirred and started hitting controls. "Sir, we just received comms from the Vaaach ship. And text, sir, not visual. Coming up on Commandcom."

The butterflies in Max's stomach turned into a flock of condors. If the Vaaach wanted to talk, they generally waited about a minute and a half and then established visual comms, usually on channel 7. No one ever received text comms from them. At least, no one who lived to file a report.

Max read the text as it came up on the display. "YOU HAVE MADE CLANDESTINE INCURSION INTO VAAACH TERRITORIAL SPACE STOP EXPLAIN QUICKLY WHY WE SHOULD NOT IMMEDIATELY DESTROY YOU STOP MESSAGE ENDS."

"They certainly do not waste words," said the doctor.

"Not usually, no," Max said. The doctor didn't know the half of it. The message contained none of the formalities of a Vaaach communication between hunters: no greetings, no announcement of the sender's identity and his credentials as a warrior/hunter, and no ritual insults to the recipient. Just the combined demand and threat. That was bad. Very, very bad. The Vaaach were pissed.

Max needed to send a reply. Now. And without much time to think about it. What to say? Think *honor*. The Vaaach were all about honor and their Rules of the Hunt. Max spent a few minutes typing on his console, made a few revisions, and then said, "Mr. Chin, send the text that's on CommandSend."

"Aye, sir."

Only after it went out could just about everyone in CIC read: "THIS VESSEL WAS FOLLOWING THE BLOOD TRAIL OF WOUNDED PREY THAT WE DESTROYED JOINTLY WITH VAAACH SCOUT VESSEL STOP ENTRY NOT CLANDESTINE BUT ANNOUNCED BY REPEATED BROADCASTS ON STANDARD INTERSPECIES COMM CHANNELS STOP MESSAGE ENDS."

"You're not going to ask them not to kill us?"

"Absolutely not, Doctor. Not unless I have a strong desire to die in the next five seconds. From the Vaaach perspective, any kind of pleading is at least a sign of weakness and, very likely, a sign of guilt. If you are innocent, why plead for mercy rather than simply demonstrating that you're innocent? What you do in this situation is tell the Vaaach the facts that *mean* they should not kill you: in this case, first that we were in active pursuit of wounded prey, which under their rules gives us the right to enter their territory; and second, that we didn't sneak in but announced our presence honorably."

Major Kraft and his Marines cycled in through the hatch. Having deduced what Max wanted them for, DeCosta arranged them behind the skipper so that if visual communications were established, the Vaaach would see six hardened warriors and their immediate commander arrayed behind their captain, ready to engage in personal combat.

Once the Marines were suitably arranged, no one said a word. Either the Vaaach would respond to the message, or they would activate their antimatter cannon and vaporize the *Cumberland.* Max had to will himself to relax his grip on the arms of his chair. He was sure his fingers had left permanent impressions in the metal. The wait seemed endless. Time oozed forward like a tired snail going uphill.

BEEP.

Because of the usual murmur of voices in CIC, the soft electronic alert from the Comms console was generally inaudible to anyone but a man sitting right in front of it. This time, it sounded almost as loud as the general quarters klaxon. Every man let out the breath he didn't know he'd been holding.

"On Commandcom, sir," Chin said.

"PRECISELY IDENTIFY PREY YOU CLAIM TO HAVE WOUNDED AND SPECIFY DAMAGE INFLICTED TO IT BY YOUR VESSEL BEFORE ENTERING VAAACH SPACE STOP MESSAGE ENDS."

At least it wasn't a blast from their antimatter cannon. Max typed. A bit longer than last time. "Send this."

"Aye, sir."

"PREY IS KRAG MEDIUM CRUISER UNION NAVAL REPORTING NAME CRAYFISH CLASS STOP DAMAGE INCLUDES DESTRUCTION OF METASPACIAL TRANSCEIVER ARRAY DAMAGE TO MULTIPLE MISSILE TUBES AND PROBABLE SMALL HULL BREACH STOP QUERY DO YOU WISH US TO MAKE SENSOR SCANS OF KRAG VESSEL OR SENSOR RECORDS OF BATTLE AVAILABLE TO YOU STOP MESSAGE ENDS."

Again the waiting. Clouseau stood up and stretched languorously, investing the familiar series of motions with the unaffected sensuality possessed only by cats and sexually confident human females. He sprang lightly to the deck and, continuing to stretch while he walked, sauntered onto the command island and lay down with his head resting on Max's left foot.

Max could not help but smile at the situation: the domesticity of having a cat using one's foot for a pillow, not in a living room in front of the fire, but on a heavily armed warship at battle stations facing possible annihilation by an advanced alien race nearly a thousand light years away from the blue and green world on which the respective owners of the head and the foot had evolved.

"Sir?" It was Ensign Bales, the seldom-heard-from officer who oversaw the ship's computer systems and data network.

"Yes, Bales."

"It's hard to tell, but I think that the Vaaach just pulled a dump from our computer."

"What did they get?"

"It looks like they scanned the whole MDC," he said, his voice tinged with incredulity.

Most of the heads in CIC turned at that one. The *Cumberland*'s main data core contained a stupefyingly enormous quantity of data. The most rapid data transfer technology available in the Union—the fastest computer in existence reading the data, transmitting it over a high-bandwidth, 2.5 million channel, polyphasic quantum-differentiated laser "pipeline"—could probably accomplish it in half a day. The Vaaach had done it without permission in nearly undetectable fashion, from kilometers away, without any physical connection, and in only a minute or two.

"I would not have spotted it at all," Bales explained, "but we did a super high-resolution scan of our data drives after the last encounter and came up with a subtle signature made by the kind of sensor they use that gets left in the nanomagnetic substrate. Basically, they employ a sophisticated quantum scan to take a snapshot of each one and zero molecule orientation in the memory matrix, which would mean that their sensor resolution is down to the molecular, if not atomic, level.

"Then, they just convert the scan back into data, using some kind of translation algorithm. If that's what it is, they have sensor technology like we never imagined. Of course, we may be sitting here for a while waiting for any response—it will take them hours just to resolve the image into a machine-readable data stream, and I can't begin to predict what it will take for them to work their way through the operating system, find the files they want, translate them into their own language, and read them."

Max shook his head. "No, Mr. Bales, I don't think it will take them long at all. I think I may have time to take a leak, though. Barely." Max got up and went to the head.

He had just come back, had sent midshipman Gilbertson fetch him some coffee, and had taken a few sips, when Chin announced, "Skipper, I'm receiving a request to establish visual communications, channel 7."

"By all means, Mr. Chin. Let's not keep the mighty hunters waiting."

Chin nodded, and Max's Commandcom display and a dozen other displays around CIC punched into that channel showed the furry face of the Vaaach commander. It looked like the same one they had encountered a few months before, but it was hard for humans to tell one Vaaach from another. Basically, they all looked like koala bears. Enormous, ferocious, carnivorous, long fanged, very short-tempered koala bears. Koala bears that made an Earth grizzly bear look like the kind of bear you tuck under the quilt with your four-year-old-daughter at bedtime.

The average fully grown Vaaach was 4.5 meters tall, with razor-sharp, retractable claws the size of carving knives, six fangs about as long as bayonets, and hard-staring, yellow-green eyes that looked as though their owner were deciding how you would be at your most flavorful: fast grilled, slow roasted, or raw.

The Vaaach began to speak: a series of growls, roars, snarls, and similar sounds, like a fight between a polar bear and a mountain lion. Lagging by about ten seconds, the computer provided a written translation on an adjacent screen, occasionally throwing in what was intended to be helpful explanatory material. The first few growls sounded as though there were some Standard words in there, mangled by the Vaaach's incompatible vocal apparatus.

"Lieutenant Commander Maxime Tindall Robichaux, Union Space Navy, of the planet Nouvelle Acadiana, I greet you. [Voiceprint matching positively establishes that the speaker is Forest Victor Chrrrlgrf, encountered by this vessel on 22 January 2315 in the Tesseck A system.] Our statement that you entered Vaaach space in a dishonorable fashion is no longer operative. We received your transmission. A member of my crew logged it improperly. The individual responsible is undergoing punishment. Does this satisfy the affront to your honor?"

The Vaaach leaned back in his seat and flexed his claws over and over: extend, retract, extend, retract, extend, retract. Each cycle took nearly a second. Max wondered what those claws would do to human flesh.

"Not much of an apology," DeCosta observed.

"For a Vaaach, that was practically groveling in abject guilt." Max keyed the audio pickup for transmission. "Forest Victor Chrrlgrf of the Rawlrrhfr Forest, Victor of the Battle of Hrlrgr, I greet you. I consider honor to be satisfied in this matter. I hope the punishment being given to the individual who made the error is not too severe. We were not greatly harmed."

When Max finished talking, he leaned back in his chair, adopted the most relaxed posture he could make himself adopt, and watched Chrrlgrf read the translation. At one point, he stopped flexing his claws, extended them fully, and made a slight sweeping motion with one of his hands. Intel said that the motion indicated anger—a suppressed reflex to reach out with his hand and rip open his opponent's chest. He finished reading, considered for a moment, and looked up, those alien and yet so obviously intelligent and perceptive eyes leveled right at the camera. He could only imagine how intimidating it would be to have the immense, powerful Vaaach in the same room.

The Vaaach, gave off what sounded like a sigh. An almost pensive sigh. *What's that about?* Then, the polar bear versus mountain lion match resumed and translation started to scroll up the display.

"I am no longer to be addressed as 'Forest Victor.' My present rank is 'forest commander' [a rank believed to be roughly equivalent to rear admiral]. You are blameless for the error in addressing me. Such changes are military matters we do not often reveal to fruit eaters.

"Regarding the negligent member of my crew, his punishment is not a matter to be discussed with frivolous monkey offspring. Be satisfied with knowing that neither you nor he has been put to death. Do not give me cause to regret either decision. As to what to do with you, because the Krag vessel just destroyed here died bearing the marks of your claws, there is a fine point of honor and the Hunters' Rules we must resolve, based upon a further review of the computer records we have obtained from you. We will advise you when we have decided. It should not be long, even for one with a primate attention span. Do not attempt to leave. This communication ends now." The carrier cut off, and the displays tuned into it went blank.

"What the *hell* was that about?" Everyone was staring at the doctor not just because of the unaccustomed vehemence with which he stated his question but also because he almost never uttered any kind of curse. "None of that makes any sense at all."

"Actually, Doctor, it does," Max said calmly. The sometimes excitable Sahin injecting additional fear and anxiety into the CIC was the last thing he needed. The men were nervous enough with the ship caught like a bug in a jar, waiting to know whether the entomologist with his hand on the lid was going to set them free or dissect them.

"The Vaaach are bound, on penalty of swift death, to a strict code of honor, which they apply consistently and—by their standards at least—fairly. Sometimes, the right thing to do can depend on some seemingly trivial detail, just as in a law case. So, they're looking at what happened. In detail. It won't take them long to make up their minds. They are decisive. They make Admiral Hornmeyer look wishy-washy."

A few people chuckled at that. *Good. If people are laughing, they aren't too scared to think. And they should always be thinking.* "They'll learn what they need, announce what they found and what they decided based on what they found, and then they'll act on it."

Only a few minutes passed before Chin announced, "Carrier on channel 7, sir."

"Let's have it."

Chin made the requisite connections causing the bizarre interweaving of complex geometric patterns and color progressions that the Vaaach used for a test pattern to appear on a dozen or CIC displays. He tied the CIC visual and audio pickups into the transceiver, which notified the Vaaach that the *Cumberland* was ready to engage in communication. A moment later, the test pattern was replaced by Vaaach commander, his fuzzy face and tufted koala bear ears looking cute and cuddly as ever, with his dagger-like fangs and deadly, alien, yellow-green eyes even more dangerous. A few short roars and a snarl followed.

"I greet you, Commander Robichaux," said the translation.

"I greet you, as well, Forest Commander Chrrlgrf."

"We have reviewed your activities since we last met, including your recent battle with the Krag. We will not kill you. Not today." Max could feel an immediate dissipation of tension in the compartment, like a spring uncoiling.

"We are pleased to learn of your decision."

A few short, barking growls, perhaps the Vaaach equivalent of laughter. "Of course you are. You will continue to hunt the Krag. We hope you kill many of them. It seems you were born for that purpose, as Forest Commander Vllgrhmrr said twelve seasons ago when you spent time among the Hunters of Vermin.

"Now, regarding the hunt, you have forced us to do something for which there is no precedent. Although a Vaaach youngling inflicted some wounds on the prey, you killed it. And when the youngling encountered it, the prey was suffering from many wounds, including wounds you—not just your hunting brothers—but you and your ship, inflicted on it. And of all the wounds suffered by this prey, the ones inflicted by you and your ship were the most recent. We now also know that the prey was fleeing you when the youngling pounced on it. Under our law, although the hunter who controls the territory in which a kill is made has the primary rights to the prey, the hunter who kills prey in the territory of another hunter or who drives it into that territory where it is then killed has rights of blood, the right to take some of the meat from the kill."

The forest commander paused once again. He contemplated one of his claws. Perhaps it was duller than the others. Perhaps it was sharper. Perhaps there was something about its wicked curvature and its long, knife-like cutting edge that he found particularly appealing.

After a few seconds, the CIC transducers started to put out more feeding time at the tiger cage sounds. "Unfortunately, you cannot exercise this right in the usual way because the kill has been made and the prey utterly destroyed, to the last atom. Even so, failing to grant your rights of blood would be an act of extreme dishonor and is not even to be considered. I have just spoken with the Loremaster and the Lawspeaker on our homeworld, and they are in agreement with me and with each other: our traditions and law allow no exception. You must share—in whatever manner is possible—in the meat from the beast, even if you are a tiny, pink, fangless, scampering primate."

At least the Vaaach was being insulting. That was always a good sign. He broke eye contact with the camera for an instant, as though he were concealing an emotion. Amusement? Feigned reluctance to do something he had planned to do all along? Reading humans is hard enough, but a fur-faced, technologically advanced, tree-dwelling, carnivorous alien?

"According to the Loremaster and the Lawspeaker, before you may receive your meat, you must first be proclaimed a Hunter. We do not suffer hard-won meat to be passed to the scavengers. As the leader of the hunt in which you took your first Kill of Honor, it is my duty to give you a Hunter's Name. It is a duty I must fulfill well, as the name's fitness for the hunter is a measure of the honor of he who bestowed it."

The Vaaach paused, as if pondering something. He bared some of his lower teeth, revealing that they were all needle sharp. A smile, perhaps? "Your records tell an interesting tale of your hunts since we last met. You have been a busy little primate, very much a *bglrrmlmp* [a burrowing parasite, much like a tick, that causes extreme irritation to Vaaach skin and is very difficult to remove] in the flesh of the Krag. Your nature as a hunter and a warrior is clear to me. I know the kind of name to give you, but I have not had time to find the words in your primitive, poorly organized database. So, I must ask you: What is the primary form of terrain near the place of your birthing?"

"Wetlands primarily. Swamps, marshes, bayous. Some low-lying plains and grasslands. Occasionally woods," said Max, wondering where this was all going.

"Swamp. Very well. I also need to know the name of a creature on your world like our *hrllarlemar*—virtually all complex ecosystems have such an animal. The *hrllarlemar* is small, quick, and crafty. It has a peculiar kind of genius for getting through fences, for entering and raiding closed outbuildings where we keep our small domestic animals, for defeating and penetrating the most elaborate means used to keep it out. When hunted, it is highly elusive and has a great many tricks for evading and escaping hunters. It doubles back on its trail to send us in circles. It leaps from tree to tree so as to leave no scent. It leads our hunting animals into bogs and then scampers away. In our language, its name stands for its qualities. We often say that a crafty warrior is a sly old *hrllarlemar*. Do you have such an animal?"

"We do. It's called a fox."

"Fox. The name suits the beast. Come to your feet, Hunter to Be."

Max stood. This was starting to feel as though it might be important.

"Maxime Tindall Robichaux, of planet Nouvelle Acadiana, henceforth and so long as claws and fangs shall yearn to find the flesh of prey, you shall be a Hunter of the Vaaach. Your current rank is that of peer [the lowest rank in the Vaaach Hunter hierarchy]. You shall be called by the name 'Swamp Fox.' Is that an acceptable name?"

"Forest Commander, I'm afraid that it *has* been used before. That was the nickname of General Francis Marion, an American Rev—"

Max was stopped in mid-word by an almost deafening roar so loud that it triggered the sound system's protective circuits to prevent damage to the crew's hearing. Max looked anxiously down at the translation.

"I care not that it has been borne before by some long-dead fruit-eating monkey. The Vaaach did not confer the name on him. It has no meaning to us. The Vaaach do not recognize it. Your choices are simple. You may accept the name, or you may refuse it. If you refuse it, you must earn the right to claim your own name by vanquishing me in single, unarmed Honor Combat in the treetops. Such combat usually results in the death of one of the combatants. My ship has an arboretum with trees grown for just that purpose. Speak now. How do you choose?"

"I accept the name."

He made a few more of the short, barking growls that Max was even more convinced were laughter. "Wise choice. Here is your share of the meat. May it give you strength for many hunts. The voices of my ancestors whisper to me that your hairless face awaits me around many turns of my life's journey. I have no doubt that I will find you as much a nuisance then as I do now. Until then, hunt well. Unless you seek swift and certain death, leave our space immediately by the most direct route. This communication ends."

The carrier cut off, the grappling field collapsed, and the enormous black, menacing arrowhead of the Vaaach vessel pivoted in its own length, pulled away from the destroyer, engaged its compression drive, and was gone.

"What does 'Here is your share of the meat' mean? I don't see any meat anywhere." The doctor sounded irritated, as though he had been looking forward to meat furnished by the Vaaach.

"I think I do," said Gilbertson, pointing to two dark green boxes on the deck right behind Chief LeBlanc's station, in the precise center of CIC. They had apparently appeared out of nowhere. Clouseau was standing near them, his back arched, hair standing on end.

"Fantastic," blurted Bhattacharyya. "Positive confirmation that the Vaaach have matter translocation technology!"

Everyone looked at him as though he had started reciting Tri-Nin courtship poetry. Seeing all eyes on him, he raised his hands defensively. "That's been a major intelligence question for years."

"I'm sure it has been, Mr. Bhattacharyya. I'll need you to draft a paragraph or two on the issue for my report," Max said warmly. After all, geeky enthusiasm for minute details about the militarily relevant capabilities of other species was a desirable trait in an intelligence officer.

At the Fire Fighting and Hazard Control console, Chief Ardoin stuck Spacer Sanders in the ribs with his elbow. Sanders did not appreciate the interruption, as he was immersed in untangling a malfunctioning toxic gas alarm.

"What?"

"I've got it," said Ardoin.

"Got what?"

"The nickname."

"What?" Sanders was starting to sound monotonous.

"The nickname. For the skipper, dummy."

"Okay, Ardoin." Sanders made a point of pronouncing the name to rhyme with "coin" instead of ending it correctly—with a sound like the "a" in "plant." "Let's have it."

Ardoin held up his hand, palm out, moving it in a sweeping motion, in time with his words, as though reading the name written in enormous letters on a gigantic sign or the side of a mountain, "The Swamp Fox. We need to start using that Vaaach name when we talk about him. Whaddya think?"

Sanders thought for a moment. "Ardoin, you have never had one good idea in your whole life. Not one. Ever." He paused. "Except, maybe, for this one." They both smiled.

Max walked over and looked at the alien gear. After about a minute, he turned to Bales. "All right, get a dolly in here and get these things rolled—very carefully—into Captured Hardware and let's see what we've got. The Vaaach have sent us some meat. I'm betting we're going to like the flavor."

They liked the flavor. A lot.

"This box," Bales explained just over an hour later and pointing to the larger of the two, "is probably a standard memory module from the Vaaach ship. It's got traces of metal from the mounting brackets that used to hold it in place. The shape is consistent with the kinds of brackets we use to hold racks of similar-sized components in an array. We don't know for sure, but it's a reasonable hypothesis that the Vaaach may have dozens, even hundreds of these things and use them as the primary storage device for their computer system. God knows their ship is big enough that they could have ten thousand of the dang things for all we know."

He pointed to what looked like a small blue light attached to one end. "This tiny, glowing blue bump stuck on the back is a power supply. Don't ask me how it works. There's no opening in the case of the main unit, so we've got no idea about how the power gets from the power unit to the inside of the data unit. For all I know, the thing runs off of bright blue fairy dust, and the fairies transfer the power by waving their tiny pink wands. I've measured the rate of decay, though, and from all appearances the power will last something on the order of a thousand years. Maybe two thousand. Maybe more. Forget the memory unit, Captain, the Vaaach's freaking *battery* is five hundred years ahead of us.

"The memory unit is shielded from external scans by some sort of scrambler on the inside. So we have no idea of how it works. The case is one solid metal piece. No rivets, fastenings, bolts, or welds. Just smooth metal all the way around without any openings of any kind. We haven't a clue as to what the metal is. The scrambler keeps us from getting any kind of useful readings from any kind of scan we can put together, including the ones we have that are designed to defeat scramblers, and the material is so hard that we can't scrape off a sample for the mass spec. Not even a few molecules. We even poked it ten or twelve times with an old alpha proton X-ray spectrometer and got zilch."

Max broke in. "Okay, Bales, that's good, but I'm a lot less interested in what the box is made of than I am in what's inside it." Bales, far and away the best computer man on the ship, had a tendency to get drawn into technical issues because they were intellectually interesting, not because they materially related to killing Krag and winning the war.

"Right, sir. Sorry. We don't know what's inside this box and we're never going to know what's inside this box. All we will ever know is what we get out of it through *this* box." He pointed to the second, smaller box. The two had no connection that anyone could see.

"As near as we can tell, this smaller box is an adaptive interface. It communicates with the big box. Somehow. We can't read any RF between the two, and there are no metaspacial modulations, so the only thing we can think of is that there's some sort of controlled, artificial quantum tunneling effect between the two, but that's only a wild guess. Or maybe it's fairies with tiny crystal balls. I'm thinking we'll never know, at least not in my lifetime.

"Anyway, the two boxes talk to each other. The small box has got the same kind of magic blue thousand-year battery on the back powering it. And here is the only part of the whole package that we recognize. The small box has got a standard IDSSC Type 17 FODIC coming out of it. I suppose the Vaaach have scanned enough of our computers to know exactly how our systems work because the dang thing is totally plug and play, sir. I mean, the Vaaach made it so any hatch hanger could make it work. I just take this cable coming out of the box, stick it into a fiber optic data interface cable outlet, and it just boots up as a standard external device, just like I plugged in one of our secondary data modules."

He touched a key that brought up a menu on one of the wall displays. "Right now, we've got it running but under level 5 digital sequestration. I've got it hooked into one of the quarantined computers we use to interface with alien gadgets—you know, absolutely no connection whatsoever with the computers that run the ship. Even a totally separate power supply, plus devices with any data storage or wireless transmission capability that come into this room can never leave, all to keep any alien malware from getting into our system, which is why you had to leave your percom—"

"Bales," Max interrupted, "they don't give you command of a rated warship just because you have a loud voice and a charming personality. I know the elements of level 5 data sequestration. Now," Max said, pointing to the wall display, "that's not our standard menu format. Why the change?"

"Because, sir, that's not our menu. That's a Vaaach menu generated, presumably, by the interface device. Except for differences in the colors, the type faces, and some of the formatting conventions, it could easily be something that my department would put together using one of the standard Navy templates. This is the top level menu. We've got two options: 'Access Database Directly,' and 'Access Database through Linguistic/Symbolic Translation/Transliteration/Conversion Matrix.' Naturally, we've done both. The Conversion matrix lets us read the database, including all the scientific symbols, translated into Standard and converted into the symbol set and units we use. So we can read it all. For the first time!"

"Read *what*, Bales?"

"Captain, don't you get it? Remember how the Vaaach read our entire main data core the moment they snagged us? Well, that little Vaaach scout ship did the same thing with the Krag ship before we destroyed it. They put the whole freaking thing in that little box, gave us a way to read it, and gave it to us as a present. Or maybe a reward. Anyway, we have the *entire database* of a Krag *Crayfish* class medium cruiser sitting right there. We've never gotten even a part of one of these before. The best we've done is pull a partial dump from some of their base mainframes and get some logistics data and some low-level decryption keys. Their warship memory cores have a quick reset. They just hit a button, and all the bits instantly go to zero, leaving not a trace of the data. We've got a whole main data core! Sir, it's the biggest intelligence haul in—well, I'm no Intel guy, sir, but—"

From the back of the room, Bhattacharyya spoke up. "I am. And sir, the intelligence implications of this—well, they take my breath away. Literally. I feel like I might need to lie down." He steadied himself by grasping the edge of a work table.

"Sir, if that box is what Bales says it is, this represents the most important involuntary transfer of information from one belligerent power to another in the history of Intelligence. Ever. I don't just mean space combat; I mean going back to guys like Hammurabi and Ramesses. Sir, think about what's in our MDC and imagine an enemy getting his hands on it. It means . . ." He trailed off, overcome by the implications of his statement.

He was right. The implications *were* breathtaking. "Thank you, Mr. Bhattacharyya. I get it. What we've got sitting on that table right there can change the course of the war." He walked over to the comm panel and punched up a voice channel to CIC.

"CIC, DeCosta here."

"XO, this is the skipper. Are we back in Union space yet?"

"Yes, sir. Even by the most expansive reading of the Vaaach territorial claims, we've been in Union space for the last four minutes or so. We're now on direct course to rendezvous with the pennant."

"Change in plans. Alter course to rendezvous with the *Halsey.* We've got a delivery to make to Admiral Hornmeyer and his N2 Section. Tell Engineering to crack on everything they've got."

"But sir, we've just got orders from Commander Duflot to rejoin the pennant ship and escort it to the repair yards at Pfelung."

"Not gonna happen. Our possession of this device triggers a standing order that now takes precedence. XO, could you please punch Chin in on this circuit." There was a click and a quiet beep.

"Chin here. What can I do for you, Skipper?"

"Chin, please signal Commander Duflot that we are unable to comply with his order due to Naval Regulations, Article 15, Paragraph 5. Have the signal state further that due to security requirements, we are unable to provide further explanation at this time but that a full justification of my actions will be provided at the earliest opportunity."

"Aye, sir," said Chin, reluctance showing in every tone. "He's going to be hot."

"Don't I know it. But not nearly as hot as the potato we're carrying. Not even close.

"And send the following to Admiral Hornmeyer and to the Chief of Naval Operations in Norfolk. Priority: *Flash Z*."

"*Flash Z*, sir? That's reserved for the highest, highest priority communications. Stuff on which the entire course of the war could turn. Are you sure, sir?"

"Mr. Chin," Max said with perfect and patient calm, "I know what *Flash Z* means. This message easily meets the criteria. If they had a higher priority than that, I would use that one instead. Now, are you ready to take the message?"

"Yes, sir." He actually sounded a little shaky. Chin had never sent anything higher than "Urgent." The man knew his job, but he tended to be a bit on the twitchy side.

"All right, Chin. Message begins. Enigma. Repeat. Enigma. That's Echo, Nebula, India, Galaxy, Mike, Alfa. Got that, Chin?"

“Aye, sir. ‘Enigma. Repeat. Enigma.’ The message will go out in less than three minutes, sir.”

“Chin?”

“Yes, Skipper.”

“Make it two.”

“I don’t see why we are in such a furious rush to rejoin the task force,” said Dr. Sahin while sipping his coffee. “It’s not as though we have just been handed the keys to the kingdom and we have to rush to put them in the right hands to open the gate.”

“Actually, Bram, that is pretty much what we do have.” Max paused to take a sip of the steadily improving ship’s beer. Spacer Bud Schlitz was proving to have a true gift for the art of brewing, and there were rumors that the crew was pressuring him into trying his hand at brewing more varieties of beer than just the standard medium tan lager that he was now making. The two men were sitting companionably in Max’s day cabin after having eaten a late supper, the *Cumberland* having completed the first day and a half of the seven-day high-speed run to the rendezvous with Admiral Hornmeyer’s flag ship.

“I was sitting down with Bhattacharyya this morning. He’s had a better look at what’s in that database, and here’s just some of the major strategic implications of this data. First, the Krag ship used its computer to read encrypted signals, so we’ve got all of their military encrypt keys until they decide to change them, which may be up to one of their years, or 377 of our days. We’ll be able to read every transmission we intercept immediately, rather than after days or weeks in decrypt. That’s going to make a huge operational difference right there.

“Second, there’s a huge database of technical specifications: ships, weapons, area sensors, communications equipment, computers, the whole lot. With those specs, we’ll be able to find hundreds, maybe even thousands, of exploitable weaknesses in those systems. We'll know how to confuse the computers, jam the comms, deflect the weapons, blind the sensors, defeat the ships—the whole nine yards. Who knows? We might be able to find holes in their sensor net that will let one ship or maybe even a task force walk right through without being detected."

"That would certainly be useful."

"That's just the beginning. When we had relations with them, the Krag were very cagey about some things. We never learned the exact location of their homeworld, their economic centers, the layout of their hegemony. All that stuff's in there. If we can penetrate their defenses and get into their space, now we know where to go, where the assets are, what to attack that will hurt them the most.

"Add to that, we now know the location of their comm relays, fuel production facilities, logistics nodes, convoy routes, the makeup and location of their theater and strategic reserve forces, and a thousand other details that tell us where and how to hit them. And my friend, the icing on the cake is that *there is no way in hell the Krag know we have it.* So when we start putting this information to use, they will be completely surprised." He paused to marvel at what it all meant.

"That's just scratching the surface. There's information in that box and implications of that information that we can't even guess at yet. It changes everything."

"Will it win the war for us?" Bram was starting to catch on.

"Likely not. Not by itself. But I'm confident that, used well and absent some kind of major battle defeat that destroys one of our two task forces in operations against the Krag—the one under Middleton or the one under Hornmeyer—it will keep us from losing it. At least for the next year or so. Long enough for us to accumulate more allies or to come up with something else that will give us some kind of resource or manpower or technological advantage."

"You say that we now know the location of their homeworld."

"Yes, I'm afraid so."

"Why 'afraid,' my friend? Why wouldn't possession of that information be unambiguously good news, Max?"

"Because it's a lot further away than we thought. When we encountered them in 2183, it wasn't by finding a planet that they occupied. Instead, one of our long-range exploratory ships ran into one of their long-range survey ships taking readings on the same pulsar. When we traded information, both sides disclosed a fair amount of information about their homeworlds, but we both studiously did not disclose their location. They found out the location of Earth from some of our trading partners easily enough. We've never done a very good job of keeping ours concealed. They have.

"When the war broke out, we just assumed that their core worlds were about the same distance from the FEBA as ours. Turns out, they are more than 2500 light years back from the initial front, and that front has moved about a thousand light years closer to our Core Worlds since then. So, there's no question for the foreseeable future of any offensive that would knock them out of the war by putting their heartland directly at risk. Even if we turn the tide and start taking great chunks of their space, we'd be years away from being able to force a surrender, much less attain what I suspect our overall war aims are."

"And what might those be? I don't think I've ever heard them discussed, outside of 'ultimate victory,' 'utter defeat of the enemy,' and other similar verbal formulations 'full of sound and fury, signifying nothing.'"

"That's because I don't think a lot of thought has been given to them. For so long, our only reasonable objective has been to stave off defeat until we can muster whatever it takes to turn the tide and push the Krag back. How far we would push them and under what circumstances we would stop pushing them in order to make peace have been categorized as bridges to be crossed when we get to them. But we don't have much of a choice as to our war aims, don't you think?"

"I'm not sure what you mean."

"Well, the Krag have said that they have a religious obligation to destroy us down to the last child, to eradicate us from the galaxy forever. So long as they believe they have a duty to wipe out our race, we'd have to be crazy to do anything short of obliterating their military, destroying their colonies, vaporizing every space vehicle they have and the means to produce them, and parking a constellation of battle stations in orbit around their homeworld, armed to the teeth, with instructions to blow to flaming atoms anything that gets more than a hundred kills or so above the surface. That's the minimum. A good case can be made for bombing their homeworld back to the Stone Age or even rendering the planet uninhabitable."

"You mean genocide? Total genocide of the entire Krag race?"

"When and if we get to that point, it's going to have to be on the table. After all, that's *their* objective in this war, isn't it? If all we do is inflict a few major military defeats on them, maybe destroy two or three battle groups, and they sue for an armistice or a peace treaty, how can we reasonably give it to them? What assurance do we have that they won't just use the time to rebuild and rearm and come at us again and again and again until they finally catch us when we are weak and vulnerable and they get the upper hand and wipe us out?

"We're dealing with our survival as a species. We can't afford to take any chances. If we could make a peace treaty with them and believe that they aren't going to come at our throats at the first chance, that would be one thing, but given that their stated aim to kill every human being in the galaxy and then to sterilize the Earth and every Earth-settled world so that no trace of our genome remains, I can't see how we can tell ourselves that we have done our duty to protect generations of human beings to come if we leave them with any kind of space capability at all. And I wouldn't be surprised if we wind up having to wipe them out altogether."

"That is almost too monstrous to contemplate. The complete elimination of another sentient species from the universe. Has it ever been done?"

"The short answer is, yes, we're pretty sure that it has, and right here in the Orion-Cygnus arm too. But you know that our knowledge of the galaxy is very, very incomplete, even in terms of astrocartography, much less the histories of the sentient races. We hardly know anything of what took place before we came onto the galactic stage.

"Other races are very close-mouthed not just about their own history but the history of other races too. Of course, they particularly don't trust us with that kind of information because we have a way of taking information and using it in unexpected ways—like the way we took the jump drive technology we got from the Ning-Braha and made the intuitive leap to metaspacial radio, something that no one else in this part of the galaxy had except for the Vaaach.

"Speaking of the Vaaach, we've gotten some sketchy information on this subject from the Tri-Nin, who have been engaging in interstellar travel since about the time Columbus sailed for the New World. According to them, there used to be a race called the Bhandka-Hamp-Her that they say that the Vaaach wiped out."

"The Vaaach wiped out an entire race? When did this happen?"

"Sometime around the time of the American Revolution—late eighteenth century. Interesting story, though, what little we know of it. The Tri-Nin are saying very little, and the Vaaach are saying less, but from what we've heard, they had it coming."

"How can an entire race have earned extinction?"

"By wiping out hundreds, maybe thousands, of other races."

The doctor took several breaths before he could speak again. "Hundreds? Thousands?"

"That's right. Haven't you ever wondered why every race in this part of the Orion-Cygnus arm of our galaxy is at about the same technological level, with the exception of the Sarthan and the Vaaach, who aren't from around here but come from the Sagittarius arm?"

"Actually, I have wondered about it and thought it a peculiar coincidence."

"It's no coincidence. The tall trees in the forest are all the same height because all the taller ones got cut down. This race—let's call them the Bhandka for short—had got their society just the way they wanted it—no wars, no strife, no upheaval—and wanted to preserve it. Exactly as it was. I mean exactly—no cultural change, no technical innovation, nothing. So, they made cultural stability their overriding social priority.

"As you can imagine, you can't have that kind of cultural stability when you are in contact with alien races. If you have friendly contact with them, they introduce new ideas, art, music, fashion, literature, products, and who knows what else. If you aren't friendly with them, you have to keep your technology up to par and your military forces to match theirs, or one day they might decide to enslave or kill you. And even if you win the war, we all know wars bring cultural upheaval.

"There never would have been a Russian Revolution without World War I, an American Civil Rights Movement without World

War II, a Revolt of the Estates without the Lamoni Conflict. Or if those things happened, they would have happened years later and probably more gradually.

"The Bhandka decided that perfect stability required perfect isolation, which in turn required that they be alone in this part of the galaxy. That's just what they achieved. They periodically surveyed all the habitable worlds for about five thousand light years in every direction, and whenever they found an industrial civilization on one, they would simply wipe it out, usually by smacking the planet with a big rock or two from its own asteroid belt, rendering just about every large animal on the planet, as well as a lot of the rest of its life, extinct. A lot like what happened to the dinosaurs on Earth.

"The only local race they spared were the Tri-Nin and only because they've got all those advanced nonviolent defensive technologies that render them impervious to attack. That hive mind thing that all their females have with each other let them progress a lot further from one survey to the next than the Bhandka figured they could—so by the time they checked back, the Tri-Nin were too advanced for them to wipe out.

"Bhandka civilization endured without meaningful change or advancement for *a hundred million years*, maybe even longer. Could be billions of years. They even used genetic engineering to keep themselves from evolving further. Who knows how many civilizations they wiped out? For all we know, it might be thousands, even tens of thousands. It's impossible to get your brain around.

"Anyway, when the Vaaach arrived in the vicinity and figured out what happened, they went practically insane with rage, swept the Bhandka fleet out of their way like a formation of paper airplanes, and threw the largest forty-five or fifty asteroids from the Bhandka system at their planet, giving them more than a taste of their own medicine. Their planet looks like an overgrown version of the Earth's moon now. Supposedly it doesn't even have an atmosphere anymore. And the Bhandka, destroyers of more cultures than we will encounter if we explore the galaxy for a thousand years, are gone forever. May they roast slowly in hell.

"On the other hand, the Bhandka did us a favor. Until about the year 1780, every industrial civilization that arose in this part of the galaxy was destroyed, which is why there are so many races now stepping out into interstellar space at roughly the same technological level—these are the races that were on the verge of industrialization when the Vaaach took down the Bhandka. There isn't anyone who was more than fifty to a hundred years ahead of us technologically when the Bhandka were sent into oblivion."

"So then, the Bhandka are the explanation for the Fermi Paradox," the doctor said.

"The Fermi Paradox?"

"Yes. It's named after Enrico Fermi, the famous physicist who helped build the first fission reactor, the first fission weapon, and many other seminal contributions to physics that are far beyond my limited understanding of the field. It is said that after discussing alien visitation during a walk with a few colleagues, he sat down to lunch with them and suddenly asked, 'Where are they?' One of the other diners responded, 'Who, Doctor Fermi? Where are who?' He replied, 'The extraterrestrials. Where are they? They should be here by now.' He then proceeded to do some calculations showing that, given the age of the galaxy and the number of stars in it, the Earth should have been visited many times over. And as I understand the time line of such things, it was a good point."

"You bet it was a good point," said Max. "The thin disk of the galaxy, the part where the core and the spiral arms are, is something like eight billion years old. The Earth's age is 4.2 billion, and has evolved intelligent life that is now exploring the stars. Assuming that the evolution of intelligent life and the period for that life to develop interstellar travel is roughly the same from race to race, that leaves nearly four billion years for some star faring race to do what the Western Europeans did on Earth: spread their culture and technology throughout this part of the galaxy, if not the whole thing.

"So, Fermi was right in wondering where they were, because by all rights they should have come. There should have been some highly advanced race that had come to Earth and brought us primitives under its sway or at least had its version of anthropologists in pith helmets and khakis studying us."

The doctor nodded his understanding. "But the Bhandka never let that happen—they created a five-thousand-light-year-wide 'nature preserve' where we and the Tri-Nin and the Pfelung and the rest could develop without interference, and then, when we were about to reach the point where we were to be destroyed, the destroyers were themselves wiped out. That explains another thing too."

"What's that."

"The Vaaach. Most of the time they are the embodiment of the superior attitude that comes from being truly superior, as well as showing their instinctive territoriality derived from their heritage as predators, and their highly developed ethical sensibilities; but sometimes you get a whiff of paternal concern. I think it's because they know they saved our culture from extinction. Every time we impress them or show some promise, they look at us and think, 'But for us, these people would be gone.' They are a very emotional race you know. That is likely why they bind themselves so strictly to act by their rules and code of honor, because without them they would be killing each other right and left."

"I'd never thought of it that way, but it makes sense. Bram, sometimes, I wish we could sit down and talk, really *talk* to the Vaaach. Leave all of this 'puny pink monkey' and 'Warrior of Honor' crap in the hall and just carry on a conversation like sentient beings. The things we could learn from them!"

"Indeed. As extensive as their explorations have been, they must have made contact with hundreds of other races. The genetic and biological information they have collected over the course of their travels would be enough to revolutionize our understanding of exobiology, comparative anatomy, comparative biochemistry, the similarities and differences between the evolutionary paths taken on different worlds." He hastened to add, "And I'm sure that there would be a few interesting things to learn in other fields as well. Perhaps even a little physics or maybe a smattering of engineering, if you place value on such things."

"I wouldn't be surprised."

CHAPTER 14

04:04Z Hours, 03 April 2315

During his years of naval service, Max had seen orders that struck him as odd. He had seen orders that had struck him as crazy. He had, in fact, seen orders that were insane—and not just a little bit insane either, but totally screaming wack job, "someone should be taken out of the Fleet Operations Center and then put in a rubber room and shot up with half a gallon of happy juice"-type insane.

But in virtually every case, he understood what was going on behind the orders—what the person who wrote them was thinking and what he was trying to accomplish. In this case, however, he didn't have a clue.

He followed them regardless. In this case, his orders, sent *Flash Z* priority, directed him to take his ship, at the highest speed consistent with the importance of the cargo, to a set of coordinates located in deep space 3.72 light years from the nearest star system, to rendezvous with some Union naval vessel to be identified later, with which he was to initiate contact by sending the challenge code "Glorious First of June" and receiving the response "Trafalgar" in addition to the standard IFF recognition protocols. Someone, somewhere, was really into the British Royal Navy of Admiral Nelson's era.

What perplexed Max was that the capture of the main data core from a Krag warship was a contingency for which every Union warship, and indeed people with ranks running up to Task Force commander, had titanium-clad standing orders from none other than the most high and exalted Chief of Naval Operations in Norfolk. The vessel obtaining the core was to transmit the code word "ENIGMA" and then race at top speed to rendezvous with the nearest Comprehensive Technical Intelligence Unit, which, in Max's case, was on board the *Halsey*.

This business of rendezvousing in deep space with an undisclosed vessel was a deviation from the standard protocol. When Max himself broke the rules in order to win a battle it was one thing, but when flag officers started violating rules pertaining to super-high-priority intelligence objectives, Max started to get an unsettled feeling in his stomach and an annoying tingling sensation between his shoulder blades. They told him something odd was afoot. Or at least, something very, very different.

Max didn't like "different."

The *Cumberland* arrived at the designated coordinates, literally in the middle of nowhere, with her passive sensors tuned to the highest pitch of alertness.

And detected nothing.

Three hours passed, the watch changed, and still *Cumberland*'s exquisitely sensitive sensors detected nothing but the distant stars and the vanishingly tenuous gases of interstellar space. The senior officers had long ago left CIC to the attentions of the regular watch standers and the Officer of the Deck.

It was Ensign Menachem Levy's second turn in the Big Chair, and his first with the ship at Condition Amber, a heightened state of alertness in which missiles rode in launch tubes with fully energized launch coils, their drives enabled and their warheads armed; the pulse cannons stood on Ready; and half of the crew was either at stations or awake and dressed, ready to dash to stations at a moment's notice. When the ship was at Amber, there were reports to CIC every half-hour confirming the readiness of every battle station, which reports it was Levy's responsibility to log, there being no XO in CIC at the moment.

Accordingly, he regarded himself as pleasantly busy for the first two hours and nineteen minutes he sat in the genuinely comfortable seat provided for the destroyer's CO, drank coffee fetched for him by Midshipman George, and pondered the notion of considering OOD to be a pleasant duty.

The twentieth minute of the hour changed his mind. He noticed Hobbs, standing watch at Sensors, turn quickly to look to the ATTN SSR display, punch up a few different displays, and exchange a few terse words with his back room.

The process took all of three seconds before he announced, "Contact! Unidentified contact approaching under compression drive, gravity wave detection only at this time, approximate bearing two-five-two mark one-one-eight. No bearing change, no target motion analysis possible. Designating contact as Uniform One. Strength of reading increasing, still no change in bearing detected. Contact is likely at constant bearing decreasing range."

No tricky command decision here. The book was clear on that one. "Mister Laputa, sound general quarters."

The klaxons were still braying when, less than a minute later, the skipper cycled through the hatch along with the XO and Kasparov. After the con had been transferred, Max decided, instead of uttering the seemingly obligatory "status" or "report" inquiry, to throw Levy a curve ball. The place to train combat officers was in combat, or at least under the reasonable threat of possible combat, and they don't learn anything by always being confronted with the expected.

"Well, Mr. Levy," the skipper asked breezily, "what formal justification for sounding general quarters do you intend to enter in the log?"

It took Levy no more than a second and a half to realize he was getting a curve instead of the fast ball he had been expecting. He swung. "Sir, Sensors reported a gravity wave detection of a likely compression drive source evaluated to be at a constant bearing and decreasing range. An unidentified intercepting contact is a mandatory GC condition for any unescorted destroyer."

Line drive deep into right field, a stand up triple. "Outstanding, Mr. Levy. Exactly correct. You may take your station." Max pretended not to notice the young man's sigh of relief when he stepped off the command island in the direction of the Intel Station.

"All stations report secure at general quarters," reported Petty Officer Laputa at Alerts.

"Very well. Maneuvering, turn to face the contact, both axes. Attitude change only. Do not translate the ship." Max was ordering that the *Cumberland* reorient herself so that her most powerful weapons and her most acute sensors were pointing at the target, without changing the ship's location. Max was turning the ship in the direction best calculated to learn about the target or to fight it.

"Target has gone subluminal," said Kasparov. "I have mass detection of a subluminal target, congruent with the prior compression detection. Bearing is two-five-five mark one-one-seven. Range forty-eight thousand kills. Speed, very slow sir, five thousand meters per second. Mass is . . . it's big, sir, 87,900 tons. We've got an optical scanner on it, and my people say it looks . . . looks like one of our fleet tankers, one of the big ones, *Sevastopol* class maybe. That would be consistent with the mass reading."

Max turned to Chin. "IFF?"

"None yet, sir. Our box has sent the interrogation pulse. Nothing back yet."

"Reinterrogate."

"But sir, if we receive no response, the box will automatically—"

"I'm aware of that, Mr. Chin, but I don't want to wait another sixty-five seconds."

"Aye, sir. Manual instruction for reinterrogation sent."

"Those tankers are fifty or sixty years old. Their old IFF boxes can be a bit balky. I think some of them work on *transistors*." Max wondered how many people on board actually knew what a transistor was.

"IFF received, identity checks out. Union Naval deuterium tanker, USS *Singapore*, registry TMG 0088."

"Target posident as friendly and redesignated as Charlie One," said Kasparov who had relieved Hobbs at Sensors.

"Something tells me we're not here to rendezvous with that."

"Pretty safe bet, XO," said Max. "But you never know. We'll follow the protocol. Mr. Chin, signal the tanker by lights. Send 'Glorious First of June.'"

"Aye, sir. 'Glorious First of June.'" He ordered the computer to slew the forward signal lamp to point at the tanker, checked its aim manually, input the message, and instructed the computer to send the string of short and long flashes, using Morse code. By the time he had sent the message, his back room had already slewed an optical pickup around to focus on the tanker's signal lights and routed its feed to Chin's SSR ATTN display. A few seconds later, one of the tanker's lights began to flash. Chin took down the message the old-fashioned way, with pen and paper, in case it was something longer than a sentence or two that he could easily remember. It wasn't.

"Skipper, the tanker sends, 'NEGATIVE.'"

"That would mean they are not who we are here to meet." Max said. "I expect they'll be along shortly."

"Skipper?" Chin was clearly uncomfortable. "Sir, what about the tanker? Shouldn't we be hailing her, establishing a laserlink, signaling with lights, or something?"

"Negative, Chin." Max said. "We have orders from Admiral Hornmeyer to come here and execute a specific recognition protocol. We are neither ordered nor authorized to engage in any other communications, so we are not going to engage in any other communications with any other vessel. With what we have on board, we don't need to be passing the time of day with every deuterium tanker we run into. We're going to sit here and wait, if not patiently, then with the best facsimile thereof that we can manage."

It actually took no small measure of patience. Another incoming contact presented itself three and a half hours later as a gravity wave detection that soon thereafter went subluminal seventy-five thousand kilometers from the destroyer.

"It's small, sir," Kasparov announced. "Mass is approximately eighty-five hundred tons. We've got optical on it but can't distinguish anything at this range."

Before Max could ask about the IFF, Chin spoke up, "IFF confirms as friendly, Skipper. A fast Courier-Scout assigned to the Task Force, registry number CSR 8655."

"Sir." It was Bhattacharyya, not a man from whom the captain would typically be hearing at this point.

"Yes, Bhattacharyya?"

"That particular ship is the one Admiral Hornmeyer uses when he needs to leave the *Halsey.* Just a registry number—no official name for something that small, but they call themselves the 'Yellow Cab Company.'"

In theory, a truly capable intel officer developed "assets and resources" that allowed him to keep his skipper a few steps ahead of what the good guys were doing as well as the bad, but few men who held that billet on a mere destroyer took that part of their job seriously. Apparently, Bhattacharyya had a different outlook.

"Thank you, Intel, that's good to know. Mr. Chin, as soon as the Yellow Cab Company is within *hailing distance*," he leaned on the words to be sure no one missed the joke, "give them the same recognition signal." The smaller vessel quickly closed most of the gap that separated the ships and in short order replied with the countersign "TRAFALGAR."

A few seconds after that Chin announced, "Courier is establishing a laserlink. Incoming signal from the Courier. On Commandcom."

Max read the message from his console. "I am coming aboard your vessel ASAP to view the package. If you make me wade through all that fife, drum, and honor guard ceremonial happy horseshit when I board, I will have your hide. You are ordered to prepare your vessel for a high-speed run back to Pfelung. The tanker is here to top you off and to refuel the other vessel that will arrive presently. Hornmeyer. Message ends."

"I thought you said that there was never a redundant word in any communication received from the admiral," said Bram, who had come into CIC a few moments earlier.

"I did. I don't see any redundancy," Max replied.

"There most certainly is a redundancy: 'Hornmeyer.' It is evident from the remainder of the signal who wrote it. Who other than he would call the piping aboard, the presentation of arms, the playing of whatever the name of that piece is with the lyrics 'Rule the Union, the Union Rules in Space,' and the ritual inspection of the men at arms 'ceremonial happy horseshit'?"

"Redundancy or not, I am glad to be shed of the 'happy horseshit.' Apparently the admiral wants to conclude his business with us and send us in a great big tearing hurry back to Pfelung for some reason. I suppose that's what's behind all of this meeting-in-deep-space, double-O spy stuff. He wants to get his hands on the package ASAP and then send us on this errand, whatever it is. It's probably another VIP escort or some such nonsense because we helped save the last one from unmitigated catastrophe."

The admiral arrived without the usual ceremonies. As soon as he was aboard, salutes exchanged, and introductions made, he said, "All right, Robichaux, enough of this Naval Auxiliary Garden Party crap. Let's see the package."

"Yes, sir. Right this way." Max led the admiral from the hangar deck, wondering if Admiral Hornmeyer had ever so much as showed his face at a Naval Auxiliary Garden Party. He doubted it.

"You should know," the admiral said as they were making their way through the ship, "that I've squared the situation with Duflot for you. I issued orders confirming your failure to rendezvous with the *William Gorgas*, so you won't have to jump through all those hoops to satisfy him that you were acting within the scope of Article 15, Paragraph 5."

"Thank you, Admiral. That saves me a great deal of paperwork."

"Fucking paperwork. The goddamn bane of the Navy. I'd rather you focus your attention on making life difficult for the Krag than on jumping through a bunch of bureaucratic hoops. After all, you're one of my most productive commanders right now. I mean, son, have you looked at the score?"

"Score?"

"Score, son, score. War is a goddamn numbers game. Ships, tonnage, weapons, supplies, manpower, fuel, speed, distance, time. Missing. Wounded. Killed. All numbers.

"Here are some of yours. If I am remembering correctly, under your command, the *Cumberland* has destroyed one battlecruiser, five cruisers counting one where you got some help from the Vaaach, two corvettes, and two destroyers, as well as assisted on two more destroyers killed by the Pfelung, and played a significant role in the twenty-five destroyers the enemy lost at Rashid V B, all in just a few months. Plus two freighters captured whole, with cargo, as prizes. That's more enemy losses inflicted than some battle groups under my command. And with crew performance ratings that are just barely in the 'Fair' range." He shook his head in wonder.

"On top of that, that little stunt that you and Kim Yong-Soo pulled right under Duflot's nose undoubtedly saved the envoy's life. Sue was able to deliver the smooth-talking son of a bitch to the conference, where the other three envoys immediately elected him chairman and hammered out a Four Power Joint Forces Agreement in three days flat. That's got to be a new record. By the way, he told me he thinks very highly of you. You must have filled him full of that goddamn Cajun food of yours—that shit's so good it'll turn your worst enemy into your friend.

"Even Duflot doesn't want your head on a pike. Anymore. Not that it matters much now. After he almost got the envoy killed, I got him transferred to my command, and the only way that human clusterfuck is seeing the CIC of a rated warship is if he's with a flock of Wilderness Girls on a goddamn Union Day tour. I've yanked all of his combat and command qualifications and assigned him to Convoy Routing and Logistics. Punctilious little son of a bitch is actually good at it too.

"But you, Robichaux, are either a budding tactical genius or the luckiest motherfucker who ever put on a uniform. I'm leaning toward the latter. Anyway, you know how I like to bet on the winning horse, so my money is on you in the next race. With what we've got up our sleeve over the next several months, there will be some very interesting work for ships like yours."

He grinned broadly. "Very, very interesting work. If you can keep from being court martialed between now and then, you are going to help me make history."

They came to the hatch that led in to Captured Hardware. Outside the main compartment was a smaller compartment with a spacer and a Marine. The spacer politely but firmly asked both men to leave their percoms behind and pointed a hand scanner at both of them to be certain that they weren't carrying any electronic devices that would violate the compartment's electronic quarantine. Once cleared, they went in.

Captured Hardware was crowded: fifteen people packed into one of the humbler spaces on the ship. Computer, weapons, and engineering wonks tinkered with pieces of equipment obtained from the enemy, trying to extract their secrets. The only thing that marked the compartment as different from several other such spaces was the presence of three compact computer cores, totally isolated in every conceivable way from the data and power networks for the rest of the ship.

You can't just plug a captured Krag data module into your ship's computer and expect anything but disaster to ensue. Accordingly, these cores were purpose-built to probe and operate alien computer equipment and to access alien databases and storage devices, without putting the rest of the vessel at risk from enemy viruses, Trojans, parasites, data shredders, digital con artists, lying Louies, Alzheimer's bugs, bit rotters, succubi, incubi, turncoaters, sirens, saprophytes, mole makers, sappers, egg suckers, termites, and the full panoply of malware and other digital weapons deployed by the combatants in a war in which attacks on computing systems and databases had been nearly as important as attacks on ships and fixed installations.

Bales, in charge of probing the Krag database, walked Hornmeyer through what he had learned so far about the menu structure and the locations of the most important data he was finding. He managed to keep his discussion more germane than was usual for him, but Max could tell that the admiral was starting to get a bit annoyed at his occasional digressions into matters of interest only to people immersed in the science of data storage and processing. Surprisingly, the admiral mostly managed to conceal his impatience, and where he would have cut Max off at the knees, Hornmeyer was patient with Bales. Max couldn't figure it out.

Bales was on his way to the section on countermeasures protocols, scrolling through a menu that appeared to consist mainly of cartographic information, when the admiral stopped him. "Son, whoa. Stop right there. Back it up. A bit more. There. See that entry for 'Special Navigational Protocols'?"

"Yes, sir."

"Open that up for me."

In his own researches, Bales had already scrolled past it a dozen times, had opened it up once, and hadn't seen anything interesting.

"Admiral, it's probably just some sort of Rules of the Road for how to keep warships from running into each other."

"Probably. Humor me."

"Yes, sir."

Bales opened the menu. That menu was an umbrella for other menus at a lower level of the file hierarchy. Special Navigation Protocols was divided into: Providing Escort to Logistics Convoys, Providing Escort to Personnel Convoys, Providing Escort to Mixed Convoys, Providing Escort to High Officials in Secured Areas, Providing Escort to High Officials in Unsecured Areas, Ceremonial Reviews, Inspection Reviews, and Other.

"Click 'Other,'" directed the admiral.

This did not look promising, and Bales almost said something, but he took one look at the admiral and decided against it. Wisely.

"Other" consisted of Navigating in Close Company with Vessel Carrying Hazardous Material, Navigating in Close Company with Damaged Vessel in Danger of Exploding, Navigating in Close Company with Vessel Unable to Steer Straight Course, and Multivessel Transfer Procedures.

"Click on Multivessel Transfer," Hornmeyer ordered, the barest hint of an excited quiver in his voice. Everyone in the compartment who wasn't already looking at the wall display snapped his head around. The tension in the room suddenly jumped eight or nine notches.

The emotion communicated itself to the usually clueless Bales. The flicker of feeling from the admiral was more powerful than the most overt demonstration from another man. He clicked on the item.

It was a densely written procedural checklist, setting forth some fifty-three steps and check-offs for the accomplishment of what must be a technically demanding operation. As the men read further, they saw that it was the procedure to be used by up to eight ships when they simultaneously executed some sort of maneuver or other in close company. They read further, through steps involving synchronization of clocks to the nanosecond, relative orientation of the ships' center of mass in the same plane to within .003 seconds of arc, and precise alignment of the plane of the formation with the metaspacial "grain" of the galaxy. Suddenly, a frisson passed through the group, as though a veil had just been snatched away to reveal to their eyes for the first time a dazzling gem of extraordinary and unexpected beauty. Some actually gasped. Five or six let out an almost breathless "Oh!"

That's what the list was: a detailed how-to description of the most important group maneuver-procedure in the Krag arsenal, sending up to eight jump ships at the same time through the same jump point. The Krag had been using that little trick to kick the Union's butts since day one of the war, and the Union had never managed to uncover its secret despite trillions of credits worth of research over more than thirty years.

Everyone stood in silence for a few moments. The same idea hit everyone at the same time.

This changes *everything.*

The admiral summed it up for everyone. He uttered the expression slowly, drawing it out for a full four seconds, maybe five. "*Oy*. Fucking. *Mekheye*." He borrowed some of his ancestors' Yiddish, the rich and colorful language of a displaced people.

"*Regardez donc*," said Max, borrowing some of his ancestors' Cajun French, the rich and colorful language of another displaced people.

"You know what this means, son?"

With an effort, Max managed to keep himself from telling the admiral that he did indeed know what *oy mekheye* meant. Instead, he said, "Yes, sir, I do. It's a whole new war."

The admiral ordered Bales to copy all the files in the Krag database pertaining to the jump procedure onto a data chip, which the admiral had a crewman sew into the left breast pocket of his pilot's uniform so that there was no possibility of its getting lost. He then ordered the pilot to take the scout ship at maximum velocity back to the Task Force.

The admiral would have liked to copy the whole database, but it was so huge that it would not fit into the *Cumberland*'s MDC, much less on something that would fit on the scout. The jump procedure chip was accompanied by Hornmeyer's marching orders to his staff to find a way for Union ships to implement the procedure "with the utmost celerity and in the deepest secrecy." The tiny vessel had disappeared in a wave of compressed space, moving as fast as any ship ever designed by human minds and built by human hands.

The admiral and Max sat in CIC, with Max at his station and the admiral actually putting the Commodore's Station to its intended use. The doctor sat in the spare seat at Comms.

"I'm surprised that you didn't send the Vaaach data module on the scout along with your pilot," said Max.

"Put the most significant intelligence coup in human history—one that we can't duplicate until we can attach it to something as big as the main data core on a carrier or a battleship—in a ship that doesn't even have a missile tube? Not a chance in hell. No, son, that data core is the solid platinum, diamond-encrusted, copper-bottomed, motherfucking lode. That little jewel and I are going to arrive at the Task Force in style. It's going to be a hell of an entrance."

He smiled. It was the kind of smile a wolf gives just before the object of his gaze makes the permanent change in status from being a living organism called a "sheep" to being a meal called "lunch."

"But not nearly the entrance I'm going to make the next time I hit those rat-faced Krag motherfuckers. Not nearly." He looked at his wrist chrono, then stood up. By that sort of commanding dynamism some leaders have, his force of will, combined with his mere intention to speak, quieted the compartment without his having given any sign.

"Gentlemen, in about three minutes, you're going to get a mass reading at about two-four-three mark zero-one-seven. A huge fucking mass reading. Don't shit your pants. You're about to see something you'll remember the rest of your lives."

True to the admiral's prediction, two minutes and forty-eight seconds after the announcement, Kasparov announced a gravity wave detection exactly on the predicted bearing. He designated the contact as Charlie Two based on "circumstantial classification," meaning that he had no sensor evidence that it was friendly, but because the contact was where a friendly was expected, doing what a friendly was supposed to be doing, it was probably a friendly. After all, that bird swimming around in your duck pond during duck season and making quacking noises is almost certainly not an eagle.

One minute and nine seconds later, Kasparov gasped loudly. Just as everyone close enough to have heard him turned their heads at the uncharacteristic reaction, he croaked "Contact! Mass detector. Stand by while I change to a different scale." Then to his back room. "No, bigger than that. Even bigger. There. Okay. Harbaugh, you sure that's right?" A pause ensued. "It made its own gravity waves when it went subluminal?" Another pause. "Sweet jeeeeezus." He took a calming breath and then announced to the CIC as a whole.

"Mass detection, dual phenomenology, bearing concurrent with gravity wave detection of Charlie Two. Mass of contact is…approximately five million tons. Saying again…Five. Million. Tons." Heretofore, the largest warships ever made by the Union were the *Nimitz* class fleet carriers and the *Victory* class command carriers that came in right at a million tons.

"Mr. Kasparov, fire up the Arnaz scanner and let's get a realistic number," Max said, a trace of annoyed disbelief in his voice. "You can't generate a compression field big enough to enclose and move a five-million-ton ship."

"Belay that, son," said Admiral Hornmeyer. "God help me for overriding a captain's order in his own CIC, but you can keep the Arnaz scanner off-line. It really is five million tons." The crusty old bastard was beaming. "And it's ours."

Chin broke in. "IFF, sir. Sirs. Confirmed Union transponder code, identity: USS *Winston Churchill*, registry number BSD-0001, Type: battleship." Pause. "Classification... Super Dreadnaught."

Admiral Hornmeyer looked eleven feet tall and ready to beat the entire Krag Hegemony in single combat. "There she is, gentlemen, my new flagship, fresh from the fleet yards at 40 Eridani A. She's still got contractors on board calibrating some of the electronics and ironing out the bugs, but she's a warhorse born and bred, and she is foaled at the turning of the tide. Because, gentlemen, *the tide has turned*. From now on, we take the initiative. We go on the offensive. We're done second guessing where the Krag are going next. Let the Krag worry about where *we're* going to attack *them* next.

"And we're done with falling back. Let them worry about Defense in Depth and staged retreats and evacuation corridors, because *we* are going forward. Forward to engage and destroy their fleets. Forward to wipe out the Krag's supply nodes and fuel dumps and their mines and war factories. Forward to retake our systems and free our people. Forward, men! Forward to victory!"

Only the strict "no outbursts or demonstrations" rule in CIC kept the men from cheering. Max could see the confidence in their eyes: if anyone could lead the fleet to triumph, it would be this brilliant, ass-kicking, profane, iron-assed son of a bitch.

"Admiral," Max said, almost breathless, "I thought the upper limit of what you could get a compression field around was about two million tons. That was going to be size of the *Churchill* class carrier we kept hearing all those rumors about. What happened to the carrier?"

"The *Churchill* class carrier project was the cover for the *Churchill* class battleship project." The admiral spoke as though he were confiding a great secret to Max and his men. "There's no fucking way you can hide a great goddamn battleship, son, and you can't hide the appropriations, the millions of tons of matériel, the tens of thousands of workers, and the city's worth of infrastructure, so we hid the fucker in plain sight, along with the other battleships being built in other yards around the Union.

"We compartmentalized the work, so most men never saw the big picture—hid the shape behind enough Zero G scaffolding to build half a dozen skyscrapers. We even had a thousand workers fabricating dozens of launch catapults and flight decks to go on a giant carrier. Won't go to waste, though. We'll put 'em on the next carrier we build. Biggest goddamn warship mankind has ever produced, and we've got four more of the motherfuckers to be launched in the next forty-five days: *Leonidas*, *Charlemagne*, *Shaka*, and *George Washington*. More after that. Maybe smaller and faster, maybe bigger and meaner. Haven't made up our minds yet."

"But how do you get it to go anywhere except on sublight and jump?" Max asked. "No one can sustain a compression field that big. So much energy is lost between the center and the periphery—"

"Son, son, son," the admiral interrupted. "You've got your feet stuck in the old goddamn paradigm. We don't sustain *a* field. We sustain *four*."

"Four?" He was incredulous. Then the light went on. "You mean, we solved the problem of field synchronization? But I thought the mathematics and physics of that were supposed to be fifty years out. Maybe a hundred."

"I hate to break it to you, Robichaux: they still are. We bought the field synchronization algorithms from the Sarthan. You know how they are. If they have it, it's for sale, and the price has lots of zeroes in it."

"I know, but the word is that they wanted three and a half *trillion* credits for the algorithms. No credit, either. Cash on the barrelhead in Tri-Nin Depositary Instruments, or gold, platinum, palladium, uranium 235, or plutonium 239."

"This is one of those cases in which the rumor was abso-fucking-lutely accurate. Happens more often than I like to think about. The greedy motherfuckers would also have accepted payment in antimatter, although why anyone would want to be within a parsec of the hellish stuff, I'll never know. But we managed to talk them down from three and a half trillion to two and three-quarters, along with waiving our claims to an uninhabited star system we've had in dispute with them.

"It cleaned out just over a quarter of the gold and platinum reserves of the entire Union. Goddamn blood suckers. Anyway, we've got a whole new generation of ships being designed and built around dual and quadruple field generators. On vessels of equivalent displacement with equivalent power plants, we're getting 30 percent more speed and a 50 percent increase in fuel efficiency. The sky is now the limit on displacement. Now we can build them big enough to carry weapons with the punch to get through the Krag defenses, deflectors powerful enough to shrug off anything they throw at us, and gigantic fusion power plants big enough to power the lot.

"When you add in this new jump thing, we're going to move faster and hit harder. My friends, we're going to fucking kick some Krag ass. Given a year or two, we're going to kick the bastards back at least two hundred light years. Maybe three hundred."

Then, his enthusiasm muted somewhat. "It's no guarantee of victory. It's not even a guarantee that the bastards won't defeat us in the long run, but they're not going to beat us in the short run now. They've still got an advantage in population, population growth, and industrial capacity, but our new ships are going to give us a qualitative advantage. What's in that memory core is going to give us a whole toolbox full of dirty tricks to use against them. The multiple ship jump is not only going to let us throw more firepower at them faster, but the first time we use it on them, they're going to piss themselves with surprise.

"When we start rolling them back, I bet that we start picking up allies like the Ghiftee and the Texians and the other independent human powers, and maybe even some more aliens. Everybody loves a winner. It's a new fucking war, gentlemen, and we're going to be serving the Krag some of what they've been serving us all these years.

"Now, Robichaux, you and I have a few things to discuss out of the hearing of the children, and then I'm going to take command of my new flagship. This time, if the captain over there asks me nicely, I just might let them break out the white gloves, flags, fifes, bugles, drums, and all that other happy horseshit. After all, it isn't every day that a man takes possession of the biggest goddamn warship in Known Space."

CHAPTER 15

09:42Z Hours, 15 April 2315

"So, gentlemen," Max said, "in conclusion, it appears we are bound for what has got to be the strangest rendezvous in the history of the Union Space Navy. The men are acting spooked about the whole thing, and it's our job to reassure them. We need to project calm and assured confidence, to let them know we believe that everything is bound to come out fine. They look to us as examples not just of how to act and how to comport themselves but also of what to think and feel. They must see in us the traits we want to see in them. And right now, that's courage and confidence."

Max was meeting with his "brain trust" in his day cabin. The assembly was powered by sugar, in the form of an impossibly delicious pound cake, and caffeine, in the form of the sublime Wortham-Biggs Four Planet Blend coffee. If only the news he had just delivered had been one-tenth as good as the refreshments.

"I am not in the least certain that I am capable of engaging in so profound a deception," said the doctor. "I have no confidence whatsoever that the outcome of this series of events is going to be favorable. I would be much more courageous and confident were we still in the Pfelung system, training fighter squadrons to go into battle with a Union destroyer as their battle coordination vessel. That was looking as though it would turn into a truly effective gambit."

"*Tactic.* A mode of operations or combat procedure is a 'tactic.' 'Gambit' refers to a particular stratagem or maneuver, especially the opening move in an encounter, particularly if it is designed to deceive or manipulate the enemy."

"Tactic, gambit, stratagem, maneuver, ploy... You naval people have so many different words for what is essentially the same thing: a means of killing your adversaries. It seems redundant.

"In any event," said the doctor, "I'm worried about this rendezvous. The Vaaach asking for you, Max, by name, and wanting to get together out in the Great Inner Gap for an unspecified reason. Why the Great Inner Gap? No one goes out there."

The region of the Milky Way Galaxy known to humanity and the races with which humans had commercial and cultural relations, called Known Space, lay in the Orion-Cygnus arm of the galaxy. Coreward and rimward of this area were two relatively star-poor areas separating it from the adjacent galactic arms: the Great Inner Gap, between it and the Sagittarius arm, and the Great Outer Gap separating it from the Perseus arm.

The star systems in the gaps were too few and far between, not to mention too poor in jump points that connected together in a useful network, to make them attractive targets for colonization and conquest; accordingly, military operations in the Gaps were very rare. "And why ask for you by name, anyway?"

"Elementary, my dear Doctor," said Brown. "They know him. And what's more, he is now a 'peer hunter.' They can deal with him as a low-ranking one of their own rather than as an inferior with whom they are not supposed to have anything but the most cursory contact."

"At any rate, we'll know very shortly," said Max. "To stations."

They left, everyone but Brown going to CIC. Brown took his station in Engineering.

After the transfer of the con from Hobbs to Max, Max sat in the Big Chair and eyed the navigational display. "Maneuvering, alter course to take us to a point in a line extended from galactic center through the RP, two AU rimward of the RP. Then approach the RP from the rimward direction at point five c, standard decel at the end."

Chief LeBlanc acknowledged and began to implement the order. After twenty-eight minutes, as the ship was decelerating near the end of the subluminal run, Max turned to Chin and said, "Chin, One MC."

"One MC, aye."

The light went on. Max's calm, confident voice reached out from every speaker in the ship to every heart and mind on board. "Shipmates, this is the skipper. You know where we are and as much about what we are doing as I do. We know the Vaaach asked for us by name, and we know that the Vaaach are not ones for frivolities. We would not be here if there weren't something important for us to do.

"Everyone be sharp. Keep your eyes, as well as your mind and your attention, focused where they are supposed to be. You, gentlemen, are my eyes and ears. My arms, hands, fingers, and legs. I make the decisions, but only with the information you give me. Those decisions have meaning only because you carry them out. We're all mountain climbers, roped together on the rock face—dependent on each other. You do your part. I'll do mine. We'll come through this together. Skipper out."

Max was always of two minds about these little pep talks. He knew he wasn't a great orator, or even a good one, and that a lot of modern commanders thought these kinds of speeches silly or pointless. He always felt a bit foolish giving them. On the other hand, Max remembered being an ensign on the *Margaret Jackie* as she was racing to get to the Battle of Dupuy III in time to stop the rout and maybe turn the tide.

Max was scared stiff when Commodore Middleton came over on One MC and delivered five or six sentences that left him feeling calm and centered and able to do his job. Max understood from that experience that many of the men needed to hear from their skipper not just the words but the tone of voice and manner of delivery to tell them that the skipper was confident. A commander must be confident, and he must communicate that confidence to his men. People always talk about how the men support the leader. They forget that on the precipice of danger or during the fearful prelude to battle, it is the leader who supports the men. He must have enough courage not only for himself but to give an infusion of it to everyone under his command.

"Station keeping at the rendezvous point," LeBlanc announced a few minutes later.

"We're still three minutes early," Max observed.

Two minutes and fifty seconds passed. At the stroke of the appointed time, Kasparov called out, "Contact, designating as Uniform One, bearing triple nipple by triple nipple."

One of the cruder bits of Navy jargon, it meant zero-zero-zero mark zero-zero-zero. The target was directly between the ship and the center of the galaxy.

"Range, ten kills. Exactly ten kills. I mean to the tenth of a millimeter. No drift, either. Perfectly stationary. God knows where he came from. He just appeared. Maybe he was stealthed brilliantly and he turned it off."

He paused to listen to someone in his back room. "Okay, okay. Now classifying as Vaaach: mass and EM emissions are all consistent with the last vessel we encountered."

Chin spoke. "Visual carrier, sir. Channel 7."

"Let's see it."

A moment later, the now familiar ferocious koala face filled several CIC screens, followed by the now familiar roaring and snarling. This time, however, there was something about the ferocious lions tearing at their meat sounds that struck Max as hinting almost of friendliness. It did not take long for the translation to appear.

"This is Forest Commander Chrrrlgrf. I greet you Forest Peer Swamp Fox. I have no doubt that your tiny primate brain is filled with the question of why you were asked to meet with me at this time and place."

"And I greet you Forest Commander Chrrrlgrf. It did occur to me, yes."

"The Vaaach have been asked to summon you to this meeting and to guarantee safe conduct. The meeting is not with me but with the vessel that will arrive in slightly more than two minutes. It is a Krag vessel. The Krag will arrive and advance to within ten kilometers of your vessel and mine. They will transmit a message for delivery to the leadership of your people. You will confirm receipt of their message. The Krag will depart on a direct path to their space. You will depart on a direct path to your space. This will be a peaceful encounter, on pain of death. If you fire on the Krag vessel, you will be destroyed instantly. If the Krag vessel fires on you, it will be destroyed instantly. Is this acceptable?"

"It is."

"Very well. Prepare to receive the Krag."

At the promised moment, the Krag vessel appeared on gravity wave sensors, then went subluminal and approached the rendezvous point, stopping exactly at the prescribed point, though without quite the same precision as the Vaaach; the Krag positioned themselves with the precision of about half a meter.

"Carrier wave from the Krag," said Chin. "Now, an attention signal. Sir, they're using the old Krag-Human comm protocols we worked out with them back when we were in contact. They're telling us to prepare to copy text, Language is Standard, encoding is Formatted Text B. In thirty seconds."

"Acknowledge the message." Max's voice was even, quiet, grim. He had a bad feeling about what the Krag were sending. He had an even worse feeling about the eventual reply.

Chin called up the old transmission protocols and punched them into the ship's ENcoder/DECoder. "Receiving transmission." A few seconds later, "I'm getting readable text from the ENDEC." About twenty seconds later, almost under his breath, "Holy fucking shit."

"Mr. Chin," Max rebuked him in a low but even voice. "No profane editorializing on the contents of comms." Then, to calm the twitches he was getting from his hypocrisy detector, he added, "That's my job."

Chastened, Chin responded, "Yes, sir. But you've got to see this."

The transmission ended. Max read it.

Holy. Fucking. Shit.

"What do you think the president and the Senate will do?" Dr. Sahin took a deep drink of his "fruit punch potpourri," made from a mixture of undisclosed and various fruits, the kind of mixture generally served by the galley when it was trying to get rid of the tail ends of several different varieties of frozen fruit juice at the same time to clear out a freezer unit.

Max was a bit deeper into his precious supply of Kentucky bourbon than he usually allowed himself to get, and was more loquacious than usual. "How the fuck do I know? I don't trust those greasy, double-talking bastards as far as I could throw Hornmeyer's new flagship. No, that's not true. I trust President Lee. He's one of us. Retired cruiser commander. I even met him once. Of course, that was the first time I was court martialed. He was a member of the panel that tried me. He voted to acquit. They all did."

"For what could you have been court martialed?"

"Insubordination. It was that time when I commanded a PC-4 and Commodore Barber, that was before he was the famous throughout the fleet Admiral Barber ordered me to disengage and withdraw when—"

Max was cut off when the comm buzzed. "Skipper."

"This is Lee in the Intel SSR."

"Okay, Lee Hwang-Sik, right? Philologist and LingAn expert. Got something?"

"As a matter of fact, sir, I think I do. How do you want it?"

"Face to face, with the bark still on, as always. Come to my day cabin."

"On my way. Lee out."

Max drained his glass but did not pour another. He took a few sips of the coffee that had also been poured for him. Lee arrived a moment later and exchanged salutes with his commander. Lee's was adequate but was not what one would call exemplary. The young man always got stratospherically high FITREPS on how he performed the analytical functions that went with his billet, but mediocre ones in those categories that measured the shininess of his boots, the sharpness of creases, and the snappiness of his salutes. Max liked a man who had shiny boots, sharp creases, and snappy salutes, but he positively loved a man who was good at his job. Lee was another one of the officers handpicked for this ship by Admiral Hornmeyer.

"Well, Lee, what've you got for me?"

"Sir, we've done a linguistic and psychological pattern analysis on the Krag message and have come to what we regard as some highly reliable conclusions."

"Such as?"

"Well, sir, as you know, Standard and the Krag language are far more different from one another than any two human languages. Not only are the modes of vocalization completely different, but the two languages describe the world in ways that are so different that some things just don't translate. Standard has about eight or nine fairly close synonyms for the verb 'to run,' most of which describe different kinds of gait while running: scamper, trot, sprint, lope, and so on. The Krag have more than forty, describing minute variations in speed, gait, the extent to which the runner weaves from side to side or uses cover or burrows below and then goes on the surface, doubles back on himself to confuse his pursuer, and so on. They have a dozen words for 'obedience,' but no word for 'loyalty.'"

"So? How does that help us? The message isn't in Krag; it's in Standard."

"But sir, that's just it. It's *really* in Standard. I mean, if it had been originally written in Krag and translated to Standard, there would be traces of Krag syntax and Krag usage. But more than that, there are fundamental differences in thinking between the two species that show up in their writing. For example, we tend to tell a narrative from the beginning, whereas Krag tend to start with the event that produced the most emotion, particularly when the emotion was fear. We usually begin a syllogism with the major premise; the Krag typically begin with the conclusion. And Skipper, this message was clearly written in Standard by a native speaker—by someone who grew up speaking it from the cradle. Not only that, as far as such things go, sir, it was written well, by someone who has a talent for written expression. Whoever wrote this is a good writer."

"So, the Krag have at least one human working for them. There are always collaborators or people who can be beaten and tortured into cooperation. That's not really news."

"It might be more news than you think, Skipper. We can tell a lot about a person from how he writes. Some of the things we can almost always work out from a writing sample of sufficient length are intelligence, education, vocation, capacity for abstract thought, whether the person's primary decision-making mode is logical or emotional, how organized he is intellectually, and whether his main perceptual mode is visual or auditory or tactile.

"Writing can be almost as individual as a fingerprint. Think about how you always know whether orders come directly from Admiral Hornmeyer rather than his staff. Even if you took out the 'goddamns' and all that, you'd still recognize his writing. The computer can develop a prose profile from a document and can sometimes match it to an individual."

"I'm getting the sense that you have a match."

"We do. According to the computer, there is an 89 percent chance that the author of the message is Senator Wesley Exeter."

"Senator Exeter! You've got to be kidding me! Wesley Exeter would rather starve to death, be beaten to a pulp, or slit his own wrists than give the Krag the time of day. He was always pushing for larger appropriations for the Navy and then turning around and criticizing us for not being aggressive enough in the war.

"Every year, he would get one of his friends in the Assembly to sponsor legislation withdrawing the Union from the Convention Prohibiting the Development and Deployment of Antimatter Weapons so we could throw some of the hellish things at the Krag. He lost his mother, wife, and four—count 'em—*four* daughters in the Gynophage attack. One of them was a four-month-old baby. Everyone knows that the Krag took Dommert III when he was there to be with his dying father, but no one thought they would take him alive. The profile has got to be wrong. You said that it's an 89 percent match. That means there's an 11 percent chance that it is someone else. This has got to be the 11 percent."

"Captain, I believe that Mr. Lee might be correct," said the doctor calmly. "We have been at war with the Krag for more than thirty years but have never recovered anyone who has been in their hands for more than a few weeks. Not one person. We do not have any idea what they do to prisoners except for your testimony, some of which—as I interpret what you saw on board the *San Jacinto*—sounds like the beginning stages of a very slow but very thorough brainwashing and conversion process. I do know that if we had captured Senator Exeter and that if we were totally devoid of scruples, we could turn him into a fervent believer in any philosophy we chose or make him loyal to any cause we wished. It would take six months, maybe as much as a year, but it could be done effectively and permanently.

"If the Krag have such techniques, and we have no reason to believe that they do not, then it is not surprising at all that they have obtained the cooperation of Senator Exeter or that of anyone else who fell into their hands and whose assistance they desired strongly enough. The explanation for 11 percent uncertainty likely lies first in the identification method itself. Lee, what is a typical match that is later confirmed to be accurate?"

"Occasionally we get a ninety-six or ninety-seven, but a ninety-two or ninety-three is more typical."

"That is roughly what I surmised. And the remainder of the difference in this case is probably the result of the brainwashing and conversion technique. When one alters a person's belief system so fundamentally, there will be some noticeable, though not fundamental, changes in the way his brain constructs chains of reasoning and then translates them into persuasive language. Senator Exeter has been made into a different person, so his writing is going to be different, at least to a certain degree."

"I suppose that makes sense." Max shook his head sadly. "It's just that it's hard to think about what you would have to do to a man like that to get him to work for the Krag. I'd rather think of him dead than turned into their lapdog."

"I am highly confident that they do have many humans working for them in many capacities, on a highly organized and systematic basis, and providing them excellent service, I might add."

"Doctor, what makes you say that?" Max was a bit confrontational. "I truly detest the idea of there being a force of human beings in some kind of Bureau of Quislings sitting in offices and writing reports and memos and going to meetings where they drink coffee, eat boysenberry danish, and plot the extinction of the human race."

Sahin sighed, as though it pained him to have to explain so obvious a matter or, perhaps, because he would prefer not to have to explain these kinds of truths to someone who would find them painful.

"Max, I know they have humans working for them because they have displayed an understanding of us that is too sophisticated and too well-informed to be entirely the work of an alien race. Time and time again, they've played us politically and diplomatically in ways that show they understand humans far better than they could from the brief contact we had a century ago. They must have humans advising them. Not only that, they must have humans who are intelligent and well informed, and who have a detailed and sophisticated understanding of the workings of our societies, our governments, our economy, and other aspects of our civilization."

"In other words," consented Max, "not only do they have people working for them, but they've got talented people, and they've found a way to get good work out of them. I don't like that conclusion, but I suppose that the evidence supports it."

"Sir, this communication certainly supports that conclusion," said Lee. "There are textual cues that show when something is written under duress. None of those are present. To the contrary, there are also textual cues that show when a writer is doing his best work and has put his heart into it. Those cues *are* present here. In fact, there is evidence that the document was written with a certain enthusiasm and genuine agreement with what it says."

"Is there anything else in there that I need to know about?"

"I suppose the fact that it shows that our military and our government are apparently laced with Krag spies is self-evident, so no, sir."

"Lee, the president is supposed to be some sort of cousin or yours, isn't he? What do you think he's going to do?"

"Sorry to burst your bubble, sir," Lee said with an embarrassed smile, "but that's just one of those rumors based on our both being Korean and both having the same surname."

"But he *is* a countryman of yours. I'm not even from the same planet as he is." Max looked at the young man with genuine curiosity. "You would have a better read on him than I do. Besides, I hear you're some kind of expert on Union politics and have a way of telling what a politician is going to do by dissecting the language in his speeches."

"It is sort of a hobby, sir. Studying philology gives one an appreciation for the nuances of language and politics that is, to a great extent, a dance of language. I've studied the speeches of President Lee quite extensively, and I think they reveal that he is mostly bravado covering a fundamental lack of courage and resolve. As a warship captain, he may have been strong and decisive, but he is over his head leading the entire Union. He doesn't have the confidence in his own judgment to allow him to make clear, bold decisions for billions of people. I think he's weak, sir. I'm afraid he might cave. That's my best opinion, sir. I pray that I'm wrong."

"I pray that you're wrong too, son. Thank you. Excellent work. That will be all for now." Lee saluted and left. He had not been gone for more than three or four minutes before the comm buzzed.

"Skipper."

"Skipper, this is Chin. We finally got a confirmation from the *Lee Janot*, the task force's comms vessel, confirming receipt from us of the Krag message. The admiral also signaled 'No rush now, Robichaux. Rendezvous with the *Churchill* at standard cruising velocity.'"

"Thank you, Chin. Please give the word to Maneuvering to reduce speed to 1575 c and alter course to rendezvous with the *Churchill*."

"Aye, sir. Chin out."

A few seconds later, Max could feel the vibrations and other sounds of the ship's engines, fusion reactor, and the reactor's cooling system all drop to a lower pitch as speed was reduced from Emergency to Cruise. The ship had been rushing back to Union space to rendezvous with a comm relay or to get close enough to one to establish a comm channel.

"Speaking of the *Churchill*, I'm not certain why everyone seems to be talking about it with such rabid enthusiasm. I saw it on the visual display and it impressed me no more than did the other battleships I have seen, the *Wessex* or the *Michigan*."

Max almost choked on his coffee. "You can't be serious."

"I'm entirely serious," he replied. "I was watching when the admiral made that 'fly by' before zooming off to join the task force, and I am telling you that the *Churchill* looked no larger, nor more formidable, than the *Michigan*, which I saw several years ago. In fact, the two ships looked rather alike, to my mind. I must admit to being rather disappointed."

"I'm sure the admiral would be grieved to hear that seeing the largest and most powerful warship ever built by the human race was a letdown to you. I'll let him know that he should have brought with him an accomplished tridvid director to make the experience more impressive and memorable. Maybe a long scene full of shots of the immense ship turning on its running lights one after the other and slowly pulling out of the orbital construction dock. Then, accompanied by a swelling fanfare full of trumpets and French horns—lots and lots of French horns—the ship passes by the camera, making a distinct 'whoosh' sound, in the soundless interstellar vacuum mind you, and engages its compression drive, causing it to disappear in a dramatic flash. Then, you might have been impressed."

"You are making a jest at my expense."

"Absolutely. The point is, Bram, you had nothing to show you the scale of the ship. It looked like the *Michigan* because the two vessels are of similar design. From what I could tell, the *Churchill* is very much like a scaled-up version of the *Michigan*. The *Churchill*, though, has more than ten times the mass. *Ten times*. Her *secondary* pulse cannon batteries are twice as powerful as the mains on the *Michigan*, and the mains have twelve times the power rating. That ship's so huge, it has a hangar deck for a fighter wing as big as the one flown off an escort carrier.

"And it's almost as fast on compression drive as we are, so it can take off with a screen of fast cruisers, frigates, and destroyers; go straight across deep space to a Krag-held system; and take it without having to jump in right under the huge guns of a fixed battle station zeroed in right at the jump point. That kind of force could take some of these Krag systems without any warning, turn their flanks, punch holes in their defensive perimeter... any number of things. Can you imagine a weapon like that in the hands of an aggressive, creative, unpredictable, unorthodox tactical genius like Admiral Hornmeyer? I'd hate to be the Krag commander who had to deal with that."

"I had not taken the scale issue into account. I suppose it would be like examining a microorganism through a microscope without knowing the level of magnification—one would not know the size of the thing just by looking at it. I had no idea how much larger and more powerful this new ship was than our older ones."

"Bram, it's literally an order of magnitude."

"Perhaps that will be enough to persuade those individuals who will make the grand decision to do what they should do. At least Chin's news has got to be some kind of relief," said Sahin. "We are not under pressure to get to the comm relay to alert the rest of the human race what's happening."

"Oh, yes, sure. Huge relief. Great load off my mind. In any event, we'll be back at the task force in three days. In order to make the rendezvous to deliver the answer, we will have to depart no later than ten days after that. We'll know the answer then. For good or ill."

"What do you think will happen?"

"I honestly don't know, but I am very much afraid that President Lee will agree. You? You seem to have better insight into these things than I do."

"I don't know about that. I may understand the formal process in more detail, but that does not necessarily mean that I can predict the outcome more accurately than you or than anyone else, for that matter. For one thing, it is not going to be up to the president. On something of this magnitude, the decision will be made by the Senate in Executive Session.

"The president, as an *ex officio* Senate member and *de facto* leader of the Social Democratic Party, will have a say, and it will have a great deal of influence. It may even be decisive. But it is fundamentally the Senate's choice. And as you know, the Senate is not constructed on party lines except for the Popular Members. The Members representing the other Estates vote the interests of their Estates—you know, Manufacturing, Shipping, Mining, Agriculture, Academia, Media and Communications, and the others—or what they perceive to be the best interest of the Union as a whole. How the Senate will receive this is hard to predict. I concur with you. I am very much afraid that they will agree. I have detected a certain exhaustion and want of courage in their actions lately. I will continue to pray most fervently that I am wrong. But what if I am right?"

"Between you and me, I think this ship ignores a surrender order. I kept half of my share of the gold from that freighter we captured in January here on board, and we use that to buy all the supplies we can stuff into the ship, and we go rogue. I bet there will be others. People like Captain Kim. Hell, can you see Hornmeyer meekly turning his ships over to the Krag? Not in this lifetime. We find a way to keep fighting."

"I pray that it does not come to that point."

"Amin to that, my brother."

"And with that, my brother, I take my leave of you. I have a few patients on whom I must check. Good night, Max."

"Good night, Bram."

He left. Max reached again for his bourbon. Like a small boy picking at a scab after having been told by his mother several times to leave it alone, Max called up the Krag message that was causing him so much unease. He put it on the smaller display of his workstation rather than on the display wall. Somehow, displaying it on the wall gave too much dignity and importance to the chilling words.

From the Hegemon and High Privy Counsel of the Sovereign and Supreme Viceroys of Creation, known to you as the "Krag," to the President, Senate, and Assembly of the Union of Earth and Terran Settled Worlds, we send greetings and the following message.

When we initiated the present Holy War against you, it was in the sincere and faithful belief, informed by authoritative revelation, that you were unholy blasphemers and that your very physical form and genome were demonic creations of the Evil One brought forth into the Universe to challenge the Vice-Regency of Creation for which the Creator-God made and destined us. We now have increasing reason to believe that our interpretation of events and of the holy revelations we have received may have been in error.

Your ability to resist our initial attack and subsequent offensive operations was far greater than expected. Your ability to challenge us with a continuing series of new strategies, new tactics, new weapons, new ships, and new technologies has led us to the inevitable conclusion that the Creator-God has not decreed that we must, necessarily, be the instrument of your destruction at this point in history.

We have reexamined the evidence upon which we made our initial determination and have concluded that you are not demonic creations of the Evil One, nor are you, as we first thought, inherently and incurably evil. Rather, as is the case of all living things, and—in particular—all living things that share our common genetic heritage, you are children of the Creator-God as we are. Accordingly, we are now of the view that to seek your unconditional *eradication from the Universe would be sacrilege, as the Creator-God abhors the needless death of any sentient beings whom he has brought forth.*

We do, however, believe that you are dangerously and blasphemously deluded. You do not worship the Creator-God. You do not recognize the overlordship of the superior beings whom he has created and chosen to rule over you. You refuse to recognize that it is His plan that you submit to our authority. You continue to believe that your life form and ours originated on your world, that our world was populated with life forms evolved on your world, and that we are not the Creator-God's chosen creations, but merely an animal evolved from an ancestor of the lowly pests that infest your homes and granaries.

Therefore, rather than exterminate you, we have concluded that the Creator-God wishes us first to humble you, then to rule over you as just and wise overlords, and finally to convert you from your various unholy, idolatrous forms of worship to the eternal glorification of the Creator-God who spawned the Universe and all life in it.

You may be of the belief that you, rather than we, are the recipients of divine favor, based on certain recent events that, admittedly, would appear to show that events have turned in your favor. The advantages you believe they confer upon you are illusory. We know of your recent purchase from the Sarthan and what that will mean in terms of your vessel design. Although the Sarthan will not give us the benefit of a similar sale, irrespective of cost, the simple knowledge of what you now have will enable us to eliminate much of the strategic benefit you expect to gain from this technology. When your larger ships appear, we will be ready for them and will have countermeasures adapted to destroy them. We have new and more capable weapons that have not yet been used in combat against you. These weapons will be particularly effective against your new vessels.

Further, we retain our previous advantages of greater population, greater rate of population growth, more worlds, more natural resources, and greater industrial capacity. Recent events, in fact, have made these advantages even more formidable. Unknown to you, our civilization has been at war with another race known as the Thark since the second year of our war against you. This war has consistently consumed nearly a third of our personnel and the output of our military-industrial complex. We have just conquered the Thark, which will allow us to turn all of the resources we have been devoting to fighting them to the war against you and, in the fullness of time, will also allow us to turn against you all of the resources and production capacity formerly controlled by the Thark.

If the war continues, our victory is inevitable. You will be defeated. If we defeat you, we will exterminate you.

In light of the foregoing, we offer to accept the Union's surrender on the following terms:

1. Complete disarmament of all humans subject to Union jurisdiction. All Union naval vessels, all bases and installations, and any other military assets will be surrendered to us. We will transport vessel crews and other combat capable personnel to detention centers for reeducation and, provided that they are found not to be a threat to our rule, later transport to their homeworlds. Military personnel who cannot or will not be reeducated will be humanely detained for life. No human will retain any firearm or other weapon capable of military use for any reason. Civil law enforcement will be provided by armed Krag military and unarmed Human police. Human police and paramilitary units may be provided with arms at some time in the distant future when your descendants are contented subjects under our just rule.

2. Complete dismantling of all apparatus of government in the Union at higher than the city and county levels. Government and administration will be provided by wise and just Krag overlords appointed by the Hegemony. Their rule will be absolute.

3. The purely Human concept of "Civil Rights" will have no place in the new order. Humans' place in the Universe is as a subject people. Subjects have no rights other than those conferred by their superiors. Our rule will be just and humane, but only because we choose to rule in that manner, not because of any inherent or innate entitlement on the part of Humans to be ruled by their superiors in any particular manner.

4. The practice of all false religions will cease. All clergy will be detained and reeducated. All other Humans will be instructed in the worship of the Creator-God. Those who refuse will be executed. Their deaths will be brought about humanely, but without delay. There is no place in Creation for children of the Creator-God who are blasphemers.

We understand that these terms seem harsh. This is because the Creator-God has decreed that you be humbled and reformed. Doing so requires that our rule at first be with an iron hand. Once your race has been humbled, and once your people are reformed and have grown to adopt the true faith, you will find that we can be benign and gentle rulers who will allow you to retain much of your culture and autonomy. Later generations will fail to understand why there was such enmity between our peoples and will regard us as wise overlords. Your descendants will be happy subjects of the Krag Hegemony. And more importantly, you will have descendants. Your race will continue. Your billions of progeny will live on, most enjoying long, healthy, productive, and happy lives—working, having families, and living in a manner unchanged in most particulars from how you live now.

If you do not accept these terms, we must conclude that you will not accept humbling and reformation. In that event, your blasphemy and offenses cannot go unpunished. We will continue the war against you until your race is forever removed from creation. Because this is an outcome that we would deeply regret, we earnestly and sincerely pray that you accept our overlordship and religious instruction so that your people need not be destroyed.

Communicate your acceptance or rejection of these terms by sending the same ship to the same rendezvous point at 12:00Z Hours, 2 May 2315. If the designated ship is not present, we will conclude that you wish the war to continue. Not one of you will survive. Each of your worlds will be sterilized down to the last bacterium. So, the question we pose to the Union is this: Will you save your race, preserving the lives of yourselves, your children, and the generations to come by tendering your surrender and accepting the overlordship of the Krag?

Even in the heat of battle, in the face of the enemy with the odds against him, Max had never as an adult been truly, abjectly afraid.

He was afraid now.

CHAPTER 16

11:50Z Hours, 2 May 2315

Max had experienced tension in a CIC before: on capital ships before major fleet actions where the admirals were rolling the dice with three or four carrier battle groups and the stakes were an entire sector or sometimes even two. Once, he had been present when Admiral Middleton had quietly put his whole Theater Task Force on the table to be victorious or to be obliterated. None of those compared to this.

Cumberland was at the rendezvous point. Ten minutes early. The Union's answer to the Krag surrender demand had been decided by the Senate in a closed session that lasted for nineteen straight hours. It was known that the president attended the entire debate and made use of his rarely exercised privilege to speak personally on the issue.

It was also known that the vote of the Senate had been unanimous and that the text of the message communicating the decision to the Krag had been drafted by the First Senator (what the Senate called its Chair), Alexander Conway, a short, balding, fastidious man known more for his mastery of the legislative technicalities than for any particular wisdom or strength of character. Lee and Conway were advised by Union Foreign Minister Judith Bernard, a retired admiral who had fought in the early days of the Krag war, before the killing of billions of females by the Krag biological weapon known as the Gynophage caused the Admiralty to remove women from all front-line service.

Bernard, known as the "Smiling Executioner" for her habit of wearing a small, tight smile on her face while cutting the enemy into small slices and bite-sized chunks, had enough toughness to make up for any deficiencies in the two men, with a generous quantity left over for the rest of the Senate. Unfortunately, she was not in charge. In an unprecedented move to guard the security of the Senate, that body had held this crucial session in the Pete Conrad Convention Center on the Earth's Moon.

What was not known was how the vote had turned out. That was the most closely held secret in the history of the Union. Only President Lee, the Senate, and Minister Bernard knew the outcome, and they were all secluded on Luna Base under Marine guard, with all the long-distance comms on the whole Moon shut down so that no one could leak the result. It was feared that disclosure of the outcome, before it became a *fait accompli* by transmission to the Krag, might spawn demonstrations, riots, even secession of worlds from the Union, detracting from the unanimity of the response and rendering it ineffective. This step, standing alone, made Max lose almost all hope.

The response to the Krag had been encrypted with a time-lock code that would not allow it to be read until the appointed moment, the time-lock encrypted data encrypted again in ICEPACK, the Union's highest level encrypt, and placed on a data chip to be carried to the rendezvous in the *Cumberland* and transmitted.

That chip was now plugged into the captain's console, which had been programmed to read the chip and transmit the message when Max pressed the recently repaired and now famous "SUMMON STEWARD—COFFEE" button. Max was on the verge of being physically ill. The mood in CIC was not only tense but grim. Most of the men had picked up on the skipper's pessimism and now believed that the Senate had voted to preserve the existence of the human race by sending it into eternal slavery under the lash of the Krag.

The result of the vote would be released to humankind at large by means of a presidential address beginning at the instant the answer was scheduled to be transmitted. On board the *Cumberland*, every console throughout the ship had been configured to display the answer when it was sent, so no man need wait in suspense a second longer than necessary. Two hundred and fifteen men would know the fate of the human race in a single, shared moment. Until then, it was agony.

At 11:55, the Vaaach vessel seemed simply to wink into existence, exactly ten kilometers away, just as it had the last time. After the usual steps, the forest commander's face appeared on the displays. His demeanor seemed subdued. The normally gut-shaking roars were quiet and deliberate. Then, the translation: "Peer Swamp Fox, I greet you."

"And I greet you, Forest Commander Chrrrlgrf."

"This is an important day in the history of your race. Although I am here only to bring Human and Krag together to exchange their messages in safety, I wish you to know that I do not welcome the thought of your troop of absurd, chattering primates going into the long silence of oblivion, nor do I welcome the thought of them being chained and marched into the cages of slavery."

He stood, placed his long arms (which reached well past his knees—a sign of his arboreal heritage) at his side, claws fully extended, and bowed his head for just under five seconds. Salute? Prayer? Mourning? There was no intel brief on this gesture. Then, he leveled his unnerving yellow-green eyes at the camera. It felt to Max as though the Vaaach were meeting his own eyes. There was genuine emotion in the alien gaze. Max could not read it, but it was certainly present and it was undoubtedly powerful. "The Vaaach wish you well."

"I thank you for your good wishes, Forest Commander. I do not know what the answer of my people will be. We will all learn it together."

"I await this revelation with interest. Today, we will learn the true nature of your species: hunters or prey."

The Krag vessel appeared at 11:59 and slid into its appointed place. At the stroke of 12:00 Chin announced, "Sir, the Krag send 'Ready to copy transmission.'" His voice was like death.

High noon. The hands of the old-style twelve-hour watch clock mounted on the bulkhead pointed straight up because, at that moment, more than a thousand light years away on Earth, the sun was at its highest point in the sky as viewed from the meridian of Greenwich, England. Over the thousands of years of human history, how many confrontations, how many meetings, how many ultimatums, how many pivotal events had been scheduled for just this hour and minute? Could any of them—could all of them put together—be any more important than what was about to happen at high noon, today, 2 May 2315?

No. Probably not.

Max steeled himself to push the button that would cause his console to lock in the decrypt, interrogate the chip, extract the response, and transmit it to the Krag. He laid his finger on top of the button without pressing it. It was bad enough that he was the one who had to send the message he was certain would begin humankind's subjugation to the Krag. He could not make himself watch it happen. The almost unbearable emotion of the moment making Max literally unable to breathe, he closed his eyes and forced his finger to exert the necessary pressure. The button engaged the contact that closed the circuit, making a click that, although almost inaudible, echoed in Max's mind like a rifle shot.

There. It was done.

Max felt a coldness run through his veins, as though he were receiving an intravenous drip of liquid helium. He knew the people around him were reading the response. Eyes still closed, he listened for changes in their breathing, speech, anything that would give away the answer without his having to look at the fateful words on his display. Nothing. The CIC crew was always a stoic lot.

A warship is essentially a hermetically sealed metal tube containing equipment, air, consumables, and human beings. The hull, the airtight bulkheads, and the decks that transect that hull are made of metal so thick and so sturdy that sounds made by the unamplified voices of the humans within or by the direct actions of their limbs in one compartment of the ship are usually inaudible in any other. But if enough noise is made of the right kind, the ship can be turned into an enormous reverberation chamber that amplifies and multiplies sounds rather than dampening them. Max had never encountered that phenomenon.

Until that moment.

At first, he could barely hear it, an almost subliminal suggestion of a sound, like the thunder of a distant storm. Undifferentiated in the beginning, it resolved into a series of *BOOMs* that got louder and louder and more and more powerful until the ship and the very air within it seemed to shake with each one. Only one thing could make that sound, Max thought: every member of the crew stomping his feet and banging on the bulkheads in unison. Also, faintly, he heard voices echoing through the bulkheads and vibrating the decks both above and below him. The men were shouting something in rhythm with one another. One word. Two syllables. He could not make them out.

Max's heart was beating so hard that he could feel each individual contraction not just as a motion inside his chest but as a throb of pressure inside his head—pressure so great he felt as though his head might explode. He opened his eyes, assembling the courage and the patience to wade through a lengthy Senatorial reply, the verbosity and obscurity of which would prevent him from knowing until the very end of the document the answer to the Krag's deadly question. The Krag had asked: *Will you save your race, preserving the lives of yourselves, your children, and the generations to come by tendering your surrender and accepting the overlordship of the Krag?*

The answer of the Union and of the human race to the Krag's question, shown on hundreds of displays around the ship, was a single word: the same word that the men were shouting over and over in time with the cannon-like booms that shook the ship, the same word that—for good or ill—would shape the destiny of the human race for all time:

NEVER.

The Union would fight on. Mankind would live free.

Or die.

The story of Captain Max Robichaux, Doctor Ibrahim Sahin, and the USS Cumberland *continues in the concluding volume of the "Man of War" Trilogy,* Brothers in Valor, *scheduled for publication in April 2014. The author plans more adventures for these characters; readers can look for the "Flames of War" trilogy (tentative title) beginning in late 2014.*

GLOSSARY AND GUIDE TO ABBREVIATIONS

Alfvén wave A low-frequency travelling oscillation of ions in a magnetic field, resulting when ions are injected or inserted into the field, with the ion mass density providing the inertia and the magnetic field line tension providing the restoring force. Alfvén waves travel along the lines of force of the magnetic field.

Allah askina (Turkish) For God's sake. An expression of shock and dismay.

Alphacen Alpha Centauri, as viewed from Earth the brightest star in the constellation Centaurus (the Centaur) a trinary star system and the star system nearest to the Sol System. Primary star: Alpha Centauri A, a type G2V main sequence star.

Article 15, Paragraph 5, Naval Regulations The provision of Naval regulations giving the commander of a rated warship the authority to disobey a direct order from a superior when an unforeseen event triggers the operation of a superior and countermanding standing or other preexisting order. In such an event, the officer disobeying the order is required to provide, as soon as practicable, a full and complete explanation and justification of his actions, in writing, to the superior officer whose order was disobeyed. The disobeying officer invokes this regulation at his peril, as there is no "good faith exception" to excuse his disobedience if his interpretation of the orders in question turns out to be in error.

AU Astronomical Unit. A unit of length or distance, defined as the mean distance between Earth and the sun, most commonly used in measuring distances on an interplanetary rather than an interstellar scale because it yields manageable numbers for such distances. For example, Mercury is about 0.35 AU from the sun, whereas Neptune is about 30 AU from the sun. One AU is equal to 149,597,870.7 kilometers, or 92,955,807.3 miles.

back room *See* SSR.

battlecruiser A large, powerful warship carrying offensive weaponry of the size and power of a battleship but intermediate in size between cruisers and battleships. Typically massing between forty thousand and sixty thousand tons, battlecruisers possess shielding, armor, speed, maneuverability, and defensive capabilities more equivalent to those of a cruiser than a battleship. Naval officers are split on the utility of this type, with some believing that with the killing power of a battleship and the speed of a cruiser, it offers the best of both; others believe that its large guns make it as tempting a target for the enemy as a battleship, but lacking in the armor, shielding, and point defense capabilities of a battleship to defend itself, it thereby combines the worst of both. A battlecruiser is generally under the command of a full captain.

battleship The largest and most powerful type of weapons platform ship (carriers are larger and with their fighter groups, arguably more powerful, but do not mount heavy offensive weapons). Typically massing sixty thousand tons and up, battleships mount large batteries of the most powerful offensive weapons carried on starships and are equipped with the heaviest armor and defensive shielding. The firepower and toughness of a battleship rival those of a battle station. Although capable of fairly high sublight speeds, they are very difficult to maneuver. In addition, their enormous bulk means that under compression drive, they are limited to fairly low c multiples. Accordingly, battleships cross interstellar space almost exclusively by jumping. A battleship is typically under the command of a full captain or a commodore.

Battle Star An award conferred by a fleet or task force commander upon a vessel that has comported itself honorably in direct combat with the enemy. In the days of the saltwater navy, vessels displayed their Battle Stars on the hull or superstructure where other vessels could see them. Union warships display their battle stars by the use of colored running lights on their hull, arranged in the shape of a star, and illuminated when they are not stealthed. Battle Stars come in three grades: Bronze (orange lights), Silver (white lights), and Gold (yellow lights). The Battle Star is a permanent award displayed by the vessel as long as it remains in service. Not to be confused with a battlestar, which is an archaic name for a former type that was essentially a cross between a battlecruiser and an escort carrier, mounting heavy pulse cannon and missiles while also carrying fighters. This type fell into disfavor because of the difficulty in conducting fighter operations while firing guns and missiles through the fighter formations.

bearing The position of an object relative to another object, measured as degrees of angle on a horizontal and a vertical plane, with the two numbers separated by a slash that is pronounced as "mark" when giving a bearing out loud. The zero reference in both planes is the geometric center of the Milky Way Galaxy. Hence, a sensor officer will say that a contact is at bearing two-three-seven mark zero-four-five. Also, a sphere, usually made of some hard metal alloy, used in conjunction with several similar spheres to provide lubrication between a rotating shaft and its housing (ball bearings).

boarding cutlass A sword made of high-tensile-strength steel, in fashion similar to the United States Navy's Model 1917 Cutlass. It is 63.5 centimeters long (25 inches), weighs approximately 935 grams (33 ounces), and is slightly curved. The boarding cutlass is primarily regarded as a slashing weapon but can be used as a thrusting weapon as well. It is carried by naval personnel for close order battle in confined quarters on ship, particularly in locations where gunfire might puncture pipes or pressure vessels, releasing toxic or radioactive substances, or might cause the venting of atmosphere into space. A boarding cutlass and a sidearm of his choice (either an M-1911 or an M-62) is issued to a midshipman when he is promoted to midshipman first class.

Bravo The second letter of the Union Forces Voicecom Alphabet; a colloquial name for Epsilon Indi III (*see*).

BuDes (pronounced "bew-dess") Bureau of Design. The naval office responsible for designing warships and warship power plants. Its most important component offices are OfSpaF (pronounced "off-spaf"), Office of Space Frames, responsible for fabricating the hulls and the interior support structure that gives them strength and rigidity; OfPropSys (pronounced "off-prop-sis"), Office of Propulsion Systems, where the engines and drives are designed; OfHab (pronounced "off-hab"), Office of Habitability, which configures the interiors of the ships, including location and arrangement of compartments and furnishings; and OfSupSys ("pronounced "off-soup-sys"), Office of Support Systems, which oversees life support, plumbing, and similar systems necessary for sustaining life in space. Weapons, sensors, navigation systems, communications systems, and building of the ships after they are designed are all supervised by separate bureaus.

BuPers (pronounced "bew-perz") Bureau of Personnel. The naval department responsible for managing naval personnel assignments, recruiting, and similar matters.

c The speed of light in a vacuum, commonly stated as "lightspeed," 299,792,458 meters per second, or 186,282 miles per second. Unless a warship is travelling very slowly (in which case, its velocity is given in meters per second), its speed is generally given as a fraction or multiple of c, for example, .25 c for one-quarter of lightspeed or 325 c for 325 times lightspeed. In common usage, only the number is given. Hence, a tactical officer might inform his captain that a "bogie is approaching at point 25," or an engineer might advise that the ship "should not exceed 250."

ça c'est bon (Cajun French). That's good. Equivalent to *c'est bon* in Parisian French.

Cajun A person descended from the French-speaking Roman Catholic residents of Nova Scotia (which they called Acadia) who were exiled by the British at the end of the French and Indian War because of concerns regarding their loyalty to the British crown, and who settled in what was then the French Territory of Louisiana. Most Cajuns spoke their own version of French well into the twentieth century and maintain a distinctive culture to this day. On Earth, Cajuns mostly reside in the Parishes of South-Central and Southwest Louisiana, centered on Lafayette. Cajuns are often referred to by each other and by their friends as "Coonasses." The word "Cajun" is a worn-down form of "Acadian."

carrier A large vessel designed to launch, retrieve, arm, fuel, and service fighters and other smaller ships. Large fleet and command carriers can carry as many as two hundred fighters, whereas smaller Escort and Attack carriers as few as thirty. Carriers range in size from 40,000 to 1 million tons. As of January through March 2315, there were rumors that the Navy was currently constructing a new class of carriers massing 2 million tons, with one being built at the Luna Fleet Yards, one being built at Alphacen, and two at 40 Eridani A. These vessels are supposedly to be known as the *Churchill* class.

c'est pas rien (Cajun French) It's nothing, think nothing of it. Equivalent to *de rien* in Parisian French.

Cherenkov-Heaviside radiation The burst of radiation emitted as an object emerges from a jump. So named for its two components: Cherenkov radiation, which is the radiation emitted when a charged particle passes through a dielectric medium at a speed higher than the normal speed for the propagation of light in that medium; and Heaviside radiation, the radiation emitted when a particle travelling faster than the speed of light in a spatial regime in which that can occur (e.g., in *n*-space) is decelerated to subluminal velocities in our own spatial regime.

Chief of the Boat The senior noncommissioned officer on board any naval vessel. He is considered a department head and is the liaison between the captain and the noncommissioned ranks. Sometimes referred to as COB (pronounced "cob") and informally known as the "Goat."

CIC Combat Information Center. The compartment on a warship from which the ship's operations are controlled, analogous to the bridge on an old seagoing vessel before the functions of that space were split between the Bridge and CIC with the introduction of radar to combat ships in the years leading up to World War II.

CIG Change in grade. Promotion or demotion. Official orders never state that a person is "promoted to commander." Rather, they say that the person is "CIG to commander." A CIG order always states the date, hour, and minute the CIG becomes effective so that there is no question of the relative seniority (and therefore who gives orders to whom) of two officers of the same grade.

Clarke Orbit Synchronous or stationary orbit. An orbit in which the orbiting body remains stationary relative to a point on the surface of the orbited body on the latter's equator, also defined as an equatorial orbit in which the orbital period is equal to the rotational period of the orbited body. Known as a "Clarke Orbit" because the concept was first described in detail by British science and science fiction author Arthur C. Clarke in a 1945 article published in *Wireless World* magazine.

class A production series of warships of highly similar or identical design, designated by the name of the first ship of the series. Accordingly, if a series of heavy cruisers is produced from the same design, and the first ship of that design to be produced is the USS *Faget* (pronounced "fah-zhay"), then the vessels of that class are known as *Faget* class cruisers. Vessels of the same class are usually named after the same thing. For example, *Faget* class cruisers are all named after influential designers of aircraft, launch vehicles, and space vessels: Hence the class contains the *Faget, Wright, Bleriot, Langley, Kelly Johnson, Von Braun, Korolev, Caldwell Johnson, Northrup*, and so on.

class (Krag vessels) The Krag apparently have a class system similar to the Union's, producing warships of similar design in series. Because Krag vessel names are, however, unknown, difficult to pronounce, or impossible to remember, the Navy uses a system of "reporting names" for Krag vessel classes. Essentially, when a new class of Krag vessel is identified, a name is assigned to that class by Naval Intelligence. Class names generally start with the same letter or group of letters as the name of the vessel type, with the exception of battlecruisers, the class names of which begin with "Bar" to distinguish them from battleships. In this way, a ship's type can immediately be determined from its class name, even if the name is not familiar. Examples of class names for each major warship type follow:

> *Battleships:* Batwing, Battalion, Battleax, Baton.
> *Battlecruisers:* Barnacle, Barnyard, Barrister, Barsoom, Barmaid
> *Carriers:* Carousel, Carnivore, Carpetbagger, Cardigan
> *Cruisers:* Crusader, Crucible, Crustacean, Crumpet
> *Frigates:* Freelancer, Frogleg, Frycook, Frigid
> *Destroyers:* Deckhand, Delver, Dervish, Debris
> *Corvettes:* Corpuscle, Cormorant, Cornhusker, Corsican, Cordwood

Comet Colloquial term for the Warship Qualification Badge, a medal, shaped like a comet with a curved tail, indicating that the wearer has passed either a Warship Crew Qualification Examination or a Warship Officer Qualification Examination, showing that he can competently operate every crew or officer station on the ship, perform basic damage control, engage in close order battle with sidearm and boarding cutlass, use a pulse rifle, and fight hand to hand. The Comet was created in the early days of space combat to be the equivalent of the "Dolphins" from the United States Submarine Forces.

compression drive One of the two known technologies that allow ships to travel faster than lightspeed (the other being the jump drive). The compression drive permits violation of Einsteinian physics by selectively compressing and expanding the fabric of the space–time continuum. The drive creates around the vessel a bubble of distorted space–time with a diameter approximately thirty-four times the length of the ship. This bubble in turn contains a smaller bubble of undistorted space–time just large enough to enclose the ship itself. The density of space–time is compressed along the ship's planned line of travel and expanded behind it (hence the term "compression drive," which was thought to sound better than "expansion drive" or, heaven forbid, "warp drive"), creating a propulsive force that moves the ship forward faster than the speed of light as viewed from the perspective of a distant observer. This superluminal motion does not violate Einsteinian physics because the ship is stationary relative to the fabric of space-time inside the bubble, and therefore, from the point of view of an observer located there, does not exceed the speed of light. Because the volume of distorted space rises as a geometric function as ship size goes up under the familiar $V = \pi r^2$ formula multiplied by thirty-four (pi times half the length of the ship squared times thirty-four), even a small increase in the ship's dimensions results in a substantial increase in the energy required to propel it through compressed space. Accordingly, only smaller ship types can move at high speeds or for any appreciable distance using compression drive, which means in turn that major fleet operations and planetary conquests require the taking and holding of jump points so that carriers, battleships, tankers, and other larger or slower vessels can be brought into the system.

compression shear A dangerous phenomenon caused by a compression drive experiencing poor speed regulation, a common occurrence at speeds of less than about 80 c. Compression shear occurs when radical fluctuations in the degree of space–time distortion, caused by a poorly regulated drive, exert variable and rapidly fluctuating force against the "bubble" of normal space-time surrounding the ship. As the small undistorted bubble around the ship must exist in precise equilibrium with the larger zone of differentially compressed and expanded space that surrounds the smaller one, sharp variations, or "shear," along the boundary rupture the bubble and destroy the ship.

Core Systems The fifty star systems located near the astrographic center of the Union that, although constituting only about 10 percent by number of the Union's inhabited worlds, are home to 42 percent of its population and 67 percent of its heavy industrial capacity.

cruiser A large, heavily armed, and heavily armored vessel providing an excellent mix of firepower, armor, speed, and endurance. Cruisers are highly powerful and flexible warships that can operate as component parts of large task forces or as the center of small task forces of their own. Cruisers are capable of delivering heavy doses of sustained weapons fire against warships, orbital installations, and surface targets, and can operate without support for more than a year. Most cruiser types mass between 25,000 and 40,000 metric tons and are often loosely divided into the subtypes of light, medium, and heavy. A heavy cruiser is only slightly smaller and less powerful than the smaller classes of battlecruiser.

DC Damage Control. The set of duties and techniques associated with limiting and repairing damage to a ship sustained in space, particularly battle damage. The term is also used to refer to the CIC station used to display damage to the ship and coordinate the efforts of damage control parties, as well as to the person who mans that station.

delta V Change in velocity. Delta is the physics/aerospace symbol for "change," and V is the symbol for velocity (velocity technically being both speed and direction). Space vehicle maneuvers are typically measured in terms of the delta V necessary to carry them out, as that number immediately tells a pilot whether he has enough fuel and thruster power to complete the maneuver.

destroyer The most numerous type of rated ship in the Navy, destroyers are comparatively small vessels (as measured against cruisers, battleships, and carriers), optimized for speed, maneuverability, and firepower. Known as the "workhorses of the Navy," destroyers typically mass in the range of 16,000 to 20,000 tons. They are not heavily armored and are not capable of carrying enough stores, fuel, and munitions to operate for long periods of time without resupply, but carry pulse cannons equal in power (though usually fewer of them) to those carried by most frigates. Destroyers are typically operated as escorts to larger vessels as part of a fleet or task force. When a destroyer encounters a ship of greater force, it is supposed to either call upon a heavier vessel with which it is operating or, if none is available, rely on its maneuverability and speed to evade and run away (ELEVES or "elude, evade, and escape). The CO of a destroyer is typically a commander, although ships in the smaller destroyer classes sometimes have an unusually able lieutenant commander as a skipper.

deuterium separation plant A facility for producing deuterium fuel for fusion reactors. Such plants function by separating naturally occurring deuterium oxide, also known as heavy water, from ordinary water, taking advantage of the two substances' differing densities, through the use of a series of high-speed centrifuges. Once heavy water of suitable concentration (more than 95 percent) is obtained, the deuterium is then broken down by electrical hydrolysis into elemental oxygen and deuterium. Such facilities tend to be located on water-covered moons similar to Europa in the Sol system because they provide a large supply of relatively high-deuterium water, a shallow gravity well, and some kind of large hard surface (either ice or rock) on which to construct the facility.

droga, merda, porra (Brazilian Portuguese) Bummer, shit, fuck. An exclamation of shock and dismay.

"E" for "Excellence" An award conferred upon a vessel by a Task Force commander or higher authority for conspicuous excellence or achievement in any area of endeavor. The award is displayed by illuminating running lights, arranged in the shape of a large letter "E," when the vessel is not stealthed. The award is typically made for some demonstration of outstanding proficiency by the vessel and is authorized to be displayed for a limited number of days, usually sixty.

EM Electromagnetic. Usually short for the term "electromagnetic radiation," meaning visible light, radio waves, ultraviolet, infrared, and similar forms of energy forming a part of the familiar electromagnetic spectrum. Often used to distinguish sensors that detect EM radiation from those that detect other phenomena such as gravitational effects or neutrinos.

EMCON Emissions Control. A security and deception measure in which a warship not only operates under what twenty-first century readers would call "radio silence" but also without navigation beacons, active sensor beams, or any other emissions that could be used to track the ship.

Emeka Moro Emeka Moro, USS Union Space Navy Frigate, *Edward Jenner* class, registry number FLE 2372, commissioned 8 December 2295. Currently (as of 20 February 2315) undergoing extensive repairs and refit at James Lovell Station to repair damage sustained in battle against a Krag *Barsoom* class battlecruiser on 11 November 2314. For the person, *see* Moro, Emeka.

Enlisted Ratings The ranks of enlisted men in the Union Navy are listed below, in order of increasing rank. Within each rank, not separately listed here, are three classes—first, second, and third. So, within the ranks of able spacer, one can rise through the ranks of able spacer third class, able spacer second class, to able spacer first class.

recruit
ordinary
able
petty officer
chief petty officer

Epsilon Indi As viewed from Earth, the fifth brightest star in the Constellation Indus (the Indian). A main sequence star, class K, orbited by two brown dwarf stars and seven planets, located approximately twelve light years from Earth. The name is also used to refer to the third planet of this system, Epsilon Indi III (sometimes referred to as "Bravo" for the letter "B," as it was the second Earth colony outside the Sol system, coming after "Alpha," or Alpha Centauri).

FEBA Forward edge of battle area. The "front line," or, in three-dimensional space, a plane or other two-dimensional surface, marking the boundary between space controlled by friendly forces and space controlled by enemy forces. Alternately, the surface marking the forward-most friendly forces. Sometimes referred to as FLOF, or forward line of own forces (from forward line of own troops in pre-starflight Earth ground combat).

fils de putain (Cajun French) Son, or sons, of a whore. Used as an insult when an English speaker would say "son of a bitch" or "bastard." It is not, however, appropriate to use this expression in those places where an English speaker uses "son of a bitch" as an impersonal expletive as in, "Son of a bitch, I left my wallet at home."

flagship The ship from which a commodore or admiral exercises command of a task force, fleet, or other group of vessels. The flagship of a major task force is typically a command carrier or a fleet carrier. The flagship of a smaller task force may be a battleship, a battlecruiser, or even a cruiser.

frame A vertical cross section of a warship, numbered from bow to stern for the purpose of describing the location of damage the ship's structure or to large areas. A destroyer might have as few as eight frames, whereas a carrier has hundreds.

frigate A type of warship with a slightly higher displacement range than destroyers (frigates typically mass between 18,000 and

26,000 metric tons; note, the largest classes of destroyer are heavier than the smallest classes of frigate), but usually somewhat slower and less maneuverable, more heavily armed (particularly in the matter of the number of missile tubes—most destroyers have only two forward-firing missile tubes, whereas most frigates have at least four, and many have six or eight) and armored, and carrying a larger supply of consumables and weapons reloads to give them significantly higher endurance on station without resupply. Frigates are most commonly used in detached service. Frigates are typically skippered by a full commander.

FTL Faster than light. Superluminal.

gash duty The assignment or duty of performing menial chores, especially those involving cleaning up accidental spills, leaks, overflows, and human bodily fluids. Although the term is of saltwater navy vintage, its origin is otherwise obscure.

Gates The traditional naval nickname for a respected and highly able computer and information systems officer. The name is taken from that of William "Bill" Gates (born 28 October 1955; died 23 August 2044) the founder of the Microsoft Corporation and one of the architects of "the personal computer revolution." The term was first applied to computer officers upon the formation of the UESF (*see*) in 2034.

genau (German) Exactly, precisely. Often used to express agreement.

Gott im Himmel (German) God in heaven! An exclamation of shock and dismay.

Gynophage An extremely virulent genetically engineered viral disease launched by the Krag against the Union in 2295. The disease organism is highly infectious to all humans, but a gene sequence unique to the human "Y" chromosome prevents disease symptoms from manifesting in all but a tiny fraction of males, thereby keeping infected males contagious but asymptomatic. It is 99+ percent fatal to human females. It is believed that, left to itself, the disease would have killed all but a few of the human females in the galaxy and resulted in the virtual extinction of the human race. It was disseminated by thousands of stealthed compression drive drones launched by the Krag in the early days of the war, each of which launched thousands of submunitions that exploded in the atmosphere of human-inhabited planets. The disease functions in a manner similar to Ebola, by breaking down the tissues of the internal organs, but kills much more rapidly. Once the disease begins to manifest, the subject is dead within minutes. The disease is currently treated and prevented by the Moro Treatment, a combination vaccine and antibody devised by a team led by the brilliant Dr. Emeka Moro (*see*).

Goat Informal name for the Chief of the Boat (*see*).

greenie Colloquial term for a recruit spacer. So called because the Working Uniform for that grade is light-green in color.

Hamilton, Ian (Sir) [full name: General Sir Ian Standish Monteith Hamilton GCB GCMG DSO TD.] Born 16 January 1853; died 12 October 1947. General in the British Army and Commander of the Mediterranean Expeditionary Force at the disastrous Battle of Gallipoli. Among the multitude of acts for which he has received severe (and well-deserved) criticism is his disparate treatment of troops under his command of different nationalities, favoring British troops at the expense of troops from the British colonies, particularly those from Australia and New Zealand.

Hotel Union Forces Voicecom Alphabet designator for the letter "H." Sensors and Tactical designation for a hostile contact or target.

"hottie Scotty" A particularly industrious or capable member of the Engineering crew, sometimes used disparagingly regarding a person who, for the moment, is the favorite of the chief engineer for reasons unconnected with merit (*see* "Scotty").

hypergolic Two substances that, when combined, will ignite and combust without need of an ignition source, a term used in the Navy primarily to describe fuels for missiles and thrusters. Rocket motors employing hypergolic fuels are mechanically simpler and inherently more reliable than those that do not, because no ignition source need be provided in the design. On the other hand, hypergolic fuels provide a lower specific impulse (essentially the amount of thrust developed per unit of fuel and oxidizer) than cryogenic fuel/oxidizer combinations such as hydrogen/oxygen.

IDSSC Interstellar Data Systems Standardization Convention (pronounced "id-sick"). An informal agreement among the major computer and data systems manufacturers of the Union, most human worlds, and several alien races, providing for standardization of data formats, transfer protocols, design of cables and connectors, and other matters to allow interchangeability and transferability of data and computer equipment from one star system to another. Because of IDSSC, a Pfelung printer can be attached to a computer made on Alphacen and used to print documents written and saved to a data chip on Ghifta Prime.

IFF Identification, friend or foe. A general descriptive term for any system that allows vessels to identify each other as being friendly or hostile, usually involving an exchange of coded electronic transmissions.

inertial compensator The system on a space vessel that negates the inertial effect of acceleration on the crew and vessel contents (known as "G forces"), enabling the ship to accelerate, turn, and decelerate rapidly without killing the crew and ripping the fixtures from the deck.

Jellicoe, Sir John [full name: Admiral of the Fleet John Rushworth Jellicoe, First Earl Jellicoe GCB OM GCVO SGM] Born, 5 December 1859; died, 20 November 1935. Commander of the British Grand Fleet at the Battle of Jutland fought on 31 May through 1 June 1916, during Earth's First World War. During the war, it was said of him that he was the one man in the Empire who could lose the war in an afternoon.

jump drive One of the two systems that allows a space vessel to cross interstellar distances in less time than it would take to travel at sublight speed (the other being compression drive, *see*). The jump drive transfers the vessel in a single Planck interval from one point in space, known as a jump point, to another jump point in a nearby star system, and never less than 3.4 nor more than 12.7 light years away. Jump points are generally located between 20 and 30 AU from a star and almost always lie at least 45 degrees away from the star's equator. For some unknown reason, systems either have no jump points, three, or a multiple of three—but most commonly three—usually located several dozen AU from each other. Jumping is always more energy efficient and much faster than traversing the same distance with compression drive. However, it is almost impossible to jump into an enemy-held system, because the enemy will almost always have weapons trained and ranged on the jump points and the process of jumping requires that the jumping ship power down all sublight drives, weapons, shielding, and point defense systems, making it virtually helpless when emerging from a jump. Accordingly, in order to take a system, it is usually necessary to send in ships from a system within ten light years or so under compression drive and take the jump points, thereby allowing heavier ships, troop carriers, and supply vessels to jump in.

Jurassic Space The period, technology, or practices associated with human space exploration, particularly manned or crewed space exploration, before humanity acquired the technology to explore interstellar space by defeating the Ning-Braha at the Battle of Luna (circa 1960 to July 2034).

***Khyber* class** A class of destroyer, the first of which, the USS *Khyber*, was commissioned on 24 April 2311, making these vessels a "new" class in 2315. The *Khybers* are exceptionally fast and maneuverable, even for destroyers. The thrust-to-mass ratio of these ships is in the same range as those of many fighter designs; accordingly, it is said that they handle more like large fighters than escort vessels. They are equipped with pulse cannon as powerful as those on many capital ships (although they have only three of these and a smaller rear-firing unit, whereas a capital ship might have a dozen or more). Ships in this class are extremely stealthy, possess a sophisticated ability to mimic the electronic and drive emissions of other ships, and have a highly effective sensor suite. They are also equipped with SWACS (*see*). The trade-offs made to optimize these characteristics include highly Spartan crew accommodations (Spartan even for a destroyer), a radically reduced number of reloads for her missile tubes (twenty Talons and five Ravens versus a typical destroyer loadout of sixty and twelve); a small crew, making for a heavy workload for all personnel; modest fuel capacity; and a reduced cargo hold. Unsupported endurance is rated at 75 days (as compared to 180 days for most destroyers) but in practice is somewhat shorter. It is believed that the class was designed to make quick stealthy raids into enemy space and destroy his supply lines and means of communication, thereby disrupting his logistics and command/control/communications. Mass: 16,200 metric tons. Top sublight speed: .963 c. Compression drive: 1575 c cruise, 2120 c emergency. Weapons: three forward-firing Krupp-BAE Mark XXXIV pulse cannon, 150-gigawatt rating, one rear-firing Krupp-BAE Mark XXII pulse cannon (colloquially known at the "Stinger"), 75-gigawatt rating. Two forward- and one rear-firing missile tubes. Standard missile loadout of twenty "Talon" (*see*) and five "Raven" (*see*) antiship missiles. Ships in this class are named after historically significant mountain passes and ocean straits. Length: 97 meters; beam: 9.5 meters. Commissioned ships in this class as of 21 January 2315 are *Khyber, Gibraltar, Messina, Cumberland, Hormuz,* and *Khardung La.* The projected size of the class is eighty-five ships.

Known Space That portion of the Milky Way Galaxy explored by humans or of which humans have reasonably reliable information from alien races, mostly consisting of a portion of the Orion-Cygnus galactic arm centered on the Sol System.

Kuiper belt (rhymes with "piper") A belt of bodies, made mainly of frozen volatiles such as water ice, methane, and ammonia, found in the outer regions of many star systems. In the Sol system, it begins about 30 AU from the sun (the orbit of Neptune) and extends out to approximately 50 AU. Kuiper belts typically contain several planet-sized objects, known as *Plutinos*, a name taken from Pluto, a Kuiper belt object discovered in 1930 and classified as a planet for more than 70 years. Kuiper belts are tactically important mainly because the large number of massive icy objects provide a good place to hide a warship's mass and heat signatures.

lubber A person unfamiliar with space and not possessing the skills and knowledge associated with service on a space vessel. From the old saltwater navy term, "landlubber," which is itself of obscure origin.

lubber line A space vessel course consisting of a straight line through space, from the point of origin to the destination.

Mark One Eyeball Naval slang for the human eye without any artificial aid of any kind. Called "Mark One" because it is the original unimproved model (often, naval systems are numbered Mark I, Mark II, Mark III, and so on, as new versions are introduced).

M-62 Model 2062 Pistol. One of the two sidearms approved for use by Union Space Navy personnel (the other being the M-1911), the M-62 is a 10-millimeter, semiautomatic, magazine-fed handgun. It was introduced to naval use in 2062, during the First Interstellar War, when the Glock polymer-framed weapons then issued were found to become brittle, to warp, and even sometimes to melt in the temperature extremes of space combat, requiring that the Navy issue an all-metal handgun to supplement the M-1911. The resulting weapon, designed by the Beretta-Browning Arms Corporation, was based largely on the venerable Browning Hi-Power design, modified to fire the larger cartridge (the older weapon was originally designed for the 9 mm cartridge but was also manufactured for the .40 S&W round). It has a 14-round magazine.

M-72 Model 2072 Close Order Battle Shotgun. The Winchester-Mossberg Arms Company Model 2072 is a semiautomatic 12-gauge shotgun designed for close order battle against boarding parties or for use by boarders. It has a "sawed-off" 13-inch barrel and is fed from a 10-round box magazine rather than the traditional tube magazine so that it can have a short barrel for use in close quarters while retaining high magazine capacity. The most common load fired in this weapon is a high-velocity 00 buckshot shell that propels ten .33-caliber (8.322 mm) hard-cast lead balls at a muzzle velocity of approximately 350 meters per second. The weapon is also capable of firing various slug, slug-sabot, dart-penetrator, and exploding rounds. It is of steel and composite construction (no polymer parts) and is equipped with fixed military aperture sights.

M-88 Model 2288 Pulse Rifle. The Colt-Ruger Naval Arms Corporation Model 2288 is a 7.62 × 51 millimeter, select-fire, magazine-fed battle rifle issued to Navy personnel for boarding actions, ship defense, and ground combat. It is similar in form and function to the M-14 battle rifle issued by the United States of America in the mid-twentieth century but made significantly lighter through the use of aluminum and composite materials (5.56 mm rounds were found to lack sufficient penetrating power to reliably kill Krag wearing combat gear). It is also the standard-issue personal weapon of the Union Space Marine Corps. The rifle is fed from a 35-round box magazine and is of all metal/composite construction (no polymer parts). The naval version has standard military aperture sights adjustable for range only (not windage), whereas the Marine version is equipped with a detachable optical aiming device that operates either as a red-dot reflex sight or a low-light-capable zoom telescopic sight. Muzzle climb and recoil in full-auto mode are nearly eliminated by a miniature, power cell–driven, inertial compensator unit in the stock. The weapon has four firing modes: semiauto, three-shot burst, six-shot burst, and full auto. It is called a "pulse rifle" because, coaxially mounted below the rifle barrel, is a launcher from which can be fired the MMD ("Make My Day") pulse grenade, a 35-millimeter, self-propelled, short-range projectile containing a shaped charge–equipped pulse slug capable of penetrating the armor on a Krag fighting suit at a range of 50 meters and then exploding, killing the occupant. The MMD is also effective against lightly armored ground vehicles.

M-1911 Model 1911 pistol. One of the two sidearms approved for use by Union Space Navy personnel (the other being the M-62), the M-1911 is an 11.48-millimeter (sometimes referred to by the archaic designation ".45-caliber") semiautomatic, magazine-fed handgun invented by perhaps the most brilliant firearms designer in Known Space, John Moses Browning, who was active in the United States of America on Earth in the late nineteenth and early twentieth centuries. The M-1911 was the official sidearm of the armed forces of the United States during

World War I, World War II, the Korean Conflict, and the Vietnam Conflict. It has remained in use by certain units in the United States armed forces, later by at least some units and personnel in the armed forces of United Nations of North America, United Earth, the Terran and Colonial Treaty Organization, the Earth and Colonial Confederation, and the Terran Union. The current version is only slightly different from the Model 1911 A1 used by American Forces in World War II. The changes include an ambidextrous thumb safety, lightweight alloy frame (the original frame was made of ordinance steel), extended beaver tail, three-dot luminous/fiber optic sights and a laser sight, bushingless barrel, and 12-round magazine. This weapon continues to be used more than four hundred years after its introduction because it is powerful, accurate, well balanced, and easy to shoot. It is effective against humans and most aliens against whom humans have fought (it is especially effective against Krag) and offers an excellent combination of high stopping power with low muzzle flash and reasonable recoil.

midshipman A boy between the ages of 8 and 17 taken on board ship both to perform certain limited duties and to be trained to serve in the enlisted or officer ranks. Commonly referred to as "mids."

midshipman trainer A senior noncommissioned officer, typically the second most senior chief petty officer on the ship, in charge of the training, housing, discipline, and welfare of all midshipmen on board. Also known as "Mother Goose" (*see*).

MMD *See* M-88.

Moro, Emeka (for the ship, see *Emeka Moro*) Physician and medical researcher born in Mombassa, Kenya, Earth, on 15 April 2241. Winner of the Nobel Prize for Medicine in 2295. Perhaps the foremost expert in human infectious diseases in the galaxy, Dr. Moro headed the effort to devise a treatment or preventative for the Gynophage (*see*), an effort that involved more than a million physicians and researchers on more than four hundred planets, at its peak consuming 43 percent of the interstellar communications bandwidth and 15 percent of the computing capacity available to the human race, and costing more than 300 trillion credits. When early research work began to indicate that neither a vaccine nor an antibody-based treatment would be more than 25 percent effective, it was Dr. Moro who personally had the insight of combining a vaccine with a set of broad spectrum antibodies synthesized not only to match the current disease organism but also the nine most probable mutations of its external protein coat, thereby creating a vaccine that prevents infection in those who are not infected and prevents manifestation of the disease in those who are infected but are asymptomatic. Dr. Moro is literally the most honored human of the last thousand years, being the namesake for one inhabited planet, two colonies on inhabited moons, five medical schools, dozens of hospitals, and hundreds of schools. For decades "Emeka" was the most popular male given name in Human Space. Dr. Moro currently lives with his spouse, famous molecular biologist Dr. James Warington, in London.

Mother Goose The semi-official title for the midshipman trainer (*see*).

N2 Naval Intelligence Staff, the equivalent of G2 in the old Army general staff system.

Officer rank abbreviations:

GADM: Grand Admiral (five stars)
FADM: Fleet Admiral (four stars)
VADM: Vice Admiral (three stars)
RADM: Rear Admiral (two stars)

CMRE: Commodore (one star)
CAPT: Captain
CMDR: Commander
LCDR: Lieutenant Commander
LT: Lieutenant
LTJG: Lieutenant junior grade
ENSN: Ensign

One MC (also written 1MC) One main circuit, the primary voice channel on a naval vessel, allowing a properly authorized speaker to be heard over every audio transducer in the ship. The term dates back to the saltwater navy.

oy mekheye (Yiddish) an that does not translate well into Standard expressive of supreme joy or exaltation.

oy veh (Yiddish) "Woe is me." An expression of sorrow and dismay.

pas aujourd'hui (Cajun French) "Not today."

PC-4 Patrol Craft, Type 4. A sublight only high-speed patrol and light attack craft used for system and planetary defense as well as for light intrasystem escort duties. Length: 72 meters. Beam: 5 meters. Crew: two officers, ten enlisted. Armament: one 75-gigawatt pulse cannon, six Raytheon-Hughes "Talon" ship-to-ship missiles (*see*). Top speed: .97 c.

pennant In a multivessel group commanded by an officer below the rank of commodore, the vessel from which the group is commanded and in which the overall commander of the group is stationed.

percom A wrist-carried communication, computing, and control device worn by all naval personnel when on duty.

pigeon In a formation of military vessels, the vessel being protected or escorted by the others, particularly if there is only one such vessel and it is of particular importance.

posident POSitive IDENTification.

pulse cannon A ship-mounted weapon that fires a pulse of plasma diverted from the ship's main fusion reactor and accelerated to between .85 and .95 c by magnetic coils. The plasma is held in a concentrated "bolt" by a magnetic field generated by a compact, liquid helium–cooled, fusion cell–powered emitter unit inserted in the bolt just as it is about to leave the cannon tube. The bolt loses cohesion and expands explosively when the emitter stops generating the containment field resulting from: (1) the emitter's exhaustion of its coolant supply, resulting in the plasma vaporizing the emitter; (2) the emitter's timer shuts down the emitter at a set range; (3) the bolt strikes a target destroying the emitter. Pulse cannon are rated based on the power output of their coil assemblies, which determines how much plasma can be fired in a given pulse; the explosive power of a pulse cannon bolt, measured in kilotons, is roughly 1/300 of the power rating in gigawatts. Accordingly, a maximum power bolt from a pulse cannon with a 150-gigawatt rating is approximately 0.5 kilotons. If the firing ship is travelling at a high fraction of lightspeed, the speed of the plasma pulse can exceed .99 c.

Raven A large antiship missile carried by Union warships. Much larger than the Talon (*see*) and with a higher top speed, the Raven accelerates more slowly, is less nimble, and is more vulnerable to point defense systems and countermeasures than the Talon, due to its larger size. Manufactured by Gould-Martin-Marietta Naval Aerospace Corporation, the Raven finds its target with both passive and active multi-modal sensor homing and then inflicts its damage with a 1.5-megaton fixed-yield fusion warhead powerful enough to destroy all but the largest enemy vessels and to cripple any known enemy ship. Ravens are equipped with an innovative system known as Cooperative Interactive Logic Mode

(CILM—pronounced “Kill ’em”). When more than one Raven is launched against the same target, CILM causes the missiles to communicate with one another and attack the target jointly, closing on the enemy from multiple vectors, to render defense more difficult, and exploding at the same instant to inflict the most damage.

regardez donc (Cajun French) An expression of awe and amazement, roughly equivalent to an extremely emphatic “Wow!” Literally translates as “look at that.”

registry numbers The unique identification number assigned to each warship, consisting of its three-letter class code, followed by a number.

Richthofens Fancy maneuvers. From Baron Manfred von Richthofen, better known as the “Red Baron,” the famous World War I German fighter pilot.

Robinson, Will (*see* Will Robinson).

RRS Royal Rashidian Ship. Used to identify a Rashidian naval vessel, much as USS (Union space ship) precedes the name of a Union naval vessel.

saltwater navy A Navy comprised of ocean-going ships as opposed to one comprised of ships that travel in space. In the Union Navy, the term is particularly used to refer to the navies on Earth, the officers and traditions of which formed much of the basis for the United Earth Spaces Forces in 2034 (the navies of the United States and Canada, Great Britain, and Japan were particularly important).

scones Small, single-serving cakes, usually lightly sweet and baked in flat pans, traditionally a part of the English tea refreshment, often served with cucumber finger sandwiches. Believed to have originated in Scotland. Likely an acquired taste, like cucumber finger sandwiches.

Scotty The traditional nickname for a warship's chief of engineering, irrespective of the national origin of his ancestors. The nickname is believed to have originated with the *Star Trek* franchise, as "Scotty" was the nickname of Lieutenant Commander Montgomery Scott, the chief engineer of the fictitious USS *Enterprise.* As the character became incorporated into spacer lore, it was said that Scotty could repair a fusion reactor with nothing but duct tape and a ladies' hairpin, drank Scotch like weak green tea, and defied hostile aliens with icy ultimatums articulated in a rich Highland burr.

SDMF Self-destruct mechanism, fusion. A fusion munition carried on all Union warships prior to the Battle of Han VII for the purpose of destroying the vessel as a last resort to prevent it from falling into enemy hands.

Senate Generally and historically, this term refers to the upper chamber of a bicameral legislature of either a state of the United States of America, or of the United States of America itself. In current usage, this term refers to the Union Senate, also called the "New Senate" (although this usage is becoming less common) one of the two bodies of the Union Parliament (the other being the Union Assembly). The Senate consists of five members chosen by the Congress from each of the Estates: the people (the "voters"); agriculture (the "farmers"); manufacturing (the "makers"); shipping and transportation (the "movers"); academia and science (the "thinkers"); extractive industries (the "miners"); the information media (the "reporters"); retail and consumer sales (the "storekeepers"); lending, deposits, and investments (the "bankers"); architecture, construction, and civil engineering (the "builders"); public employees (the "governors"); the armed forces (the "warriors"); health care (the "doctors"); attorneys, brokers, accountants, and similar professionals (the "lawyers"); and publishing, cinematic and broadcast tridvid, trideo game design and sales (the "entertainers"). The New Senate, with representation based on the Estates, replaced the Old Senate with membership consisting of two members from each Major World or Inhabited System after the Revolt of the Estates in which the Estates determined that a government in which representation was based on population and locality failed to reflect the economic communities that had arisen in Human Space and that such a government tended to impose unfair burdens on some estates in favor of others. Accordingly, all changes in taxation and declarations of war, as well as significant changes in the Union budget require the unanimous concurrence of all the Estates represented in the Senate.

SEUR Safety and Equipment Utilization Regulations (the acronym is pronounced "sewer"). Regulations promulgated by the Navy governing the appropriate use parameters for virtually every imaginable vessel, device, system, or piece of equipment issued by the Navy.

six Shorthand for "six o'clock position," or directly astern.

SOP Standard operating procedure.

Sparks The traditional nickname for a warship communications officer.

Speak, friend, and enter. A reference to J. R. R. Tolkien's *The Lord of the Rings.* The phrase was written (in secret writing visible only in moonlight and only after the uttering of magic words) over the West Door to the Mines of Moria, also known as Khazad-dûm, a vast underground realm of the dwarves, which at the time of the story had been abandoned by them, as it was occupied by an ancient and powerful monster known as a Balrog of Morgoth. The door would open upon utterance of another magic word, "mellon," which is "friend" in Elvish.

squeaker A particularly young or puny midshipman. Also "squeekie," "deck dodger," "panel puppy," and "hatch hanger" (the last for their habit of standing in the hatches while holding the rim, thereby blocking the way).

SSR Staff support room. A compartment located in the general vicinity of the CIC, containing between three and twenty-four men whose duty it is to provide support to one CIC department by performing detailed monitoring and analysis of the sensors or equipment for which that department is responsible; this monitoring is at a level impossible for one or two people assigned that function in CIC.

Standard the official language of the Union; also, the official language or a widely used second language on virtually every non-Union human world. Standard is derived mostly from the English that was the most widely spoken second language on Earth and was the language of international science, commerce, shipping, and aviation in 2034, when the first human space forces were formed.

SVR Space Vehicle Registry. Usually used to refer to the database containing registry information for every space vehicle known to the Union, including information for vehicles of friendly powers who share registry information with the Union Space Vehicle Registration Bureau. The Union Space Navy maintains a classified SVR database containing the registry information for all naval vehicles as well as the ones on file with the Registration bureau.

synchrotron radiation Radiation emitted as a result of the radial acceleration of ultra-relativistic charged particles through a magnetic field.

SWACS Space Warning and Control System. An integrated sensor, computer, and command/communications/control suite placed on various warships to provide an exceptionally high level of sensor coverage and detail and to coordinate the defense against attacking vessels.

Tabi'a (Arabic) Any formation in which multiple warriors or vessels array themselves to form a protective wall. In the Rashidian Space Navy, the term is used to denote any squadron or other unit tasked with protecting another ship.

Talon The primary antiship missile carried by Union warships. Manufactured by Raytheon-Hughes Space Combat Systems, the Talon is an extremely fast, stealthy, and agile missile with both passive and active multimodal sensor homing and a 5–150 kiloton, variable-yield fusion warhead. The Talon is designed to elude and penetrate enemy countermeasures and point defense systems, use its onboard artificial intelligence and high-resolution active sensors to find a "soft spot" on the enemy ship, and then detonate its warhead in a location designed to inflict the most damage. One Talon is capable of obliterating ships up to frigate size and of putting ships up to heavy cruiser size out of commission. Against most targets with functioning point defense systems, the Talon is a better choice than the heavier Raven (*see*). Beginning in February 2315, Talons were equipped with Cooperative Interactive Logic Mode, a technology adopted from the Raven.

Teller-Ulam soufflé A reference to the "Teller-Ulam Design," which is the fundamental architecture for every thermonuclear weapon ever built by humans. The design may be the only practical design for a true thermonuclear weapon, as it was independently arrived upon by Soviet physicist Andrei Sakharov (and was known in the USSR as "Sakharov's Third Idea"), as well as every alien civilization to have developed thermonuclear weapons whose design is known to humans. The design consists of a fusion-boosted, implosion-type ("Fat Man") fission bomb and a mass of lithium deuteride contained in a uranium casing, with a rod of fissionable material in its center. The compression of the lithium deuteride by detonation of the fission weapon, along with the neutrons generated by the weapon, plus those generated by the casing and by the rod triggered by the neutron flux created by the primary detonation, ignites a fusion reaction in the deuterium contained in the lithium deuteride.

Terran Union The common name for the Union of Earth and Terran Settled Worlds, a Federal Constitutional Republic consisting of Earth and (as of January 2315) 518 of the total 611 worlds known to be settled by human beings. Often simply referred to as the "Union." Formed in 2155 upon the collapse of the Earth and Colonial Confederation (commonly referred to as the "Earth Confederation" or simply the "Confederation") resulting from the Revolt of the Estates that began in 2154. The territorial space controlled by the Union has a shape roughly like that of a watermelon 2500 light years long and 800 light years wide, aligned lengthwise through the Orion-Cygnus arm of the Milky Way Galaxy. Population, approximately 205 billion. With the exception of the Krag Hegemony, the Union is the most populous and largest political entity in Known Space, as well as the most economically successful.

TF Task Force. A group of warships assembled for a particular mission or "task." Distinguished from a "fleet" in that a fleet is a permanent or very long-lived formation usually assigned to a particular system or region of space, whereas a task force is assembled for a limited period of time, then disbanded. Task forces are generally designated by letters of the alphabet, for example, Task Force TD or Tango Delta. Units may be spun off from a task force; these are usually designated by the name of the task force followed by a color or a number, for example, Task Force Bravo Victor Seven or Task Force Galaxy Foxtrot Green.

type When applied to warships, this term refers to the general category and function of the vessel, as opposed to class, which refers to a specific design or production run of vessels within a type. The most common types of warship are, in decreasing order of size, carrier, battleship, battlecruiser, cruiser, frigate, destroyer, corvette, and patrol vessel. There are of course, other types of naval vessel that are not categorized as warships, including tanker, tender, tug, hospital ship, troop carrier, landing ship, cargo vessel, and so on.

UESF United Earth Space Forces. The international military arm formed in 2034 by United States and Canada, the European Union, and the China–Japan Alliance to retake the Earth's moon from the Ning-Braha who had occupied it, presumably as a prelude to a planned invasion of Earth. The UESF drew its personnel primarily from the navies and air forces of the founding powers and drew its command structure, regulations, traditions, and other institutional foundations mainly from their "saltwater navies." Nevertheless, the UESF was a joint force that regarded itself as the successor to all of the armed forces of all of the nations of the Earth. The Ning-Braha technology captured by the UESF in this campaign was the catalyst for mankind's colonization of the stars. The UESF is the direct institutional ancestor of the Union Space Navy.

Union *See* Terran Union.

von Braun, Wernher Born, 23 March 1912; died, 16 June 1977. German-American rocket engineer best known for leading the development of the German A-4 rocket (commonly known as the V-2), humanity's first operational ballistic missile and the first human-created object to reach outer space, as well as for leading the team that developed for the United States the Saturn series of space launch vehicles. This series included the Saturn V that propelled the Apollo spacecraft to the Earth's moon in a series of memorable missions extending from December 1968 (Apollo 8) to December 1972 (Apollo 17).

Watch The period of time that a member of the crew who is designated as a "watch stander" mans his assigned "watch station." Also, the designation of the section of the crew to which the watch stander belongs. On Union warships, there are three watches, usually known as Blue, Gold, and White. They stand watch on the following three day schedule:

First Watch: 2000–0000 (1 Blue) (2 Gold) (3 White)
Middle Watch: 0000–0400 (1 Gold) (2 White) (3 Blue)
Morning Watch: 0400–0800 (1 White) (2 Blue (3 Gold)
Forenoon Watch: 0800–1200 (1 Blue) (2 Gold) (3 White)
Afternoon Watch: 1200–1600 (1 Gold) (2 White) (3 Blue)
First Dog Watch: 1600–1800 (1 White) (2 Blue) (3 Gold)
Second Dog Watch: 1800–2000 (1 Blue) (2 Gold) (3 White).

The Captain and the XO do not stand a watch. Rather, so that there is a designated officer with control of the ship at all times, all officers other than the CO, XO, and the CMO serve as Officer of the Deck, serving as the officer in charge of minute-to-minute operations in CIC when neither the CO nor the XO is in CIC. Officers of the Deck stand watch for eight-hour shifts on a rotating basis.

waving the flashlight Manually directing active sensor scans in a particular direction or directions, either from a fixed orientation or from a programmed scan pattern, usually as a means of obtaining more information to develop a passive sensor contact. Waving the flashlight is to be avoided in certain circumstances because doing so alerts the source of the passive contact that you are aware of his presence.

Will Robinson The traditional naval nickname given to the youngest and/or the smallest of the squeakers or new junior midshipmen in service at any given time on board a warship. The name is taken from the name of a character in the 1960s television series *Lost in Space.*

XO Executive Officer. The second in command of any warship.

Yankee search Active sensor sweep, that is, a sweep in which the ship broadcasts sensor beams and detects the reflections from objects in the vicinity, as opposed to the normal sensor mode, which is passive detection of emissions from contacts. A Yankee search omni is a sweep in all directions around the ship, as opposed to a Yankee search down a particular bearing or bearings or of a given zone. The term dates back to saltwater navy submarines but is otherwise of obscure origin.

Z (when appended to a time notation) Zulu Time. Standard Union Coordinated Time. So that all USN vessels can conduct coordinated operations, they all operate on Zulu Time, which is, for all intents and purposes, the same as Greenwich Mean Time—mean solar time as measured from the Prime Meridian in Greenwich, England, on Earth in the Sol system. When any other time system is used in any naval communication (such as the standard time of a planet on which operations are taking place or local time at some place on a planet), that fact is specifically noted.

ACKNOWLEDGMENTS

I owe all the same debts in this book as in the first. To the acknowledgments printed there, I add the following.

I am thankful to my wife, Kathleen Honsinger, for her skillful editing of the manuscripts, perceptive suggestions, and for her beautiful cover design for the original self published editions of the first two volumes of this series. I am especially thankful for her insistence in September 2012, notwithstanding my protestations that I lacked the talent to do so, that I sit down and start writing a series of military science fiction books "right now."

For his able and even inspired editing of the manuscripts of the first two (and presumably the third) books of this series, the author is very grateful to Michael Shohl, whose contribution to these books went far beyond "copy editing" to include ideas that helped these books become more focused and exciting. Thanks are also due to the highly skilled copy editing of Jill Pellarin and the people at 47North, whose detailed attention to the nuances of language, the rules of usage, and bewildering rules of English punctuation made these books more precise, more entertaining, and stylistically correct.

I am also grateful to the literally hundreds (more than three hundred as of this writing) of people who took the time to write favorable reviews of the original, self-published, versions of these books on Amazon.com. It was largely on the strength of these wonderful compliments that thousands of people were willing to take a chance on independently published military science fiction novels from an unknown author. The success that these books have enjoyed and are enjoying is largely due to these reviews.

The expression, "Stealth is life," though probably of wide currency in the Submarine Service, first came to my attention in a customer review of my first novel on Amazon.com, written by John William Hayes. I liked it so much that I made it "The First Law of Destroyer and Frigate Combat." For the expression and the kind review, I offer my thanks.

To the extent that I am able to write precise, coherent, logical prose, I owe much of that ability to two superlative teachers I encountered in Louisiana's Calcasieu Parish School system: Mrs. Mildred Hobbs, who taught ninth-grade English at Oak Park Junior High School, and Ms. Jacqueline S. Finnegan, who taught eleventh- and twelfth-grade English at Lake Charles High School. The Hobbs and Finnegan in the *Cumberland*'s CIC are a respectful nod to these two outstanding educators, who held their students to the highest standards of excellence and who accepted from me nothing less than my best work. My understanding is that Ms. Finnegan is now deceased. Mrs. Hobbs, however, at last report is still healthy, vigorous, and enjoying her retirement. Accordingly, I convey to her my respectful greetings and heartfelt thanks.

My father, Harvey G. Honsinger, passed away in March 2012 and did not live to see the publication and success of these books. He was a novelist and spent many hours talking with me about how he wrote his novels. Much of what I learned in those talks can be found in these pages. The late Mr. Honsinger had a very colorful way of expressing himself. Every now and then, one of the "Southern" characters in these books says something that he used to say or in a rhythm and a voice that echoes his. Harvey said some of those things on his citizens band radio, which he started using back in the 1960s, before they became the rage. In addition to his call letters, KMR-7239, he was widely known by his handle: "The Swamp Fox." It is in his honor and cherished memory that Max Robichaux will carry that nickname through the remainder of his adventures.

Lake Havasu City, Arizona
4 July 2013

ABOUT THE AUTHOR

Kathleen Honsinger 2013

H. Paul Honsinger is a retired attorney with lifelong interests in space exploration, military history, firearms, and international relations. Born and raised in Lake Charles, Louisiana, he is a graduate of Lake Charles High School, The University of Michigan in Ann Arbor, and Louisiana State University Law School in Baton Rouge. Honsinger has practiced law with major firms on the Gulf Coast and in Phoenix, Arizona, and most recently had his own law office in Lake Havasu City, Arizona. He has also taught debate, worked as a car salesman, and counseled teenagers. He is a cancer survivor, having been in remission from advanced stage Hodgkin's lymphoma since January 1997. Paul currently lives in Lake Havasu City with his beloved wife, Kathleen, and his daughter and stepson as well as a 185-pound English Mastiff and two highly eccentric cats.

This is his second novel.

Stay up to date on future "Robichaux/Sahin novels" as well as other developments in the Honsinger Publications universe by visiting Paul Honsinger's blog at: http://paulhonsinger.blogspot.com/. Follow him on Facebook (http://www.facebook.com/honsingerscifi) and Twitter (@HPaulHonsinger).

Contact the author at: honsingermilitaryscifi@gmail.com.